She hadn't seen him since the night they made love, and now here he was again, but she was married to another man...

Darcey had felt someone move and stand beside her as she bartered for the coral necklace. It would match the new silk blouse she had purchased before they left Agadir.

"Excuse me?" Darcey said, turning to glare at the man standing next to her holding up the pair of earrings. She fully intended to tell him to buzz off. "Quin!" she gasped as she recognized him. "Quin, what are you doing here? Where did you come from?" she asked in rapid succession, resisting the immediate impulse to throw her arms around his neck.

What-are-you-thinking? she scolded herself, immediately tamping down the urge.

"I have been looking for you for months," Quin said, placing his hand on her arm. "Let us go somewhere and talk. You can tell me all about what has happened to you since we last met." He gently maneuvered her away from the booth, sensing the two men quickly closing the distance between them. "Come, we have much to catch up on."

Darcey was too overwhelmed at seeing Quin, and also trying to understand the feelings that he had aroused in her just now, that she took no notice that he had taken the necklace from her hand, or that he had dropped it back on the table. He was now gently but firmly, moving her away from the booth and back toward the main street. When they turned the corner and headed back in the direction of the hotel, she finally realized what was happening.

She stopped and pulled her arm away. "What do you think you're doing?"

A fairytale wedding she'd always dreamed about. An unexpected "Fairy God-Father" she'd never imagined. A grandmother she'd never known. Add a deranged uncle obsessed with revenge. An impending crisis as the earth's ozone layer diminishes, which leads to a job offer for Brad that could be "out of this world." Then stir in a little romance, murder, mayhem, along with a dash of evil, and you have the perfect combination for *Inescapable ~ Tomorrow*, Book 3 in the spectacular Inescapable Series by Madge H. Gressley.

Old questions are answered, and new dangers arise as Darcey finds herself the object an evil plot of revenge on Brad, who is unaware of the dangers he faces and the choices he must make as he accepts the new top-secret job with ORCA.

has a little something for everyone. I thoroughly enjoyed it.
~ Regan Murphy, The Review Team of Taylor Jones & Regan Murphy

INESCAPABLE

Tomorrow

MADGE H. GRESSLEY

A Black Opal Books Publication

DEDICATION

This book is dedicated to God, who gave me the talent to write it; to my family and friends, who without their encouragement it might never have been written; and to my late husband, Stu, who always said, "I taught her everything she knows."

*Yesterday is but today's memories
while tomorrow is full of today's dreams.*

PROLOGUE

Six months earlier:

Quin stepped out of the shower, grabbed a towel, and wrapped it around his waist. His bare feet left a trail of wet footprints on the highly-polished, mahogany floor as he made his way to the huge wooden chest of drawers, where he yanked open one of the big drawers and grabbed his underwear, socks, and tees. Flipping the lid of his case open, he stuffed them in. Moving on, he yanked his clothes off their hangers in the closet, doubled everything over, and crammed it on top of the lumps of underwear. He packed everything, except what he planned to wear in the morning. Quin set the case on the floor and gave it a shove with his foot, sending it sliding in the direction of the door. It bounced as it hit the wall and settled a few inches from the wall. He surveyed the room one last time, whipped the towel off, tossed it through the open bathroom door, and lay down naked, spreadeagle on the bed.

Where to start looking for her? Quin wondered, staring at the ornate embellishments on the ceiling?

He had no way of contacting Vargas, the man to whom Carlos had said he had sold the woman. Last night, Quin had pressured Carlos into telling him who the man was and that he lived somewhere in Morocco. Unfortunately, he refused to disclose a phone number or address.

Quin supposed he could have physically threatened Carlos, but then again, he could not be sure that Carlos would give him the correct information anyway. He knew Carlos could not be trusted. He was too much of a coward and would swear to anything when backed into a corner. Quin drifted off with a partial plan still swirling around in his mind.

∽∾∽

Carlos tried once again the next morning to persuade Quin to stay, cajoling and pleading, just short of crawling on his hands and knees.

"You know I need you," Carlos whined. "Ricardo is good, but he is not you. You know how I depend on you to run the business." He placed his arm around Quin's shoulders as they walked down the hall to the study. "You are my number one." He grinned broadly, giving Quin a slight hug. "Let bygones be gone and stay. Why let some woman come between us? I will even increase your cut. Where else can you make such easy money? Come on, what do you say?"

Quin shrugged Carlos's arm off and walked, stiff-backed, in front of him into the study. "You are not going to change my mind. I am through. I told you that last night," he growled as he turned and glared at Carlos. "Nothing you have to say will make any difference now. I want my money, and I am taking the Land Rover."

Begrudgingly, Carlos walked to the safe and counted out Quin's cut of the money. "Are you sure about this?" he asked one more time. He held out the packet of money to Quin but still gripped it tightly.

Quin jerked the packet from Carlos's fingers. "Yeah, I am sure," he snapped.

Not even taking time to count the money, he stuffed it in his bag and strode down the hall to the front door. He took the steps down to the driveway two at a time.

Reaching the Land Rover, he threw his bag in the back,

never looking back as he sped down the driveway and out of the front gate.

Carlos watched until Quin turned out onto the road then closed the front door.

CHAPTER 1

Searching

Months had passed since Quin left Carlos and Lima behind in his search for the woman and Vargas. He had flown to Morocco, not knowing exactly where Vargas lived. He searched in several cities before finding someone who knew a Luis Vargas, who raised Arabian horses and had a ranch somewhere outside of Agadir. Quin had heard whispers that this Vargas might also be involved in the trafficking of women.

Quin drove his rental car to Agadir and started, quietly, inquiring about Vargas. Everyone who knew Luis Vargas said he was a well-respected businessman who raised Arabian horses, and it was unthinkable that the Luis Vargas they knew would be involved in such a dirty business as the trafficking of women. That was, until a tall, dark man approached Quin one day as he sat having coffee in a small alfresco café.

"You will not find what you are looking for if you proceed on your current path," the stranger offered. "For what you seek, you must look in the dark, not the light." With that, the stranger blended into the passersby on the sidewalk.

Following the stranger's advice, Quin turned to the underbelly of Agadir for answers. When he approached people about Vargas, no one was willing to talk to him, and those who did talked in whispers while constantly looking over their shoulders.

"Yes, Vargas is known as a very dangerous man—an enforcer—one you did not mess with," they cautioned Quin. "You would be better off dropping your quest," they told him. "It is too dangerous to keep asking questions. If you value your life, you will quit while you are ahead."

Quin was warned many times to leave it alone, but he stubbornly forged ahead.

Finally, after weeks of searching with no results, Quin sat in the small coffee shop not far from the dingy little room he had rented, wondering why the hell he was still in Morocco. Most of the tables were vacant as it was still too early for the evening regulars.

I have been beaten up, had my life threatened, and for what? he thought. *I am no closer to finding her than I was back in Lima. I am ready to call it quits and head back to El Salvador. Maybe I can find Ricardo, and we can take up where we left off, without Carlos, of course,* he decided.

Cradling the cup with his hands, Quin stared at the curious pattern the dark specks of coffee grounds made on the bottom of the cup when a stranger tapped him on the shoulder.

"I understand you have been asking questions concerning a certain Luis Vargas, who might be in possession of a particular woman that you are seeking," the stranger said, as he sat down, uninvited. "I might have the information you want." The stranger grinned, showing blackened teeth and gaping holes where some were missing. "For a price, of course."

"You must be mistaken," Quin, said, taken aback by the man's audacity.

"Oh, I do not think so," the stranger persisted, still grinning broadly.

Quin bristled. "What makes you think you know my business?"

"Oh, I know a lot of things," the stranger said, continuing to grin and cocking his head to one side. "I make it my business to know things. I watch. I listen. I find out what you are looking for, and then I help you find it," he said, shrugging his shoulders. "I know you have come from Peru in search of a woman. I know that you were a part of the group that kidnapped and sold her. I know that you have been asking questions in all the wrong places, places that will get you killed." His grin faded, his eyes narrowed, as he leaned forward into Quin's space. "You talk too freely. Too many people know what they should not know about you. That is why I am here to help you."

Quin scrutinized the stranger through cynical eyes. How had this low-life person found out about what he was doing? Quin thought he had been discreet in his inquiries, but the underbelly of Agadir ran on money exchanging hands for illicit activities, drugs, prostitution, murder, and information. He had been warned that asking questions in the wrong places could get him killed, but he had avoided those—he thought. "Tell me how you know these things?" he demanded.

"You have asked one too many questions in the wrong places, my friend." The stranger leaned closer, the odor of saffron and cumin permeating the air, as he whispered, covertly casting his eyes around the room. "I am here to help you."

Quin pulled back from the stranger, trying to put some fresher air between them. "Help me how?" he asked.

The stranger leaned back and shrugged, grinning again. "I have the information you seek, as I said. But it comes with a price. I must make a living, you know."

"What information do you think I am looking for?"

"You want to know where this woman is that was kidnapped in Peru and sold to a Luis Vargas here in Morocco. That is the information I have. However, I will tell you this—right now, for free—if you continue asking questions, you will be killed. It has come to my attention that there is already a price on your head in certain quarters." The stranger shrugged and continued. "As I said, I have to make a living, and that is why I will sell you the information you seek for a modest price, of course, and save you from a most unpleasant death." He continued grinning, laying his hand, palm up on the table.

Quin stared at the stranger's dirt-encrusted hand with its yellowed and broken nails extending past the end of the fingers. His stomach lurched at the sight. *But*, he thought, *what choice do I have? I have not been able to find out anything on my own, and I certainly do not want to wind up dead in some damn gutter.*

"How much?"

"One thousand—American."

"That is too much. I will take my chances on the street. There are still places I have not checked." Quin leaned back, making ready to stand up.

"That is not a wise idea, my friend," the stranger cautioned, wagging his finger at Quin. "As I have said, there is already a bounty on your head, and I could have easily claimed it many times before coming to you with my proposition. But—" He paused and shrugged. "—because I like you, I do not want to see you left to rot in some filthy alley. So, for you, I will make it five hundred American." He leaned back and traced a coffee-stained crack in the Formica tabletop with his finger. "Besides, it would have been bad for business if I had," he muttered more to himself than to Quin.

Quin eyed the stranger. Five hundred seemed like a number he could work with, and it would still leave him enough money to get back to El Salvador if things did not pan out. He studied the stained and chipped tabletop. He was in no hurry to let the stranger know he would take his offer.

Let him stew a bit, he thought and watched out of the corner of his eye as the stranger nervously repositioned himself on his chair a couple of times.

"I do not have that on me," Quin said slowly, raising his

eyes to meet the stranger's. "I will need some time to get it."

"I will wait," the stranger said, relief in his voice. "I will be back here in two hours. Have it then. Let me remind you, it is in your best interest to do this," he cautioned and stood. The grin was now gone as he looked Quin in the eye.

Quin waited a few moments and then followed the stranger out of the coffee shop, wondering how he was going to get five hundred American dollars in two hours. He looked at his watch. The banks had closed a half an hour ago.

Where else? he wondered, mentally running through the shops that lined the streets he knew. *There is that small pawnshop I pass on the way to the coffee shop. It is worth a try.*

A small bell jangled, as Quin pushed open the pawnshop door. The smell of old things, dust, sweat, and incense hung in the air. Quin walked toward the counter where an old man stood, his white tunic, spotless.

"How may I help you," the old man inquired softly.

"I need to exchange some dirhams for American dollars," Quin said, stopping at the counter, his eyes quickly evaluating his surroundings.

The old man slowly looked Quin up and down. "How much are you looking to exchange?" the old man inquired.

"Enough for five hundred," Quin answered.

The old man paused. "And you have this amount with you?" he questioned with narrowed eyes, observing that Quin carried neither satchel, bag, or briefcase.

"Yes, I have the required amount for the exchange," Quin answered, placing his hand on his waistline. "Do you have the amount I require in American dollars for the exchange?"

The old man studied Quin for a few seconds, turned, and walked through a curtained doorway behind the counter. Quin stared after him.

Several minutes passed, and the old man had not returned. Quin began to wonder if the old man was going to blow him off. But maybe not, as he heard muffled voices coming from behind the curtains the old man had passed through.

Deciding he would give the old man a few more minutes, Quin turned and rested his backside against the counter studying the pawned items that sat in no particular order on the shelves. Many of the items on the dusty shelves did not appear to have much value—just small, everyday things and, by the amount of dust that had gathered on them, gave the impression they had been sitting there for quite some time.

Observing this, Quin guessed that most of the shop's pawn business probably came from locals in the neighborhood. This worried him a bit, as he thought about it. Maybe the old man would not be able to make the exchange if he only dealt in these meager pawned items. On the other hand, if he did have the money to make the exchange, Quin was certain that it would not have come from selling these dust-covered items. That thought disturbed him even more. He had no desire to find out what might transpire in this shop after hours.

He had wandered around the shop then moved back to the counter when the old man reappeared through the curtained doorway followed by a younger man carrying a metal box. Quin quickly noticed the younger man also had a pistol stuck in the waistband of his trousers.

"Your dirham, *por favor*," the old man said, holding out his hand. The younger man placed the metal box on the shelf behind the counter, his hand now rested on the butt of his pistol.

Quin fumbled with the money belt around his waist, finally got it open, and pulled out the dirhams equal to five hundred American dollars. The old man smiled slightly as Quin counted out the money into neat stacks on the counter.

"There, that should do it," Quin said, placing the last colorful bill on the last stack.

The old man smiled. "You will pardon me if I count also, *por favor*."

"Yes, of course," Quin said, as he nervously eyed the younger man. Quin had his Glock tucked into the waistband of his jeans at the small of his back and was confident he could outmaneuver the younger man before he had time to pull the trigger.

The old man slowly counted out each stack and tallied it on a sheet of paper as he finished each one. The younger man stood behind the old man watching, only glancing every once in a while, in Quin's direction.

Quin sighed rather loudly.

The old man looked up, smiled, and went back to counting. "It appears that you have the correct amount for the exchange," the old man said, laying down the pencil. He then pulled a chain from around his neck on which a key hung and unlocked the box. As he opened the box, the younger man moved closer to the counter and watched Quin as the old man counted out five, crisp, one-hundred-dollar bills. He did not hand them to Quin but instead placed them on the counter next to the stacks of dirhams.

"The exchange is complete," the old man said. "You should find your money belt considerably lighter now." He picked up each stack of the dirhams and placed them in the metal box, one by one. He paused and looked at Quin. "A wise man does not spend his money foolishly," he said, closing the lid on the box. "Make sure you are buying wisely. What you desire today may have untold consequences, come tomorrow."

"Yeah, whatever," Quin said as he snatched up the bills, folded them, and stuffed them into his pocket.

A cold wisp of air brushed across Quin's shoulders as the old man shuffled back through the curtains. A sinister smirk played across the young man's face as he picked up the metal box before following the old man. An eerie stillness fell over the room as the curtains fluttered and then stilled. Quin could not get out the shop fast enough, stopping only to check his watch as he quickly walked back to the coffee shop. He shivered and tried to push what had happened in the pawnshop to the back of his mind.

Crazy old man, he thought. *What was all that cryptic bullshit anyway?*

Quin wondered how long he would have to wait since it hadn't taken the full two hours to get the money. Not long, he figured since the stranger seemed eager to make the deal. He sat down at his usual table, ordered a Turkish coffee, and settled back in the chair to wait for the stranger.

The stranger slipped into the chair across from Quin just moments after he had ordered the coffee. Quin wondered if he had been hiding somewhere close, watching for him to return.

"I presume you have my payment?" the stranger asked as he sat down, grinning.

"Yes, I have it, but I want the information first." Quin looked at the stranger with narrowed eyes. "If it is not what I am looking for, there will be no payment."

"Very well." The stranger leaned forward. The odor of cumin and saffron again marinated the air between them. "The woman you seek is to be married. The ceremony will be tomorrow at the Vargas ranch. It has been arranged that she will then travel with her husband to Dubai the next day and will stay there for a few days at the Grand Dubai Palace Hotel." He paused and placed his hand, palm up on the table, indicating he had upheld his part of the bargain.

A sinking feeling hit Quin in the pit of his stomach as he heard the stranger say she was to be married.

Married. The word echoed through his mind. *I am too late.* Then he thought, *But what if it is an arranged marriage? One that she was forced into. If that is the case, I can still rescue her. It may not be too late.*

His mind began racing as a plan formed to seek out the woman in Dubai, ignoring the sinking feeling that was growing in the pit of his stomach. If it were an arranged marriage, there would be plenty of guards around, and he could see it would be futile to pursue her here. No, he would wait and follow her to Dubai.

The stranger cleared his throat loudly, jolting Quin back to the present. Quin reached into his pants pocket and pulled out the folded, five, one-hundred-dollar bills, and placed them on the table. Immediately, the stranger snatched them up and stuffed them inside his tunic, leaving in their place a dirty scrap of paper on the table. Covertly, he looked around, making sure no one had seen the transaction, and quickly disappeared before the waiter placed Quin's coffee on the table.

Quin unfolded the scrap of paper. On it was written, *Use only if you need help,* and a phone number.

CHAPTER 2

A Decision

Four weeks earlier:

The sun glinted off the silver skin of the jet's wing—as it sliced through the air at thirty thousand feet—and hit the side of Darcey's glass, casting an amber glow on the table. Where had the time gone? She was not ready to meet Luis again, even under the now-presumed amicable conditions. The events of the prior months were still all to fresh in her now restored memory. She was not sure she had it in her to forgive and forget all that had gone before. As the plane sped closer to the destination she had hoped to forget, the stone in the pit of her stomach grew larger. Swallowing the last of the amber liquid in her glass, she closed her eyes and tried to empty her mind, hoping sleep would help her sort out her tangled thoughts.

⸲

Her friends—Ashley, Melanie, Wendy, her BFF Marti—and Darcey flew back to Dallas to tell everyone about the wedding and to arrange for those who would be traveling to Morocco.

Luis had told Brad to spare no expense. That he would send his private jet and arrange with ORCA to use their corporate jets as well. If more were needed, Luis told Brad to get them, he would pay for it all.

By the time she had the guest list pared down, there were still a hundred and fifty names. She felt that that was still too many, but Brad had said not to worry. Luis's instructions were to invite anyone and everyone she wanted.

Brad's list of names was small, mostly friends from ORCA, and his only family—his sister, her husband, and their daughter. Darcey's dad's side of the family would all be coming with the exception of her grandparents who had for some inexplicable reason had severed all ties after her parents' funeral. She didn't know anyone from her mom's family. Her mom had never spoken about them, and Darcey had always presumed her mom had no family left.

Brad and Darcey had decided that she and Marti should go on ahead and meet with Luis. Brad would follow in a couple of days, after wrapping things up from the opening of the Dome and then stop in Dubai to talk with Asad about the new project before arriving in Morocco.

Upon arrival in Dallas, Darcey had given her notice at the agency. Her boss expressed regret about seeing her leave and wished her well but was sorry he would not be able to make the wedding. A group of her co-workers took her out for dinner and drinks, and the gang at the Sweetwater threw a big party for her the night before she and Marti left for Morocco.

The knot that had developed in the pit of Darcey's stomach was growing tighter the closer Morocco loomed on the horizon. She looked over at Marti, who was now awake. Marti stretched and yawned.

"What did I miss?" Marti asked, through the yawn.

Eyeing the ice that had long since melted in her glass, Darcey smiled, "Nothing. I've just been thinking about the wedding." She pushed the button for Thomas. "I'm still having a problem with having the wedding at the ranch and Luis paying for it all. I'm not comfortable with knowing he still has women locked up." She looked over at Marti, who placed a comforting hand on her arm. "Oh, I know they're not being hurt physically, they live in the lap of luxury and want for nothing. It's the fact that, after being rescued if their choice was to stay, they became *his* property to do with as *he* pleased." Darcey turned and looked out the plane's window.

I have been warring with myself since I agreed to hold the wedding at the ranch. Brad has been trying to understand my reasoning, but he met Luis on a different level. Brad saw Luis as a rescuer who helped him save me. I suppose I can see it from his point of view, but I know if Brad had not found Luis and told him about me, Luis would not have had any second thoughts about putting me on the block, and that bothers me.

Although the women wanted for nothing, they were still prisoners, his property. On the other hand, Luis was doing what he could to eliminate those who trafficked in women. Those he rescued were given the opportunity of returning to their families or staying with him, an option not offered to her, she remembered bitterly. Her kidnapping had been planned and carried out by Carlos Santiago, who had sold her to Luis.

Luis still perpetuated trafficking with his Bel Ami Gala. He had just taken it to another level. She guessed you could say, even though, the women had been sold, in an abstract sense they had not. Luis had his special Elite Force that kept tabs on every woman who had ever been bought at any of the Galas.

Their welfare was a prime priority to Luis, and those who had bought a woman at one of his Galas were under constant scrutiny by his Elite Force. Should any of those women ever be mistreated, in the slightest way, Luis's special Elite Force dealt with the perpetrator swiftly, and, the woman in question was returned to the ranch permanently. After the first few incidents, the word spread fast, and Luis's reputation as an enforcer was made.

"You've got to stop worrying about this until you meet

with Luis," Marti said, breaking Darcey's train of thought. "You have to listen to what he has to say."

Marti wanted to blurt it all out, what Brad had confided to her about Luis, but he had made her swear to say nothing about it to Darcey. He said Luis wanted to explain everything to Darcey himself.

"Maybe you're right. I should wait to hear what Luis has to say." Darcey sighed. Thomas brought her the fresh drink, but it held no interest for her now.

They would be landing shortly, and she needed to freshen up. What she really wanted was a long hot soak in a tub. Absently, she wondered what room she would have. She smiled to herself, remembering the bathroom incident—and Nicho.

Besides meeting Luis, she was also worried about seeing Nicho again. She didn't know how Brad would feel about seeing him again. It wasn't exactly a cordial parting at the Gala, and she hadn't told him about meeting Nicho at the ORCA office in Lima. Things were moving so quickly for the opening, she had completely forgotten about it. Then she supposed Ty could have mentioned it to him, but if he had, Brad never mentioned it to her. Still, it bothered her that she hadn't told him about the meeting. She would tell him when he got here, hopefully before he and Nicho saw each other. She wanted no secrets between her and Brad.

Luis's limo was waiting on the tarmac when they landed. It was still light out, and Darcey could see what Morocco really looked like. Her first untimely arrival at the ranch and her chaotic departure had both been in darkness. The stay at the ranch had offered only a limited view of the landscape from the windows in her quarters, so this was a real treat. She was captivated by Morocco's charm and beauty.

Marti just finished a call to her dad as the limo stopped at the front of Luis's home. The driver stacked their luggage on the sidewalk. Darcey remembered Jose as he met them at the front door. He and Nicho had shown her to the room where she had been locked up.

"*Buenas tarde, señoritas,*" Jose greeted them, with the slight bow Darcey remembered.

"*Buenas tarde*, Jose," she said, looking around the foyer.

This was a much more welcoming entrance than the one she had first walked through those many months ago.

"If you will follow me, *por favor*. Señor Vargas is waiting for you in the library," Jose said, as he started down the hallway to the left of the grand staircase. "Your luggage will be taken to your rooms."

"*Gracias*, Jose," Darcey said, taking Marti by the hand, and they followed Jose down the hall.

Marti leaned into Darcey and whispered in her ear, "Wow!" Her eyes were going everywhere at once, trying to take it all in.

Darcey's mind, fully occupied with meeting Luis, had not paid much attention to the surroundings, so she only nodded. The knot in her stomach was now a boulder. Her palms were sweaty and her heart rate increased. It reminded her of the first night that Nicho had come to take her to that first formal dinner of the Gala—only now, she wasn't a prisoner.

Darcey must have been frowning.

Marti elbowed her. "Smile. You look like you're going to a funeral," she pointed out, "and ease up on the grip, will you? I'm losing feeling in my fingers."

"Sorry, I'm just nervous about this."

Marti giggled. "Just breathe. I'm sure he doesn't bite."

Darcey glared at her.

"It'll be fine," Marti assured her, grinning, giving her hand a slight squeeze.

Darcey halfway grinned, trying to match Marti's easy-going nature.

Jose had stopped in front of the library door, waiting for them to enter. Luis walked toward them, and Darcey hoped he wasn't going to embrace her. She didn't know if she could handle it. She was still uncomfortable in his presence.

"*Bienvenido, señoritas.*" Luis paused, staring at Darcey.

¡Mio Dios! She looks exactly like Saleem, he thought. Regaining his composure, he asked, "Did you have a pleasant trip? Some refreshments, a drink perhaps?"

Luis had stopped before he reached them. He was nervous. He did not know exactly how to read Darcey. He could see she was clearly uncomfortable, in spite of the soft smile on her lips, and he did not want to do anything to upset her further. Brad had said she was not completely sold on the idea of having the wedding here. It puzzled him why she still had not said anything to Brad about her time here.

"I would love a drink," Marti said, giving Luis a big Texas grin. "Wine, if you have it, would be wonderful. Something a little sweet, maybe?"

"Certainly. And, for you, my…ah…Señorita Darcey?" Luis asked, catching himself before he called her my dear.

"Just water will be fine." At this point, more alcohol and an empty stomach would be a bad combination for her. She was thankful she hadn't touched the Scotch Thomas had brought her just before they landed. What she needed now was to keep a clear head.

Choosing one of the leather chairs instead of the sofa, Darcey sat down, wishing this meeting were over and done with.

Marti calmly explored the walls lined with shelves full of books, seemingly oblivious to Darcey's anxiety. "You have a wonderful library, Señor Vargas. I've never seen so many books in one collection outside of the library back home, of course." Marti turned around, walked over to the sofa across from Darcey, and sat down.

"*Gracias.* I am very proud of my library. I have a passion for books, and I have read every one of them." Grinning, Luis handed Marti her glass of wine then turned and handed Darcey a glass of sparkling water. She took the glass by the stem to avoid any contact with him. She knew it was silly, but she just couldn't touch him.

Luis sat down on the other end of the sofa across from Darcey, cautiously watching her. *This is going to be more difficult than I imagined*, he mused. *Perhaps I should wait until tomorrow, let her get used to being here again. I cannot afford to do this wrong.* He cleared his throat. "How soon will Brad be following you?"

"He should be wrapping things up tonight and, hopefully, he will fly out tomorrow, or the next day, for sure," Darcey offered, avoiding direct eye contact with Luis. "He will be stopping in Dubai to meet with Asad before coming here." She could sense he was as uncomfortable as she was. *Serves him right. He should be uncomfortable*, she thought.

It was then that Darcey hatched her plan. If he wanted her to have the wedding here, and he wanted to pay for it all, then it would cost him more than money.

Darcey's terms would be: She would only hold the wedding here if—*One, he released all the women here and let them decide to go or stay and, if they stayed, he would see to all of their needs and they would be free. And, two, the Bel Ami Gala would no longer be a place where prospective buyers came, but it would be where prospective husbands came to view prospective brides.*

She figured if he could afford to dress all of his women in designer clothes and jewels, he could afford to find them husbands instead of owners. Of course, he would have to make sure his Elite Force still kept the women under projective surveillance. Yes, these would be her terms.

Luis was watching Darcey as a smile began to play around her lips. *She seems to have made a decision about something,* he thought. *I hope it is in my favor.* He cleared his throat and stood up. "Dinner will be served in a couple of hours, and I'm sure you would like to rest and change after your long flight. Jose will show you to your rooms." He walked to the door and pulled the brocade sash by the door.

A few minutes later, Jose appeared at the door. "This way, *por favor.*" He motioned and started down the hall. As he turned and started up the stairs, Darcey slipped her hand into Marti's, and they followed Jose up the stairs.

Darcey stood in the doorway of the room Jose had shown her to and watched as he opened the door across the hall for Marti. Marti smiled as she thanked Jose then turned and pointed her finger at Darcey. "You—get some rest." She closed her door.

Sighing, Darcey turned and surveyed the room. It was nothing like her old quarters. In fact, it didn't even come close to it. It was pretty enough, but there were none of the lavish furnishings her quarters had had. This room just had a bed, an antique wardrobe, some comfortable upholstered chairs, and, of course, the bathroom. She felt a little disappointed. She had imagined that these rooms would be luxurious with all of the amenities. She didn't know quite what to make of that. But now…she needed to think on that, but only after, she'd had her soak in the tub.

⸲⸳

A soft tap came on Darcey's door, then Marti stuck her head around the doorjamb. "Are you ready, yet?" she asked, slipping in and looking around. "Your room looks almost like mine. Pretty great, huh?"

"Yes, it's nice," Darcey said, giving herself one last look in the mirror. "But you should have seen my old quarters." As soon as the words had passed her lips, she immediately regretted saying anything about her old life here. She knew Marti would interrogate her mercilessly later, and Darcey wasn't ready to talk about it—not yet.

"Your old quarters?"

Oh, crap. Here it comes. "Are you ready? Let's go on down. I could use a stiff drink before dinner." Darcey ignored Marti's question, hoping she would take the hint but knowing Marti, probably not.

"What's this about your old quarters? Is that the ones you lived in here?" Marti asked, following Darcey out of the room. "Do you think we can go see them? I would love to see them."

"I wonder what they're serving for dinner. I suppose we should look for the dining room since Luis didn't tell us where it is." Darcey purposely ignored her questions. *If she asks one more question, BFF or not, I am going to tell her to back off in no uncertain terms,* she threatened.

Noticing Darcey's stiff back descending the stairs in front of her pointedly told Marti that now was not the time for more questions. *Well, you don't have to hit me with a two by four*, Marti thought. *I can take a hint.*

Ever since Brad had told Marti about Darcey's life here, she had fantasied about it and had been dying to know more. She guessed Darcey would talk about it when she was ready, but a girl could wait only so long before curiosity took over, and one just couldn't stop one's self from being a pest.

Darcey sped up going down the stairs, putting some distance between Marti and herself. Just another defense mechanism she had learned while here. She stopped at the bottom of the stairs, deciding which way to go. *What does it matter?* she thought. *We'll eventually find it.*

Her nerves were on edge, and Marti's questions just added to the tension she was feeling.

"Señoritas, you are just in time. This way *por favor*." Luis was all smiles as he walked toward them.

Darcey halfway smiled.

Marti, on the other hand, rushed forward as Luis offered his arm. "Why, thank you, Señor Vargas," she said, as she glanced back over her shoulder at Darcey who followed them into the dining room. Luis seated Marti and turned to assist Darcey, but she already had her hand on the chair back and pulled it toward her.

"I'm fine, thank you," she said, as she sat down.

"Certainly." Luis smiled. *Independent, just like Saleem. Yes, she is her daughter,* he thought, taking his seat at the head of the table.

Darcey fidgeted with her napkin, trying to settle her nerves. *I don't like being in this position wondering what to*

say next and wanting to be anywhere but here at this mo-
ment. Luis has been nothing but polite and welcoming, but I
still have reservations about this whole wedding thing, she
worried.

"Señoritas Darcey, Marti, *por favor*, help yourself to the
wonderful array of appetizers on the sideboard. There is
wine, coffee, and tea as well. But save room for the main
course," Luis said, smiling while directing their attention to
the sideboard loaded with trays of delicious-looking hors
d'oeuvres and fresh fruit.

"Oh, my," Marti exclaimed. "This is wonderful. I think
I'll sample just a little of it. I want to save room for the
main course," she said, scrutinizing a tray loaded with sau-
sage stuffed croissants.

Darcey pushed her chair back and picked up a plate from
the sideboard as she eyed the tempting array of delicacies
that Luis had had his cooks prepare, she assumed, special
for them. It was way too much food for just the three of
them, and she wondered what he did with the leftovers.

"*Por favor*, do try the stuffed crab cakes," Luis said, diverting Darcey's thoughts. "Brad said they were your favorite."

Ah, just as I thought. "Thank you, but you didn't need to
do anything special just for me, for us. It's not necessary,"
Darcey said flatly. "Whatever you normally serve for the
meals will be just fine." She didn't like where this was
headed. Luis was trying way too hard, she felt, to make up
for what had happened to her here, and he really wasn't sure
how to do it. The wedding, the gowns, the food, the transportation, all too much. *I need to put a stop to all of this—*
now!

"Senor Vargas," Darcey started to say.

"Luis, *por favor*," he interrupted her.

"Senor Vargas," Darcey started, again, "please, do not
do anything special for me. Everything you are doing for
the wedding is far too much. It's making me uncomfortable.
I don't know you, even though I was here under other cir-

cumstances for a while, I don't know you, so I'm wondering what's behind all of this and why are you doing it?

Luis slowly laid his fork down and wiped his mouth with his napkin before speaking. "I am doing all of this because I want to. Do I have to have an ulterior motive? Can I not just want to do something for my friend, Brad and his beautiful fiancé?" he queried.

He had an ulterior motive but was not yet ready to reveal it to her. He had not seen this coming, although, he should have. He had been so elated at being able to do something special for Saleem's daughter, who by all rights should have been his, he had not taken into consideration how she might react. In all of the excitement, he had forgotten the circumstances that had brought her here in the first place, and thus, had not made any allowances for her feelings in the matter. *How could I have been so thoughtless,* he admonished himself? *Brad had said she has never talked to him about her time here. Surely, it has been long enough she should have wanted to tell him about it, now. There must be something else going on that has caused her not to want to talk about it.*

Darcey could see his jaw tightening, and Marti kicked her under the table, but she ignored Marti and the sharp pain in her ankle. She knew she should feel ashamed of being rude to her host, but, in this instance, she didn't. She felt she had earned the right to be rude—well, at least to speak her mind on the matter. "I suppose that is your prerogative if you want to spend your money that way. It just makes me uncomfortable," she said, studying her hands folded in her lap. "But if you insist on having the wedding here, I have some conditions." She raised her head and looked directly at Luis.

"What are your conditions?" Luis asked, raising an eyebrow, suspicious of what her ulterior motive might be.

"If you want the wedding here, my conditions are—One, you release all the women here and let them decide to go or stay and if they stay, you will see to all of their needs and they will be free. No more locked doors. No more prisoners. And, two, the Bel Ami Gala will no longer be a place where prospective buyers come, but it will be where prospective husbands come to view prospective brides. Of course, you will still have your Elite Force keep the women under protective surveillance. Just because they are now wives does not mean the husbands will always treat them with respect." She paused, before finishing. "These are my conditions." She sat stiff-backed in her chair, her hands wringing the napkin on her lap and holding her breath, waiting for his reply.

"My dear *niña*," Luis said, "I do want you to have your wedding here, and I want you to have everything you desire to make it special, but those are mighty heavy conditions. I will have to give it some serious thought. I love Brad like a son. I see you already like a part of my family now, and I hope you will come to think of me that way, too, but I cannot agree to your conditions without considering them carefully." He watched Darcey, waiting for her reaction to what he had just said.

Darcey sat for a few minutes, the silence getting on her nerves and knowing he was waiting for her reply, she sighed. Out of the corner of her eye, she could see Marti was holding her breath.

"Very well," Darcey said. "I will not do anything concerning the wedding until you have considered my terms." She looked up, surprised to see a small flash of pain in his eyes before it was gone.

"That will be fine. I will have an answer for you in the morning."

෬෬෬

The evening meal was over, Darcey and Marti had retired to their rooms, and Luis sat deep in thought in the library, a half empty glass of Scotch held loosely in his hand.

He had never thought in his wildest dreams ever that Darcey would present him with a dilemma such as this. Luis had never thought of his women as prisoners. Property, yes, but prisoners, never. In his mind, the doors were locked for protection like you would do to protect any precious thing you owned. He had never considered that they would view themselves as prisoners. He gave them everything. They wanted for nothing. They were precious to him. Fine jewels, to be admired and enjoyed.

On the other hand, it was true he did auction them off—but to only the elite and only after they had been thoroughly vetted. No buyer, no matter how wealthy, was ever allowed to participate at any of the Galas unless they had passed a rigorous inspection by his Elite Force. Luis viewed his Elite Force as another level of protection he gave his women.

Of course, there was the little matter of "profit." But that had been purely secondary, he had convinced himself. Just another level of protection for his "jewels." The fact that it increased his coffers substantially was merely coincidental. Besides, he had reasoned, the majority of that money went back to dressing his "jewels" in the finest haute couture designs and jewels available.

Mulling over his options, Luis refilled his glass and stood, staring out the French doors leading to the patio. The moon cast a silvery sheen on the stone walkway leading to the garden. It reminded him of evenings past, sitting in the cool of the night with Saleem, his arm wrapped around her as she snuggled up close. Twenty-five years had not dulled the memories of those evenings. Nor had it dulled the memory of her kisses or the smell of her perfume. Moisture gathered in the corner of his eye and spilled over, slowly gliding down his cheek.

"Oh, my Saleem," he groaned. "What do I do? She is your daughter, through and through. I cannot deny her this request. I'm afraid if I do, it will drive her away forever. I cannot take that chance."

His decision made, Luis downed the rest of his Scotch,

turned out the lights, and walked slowly up the stairs to his bedroom. *Tomorrow*, he thought, as he closed his bedroom door.

CHAPTER 3

The Dress

The morning dawned bright and clear, just a few wisps of white clouds drifted in the azure blue sky. Darcey had tossed and turned all night unable to find a comfortable spot on the bed. She knew she looked like a mad woman with her hair every which way as she stepped out on the balcony. She didn't care. She was too worried that Luis was going to deny her conditions.

If he calls my bluff, then what will I do? I can't just pack up and leave, can I? Marti would have a cow. Then, there's Brad. Damn! Why did I back myself up into this corner?

A small bird landed on the balcony railing and hopped along the length of it until it made a turn back to connect to the wall. The bird stopped and sang Darcey a small sweet bird song and then flew off. Somehow, it made her feel better.

She hurried back in and readied herself for the day, trying to keep ahead of Marti coming to get her. Marti never liked being late for anything, and it bugged her that Darcey was never ready until the very last minute. Darcey smiled at the thought as she ran the brush through her hair.

She met Marti in the hallway, and they headed down for breakfast. Darcey dreaded every step she took down the stairs.

Luis was nowhere to be seen as they entered the dining

room. The smell of freshly brewed coffee mixed with the smell of fresh baked goods hung in the air tweaking Darcey's appetite. She hadn't realized how hungry she was until that moment. Marti had already scooped up a couple of scones and a buttery pastry along with her coffee and had sat down at the table. Darcey was taking her time deciding which of the tempting pastries she wanted when Luis walked through the door. Her appetite immediately vanished, and the boulder reappeared in her stomach.

"Buenas días, señoritas," Luis said in greeting. "Exceptionally lovely morning. Would you like to have breakfast on the patio this morning?"

Marti glanced over at Darcey and, noticing her expression, which reflected the pure agony she felt, shook her head, "Thanks, but in here is just fine." She smiled sweetly at Luis. "But thanks for asking. Maybe tomorrow?"

"Yes, I will inform the kitchen we will take our breakfast on the patio tomorrow morning. They will have it all set up out there," Luis said, placing some pastries on a plate.

He glanced nervously at Darcey, trying to gauge her demeanor. He had thought long and hard after going to bed last night about Darcey's conditions. He knew he really had no choice but to agree with them. The risk of losing her, if he refused, was too great, and then there was the matter of Brad, who he had begun to love as his son. What would it do to that relationship if he denied Darcey? No, Luis had to accept the conditions and make the best of it. He would figure something out. He always did.

Darcey watched as Luis made his way to the table and sat down. Even though she dreaded hearing what he was going to say, she sat stiff-backed in her chair and looked him in the eye. *Might as well get this over with, right now,* she decided.

Luis took a drink of his tea and slowly set the cup down before looking Darcey in the eye.

She braced herself. *Here it comes.*

"I have given this much thought, last night and this

morning," Luis said slowly. "I have come to the conclusion, that for the good of everyone, I will accept your conditions with the proviso, that I will pay for everything for the wedding, and you will not utter a word of complaint about it. I do not want to hear anything more from you on the subject. Is that understood?" His eyes never left Darcey's.

She didn't blink. She was too stunned to move. She didn't think she even breathed until he was finished. "Ye—yes, I understand," she stuttered, relieved and aggravated at the same time that he had accepted, but his proviso left her feeling like an unruly child. "Thank you. I won't mention the *outrageous* amount of money you are spending or the *extravagance* you are going to for the wedding again," she replied curtly.

"Now, that is settled," Luis said succinctly, looking at both Marti and her. "Your first fitting for the gowns is this morning at ten. Please be ready by nine as it is a forty-five-minute drive into Agadir."

Darcey and Marti exchanged astonished glances. The rest of the meal was finished in silence. Whether Luis didn't have anything else to say or because they couldn't think of anything to say, Darcey didn't know, but they ate in silence. Even Marti was quiet.

෮෨෮

Slouched in the corner of the back seat of the limo, Darcey took no notice of the beautiful countryside or the clear blue sky as they drove to the Hilton Hotel Agadir. She was still too aggravated over Luis's proviso. She knew it was a small price to pay for setting the women free, but it still rankled her nonetheless. She didn't take any interest in the conversation between Luis and Marti. She purposely tuned them out.

Following Luis and Marti into the elevator, Darcey worked her way to the back. She had no enthusiasm for the ordeal that awaited her upstairs. Luis had had some designer flown in from somewhere; she hadn't been paying any attention while he had regaled Marti with the details. Darcey just wasn't interested.

The elevator doors opened onto the penthouse floor. The rooms were filled with racks and racks of white bridal gowns and bridesmaid dresses in a rainbow of colors. Darcey stopped dead in her tracks, her eyes glazed over as her mind tried to take in the claustrophobic sea of white looming before her. She ignored Luis and Marti as they stepped around her and were greeted by some woman.

"Welcome, Señor Vargas, ladies," the woman said, extending her hand to Luis. "I am Justine, Madam Chelsea's secretary. She will be with you shortly. In the meantime, please, feel free to look around. Catherine will be in to take your measurements shortly," Justine said, addressing Marti and a dazed Darcey.

Darcey vaguely remembered hearing something about measurements.

"Coffee, tea?" Justine inquired, turning back to Luis.

"Yes, *por favor*," Luis said, smiling admiringly at Justine. "Tea would be perfect. Darcey? Marti?"

"Coffee would be absolutely wonderful," Marti gushed. "Darcey?" She looked at Darcey and placed her hand on Darcey's arm. "Darcey, you want some coffee, don't you?" She shook Darcey's arm, breaking her trance.

"Wha—what?" Darcey stammered, blinking and surveying the claustrophobic room with the hundreds of white bridal gowns, crushed together on racks, which seemed to be growing the longer she stared at them. Suddenly, there was no air to breathe. She felt like she was being suffocated, as if the racks of gowns were closing in on her.

"Do you want a cup of coffee?" Marti moved around and stood directly in front of Darcey, her concern growing. "Are you all right?"

Darcey saw the worry in Marti's eyes. "Yes, I'm fine, and, yes, I would like coffee." She wasn't fine, but she smiled half-heartily anyway, looking for a place to sit down since her knees had all of a sudden decided they didn't want to hold her up. Slowly, she made her way across the room to the ivory, brocade-upholstered winged-back chair beside one of the racks, thankful that it wasn't any farther than it was, and that Luis had his back turned toward her talking to Justine. *I don't want to be here. I don't want any of this.* She closed her eyes, trying to regain some semblance of control over her frayed emotions.

She inhaled deeply and gripped the arms of the chair. *Okay, you can do this. Pull yourself together. You've always met obstacles head-on, and you've never backed down. So, get your shit together, girl. If Luis can give in to your conditions, then, you can do this.*

Darcey opened her eyes to find Marti staring at her, a worried expression on her face. "What?" she snapped at Marti, and immediately felt sorry she had.

"Are you sure you're all right?" Marti asked. "Maybe we should just reschedule. Give you a little more time to get adjusted to being here," she suggested.

"No. Let's get this over with, *now*," Darcey said emphatically, rubbing her forehead where a headache was forming. She didn't want to put it off any longer. She *couldn't* put it off any longer and keep her sanity.

Justine returned followed by a woman carrying a tray laden with carafes of coffee and tea, cups, saucers, and a basket filled with scones. She directed the woman to place the tray on the low table in front of the ivory, brocade-upholstered sofa.

Unfortunately, it didn't look like Darcey would be getting her cup of coffee after all.

A woman with a measuring tape draped around her neck and glasses perched on top of her head emerged from the doorway on the far side of the room and whisked Marti and Darcey away to have their measurements taken.

❧❦❧

Marti was thumbing through a binder with sketches of gowns when Darcey emerged from the bathroom that was subbing as the dressing room.

"Hey, look at these," Marti said, turning the binder around. "Some of these are really beautiful."

"Yeah, they're nice," Darcey said, not really looking at the sketches. *I want to go home,* her mind kept screaming.

"Ladies," Justine said, poking her head in the door, "Madam Chelsea is ready for you now."

She held the door open, her lips in a tight little smile. Her expression said, "Move your butts, now."

Marti and Darcey looked at each other. Darcey shrugged and sauntered out the door. *If I have to endure this side-show, I'll do it on my own time. After all,* she remembered, *I'm the bride, and they are supposed to cater to me. Push me too far, and I will give them a whole new meaning for "bridezilla."*

Luis was conversing with a woman Darcey guessed to be Madam Chelsea. She was not at all what Darcey would have expected an haute couture designer to look like. The woman was, maybe, in her mid-sixties, medium height, with graying hair piled on top of her head and held with an alligator clip. She kept pushing the stray wisps of hair that had escaped the clip behind her ear as she talked with Luis. She had on a pair of patterned, chartreuse cargo pants, the kind with all the pockets, a white tank top over a short-sleeved aqua tee. Her feet, with bright red nail polish on her toes, were encased in a pair of white leather sandals. If Darcey had met her on the street, she would never have guessed she was a famous designer.

As Marti and Darcey approached Luis and Madam Chelsea, she turned and beamed at Darcey. "You must be the beautiful bride," she said, a warm, friendly smile spread across her face, her eyes crinkling at the corners. She gently took Darcey by the shoulders and turned her around. "Let me have a look at you," she said. Backing up, her hand to her chin in contemplation. "Yes, you will make a most beautiful bride. Come; let's get started. Have a seat on the sofa, and we'll get this show on the road." She strode across the room hollering on her way through the door, "Justine, are the girls ready?"

Luis had already seated himself in the winged-back chair Darcey vacated earlier, a self-satisfied smile on his face, sipping his tea, as Darcey sat down on the sofa wishing this whole thing was over.

She leaned her head back and closed her eyes. *This is a waking nightmare. The only thing that has been keeping me from going completely bonkers is knowing that Brad will be calling this afternoon.*

Marti sat down on the sofa, watching Darcey out of the corner of her eye, wishing she could do something to make this whole thing magically be over with. She decided what Darcey needed was a "fairy godmother" to wave her magic wand and, presto, Darcey would have the perfect dress for the perfect wedding, to say nothing of having the perfect bridesmaid dress.

Darcey's eyes flew open as someone plopped down beside her. It was Madam Chelsea. She reached over and patted Darcey's hand, "Let's get started," she said softly. "Justine! Let's go!" she yelled.

The double doors opposite the sofa opened, and a model floated out in a fluffy bridal gown, the first of many that followed in different styles and lengths. Darcey lost count after the first fifteen. Madam Chelsea had handed her a small notepad and pen to make notes of the ones she liked. Madam Chelsea kept looking over at Darcey to see what she had written down, and frowning as gown after gown paraded through the room, and Darcey had made no notations.

As the last of the models disappeared behind the double doors, Madam Chelsea turned to Darcey, "Didn't you find any of those to your liking?" she asked in disbelief.

"No, I'm sorry, but I really don't know what I want. All of this has happened so fast, I really haven't had time to think about what it is I do want," Darcey said, staring at her hands. "I need some time. Do you have a catalog of the gowns I could take with me? I noticed there was a binder of sketches in the room where I was measured."

"Yes, I have a show catalog with most of the dresses you saw today, and you may take it," Madam Chelsea said quickly. "However, as to the binder, those are the dresses that I'm still working on. I do not normally let those out of my sight, but I will let you take it as long as you promise that only you and your friend Marti will view its contents," she said, looking around. "This is a highly competitive business, and spies are sometimes in the most unlikely places." Madam Chelsea stood, smiling, and waited for Darcey to stand also. "I know this is overwhelming to you at the moment, but, believe me, I will get you through it. I have not lost a bride yet," she said, laughing, her arm encircling Darcey's waist as she maneuvered her toward the room with the binder.

ↄ◦ↄ◦ↄ

It was mid-afternoon before they arrived back at Mon Rêve, where Jose greeted them at the door, handing Darcey a folded piece of paper as she entered.

"It is a message from Señor Brad for you," Jose said with a slight bow.

Darcey unfolded the paper and read that Brad would be calling back this evening. He had landed safely in Dubai and was going to dinner with Asad.

"*Gracias*, Jose," Darcey said, smiling weakly. The only hope of getting through the morning was that she had known she would be talking to Brad this afternoon, and now, even that was gone. She sighed heavily. *Can't anything go right?* From somewhere in the depths of her mind, her inner voice was back. *Luis agreed to your conditions, remember. That went right.*

Darcey frowned and followed Marti up the stairs. She

needed to regroup and get herself together. She felt like an idiot for letting the morning get to her. Uncle Jack would have been ashamed of the way she acted. She could almost hear him saying, "I taught you better than that. There isn't any situation you can't handle if you put your mind to it and don't go off the deep end before you've thought it through."

Later, Marti knocked on her door carrying the catalog and binder from Madam Chelsea's. They plopped down in the middle Darcey's bed and sat cross-legged, pouring over the catalog and the binder in the golden glow of late afternoon. Darcey was much more comfortable in this setting and even found she liked some of the gowns, but nothing jumped off the page and said, "I'm the one."

Finished with the catalog, Darcey passed it over to Marti and reached for the binder.

"Hold your horses, girl," Marti said, tightening her grip on the binder. "I'm not through. I've already found two, that if I had the money right now, I'd buy one of them and save it for my wedding," Giggling, she leaned forward and whispered, "I think Ty is going to pop the question after the wedding. He was dropping some pretty broad hints before we left."

"Really?" Darcey asked, her eyes wide, a sly smile tweaking the corners of her mouth. "Tell me more." She scooted closer so she could look at the binder with Marti.

"Well, you know, like, when did I think was a good time for a wedding, did I like a big wedding or a small one, what did I think about eloping. You know, stuff like that. Just every once in a while he'd work it into the conversation, and I sorta put two and two together," she said, looking up at Darcey. "What do you think?"

"I don't know, but it does sound suspicious, to say the least. I'll see what I can find out from Brad," Darcey promised, grinning slyly.

CHAPTER 4

Dubai

Brad made his final rounds of the dome meeting with the section heads in order to make sure no one had questions for him before he left for Dubai. He was leaving Ty in charge of the dome and its daily routine for now. He would talk with Asad and recommend him as his replacement if he took the job in Dubai.

"Well, that looks like we've covered everything. Y'all should be all set," Brad said, as he and Ty walked back into Brad's office. "Do you have any questions for me?"

"Don't think so, boss," Ty said, grinning. "You just go 'n get yourself ready. We can handle it here. No need to worry. We'll catch up to you at Vargas's in a couple of weeks."

"Okay, I'll leave you to it then," Brad said, walking to the door. "Feel free to use my office if you want. All the files are easy to find."

Giving the office one last look and a nod to Ty, Brad walked down the corridor toward his quarters. He stopped briefly in front of Lilly's darkened and locked office, contemplating all that had gone on in the past few short weeks.

Has it only been that short of time since Lilly committed suicide and the dome had its official opening? he questioned. *It feels more like months*, he thought, walking on.

The closer he got to his quarters, the slower Brad

walked. He was dreading going in, knowing Darcey wasn't there but was somewhere in the air over the Atlantic on her way to Luis's. It would be another three or four days before he would be with her again. That would be three or four days too long, he decided. Brad had called Darcey, and they had talked away the hours the evening before she flew out from Dallas to Morocco. Even at that distance, he could feel their connection as strong as ever.

Brad had called Asad the next morning and told him he would arrive sometime the day after tomorrow. *No use putting it off any longer*, he thought as he packed. He was definitely interested in finding out more about the project, but he couldn't imagine any project bigger than the Bio Dome.

Suitcase packed, Brad gave his quarters one last look, picked up his passport, and closed the door. He swung by the Operations Room one last time on his way to the sub bay to say goodbye to the guys and see if they had any last minute questions.

"Have a good trip, man," Scott said, shaking Brad's hand. "Ya go on 'n check out that new project. We'll be just fine."

"Yeah, don't give us a second thought," Hot Dog grinned, slapping Brad on the back.

"Okay, okay," Brad laughed. "I can see you guys can't wait to get rid of me, so I'll see y'all in a couple of weeks for the wedding."

There was still a nagging feeling lurking in the back of Brad's mind that all was not over as he climbed aboard the sub. He still hadn't found out who had orchestrated the sabotage and neither had Luis.

⌘⌘⌘

Twenty-four hours later, the plane taxied up to the OR-CA hangar, and the pilot shut down the engines as Brad stepped off the plane followed by Thomas with his luggage. The searing afternoon sun bore down as beads of perspiration popped out on Brad's brow when the over one-hundred-degree heat hit him like a sledgehammer. The sweltering heat felt like he'd walked into an oven after the climate controlled temperatures of the dome. Heat waves were emanating from the tarmac as he walked the few feet to the limo Asad had sent to pick him up. Brad waited while Thomas placed the luggage in the trunk before saying goodbye to him.

The cool interior of the limo was a welcome relief from the overwhelming heat of the outside, making the short ride from the airport to ORCA's office, comfortable. It was a quick ride up in the elevator to Asad's office on the top floor where the receptionist greeted Brad as he entered the outer area to Asad's office.

"*Buenas tarde* Señor Daniels. Go right in, *por favor*." She smiled sweetly at Brad, indicating the two beautifully carved teak wood doors.

Asad was waiting as Brad opened the door. "*Bienvenido*," Asad said, extending his hand to Brad. "It is good to see you. I trust you had a pleasant trip?"

"Yes, long but uneventful," Brad said, shaking Asad's hand.

"Make yourself comfortable, *por favor*," Asad said, indicating the cozy seating area to the right side of the room. "Tea or coffee, perhaps?"

"Yes, coffee would be fine." Brad paused and then went on in order to get to the gritty details of the new project. "So, tell me about this project you have for me," Brad questioned. "Is it here in Dubai?"

"No, it is much farther away," Asad said, thoughtfully, handing Brad his coffee. "Yes, much farther. But that is all I'm going to tell you right now. Tomorrow you will meet with the ORCA board, and we will lay it all out for you then," Asad said, sitting down across from Brad. "Now, tell me about your wedding plans. I do hope you have persuaded your lovely fiancé to honeymoon here. It is a beautiful place with much to see and do."

"Truthfully, we haven't even talked much about that yet," Brad said, setting his coffee cup down. "What with the opening, Lilly's suicide, and planning for the wedding, the topic of where to honeymoon hasn't been at the top of the agenda. The wedding is on the twenty-sixth, and I know Darcey wants to come with me when I give you my answer about the project. Maybe we'll just stay and make it our honeymoon."

"Yes, I shall plan on that," Asad said thoughtfully. "I will arrange a reception for you on the twenty-eighth for you and your lovely bride. It will also serve as the launch of our new project and hopefully to announce you as project head." Asad looked at Brad.

"That sounds like a plan, but don't you think that might be jumping the gun since I haven't even heard what the project is?" Brad questioned.

"No. I have every confidence that you will be so intrigued by the project that you will accept without hesitation." Asad paused and took a drink from his cup. "Now you must tell me all about what has happened on the dome. I have read your reports, but I much prefer hearing you tell me. Somehow, a written report is so impersonal. I want to hear your thoughts and ideas. Things that are not easily put in a report."

For the next hour, Brad related to Asad everything that had happened since the opening. Asad let Brad talk inserting an "Ah yes," or "Hmmm," here and there when appropriate.

"…and I left Ty in charge. He is doing an excellent job of managing the dome as well as handling the technical end of things." Brad paused and finished the off cold coffee in his cup.

"Thank you for sharing your views with me. I can see now that there will be no worry about having you take on our new project. Should you decide to," Asad added with a slight smile. "Now, if you are ready, Hasan will take you to your hotel. He will pick you up around nine-thirty for dinner." Asad stood and extended his hand to Brad, indicating the meeting had ended.

Standing up, Brad shook hands with Asad. "Thank you for the coffee. I will see you at dinner, then," he said, as they walked to the elevator.

Asad stood staring after Brad as the elevator doors hissed shut. He hoped Brad would be open to the new project. He could foresee no reason why he would decline, but still, this would not be the usual engineering project and time was running short. It was this new concept based on the success of the Bio Dome Project that was going to make this project a success. Even though it would be on a much larger scale, involving a harsher environment, and a more distant location, the success of this project depended on Brad accepting the position as project head. His knowledge and expertise were the main reasons that Granston International and Aries Global had agreed to partner with ORCA.

Asad turned and walked back to his office, collected his briefcase, and turned the light out. He noticed Adara had already left for the day.

Tomorrow will tell, Asad thought, as he walked out into the deepening shades of evening.

∽∾∽

Brad called Darcey as soon as he reached the hotel. Jose, who answered the phone, told him, Darcey and Marti were with the bridal gown designer for a fitting of the gowns. Brad thanked Jose and left a message saying he would call back later that evening.

Brad was disappointed and slightly pissed off that he had to wait to hear the melodic tones of Darcey's voice. He should have known that Luis would have had the appointment for the fittings made days in advance of Darcey's arrival and that they would be at the earliest possible moment.

Brad had to admit that Luis couldn't have been more excited about the wedding if it had been one of his own daughters. He also wondered if Luis had had a chance to talk with Darcey about her grandmother.

§§§

For the second time, in since she didn't know when, probably never, Darcey was completely ready before Marti. She stepped across the hall and started to tap on Marti's door when it opened.

"Well, will you look at you," Marti exclaimed. "I thought for sure I'd have to spend another half hour prodding you to get ready. What gives?"

"Oh, nothing." Darcey shrugged. "Just didn't want to hear you giving me grief over my tardiness again," she said as she started for the stairs.

"Well, would you mind making this a habit from now on?" Marti quipped as she caught up to Darcey on the stairs. "Then I won't have to feel like I have to rush to get ready in order to make sure you're ready on time. Honestly, I don't know how you manage when I'm not around." Marti giggled.

Darcey laughed, picking up speed going down the stairs. "Well, you won't have to worry about that much longer. I'll have Brad to keep me on time from now on."

She suddenly felt light hearted. She didn't know why, after the nerve-wracking morning she'd had, but she did. Maybe it was the long nap she'd taken after lunch or the sexy dream she'd had about Brad or the final realization that Luis really had accepted her conditions. Regardless, for the first time since arriving at Luis's, she felt like maybe everything would be all right.

They reached the bottom of the stairs together. Marti linked her arm in Darcey's, and they set off in the direction of the dining room. Approaching the dining room, Darcey could hear voices, female voices. She wondered who Luis had invited to dine with them. He had not mentioned it at lunch.

Arm in arm, Darcey and Marti walked through the door to the dining room. Darcey couldn't believe her eyes. There milling around by the French doors was Marla and several of the other women who she had become friends with while under Luis's roof.

"Marla!" Darcey said, raising her voice in excitement. "Is that really you? You're still here!"

Marla turned and rushed over to her, giving her a big, warm, welcoming hug. "Yes! I'm still here," she said.

Darcey didn't miss the sly look she gave Luis, who immediately cleared his throat. "Yes, ladies, if you will be seated, I will notify the kitchen we are ready." He turned and headed for the door that led to the kitchen area beyond, a slight hint of red showing on the back of his neck.

Darcey smiled. *Why, Luis you sly old dog.* Darcey glanced back at Marla, her eyes following Luis adoringly. *Ummm. Something's afoot here, Watson.*

Marla noticed Darcey watching her and quickly walked over to a young woman whom Darcey didn't recognize. Marla took the young woman's hand and led her over to where Darcey and Marti stood. She was shorter than Darcey, with a creamy complexion and honey brown hair lying softly on her shoulders.

"Darcey, I'd like you to meet Jenny. She's new here."

Darcey shook Jenny's extended hand. "Nice to meet you," she said warmly. She couldn't help but notice the waning purple and yellowish spots on the young woman's upper arms. The exact place where they would be if someone had forcefully grabbed her.

Jenny noticed Darcey's stare. "It's okay. It's not as bad as it looks," she said, extending her arm and looking at it. "I'm a real klutz. I tripped over a loose stone in the courtyard. Nicho grabbed me before I landed in the fountain." A soft smile played on her lips as she spoke.

Ah, Nicho. "Always the gentleman. That's Nicho," Darcey said, softly, noticing a blush creeping up Jenny's neck as she studied her arm. Darcey winked at Marla, who smiled and shrugged slightly. Darcey introduced Marti to Marla and Jenny.

Luis returned from the kitchen area and announced that dinner was on its way. They took their seats just as the wait staff brought in the first course.

They were halfway through the main course when Jose came in and announced that Darcey had a phone call from Señor Brad.

She felt the butterflies explode, and her heart began to race. She scooted her chair back, nearly tipping it over in her haste, and quickly followed Jose.

Darcey picked up the receiver and placed it to her ear. Her heart beating wildly, she said, "Hello!"

"Hey, babe," Brad said, in that velvet voice she knew so well, and instantly she felt their connection. "Sorry, I missed you before. How'd the fitting go?"

Darcey related what a disaster the fitting had been and how she'd nearly lost it. Then she told him what Marti had said.

"Well, whatta you know 'bout that?" He laughed. "Been wondering when the boy was gonna get around to asking her. He's been acting like a love-sick puppy ever since you all left for Dallas."

"Well, is he or isn't he?" she asked, a little put out that he was still laughing.

He chuckled. "Yeah, I'm pretty sure he's gonna. Maybe after we leave for Dubai."

"That's super! I'll tell Marti. She's been in such a state, wondering will he or won't he. Honestly, I don't know how she'd handle it if he didn't. She is so over the top in love with him. I know it would tear her apart if he didn't, and I don't what to see her hurt."

"No, don't tell Marti just yet," he cautioned. "Let me get a firm commitment from Ty before we go 'n get Marti's hopes up. I know he's gonna ask her, just don't know when for sure."

"Maybe you can nudge him in the right direction and have him ask her right after the wedding," she suggested.

"Yeah, I can do that. I gotta call him tomorrow, anyway," he said, thoughtfully.

"Now, tell me about this project that Asad wants you on," she asked, anxious to know what it was.

"Don't know anything to tell yet. I meet with the ORCA board in the morning where all will be revealed," Brad told her. "Asad just said it was bigger than the Bio Dome Project, and a lot farther way, whatever that means."

"What time is the meeting?" she asked. "I know there's a time difference, but don't know what."

"I think Dubai is four hours ahead of your time there. It's around one here. What time is it there?"

"I don't know, somewhere around nine, I think," she said, looking at her naked wrist, She had left her watch on the bathroom counter.

"That's what I thought," he stated. "I'll meet with Asad and the board somewhere around ten. I'll call you as soon as I know what it's all about."

"Okay. I can hardly wait to hear what it is. I'm so excited for you." She smiled into the receiver. "When we go back at the end of the month to give him your decision, why don't we just take our honeymoon in Dubai? I think it would be exciting to honeymoon there."

"That's what Asad suggested to me. Oh, by the way, Asad is throwing us a reception on the twenty-eighth. Just thought you'd wanna know," he said as an afterthought.

"Reception! Holy crap! I don't know any of those people," she replied, frustration reflected in her voice. *The last thing I want is a big reception. The ordeal of the wedding is going to give me enough stress to last the rest of my life. I don't think I can squeeze in one more ounce of stress without coming apart at the seams.*

"Now don't go all bonkers on me," Brad said. She let the

calming velvet tones of his voice wash over her. "You handled the dome opening just fine," he said, "and there were a hundred seventy-five people who you didn't know there. I hardly think Asad will be inviting that many to the reception."

"Oh. Yes, you're probably right," she said sheepishly. "This day has just really been, oh, I don't know, crazy, I guess. I still haven't picked a dress. On the other hand, Marti has picked out two! She can't decide which she likes the most. I'd just like to pick one." she said, sitting down in the chair next to the phone table.

"Look, if you don't find what you like, have the designer, what's her name, make one especially for you. Luis is paying, and he wants you to have exactly what you want." Brad said reassuringly.

"Yes, I suppose you're right about that. So far he's spared no expense," she said, remembering that she couldn't say anything more about how much Luis was spending on the wedding. "Oh, I almost forgot. Guess who is having dinner with us tonight?"

"I haven't a clue," Brad laughed.

"Marla! You remember Marla, the one who tried to get me to come out of the bathroom when I locked myself in there." Too late, in her enthusiasm to tell Brad about Marla, she remembered she hadn't told Brad about anything that had happened to her while she was here.

"Nooo," he said, drawing it out. "I don't believe I know who Marla is or anything about you locking yourself in the bathroom, for that matter." He did know, however, because Nicho had told him, but Brad couldn't let Darcey know that. She would tell him everything in her own time. It was her story to tell.

Oh, crap! "No. Sorry," she whispered. "I just can't talk to you about all of that yet. I have to get it all sorted out in my mind before we talk." *And it has to be face to face, not over the phone.*

What are you waiting for? her inner voice inquired. *You*

know you are ready to talk about it, or you would have re-membered that you hadn't told him about any of it yet.

She squeezed her eyes tight. *I guess you're probably right.*

"That's okay, babe. Don't worry about it. When you're ready to talk, I'm ready to listen."

"Thanks," she said softly. She would tell him all about her time here before she told him about meeting Nicho in Lima. Somehow, she thought that would make it easier to tell Brad about Lima.

"As much as I would like to keep talking to you, I think you'd better get back to your dinner before it gets cold," he said sadly. "And I need some sleep."

"That's okay. I couldn't eat much more anyway, especially after talking to you. I can't really think about much else than you holding me in your arms and feeling your body next to mine," she said, breathlessly. She could feel the heat rising as she held the phone as close as she could, wishing he could reach through and touch her.

"Yeah, me, too. I love you so much." Brad closed his eyes and let the feeling of their connection invade his senses, his desire for her pulsating. "I'll call you tomorrow," he said, softly.

"I love you more than you'll ever know," she breathed into the phone. "Until tomorrow."

"Tomorrow."

CHAPTER 5

The Project Unveiled

It was nine-thirty the next morning when Hasan pulled the limo up in front of the ORCA building, and Brad made his way to the bank of elevators on the first floor.

Damn, he thought as he pushed the up button. *Why didn't that stupid alarm go off?*

Brad had overslept, and, in the rush to get ready, he didn't have time for breakfast, so he had opted for a to-go cup of coffee from the hotel's coffee shop on his way out the door. His stomach growled in protest on the ride up in the elevator, and he hoped that didn't happen during the meeting, but with the anticipation of the meeting and the lack of food this morning there seemed a distinct possibility it would happen.

Stepping off the elevator, he noticed that the receptionist was not at her desk, so he proceeded on into Asad's office.

"Buenas días." Asad greeted Brad with a warm smile. "You are right on time. The board members will be arriving soon."

"Morning," Brad said, still standing just inside the door.

Asad got up and moved from behind his desk toward Brad. "If you will follow me, *por favor,*" he said, as he walked out the office door and turned down the hallway to the left. "We will be meeting in the conference room," he said, opening the door to the room. "If you would, *pro fa-*

vor, place your cell phone here," he said, indicating a cloth-covered gold tray. "Just a precaution, you understand. This is a highly classified project. We do not want a repeat of what happened with the Bio Dome Project." Smiling, he glanced around the room, "Ah, I see Adara has prepared coffee and tea along with some pastries for this morning. Help yourself, *por favor*."

Brad placed his cell phone on the tray and headed in the direction of the credenza that was covered with an array of tempting goodies. He didn't have to be told twice. His stomach let out a long, low rumble as he filled his cup with the steaming, aromatic, dark coffee. He placed two of the pastries on a plate and sat down on one of the cream-colored leather sofas that lined the wall on one side of the room.

The long, teakwood, conference table was surrounded by twenty, high-backed, conference chairs, upholstered in the same cream-colored leather. On the table, in front of each chair, was a nameplate. Brad presumed those were the names of the board members as he glanced at them. None of the names that he could see from his vantage point were familiar.

The first of the board members began to arrive, each placing their cell phones on the tray as they came through the door. Many of them Brad recognized, some from the dome opening and some he knew personally. He stood and greeted them. By the time pleasantries had been exchanged, most of the board members had arrived and were seated at the table. Two chairs remained vacant.

Asad took his seat at the head of the table, and motioned to Brad to be seated in the chair beside his, then gaveled the meeting to order. On a silent signal from Asad, Adara, who must have been standing somewhere at the back of the room, stepped forward and removed the nameplates from in front of the vacant chairs. She left, taking them and the tray with the cell phones. Brad wished he could have gotten a look at the names. He had thought it odd that Asad had them removed. Maybe it was the custom here to do that, he thought, swallowing the last of the coffee in his cup.

A few seconds later, Adara entered the room again carrying an armful of navy blue binders. She placed one in front of each board member, then Asad and Brad.

"That will be all, Adara," Asad said softly. "Gentlemen, if you will open your binders, you will see the proposed project we are here to discuss. I need not remind you that everything that transpires here today must not leave this room." He looked around the table, his eyes resting on each board member for a second or two, waiting for an acknowledgment that each understood the importance of secrecy. "Please take a few minutes and glance through the first fifteen pages at this time."

Brad opened the binder, and his mind refused to comprehend what he read, *Lunar/Mars Habitat Project.* He looked over at Asad, his eyes wide in astonishment.

Asad was staring intently back at Brad, gauging his reaction. He could see that the enormity of the project had hit Brad squarely between the eyes. Asad still banked on Brad's engineering imagination and curiosity to overcome any negative aspects of the project.

"You can't be serious?" Brad said in a low, strained voice to Asad and then looked around the table and saw that the board members were intently reading the pages as Asad had requested.

"Yes, we are most definitely serious." Asad nodded as he spoke. "As you will see when I explain the project."

Brad's eyes were drawn to the image of the lunar orb ghosted on the title page. He stared at it.

Moon, he thought, *the damn Moon! They want me to build a freakin' dome on the Moon!*

His mind screamed *No freakin' way!*

Steady boy, he thought. *Let's hear this through. It may not be what you think or as bad.*

Brad leaned his head against the chair back and observed the other board members through half-closed eyelids. None of them showed any reaction to what they were reading. In fact, they all looked like they were reading the minutes from the last board meeting.

One by one, they closed their binders when they had finished reading. Asad gave the few stragglers a few more minutes before he called the meeting back to order.

"Gentlemen, we are partnering with AeroDynamics to do this project, and as you have just read, this project is highly classified. It is the first of its kind to attempt a fully functional habitat on the surfaces of the Moon and Mars. Our domes will be the bases for our new Space Exploration Program." Asad paused, glancing briefly at Brad before continuing. "We have at our disposal the resources of two of the major aeronautic research corporations in the world—Granston International that will build the engine for the spacecrafts, Aries Global that will build the spacecrafts in which all of the project components will be transported to the lunar and Mars surfaces. This project is an extension of the ocean research Bio Dome Project, and our prime directive for this project is still the same. All public communication will reflect that the Lunar/Mars Project is part of ORCA's newly developed Space Exploration Program.

"I'm sure you all are familiar with Brad Daniels, our design and head engineer for the Bio Dome Project." Asad nodded in Brad's direction. "Brad will be joining us as head engineer and project manager on this. His cutting-edge design principles for the Ocean Bio Dome will be applied to this project, as well. The first phase is to construct the modules here and transport them to the sites on the Moon and Mars surfaces. Then the second, and final phase of this project will begin—" He paused. "—construction of the modules into finished, habitable Bio Domes both on the Moon and Mars."

A soft murmur spread around the room. Brad straightened up in his chair at the mention of Mars. His mind had thrown up a wall after reading the word lunar, and he hadn't looked past it or the rest of the cover page. He now thumbed through the rest of the pages while trying to absorb what Asad was saying at the same time.

"What you are seeing in front of you now, is the first phase of the project—the construction of the modules. Those will be assembled here in Dubai. The next step will be to transport and build these larger versions of the Bio Doom on both the Moon and Mars."

No freakin' way! Brad's mind was whirling. *He can't be serious. The logistics of this is astronomical. A Bio Dome, on the Moon, and Mars? He's outta his skull. Still...*

"If you will turn to page sixteen," Asad continued, "you will see what Aries Global is proposing. They have developed an Interstellar Landing Craft—ILC—that will function as transport to and from the Moon and Mars. They will be providing four of these ILCs. Two will shuttle components to and from the moon while the other two are doing the same to Mars. The pages that follow will provide you with an overview of the ILC.

"Now, turn to page thirty, *por favor*. Here you will see what Granston International brings to the table. They have just completed intensive testing on their new Faster Than Light Hyperdrive Engine—FTLHE—and the Impulse Drive Engine—IDE. These engines will power the ILCs and will enable us to reach Mars in just over three days. As with the ILC, the following pages will give you an overview of the FTLHE, IDE, and their capabilities.

"And, finally, on page fifty-one, you will find what OR-CA engineers have developed. Our aerospace engineers have developed an Echo Guidance and Landing System— EGLS—capable of flying and landing the ILCs without a human onboard. The EGLS is programmed and remotely monitored to fly and read the Moon or Mars surface and adapt accordingly to achieve a soft landing. And, as with the other two components of this project, the following pages will give you an overview of the EGLS," Asad finished, shutting his binder, watching as the board members scrutinized the classified information contained in their binders.

"Gentlemen, we will take a short break while you read the information in your binders. You will not be taking the binders with you today. So read them thoroughly. I will try to answer any questions after you have finished. In the meantime, there is fresh coffee, tea, and pastries for your enjoyment."

Brad quickly flipped through the pages, speed reading the specs of the ILC, FTLHE, IDE, and the EGLS. Rolling it all around in his analytical mind, Brad had to admit that it might be possible that this could work. An outside chance, but still possible with his design and the resources available. *Yes,* he thought, *it just might be possible.* He felt a surge of adrenaline building as he scanned back through the pages.

He remembered reading about a government-sponsored attempt to establish some form of a habitable environment on Mars. That had been several years ago, and it had not been successful. The government had made a big production of how the environment was too harsh to sustain any form of life. The news media picked it up and ran with it, making it front page news for over a week.

A little over an hour had passed when Asad gaveled the meeting back to order, "Does anyone have any questions?"

Many of the board members had questions, such as: "When does the project start? What is the cost? What is the estimated net profit for the project? Is there a completion date? How much control over the project does ORCA have? Who has the final say on cost overruns? What type of security will there be? What will be the rate of return on our investment? Is this a three-way split on the profits? What is the profit margin? Is AeroDynamics being asked to put money upfront? What safety precautions are being taken? Who will man the ILC? Will Aries provide the flight crew? Will there be an ORCA representative on board? Who will put the modules together on the Moon? Who will put the modules together on Mars? How much control does Daniels have over the project? Will he be on the Moon and Mars?"

The questions went on for another two hours.

Brad listened intently as Asad said the project would start no later than December first. Estimated completion would be in five to eight years depending on the launch windows; approximately the same as with the Bio Dome, assuming everything ran smoothly. But because this would be opening up unknown territory, the possibility of the project running longer was feasible. A skeleton flight crew would be required, and Aries would provide or train a crew. The EGLS did not require human control onboard. The crew would be mainly a security precaution. ORCA personnel would be on all flights and at both the lunar and Mars habitats at all times. The components for the modules would be made at ORCA's manufacturing facility in Dubai and then transported to the Moon and Mars to be assembled at each site. ORCA would provide the construction crews for both lunar and Mars. The crews that worked on the Bio Dome Project would be most likely the ones to do this job as they were familiar with the concept and Brad. Brad would have complete control over the entire project.

"There will be a complete set of financials available at the contract signing. Bring any more questions relating to the financials to that meeting. There will be time for discussion before any contracts are signed. Are there any more questions?" Asad asked again.

The members remained silent.

"Then, I presume we are all in total agreement to move forward with this project. All those in favor push the button on the right end of your nameplate, *por favor*. Those not in favor, push the button on the left end of your nameplate, *por favor*."

Brad watched as a small green light appeared on the front of all of the nameplates. Now, he understood why the two nameplates had been removed. Only votes of those present could count. He guessed that the votes were recorded electronically somewhere else so no vote could be counted more than once.

Brad wondered if that was how the board had been able

to evade a takeover by the Eastern Alliance at the last election of board officers.

"*Gracias*, gentlemen," Asad said. "We have one more bit of business. I have given Brad until the end of the month to give me his final decision on coming onboard with this project. Brad is getting married on the twenty-sixth. He and his beautiful bride will be here on the twenty-seventh. I will arrange with AeroDynamics, Granston International, and Aries Global to meet with us on the morning of the twenty-eighth for confirmation of all parties involved and for the contracts to be signed. Brad will have his answer to me on the twenty-seventh. Are there any objections to this proposal?" Asad asked, glancing around the table.

Brad leaned back in his chair, studying the board members with their big smiles and nodding heads, speaking quietly to one another. They had no idea what was involved with this project—how disastrous it could be if anything went wrong. They—in their *Armani* suits and *Gucci* shoes—didn't have a clue what this project entailed. *Probably any one of them could have personally financed this project without batting an eye, and all they're worried about is profit margin? If this project heads south, there'll be no profit margin for any of them to worry about,* he thought, sourly.

Asad continued, interrupting Brad's train of thought. "Very well, if there is no further business to bring before the board, we are adjourned."

The room was silent.

Asad gaveled the meeting adjourned with a loud thwack. He stood, "Oh, yes, one more thing. I will be hosting a reception for the newlyweds the evening of the twenty-eighth at my home. Consider this your invitation to attend, *por favor*."

A soft murmur went around the room. Many of the board members walked over to Brad and offered congratulations and well wishes amid handshakes.

CHAPTER 6

Breaking it to Darcey

Boarding the ORCA jet in Dubai, Brad placed a call to Darcey's cell. The call went directly to voicemail. Deciding not to leave a message on the cell, instead, he called the ranch number. Jose answered. Brad waited as Jose went to find Darcey. The anticipation of hearing her voice building as he thought of holding her in his arms, tasting her kisses, feeling her body close to his, their passion for each other wrapping them in a cocoon of everlasting love. He closed his eyes and waited.

"Hello," Darcey said, breathing hard trying to catch her breath. She had run full speed, the last several yards from the horse barns to the house after Jose had announced over the intercom that Brad was on the phone.

"Hey, what's wrong? Are you all right?" Brad asked, immediately worried that something had happened.

"Whew," she let out a long breath. "Everything's fine," she said, between breaths. "I just ran in from the barn when Jose said you were on the phone." She exhaled, falling into the chair by the phone table, fanning herself with her hand. *Inhale. Exhale. Deep, slow breaths.*

"Are you sitting down?" Brad asked.

"Yeah, what's up?" she replied, wondering why she needed to sit.

"The job—it's building a dome just like the Bio Dome,

but on the Moon—also on Mars," Brad said, pausing first then rushing through the last part.

Silence.

"Hey! Are you still there?" Brad questioned.

Silence.

"Darcey," Brad shouted into the phone. "Answer me. Are you all right?"

"Moon? Mars?" she questioned slowly, not believing what she'd just heard. "This is a joke, right?"

"No, babe. It's no joke."

"You're not seriously considering that insane proposal, are you?" she asked in total disbelief. *I can't believe what I'm hearing. How could he even think of taking the job? The Moon and Mars? It's utterly ridiculous. No, no, it's completely insane!*

"Yeah. My first inclination was to decline, but as Asad explained more about the project, my engineering curiosity took over. I've always been challenged by the seemingly impossible. That's how I developed the Bio Dome. And now this—an even bigger challenge. Honey, I have to consider it. If I don't, I'll be forever beating myself up for not at least trying to be a part of this new beginning of a whole new era of space exploration and colonization." He paused, breathlessly waiting for Darcey's reply.

He is completely out of his skull! How could he? No, no, no! Darcey stood shaking her head back and forth. "I don't want to talk about this anymore. I think you've lost your mind! How could you even think about doing something like that? I hope you've come to your senses by the time you land." She hung up and sat there fuming. *We're just starting a life together, and he wants to go gallivanting out in space?*

Darcey was pacing in front of the phone table when Marti found her.

"Hey, girlfriend, what's up?" Marti asked, sitting down in the chair and fanning herself with the cowboy hat Ty had given her.

"Brad!" Darcey shouted. "It's Brad. Do you know what he wants to do? Do you?" she screeched at Marti.

"Hardly. You haven't told me yet," Marti quipped. "What's the old boy up and done now?"

"He-wants-to-go-into-outer-space!" she said, measured and forcefully, throwing her hands up in the air. "He wants to take Asad's job that will take him to freaking *Mars*!" she blurted out. She could feel her face turning red and tears close to falling as she turned and ran for the stairs.

Marti sat there with her mouth open. *How do you respond to that,* she wondered? *Outer space! OMG!*

♋♋

Brad heard the line go dead. *Damn! She just hung up on me,* he realized. *I've never seen her this upset. Guess I'm going to have to do some fancy explaining to get her to come around. I probably shouldn't have told her over the phone,* he decided, *but I'm just so damned excited about this, I couldn't wait. But what if she doesn't come around,* he asked himself. *How do I work around that? I don't want to be forced to choose. I want both, but if I have to choose—shit! I don't want to even think about it. She's got to come around.* He turned and stared out the plane's window.

♋♋

Sometime later, Marti tapped gently on Darcey's door. "Mind if I come in?" Marti asked quietly, as she peeked around the door at a solemn Darcey sitting in the chair by the window, her arms wrapped around her knees hugging them to her chest.

Darcey just turned, looked at Marti, and shrugged her shoulders.

"Come on, girlfriend, snap out of it," Marti cajoled. "It can't be all that bad. You and Brad will work it out. Maybe he doesn't have to be the one to go into space. Maybe his part can be done here," she suggested. "Just wait until he gets here, and you can talk it out."

"I don't know," Darcey said. "The way he was talking on the phone, he was way too excited about the whole thing, especially, the space part. I can't even begin to think about that. How could he do this without even talking it over with me?" She looked Marti in the eye, hoping to see support for her reasoning.

"Has he officially accepted the job?" Marti asked, sitting cross-legged on the floor in front of Darcey's chair.

"I don't know. He said something about beating himself up if he didn't consider being a part of the project," she said, glumly.

"You do realize that by acting like this you are forcing him to choose between you and the project, don't you?" Marti cocked her head to one side and looked at Darcy quizzically. "Don't you at least owe it to him to hear all about the project first before you go off half-cocked?"

Choose? It never even occurred to me that I would be forcing him to do that. "I suppose so," Darcey admitted be-grudgingly.

She didn't want their marriage to start on a sour note. She wanted everything to be perfect between them. Well, at least, as much as possible. She wasn't that naive to believe everything could be perfect. There were no perfect fairytale endings. Real life had its ups and downs and compromises, and she guessed this was going to be one of those times.

⁊

Brad spent the rest of the nine-hour flight to Morocco going over the project. He needed to make an airtight pro-posal to Darcey, one she could live with. He knew he was being selfish, but he was willing to make any compromise necessary with Darcey in order to be a part of this project.

The more he read, the more excited and determined he became that he had to be a part of it. If it meant that he didn't go to the Moon or Mars…well, he wasn't quite ready to compromise on that—just yet.

Luis's limo was waiting as Brad deplaned. The forty-five-minute ride to the ranch seemed like hours to him. He had his proposal for Darcey all prepared and had rehearsed it several times during the flight. This had to convince her that it was the right thing for him to be a part of Asad's project.

Brad bounded up the walkway and burst through the front door, startling Jose, who was on his way to open it.

"Sorry, Jose," Brad said, briefly stopping to ask where Darcey was.

"In the garden, *señor*," Jose said to Brad's back as he disappeared down the hallway.

"Thanks," Brad hollered back over his shoulder.

He took the shortcut through the dining room to the garden. He paused briefly on the patio, looking out over the garden searching for Darcey. His eyes were drawn to her and immediately, the electric charge of their connection coursed through his body, as he saw her at the far end of the garden, sitting with Marti under a shade tree. He bounded down the patio stairs and broke into a run toward them.

As soon as Brad stepped on the patio, Darcey knew he was there. The overwhelming feeling of electricity flowed through her body as she looked up and saw him running down the path toward her. Immediately, she was on her feet, rushing to meet him. She didn't care anymore about Asad's project at that moment. All she could think about was Brad's arms around her, his kisses, and the feel of his body, pressing against her.

Brad stopped a few feet from Darcey with his arms open wide. She ran into his arms, wrapping her legs around his waist and burying her face in the curve of his neck. Inhaling his scent that sent her world spinning out of control, she melted into his body. She heard his sharp intake of breath as he felt her complete surrender, then slowly he ran his hands up her back, pressing her closer, the heat between them growing stronger. He pulled away just enough to kiss her, but that was short-lived as she heard a loud cough coming from behind them.

"Ahem!" Marti said with a giggle. "Ah, I think you're drawing a crowd."

Darcey pulled away from Brad just enough to see over his shoulder. Several of the gardeners were watching with big grins. She could feel the blush creeping up her neck and onto her face. *Oh, crap!*

Brad was grinning as he released her and tilted her head back and planted a small kiss on the end of her nose.

"I love it when you blush," he whispered, and she buried her face in his chest.

Regaining her composure and feeling the blush receding, Darcey narrowed her eyes and glared up into Brad's eyes. "You!" she said. "You, have some explaining to do!" Her brow furrowed and her mouth in a hard straight line, she grabbed Brad by the hand, gave a forceful yank, and started for the house, pulling him along behind her.

"Hey, take it easy." He chuckled, pretending to stumble, "I might need that arm."

"Oh, just be quiet," she said, trying not to laugh, because, in her mind, she was seeing his six-foot-seven-inch frame pretending to be dragged unwillingly along behind her. She heard a couple of snickers as they passed the gardeners. She could feel the blush coming back. *Oh, crap!*

Darcey stomped up the patio stairs and, reaching the top step, she whirled around, looking Brad directly in the eye. "You!" she exclaimed, trying to keep a stern expression on her face as a giggle slipped out betraying her faked outrage. Then, seeing the feigned hurt expression on his face, she couldn't hold it in any longer—she burst out laughing. *How could anyone stay angry at that face?*

Placing her hands on either side of his face, she kissed him square on the lips. She felt his arm encircle her waist and the other under her knees as he lifted her up and carried her into the house; his lips never leaving her.

"Well, what have we here?" Luis asked, chuckling, as she put her feet down on the floor and straightened her sweater where it had crept up as Brad carried her.

"Good to see you, Luis," Brad said, leaving her side to greet Luis with a warm embrace.

"Good to see you, too, my boy," Luis replied. "When did you arrive?"

"Just a few minutes ago," Brad said, turning and reaching his hand out to Darcey. "I had to see the love of my life the first thing," he said, grinning as he kissed the palm of her hand.

She shut her eyes for fear Luis would see the passion building there. Her body was running hot and cold at the same time as Brad intentionally pulled her closer and wrapped his arm around her. She tried to pull away without making a scene, but he only held her tighter.

Boy! Just wait 'til we're alone. You're gonna get apiece of my mind! She glared up at Brad and was greeted with that lopsided grin. Her anger instantly melted away. *Damn! How does he do that?*

"I presume I'll see you both at dinner?" Luis asked on his way through the French doors to the patio. "Dinner will be at nine. Try not to be late," he said.

Darcey could tell he was laughing, even though his back was to them as he went down the patio steps. She turned, socked Brad on the arm, and huffed her way across the dining room and out into the hallway.

"Hey! What was that for?" Brad exclaimed as he rushed after her. She was halfway up the stairs when he caught up with her.

"That was for embarrassing me in front of Luis, you big oaf!" She turned and glared at him, and there was that grin again. "Damn you! How can I stay mad at you when you keep grinning that way at me," she said, throwing her arms around his neck and kissing him.

"Hmmmm, I'll have to keep that info for future reference." He laughed against her lips. "Where's our room?" he asked, pulling away.

"I don't know where your room is, but my room is right here." She smiled slyly, opening the door.

"You mean we've got separate rooms! What can Luis be thinking?" He laughed, pushing past her into the room. "Not bad, considering it's sorta on the girly side," he said, stretching out on the bed and reaching his hand out to her.

"Oh no, you don't," she exclaimed, sidestepping him and sitting herself down in the chair by the window. "We've got things to discuss."

"Oh, yeah, about that," he said, swinging his legs over the side of the bed and grinning sheepishly. "I had this whole big, long spiel all prepared, giving all the reasons why it is important that I take the job and all of the reasons, to belie your fears about it. But seeing you and holding you in my arms, I forgot all of that. Yes, I want to take the job, but I don't want it to come between us. I couldn't live with myself if that happened. You are my life."

As he was talking, Brad stood up, walked over, and knelt down in front of Darcey. Taking both of her hands in his, he turned them over and kissed the palms of both. He could feel the fire coursing through his veins, his desire for her growing.

Darcey closed her eyes and let his touch wash over her. The fire from his touch completely engulfed her. She had no will. Nothing mattered but him. Time stood still, and, she saw him leaving the earth, and it was all right. She knew it would be all right. Forcing her eyes open, bring herself back to reality, she looked into Brad's eyes and knew he had to do this. It was meant to be. Leaning forward, she whispered in his ear, "Go for it. I don't want any regrets between us."

Brad reached for her, pulling her down on the floor with him, holding her tight against his hard body. They lay wrapped in each other arms as the afternoon light slowly faded into twilight.

CHAPTER 7

Days Before the Wedding

The days leading up to the wedding were filled with: invitations, fittings, cake tastings, menu selections, seating arrangements, flowers, music and musicians, hairstyling, makeup, and an array of other things that Darcey never dreamed went into planning a wedding. By the end of the week before the wedding, she was seriously considering grabbing Brad and eloping.

Then, there were the arrangements to be made for housing all of the wedding guests coming from Dallas and Lima. Luis put Marti in charge of directing the house staff in preparing the rooms to accommodate the fifty some family and wedding party members who would be staying at the ranch. For the rest, Luis had reserved most all of the rooms at the Hilton Hotel Agadir for them.

Madam Chelsea and Darcey finally came to an agreement on the dress, a beautiful creation she designed just for her. It was a wonderful combination of silk, re-embroidered Alencon lace with tiny seed pearls and crystal baguettes, and a three-foot train. It was maybe a little over the top for Darcey, but Marti insisted it was absolutely perfect. Darcey had to agree it fit her curves perfectly, and she did feel like a princess in it.

Marti and the girls along with Marla, who Darcey had asked to be one of her bridesmaids, had their final fittings the day before. The only fitting left was Darcey's today. Luis had insisted on accompanying her to the fitting, even though she had told him for the umpteenth time on the way up in the elevator, that his being there would make her uncomfortable.

"Nonsense, my dear," Luis said, smiling slyly as he walked Darcey to the fitting room door. "I believe this is part of the agreement we made, is it not?" he said, patting her arm.

"Humpft," she snorted and slammed the door.

She could hear him chuckling on the other side, but she didn't have time to fume over it as Catherine already had her dress in her hands ready for Darcey to step into. It fit perfectly. The last few adjustments had been just what were needed. The silk clung to her body like a second skin and flowed gracefully to the floor. The crystals, hand-sewn into the lace around the hem, twinkled and sparkled like fairy lights as she moved. She felt enchanted.

"My, oh my!" Catherine exclaimed, stepping back to admire her handiwork. "Ain't you a beauty? Come, one last turn around. We want to make sure everythin's just perfect. Miz Chelsea'll have my bum if everythin' ain't just so."

Darcey made one last turn around in front of the three-way mirror. The crystals glittered and glimmered as the skirt settled back.

"You're ready," Catherine beamed as she held the door open for her.

Darcey walked out into the outer room, looking straight ahead, and stepped upon the carpeted riser in front of another three-way mirror. She stood looking at herself in the mirror, her back to Luis and Madam Chelsea. *Is that really me?*

She surveyed the girl in the mirror, running her eyes up and down her silk-clad body as the girl in the mirror looked back at her, and she knew her. No more wondering, no more worrying, no more not knowing. She had come full circle. From knowing nothing, the night Brad bought and carried her away to now, remembering it all. It did seem like a fairytale, a wild and crazy fairytale, and she had her prince charming. She slowly turned around to face Luis and Madam Chelsea. The crystals sparkled in the lace, and the silk shimmered as it settled around her body.

"¡*Dios mío!*" Luis gasp, as Darcey turned around. *Saleem. My Saleem,* he thought as moisture formed in the corners of his eyes. "You are breathtaking," he whispered, as he rose up from the sofa, a lump in his throat.

"Oh, you are just purrrrrfect," Madam Chelsea breathed, as she walked around Darcey, looking at her from every possible angle. "I believe this is the most beautiful design I've ever created." She giggled, clapping her hands in delight. "Don't move, my dear," she ordered, as she headed for the double doors across the room. In her haste, stray wisps of hair escaped from the alligator clip that held her hair to the top of her head. "This must be photographed immediately. Marshall!" she shouted. "Bring the camera now! The light is perfect. Marshall! Where is that boy?" she exclaimed as she poked her head around the doorframe. "Oh, there you are. Get in here. No, no, no. Bring the big camera. I want this as a feature in the next catalogue." She hurried back to where Darcey was standing, hastily pushing the unruly strands of hair behind her ears. "The veil," Madam Chelsea said, spinning around, "we must have the veil. Christine!" she hollered. "Bring the veil!"

Moments later, Christine appeared carrying the veil.

"Well, just don't stand there. Put it on her," Madam Chelsea demanded.

"Yes'um, Right away," Christine answered, as she placed the tiered layers of silk Tulle that was attached to a delicate circle of lace, sprinkled with seed pearls, and crystals. A teardrop shaped crystal on a slender silver chain hung delicately from the lace circle onto Darcey's forehead.

"Beautiful! Just beautiful!" Madam Chelsea exclaimed, standing back, hands on her hips, grinning. "Yes! I've outdone myself this time!"

Darcey's head was spinning as she watched all the chaos

going on around her. She felt like she was having an out-of-body experience. She looked pleadingly at Luis to put a stop to all of this, but his eyes had glazed over as if in a trance. As he stood staring at her, there was an expression on his face she couldn't read. Darcey closed her eyes and tried to concentrate on Brad, but that was short lived as Madam Chelsea shouted at her. Her eyes flew open.

"Darcey! Pay attention! I want you to smile. This is the happiest day of your life, so act like it! I can't have a bride looking like she's going to a funeral wearing my most exquisite creation ever," Madam Chelsea scolded. "You are to be featured in my new catalogue. You will be the cover! Now, smile!"

Darcey did her best to please Madam Chelsea although she wasn't sure any of her smiles ever reached her eyes. She felt on the verge of another meltdown as Marshall circled her, his camera clicking away.

Oh, pull yourself together, girl! her inner voice, that had been missing for days, scolded her. *Have you turned into a complete wuss? Where's the girl Uncle Jack raised? Remember, there isn't anything you can't handle if you just put your mind to it.*

She took a deep breath and looked again at Luis, who appeared to be back to normal and was smiling broadly at her with a twinkle in his eye. She decided then, that no matter how hard she tried to control this situation, she couldn't. This was an adventure that Fate had set her on, and it left her little chance of changing the path it had created for her. Whatever awaited her, she would meet it head on, as always—*Damn the torpedoes. Full speed ahead.*

એન્ડ

Marti was in her element, getting the guests all settled, especially Ty, whose room she managed to get right next to hers. Scott, Matt, and Hot Dog were a little ways down the hall, and Brad's sister and her family were in the room next to Ty's. Ashley and Wendy's room was across the hall right next to Brad's who's was next to Darcey's, in spite of his grumbling to Luis that it was a waste of a good room when he could easily share Darcey's. Donna and Melanie's room was on the other side of Ashley and Wendy. Darcey's family's rooms had been prepared in the west wing along Mike and his new fiancé.

Rooms all assigned and everyone settling in, Marti commandeered Marla to help her arrange with the kitchen for some light refreshments to be served in the dining room around three, in anticipation of Darcey and Luis's return from the fitting. The chef had prepared an array of finger sandwiches, sweets, and fresh fruit along with coffee, tea, and wine. It was all beautifully arranged on the sideboard as the guests wandered in.

Marti prepared a plate for her and Ty and motioned to him to follow her out onto the patio where she grabbed his hand and pulled him gently down the stairs and out into the garden. Brad watched from just inside the French doors, a knowing grin on his lips, as Marti and Ty wound their way through the garden to the gazebo at the far end. He thought about the call he had made to Ty.

He had called Ty from his hotel room in Dubai the night before Ty and the boys were to fly out of Lima for Morocco. Never one to beat around the bush, Brad went straight to the point of his call. Was he or wasn't he going to ask Marti to marry him? There was silence on the other end, and Brad wondered if he'd gotten the information wrong from Darcey.

"Hey! Ty! You still there?" Brad shouted into the phone, hoping it was just a bad connection.

"Yeah, I'm still here, and ya don't haveta shout," Ty finally replied. "Just tryin' to figure out how you knew about that."

"Well, you know, girls talk." Brad laughed, relieved. "With the weddin' and everything, the girls started comparing notes, and one thing led to another. Marti confided in Darcey that she thought you might be gonna propose, but didn't know for sure. Then Darcey got on the phone and called me to see what I knew, and now I'm talkin' to you. So, are you or ain't you?"

"Well, seein' how the cat's out o' the bag now." Ty chortled. "Looks like I don't have much of a choice."

"So when ya gonna do it?" Brad asked, still laughing.

"Well, I was gonna do it right after you all left on your honeymoon. Say, just where are you goin' anyway? Don't remember you ever talkin' about that," Ty asked, subtly changing the subject, but it wasn't lost on Brad.

"Haven't quite decided that, yet. But back to you asking Marti, when you gonna do it?" Brad persisted, chuckling.

"I gotta a week's vaca'n Marti's dad's lookin' after things in Dallas. So, I kinda thought I'd check into a week-end cruise of some sort and do it then," Ty said thoughtfully. "Whatta ya think?"

"Sounds pretty romantic to me," Brad said, leaning back in his chair and propping his feet up on the side of the bed. "You want me to do some checking for you? That could save you some time'n that'd be a real surprise for Marti."

"Yeah, man, if ya don't mind." Ty chuckled wickedly. "That'd be really great. Then I could still keep Marti wonderin'."

Now, Brad felt Darcey walk through the door, even before he turned around to find her staring longingly across the room at him. Slowly her grin spread into a sexy smile as their eyes met, and everything else around them faded away.

CHAPTER 8

Confessions

Luis couldn't put it off any longer. He had to tell Darcey about Saleem and Aicha Kaddur before the wedding. In the days before Darcey had arrived at the ranch, Luis had finally gone to see Aicha and told her the results of the DNA test. He was surprised when she simply smiled and said, "I know."

"Why did you not say something to me?" Luis asked in disbelief.

"Luis, you are not the only one with connections." Aicha continued to smile. "I have many connections of my own, and some that even find their way into yours."

"I was not hiding anything from you," Luis replied. "I merely assumed that since you did not contact me for the results of the test, you were not interested in knowing."

"Yes, at first, I was not. I did not want to feel the loss of my daughter again. I did not want to open myself up to disappointment if she were not my granddaughter. I had stored away the memories of my daughter a long time ago. Then, the more I looked at the girl's photo, the more I saw Saleem. But too much time had passed, and I was embarrassed to ask, so I had a friend of the family check for me." Aicha paused, looking past Luis at the array of photos that lined the shelves behind him. "When I had my answer, I had to see for myself. I arranged for an invitation to the opening of the dome to see what this girl looked like in the flesh."

"But you could have come to me for the invitation, that much you know," Luis said softly.

"Yes, but again I was embarrassed. What would you think of me, first not wanting to know about my grand-daughter, and then asking for a favor? I could not do that." Aicha stood and pulled a velvet sash beside the door. "Tea?"

"Yes, *por favor*." Luis sighed, pulling a gold embossed wedding invitation from his jacket pocket. He watched Aicha gracefully walk back to her chair and waited until she was settled before he stood and handed her the invitation.

"*Gracias*, Luis. I was not sure you would extend me an invitation. I would have come anyway, you know." She smiled as she accepted the invitation.

"Yes, I have no doubt."

෧෧෧

The matter settled with Aicha, Luis now had to explain everything to Darcey, but he worried that he could not fully explain everything and that Darcey might not understand. He knew she only tolerated him now because of Brad. Could she find it in her heart to forgive him for buying and selling her? He had complied with her demands about the women, but would that be enough? He did not know. He only hoped.

Luis sat in the big leather chair behind his desk. He slowly turned to watch the horses milling in the paddock, the waning light making them silhouettes against the white of the barn, a glass of Scotch held loosely in his hand. It was now or never, he thought. I can't put it off any longer.

Taking a final swallow of the amber liquid, Luis sat the glass on his desk and walked out into the hall in search of Darcey. He found her on the patio stretched out on the lounge chair in the shadows, her eyes looking skyward at the twinkling stars making their appearance in the evening sky. She jumped as he cleared his throat.

"Sorry, I did not mean to startle you," Luis said, sitting down in the matching armchair. "I need to tell you something, and I don't know where to begin," he said thoughtfully.

Darcey smiled softly. "I always find it best to start at the beginning."

"Yes, I suppose you are right, but just where the beginning is, I am not sure." Luis sighed and looked skyward also. *Dios mío, give me the right words.*

Slowly he told Darcey about Saleem, Aicha, and what led him to do the things that eventually brought her to him. He explained how he found out she was Saleem's daughter, and how Brad had tracked her to the ranch, then, how he had protected her by making Nicho her guardian until the Gala was over, and lastly how he had made sure Brad was the one who purchased her.

Darcey sat up as Luis started his unbelievable, at least to her, tale. She bristled when he described what had happened to her supposed mother. *My mother was not a prostitute! She was not this woman he is describing. My mother had graduated from Texas University with an MFA in Art, for crying out loud! She taught art. She did not come from Morocco! She was born in Fort Worth, I saw her birth certificate! No, no, no!* Her mind screamed.

Darcey was vaguely aware of what Luis had said about Brad finding her, about Nicho, and the other stuff he was saying. She just couldn't get past the part about her mother.

"*No!*" she screamed at Luis. "I won't hear any more of this. You did not know my mom! She is not your Saleem. Her name was Sara. Sara Callahan!" She stood with her hands on her hips glaring at Luis. "You can't talk about my mother like that. I won't have it!"

Darcey stomped past Luis and into the dining room almost slamming into Marti.

"Hey! What's the matter?" Marti questioned.

"Not-now!" Darcey snapped at Marti and stalked out of the dining room into the hall, leaving Marti staring after her.

Darcey needed somewhere to go and think. A place where she could be alone. She had always found the quiet of the women's courtyard late in the evening a calming place. She wandered through the halls, not sure how to find it from this side of the house. She turned a corner and instantly knew the hallway. It was the hall where her old room was. Slowly she walked on, the heels of her shoes clicking on the stone floor. The damp smell she remembered assailed her nose. She stopped in front of her old room and placed her hand on the handle. She pushed, it gave way, and the door swung open. It was dark. The drapes were drawn and no evening light shown through the windows. The room smelled musty.

Strange, she thought, *I never noticed that when I lived here.*

She stepped inside and turned on the lamp by the sofa. The room looked unlived in. A light coat of dust covered the lamp table. She checked the closet; it was empty.

Has no one lived in here since I did? I must ask Marla.

Darcey wandered through the rest of the room, remembering. She ran her hand along the back of the chair before she sat down. She laid her head back, her eyes drifted shut.

I have to sort this out. What Luis said cannot be true. There is no way my mom was kidnapped and sold into prostitution. Let alone been born in Morocco. No. No way in hell!

⋐⋑⋐⋑

Darcey must have dozed off and did not hear anyone enter the room until she felt a gentle touch on her arm. She jerked awake and looked directly into Brad's eyes. Without hesitation, she threw her arms around his neck and sobbed. He held her tight, and she felt safe.

Brad let her cry herself out until there was nothing but hiccups left.

"Did you talk to Luis?" Darcey asked between hiccups. "Did he tell you what he told me?"

"Yes, I've known all about this ever since I found you here. When you regained your memory, Luis asked me to not say anything because he wanted to tell you himself. He is quite worried just now, you know, the way you stormed out," Brad said, gently raising her head up and kissing her forehead.

"Well, he can keep worrying, for all I care," she said, shoving herself away from Brad. "Surely you don't believe him, do you?"

"Well, it's kinda hard to dispute the DNA test on this," Brad said, pulling Darcey up into his arms. "I think you need to calm down and think this through logically. You said your folks never talked about any family on your mom's side. Could this be the reason?"

"Oh, I don't know," She pulled out Brad's arms and paced. "I don't want to think about my mom being a prostitute. I've heard too many tales from some of the women here to know what Luis said could be true, but not my mom. No! It could not have happened to her. It just couldn't," she said emphatically. "It's just too horrible to think about. Mom was the sweetest, kindest person ever. No, I can't wrap my mind around something like that." She covered her face with her hands. "No," she shouted balling her hands into fists. "No, I won't accept it!"

Fuming, she paced around the room. The more she walked, the calmer she became. Her mind slowly released its hold on the word *prostitute* and let her consider that what Brad said might be true. *Could that be the reason Mom had never talked about her family? Was that why she always seemed to answer my questions without actually answering them? Was that why I could never pin her down on anything about her past? Why did both Mom and Dad keep this secret from me? What were they afraid of?*

All those questions swirled through Darcey's mind, making her doubt what she knew about her mother's life. Questions that she feared might never be answered.

Brad watched as Darcey paced around the room. His heart hurt for her, and he longed to take her in his arms to comfort her but knew it would be useless at this point. At least until she worked it out for herself. Then, once Darcey had it all sorted out, he knew she would see that what Luis had told her was true.

Darcey turned and looked at Brad. She could see the worry in his eyes. "I'm okay," she finally said, giving him a half-hearted smile. "It's just hard for me to understand why Mom and Dad would have kept this from me, and why they went to so much trouble to hide where Mom came from. I even saw what they told me was her birth certificate and her diploma from the University. It makes no sense to me why they couldn't trust me with that."

"I'm sure they had an excellent reason," Brad said, walking over to her. "Maybe if you talk with Luis, you might be able to understand it."

"I don't know," she said, reaching up and lacing her fingers behind Brad's neck. "I was pretty rude to him. He probably wishes now he'd never met me." She buried her face in Brad's neck, inhaling his manly scent and feeling safe in his arms.

Brad pulled her closer and sighed. "I'm sure he'll forgive you," he whispered in her hair.

"Will you come with me?" she asked, her voice muffled by the collar of his shirt. "I think I'm going to need some moral support."

"You don't have a thing to worry about, silly," Brad said, lifting her head and grinning that heart-stopping grin that set her heart racing. "Luis loves you like a daughter— the daughter he and Saleem would have had."

That hit her like a ton of bricks. *Me? Luis? Mom? He could have been my father?* She squeezed her eyes shut and rubbed her temples. *This is just too much. The wedding,*

Brad's new project, and now this? Her stress level was at the max. The inevitable was closing in, and she had no wiggle room. Luis had seen to that. She reached for Brad's hand, took a ragged breath, and slowly walked out of the room. "Come on. Let's get this over with."

They found Luis still sitting on the patio where he had been when Darcey had stormed out, his head resting on the back of the chair, his eyes closed.

"Luis," Darcey said softly, trying not to startle him. "I've come to apologize for my outburst."

Luis raised his head. "There is no need to apologize. I should have realized that the information might upset you." He sighed, shaking his head. "I am the one who should apologize for handling it so badly."

Darcey slowly sank down onto the lounge chair she had been sitting on before. Brad sat down beside her, still holding her hand. He gave her hand a supportive squeeze as she inhaled, preparing to hear what Luis had been trying to tell her before she flew off the handle.

"Please, tell me about my mother," she said quietly.

For the next hour, Luis told Darcey all about him and Saleem. How she was kidnapped, his desperate search for her, the forming of his Elite Force, and about her grandmother, pouring his heart out, letting his deepest feelings come through.

Although he could not see Darcey clearly in darkness, he had heard sniffing several times.

She wiped away the streaks of tears that had trailed down her face. Her heart hurt for her mother and what she must have been through. Even though Darcey had been kidnapped and sold, her circumstances had been nothing like her mother's. Thankful that God had delivered her to Luis, she felt that maybe her mom had been watching over her, too.

Luis finished his story and watched Darcey as she leaned forward. "Why didn't my parents tell me all of this?" she asked, trying to see Luis's face in the dim light.

"I do not know for sure, but I can guess, that if your father had helped Saleem escape her captors, they may have been afraid the captors would come looking for them. My guess is your father was the one instrumental in getting a new identity for Saleem. She became Sara Callahan, your mother and art teacher in Dallas, Texas. I have no idea where they may have met or under what circumstances your father helped her escape. I am sure they did not tell you, in order to keep you safe. Those people who took Saleem have very long memories." Luis sighed, looking at Darcey and wanting so much to reach out and comfort her, but he hesitated.

Cold chills covered her body as the realization of what Luis's words implied. Her mind began spinning with thousands of questions.

Did anyone else in the family know about this? Had Mom and Dad confided in anyone or had they kept the secret to themselves all this time? Maybe Uncle Jack would know. I have to have answers.

Overcoming his hesitation, Luis leaned forward and reached for Darcey's hand. He had to touch her. He wanted to hug her but knew that would be impossible right now, so he gently laid his hand on Darcey's. She did not flinch, and his heart swelled with joy. As he let his fingers slowly wrap around her hand, he felt how cold she was.

"Oh, my. How thoughtless of me keeping you out here. You are freezing. Come, let us go inside and warm up," Luis said gently, pulling Darcey up as he stood.

Darcey was conscious of Luis's hand holding hers. It was warm and pleasant. She looked down at her hand cradled gently in his and wondered what life would have been like if he were her father. Her mind refused to visualize it. The memories of her mom and dad came flooding in and pushed all other thoughts out. She felt Brand stand up behind her as Luis led her into the house.

Luis cautioned himself to take it slow. *Do not rush it,* he thought, *she is letting you hold her hand. Do not push for more now. I will let her come to me on her own,* he decided. Then, even though he had cautioned himself to wait, he could not resist the temptation and linked her arm with his.

Still not sure how she felt about Luis, she didn't resist when he linked their arms. She decided she would give him a chance. After all, he had agreed to her conditions and had already released the women. Surprisingly, though, most opted to stay, and Luis had set the date for the first Bel Ami Gala for prospective husbands to take place next month.

Luis's step was light as he walked with Darcey to the library, only releasing her as she sat down in one of the leather chairs.

"Perhaps a brandy to warm you up?" Luis asked Darcey.

"No, but I would like a small Scotch and water please," she answered. She couldn't abide the taste of brandy. Uncle Jack had always enjoyed a brandy in the evening before bed. She had asked many times for a taste, but he always replied, "When you're old enough."

Then, on her sixteenth birthday, she had raided Uncle Jack's liquor cabinet and drank a half bottle of brandy. She had been sure she was going to die, if not from the brandy, surely from Uncle Jack's wrath. But neither happened. Uncle Jack just said, "I trust you've learned your lesson."

"Something for you, Brad," Luis asked, dropping ice cubes into the glass.

"Yes, Scotch with a little ice," Brad said, sitting down on the arm of Darcey's chair.

"Your grandmother wants to meet you," Luis said, handing Darcey her drink.

Darcey's hand stopped mid-way reaching for the glass. She hadn't expected that, although she probably should have. Her grandmother had gone to a great deal of trouble to get to the dome to have a look at her but had not made any attempt to introduce herself. Now that Darcey knew that she was the strange woman at the opening, she thought it rude on her grandmother's part not to have at least tried to meet her.

"When?"

"Before the rehearsal dinner, I believe," Luis replied. "She wants to come early before there are too many people."

"Do you suppose she would come tomorrow? I'd rather meet her on a less-stressful day." Darcey didn't want to take the chance that, if they didn't hit it off, it would spoil the dinner.

"I will ask her. I am sure that will be fine with Aicha. Shall we say four o'clock?"

"That will be fine," Darcey said. "Will she come here or should I go there?"

"She is planning on coming here. Not to worry, I will have tea prepared for her visit."

"Thank you." Sighing, Darcey leaned back in the chair. She hadn't realized just how tense she had become until she relaxed against the back of the chair and let her eyes drift shut. *I need sleep.*

Luis watched Darcey, noticing how vulnerable she looked. He wanted so much to cradle her in his arms, to tell her she was safe and that his heart was filled with a father's love for her. How could he make her see just how special she was to him? She was his only connection to his lost Saleem. Even though she was not of his blood, she was of Saleem's, and that was all the mattered now. He sighed and stood up. "It grows late, and you have had a big day," he said, looking at Darcey. "I will call your grandmother and arrange for the meeting to take place tomorrow afternoon."

"Yes, I think you're right," Brad said, taking Darcey's hand and pulling her up. "It's been a big day, and you need your rest."

She didn't argue. She was ready for this day to be over. All of her energy had drained away. She was already planning that long, hot soak in the tub to put her right to sleep.

Luis watched Brad and Darcey walk out of the room.

Dios, por favor, let me get this right, he prayed.

CHAPTER 9

Sunlight filtered through the crack where the drapes didn't quiet touch letting a bright beam stab across the room, piercing the dull grayness of the interior. Darcey stretched and rolled over, staring at the dust particles dancing in the streaming light, wondering what the woman who was supposed to be her grandmother was like.

Would she like me? Would I like her?

Darcey hadn't known her dad's parents very well. They lived in Seattle, and on the few times they had visited, they seemed really nice but distant. She couldn't ever remember her family going to Seattle to visit them. Then, when her mom and dad had been killed in the car crash, she couldn't remember if they were at the funeral. In fact, she didn't remember much about the funeral at all. She just knew they had never visited again.

A gentle tap on the door caused her to jump. Marti stuck her head around the door and grinned. "You up?" she wanted to know, pushing the door all the way open and entering.

"Yeah, just lying here, thinking about meeting this woman." Darcey hadn't been able to think of her as *Grandmother*. It was all too strange.

"Well, I'm sure she is very nice," Marti said. "I know she'll just love you. How could she not?"

"Yeah, maybe," Darcey said skeptically. "We'll see.

She's a whole 'nother culture. What could we possibly have in common?" She jumped out of bed and headed for the bathroom to dress.

"Don't make any rash judgments, yet. Wait 'til you meet her. You may have more in common than you think," Marti cautioned through the closed door.

"I seriously doubt it," Darcey shouted back.

Walking back into the bedroom, she pulled a pair of Wranglers off the wardrobe shelf. She had picked up several pairs while in Dallas. Although she loved the designer stuff, there wasn't anything like a good, comfortable pair of jeans.

"You're not going to wear *jeans* to meet your grandmother, are you?" Marti asked with raised eyebrows.

"Heavens, no." Darcey glared at her. "Give me some credit. I'll wear a dress. Don't like 'em, but I'll wear one to meet her. After that, if she can't like me in jeans, then that's her problem. I'm not making myself over for anyone," she said emphatically, walking out the door. "Let's get some breakfast."

ജলে

Darcey kept watching the clock slowly tick away the minutes, her stomach churning. *What if this woman really is my grandmother? How should I address her? I would feel awkward calling her Grandmother right off the bat. But then, I can't very well call her Aicha either. I suppose Señora Kaddur will have to do for now.*

Darcey sorted through the closet for the umpteenth time for a dress that would be both suitable and comfortable. Finally, settling on a baby-blue silk dress with a scooped neckline that would show off the beautiful necklace Brad had bought her in Dubai.

Opting for a pair of flats instead of heels, she was ready to meet her *grandmother.*

Brad was waiting at the bottom of the stairs. His eyes lit

with passion as he watched Darcey gracefully float down the stairs.

"You take my breath away." Brad let out a small, slow whistle. "If you weren't going to meet Aicha, I'd carry you right back upstairs."

"Why, thank you, sir." Darcey blushed and grinned slyly. "See me after six. I'll be available then."

Stopping on the stair that put her slightly higher than Brad, she planted a quick kiss on his forehead.

"May I take that as a date?" Brad grinned, placing his hands on her waist.

Her body instantly ran hot and cold at his touch, and there was no air to breathe. He lifted her up off the step and let her sexily slide down his body until her feet gently touched the floor in front of him. They were lost in each other's eyes, the rest of the world fading away. There were only the two of them until they heard a sharp cough.

Turning quickly they saw Luis standing watching them with a knowing smile on his lips. "Now, now. You'll have plenty of time for that later." He laughed, and Darcey blushed.

Luis had been watching Brad and Darcey for several minutes remembering the love and passion that had flowed between Saleem and himself. He could clearly see Darcey was Saleem's daughter, even without the DNA test. He had known it in his heart.

"Come," Luis said, extending his hand to Darcey, hoping she would not refuse. "We will meet Aicha in the library. It is more comfortable there." He was overjoyed as Darcey placed her hand in his. He gave it a gentle squeeze as he smiled warmly at her.

Blushing, Darcey placed her hand in Luis's. It was warm and comforting, and surprisingly, it took some of her anxiety away. She walked with him down the hall to the library. Brad followed behind.

"Aicha will be here shortly," Luis said. "Jose will bring tea and coffee, but you will have to serve it. We will leave you alone to visit." Luis walked to the door, pulled the brocade sash hanging there, then motioned for Brad to follow him.

Brad turned and gave Darcey a reassuring smile as he followed Luis out the door.

Darcey paced around the room, rehearsing things to say, rejecting them all after she said them out loud. They sounded forced and contrived.

Why don't you just be yourself? her inner voice whispered to her. *There's no need to try to be something you're not. Just be you and you'll be okay.*

I hope you're right.

Jose brought in a large tray with silver pots filled with coffee and tea, and a crystal plate filled with scones. He placed it on the carved teak table in the center of the seating area.

She smiled. "*Gracias*, Jose."

"Will that be all, Señorita Darcey?"

She could only nod because suddenly her mouth had gone all Sahara Desert on her, as a movement from the doorway caught her eye. Standing in the doorway was the imposing figure of a woman dressed in a royal blue djellaba and matching hijab. Immediately, Darcey's palms began to sweat as she stared wide-eyed at the woman. Darcey was sure her feet had attached themselves to the Persian rug she was standing on as she tried to pull herself together. She only hoped she didn't look as juvenile as she felt.

Aicha stopped in the doorway studying Darcey as she spoke to Jose. Darcey's grace and beauty astounded her. In the dome, she had never let herself get close enough to see how truly beautify she was. *This is Saleem's daughter*, she thought, *my granddaughter*. Aicha's heart felt light and hopeful. She had given up all hope of finding Saleem years ago, and now fate had brought Saleem's daughter to her. *I have been truly blessed* she thought, as a slow smile lit up her face.

Regaining her composure, Darcey said, "Señora Kaddur,

welcome. Come in, *por favor*." She indicated the seating area in front of the fireplace.

Aicha inclined her head toward Darcey and moved gracefully across the floor, sitting down in one of the leather chairs, never taking her eyes off of Darcey.

Darcey swallowed as she walked over and sat down on the sofa. In that instant, what little of her resolve she had left evaporated. *Get it together, girl,* her inner voice barked at her. *She's just another woman. Be gracious, but don't let her intimidate you. Remember, it's up to you to decide if you want a relationship with her, not the other way around. Remember that.*

"Would you care for tea or coffee?" Darcey asked, not really knowing what was correct. She should have asked Luis what was customary in cases like this, but it was too late now, so she just decided to do what she would do if she were at home. She smiled and placed her hand on the pot of tea, anticipating her choice.

Aicha smiled graciously. "Tea would be perfect."

Carefully Darcey picked up a cup and saucer, filled the cup with tea, then placed a scone on a gold-rimmed china plate along with a napkin and handed both to Aicha. She filled a cup with coffee for herself.

"*Gracias,*" Aicha said, inclining her head. She took the plate with the scone and placed it on the table beside the chair. Slowly she took a sip from her cup of tea, all the while watching Darcey. She then placed the cup and saucer beside the plate. "I am your grandmother," Aicha state flatly. "Your mother was my daughter."

"Yes, I know," Darcey replied. "Luis has told me all about it."

"Very well, then," she said, looking Darcey in the eye. "There's no need for me to repeat what Luis has already told you. You know all the details then. What I want now is for you to tell me about my daughter. Leave nothing out— no matter how insignificant you may think something might be—I want to know it."

As Aicha finished speaking, Darcey suddenly became aware just how hot the cup in her hand was. Quickly. she set it down in the saucer that she had left sitting on the tray and cleared her throat, as she tried to decide just where to begin. "I can only tell you what I know," Darcey said. "What came before I was born, I have no knowledge of. I have only just found out the truth about my mother. If anyone knows about what happened before I was born, I don't know who that would be."

"That is all right," Aicha said softly. "Whatever you can tell me will be more than I know now. My memories of my daughter ended twenty-five years ago."

Darcey could feel her pain as she spoke and she saw a vulnerable, lonely woman who presented a hard, crusty shell to the world, keeping the pain of her loss deep in her soul. Darcey understood from Luis when her husband passed, her only son had gone his own way, leaving Aicha to run the family business by herself. It was a hard situation for a woman in Morocco.

Aicha listened intently, her hands folded in her lap, never moving, her eyes locked on Darcey as she continued, reliving the memories as she shared them with Aicha.

Feeling awkward about showing her feelings to a stranger, Darcey avoided looking directly at Aicha whenever possible. Several times, she had to wipe away a stray tear that escaped her eyes as she talked about the car crash that took her mom and dad's life.

Darcey didn't know how long she talked before her mouth completely dried out. She picked up her cup and took a swallow of the now-cold coffee. *Ugh!* But it was wet and unglued her tongue from the roof of her mouth. Setting the cup down, she glanced at Aicha and saw her face was wet with unchecked tears.

"I'm sorry. I didn't mean to upset you," Darcey said softly.

"You did not," Aicha replied, pulling a handkerchief from somewhere under the djellaba. "Please continue."

Darcey had finished telling Aicha about the funeral and her dad's parents and was beginning to talk about dad's sister, Aunt Maggie, and his brothers, Uncles Mark and Jack when Aicha interrupted her.

"Your father's family. They have never been back to visit or asked to take custody of you?" she inquired with a raised eyebrow.

"No. My Uncle Jack took me in and took care of me until I went to college."

"Your Uncle Jack, what did he have to say about his parents not wanting you?" she questioned.

"I don't know. Aunt Maggie, Uncle Mark, and Uncle Jack never talked about it, at least not in front of me. I had no relationship with my grandparents. They have never been a part of my life."

"How sad." Aicha sighed and looked somewhere over Darcey's head. "Family is everything. You never know just how much until they are no longer with you." She dabbed the handkerchief at the corner of her eye. "I wish to meet your Uncle Jack. I presume he is here?" Aicha said, directing her gaze back to Darcey.

"Yes. I will introduce you at the rehearsal dinner," Darcey offered.

"No. That will not do." Her demeanor shifted instantly to demanding. "I must speak with him now."

Taken aback by her shift in attitude, Darcey stammered, "I—I'll see if I can find him." Then remembering her manners, she asked if Aicha would join them for the evening meal.

"Yes, I would very much like that."

"If you will excuse me, I will inform Luis that I have invited you to dine with us and then find Uncle Jack."

Having excused herself, Darcey went in search, first, of Luis, and then her Uncle Jack.

❧❦❧

Darcey found Uncle Jack on the patio just outside the dining room talking with Aunt Maggie. She went and stood beside his chair resting her hand on his shoulder. She waited until Aunt Maggie took a breath for the opportunity to tell him Aicha wanted to speak with him.

He gave Darcey a quizzical look as he stood and followed her to the dining room.

"What's the old bat want with me?" he whispered not too quietly.

Darcey had filled Uncle Jack in right after Luis had told her about her mom, in hopes he might know something about how her parents met. But all he knew was her dad had gone to Mexico City on a job, and he came back six months later married to her mom, and ten months later she was born. He said her dad never offered any explanation, but he did know that Grandma and Grandpa Callahan were extremely upset and stopped visiting after that. It had been a closed subject, and no one was allowed to talk about it.

Darcey shrugged as they reached the library door. Uncle Jack allowed her to proceed him through the door. She stepped to the side, and Uncle Jack stopped beside her.

"Señora Kaddur, this is my Uncle Jack Callahan,"

"Señor Callahan, a pleasure," Aicha said, as she turned and looked at Darcey. "That will be all. I wish to speak to Señor Callahan in private," she said, leaving no doubt she intended to be obeyed.

Darcey swallowed, inclined her head, and left, feeling like a child again. She went to find Brad. She needed a hug.

CHAPTER 10

The Morning Of

Stepping out onto the balcony, Darcey inhaled the fresh morning air and watched as fluffy white clouds dotted the azure blue sky like cotton balls. *This is it. The day is here. In just seven hours, I will be Mrs. Brad Daniels.*

Goose bumps covered her arms, and she hugged herself, elated with anticipation of starting her new life. She didn't know what tomorrow would bring, but whatever was in store for them, they would face it together.

Brad had already called Asad, confirming he would take the job. Darcey still had mixed feelings about it but would support Brad one hundred percent on his decision.

Marti startled her as she stepped out onto the balcony.

"I knocked." Marti laughed, "Guess you were daydreaming and didn't hear me."

"Probably." Darcey turned and hugged her. "Is this really happening? I'm not dreaming, am I?"

"No. This is the day. It's your fairytale coming true." Marti returned her hug. "Let's go get some breakfast," she suggested.

"No. I couldn't keep anything down." Darcey turned and walked back into the bedroom. Her nerves were raw, and she had tossed and turned all night, worrying what Aicha and her Uncle Jack had talked about.

Marti followed. "I'll bring you some coffee, then. What

time do you want Marla and me to come help you get ready?"

"I don't know. Maybe after lunch," Darcey said, rather sharply.

Uncle Jack and Aicha had visited for almost two hours. Both had offered no explanation at dinner that evening. Uncle Jack had avoided her altogether when it looked like she was about to corner him and ask questions, and there was no way she was going to ask Aicha.

Marti backed up holding her hands up in front of her as if to fend her off. "Hey, don't go all 'bridezilla' on me now!"

"I'm sorry," Darcey said, throwing herself on the bed, pulling the pillow over her head, and screaming into the mattress.

"Darcey Marie Callahan!" Marti said sternly, giving Darcey's backside a substantial slap. "Get you butt up and act like the adult you are. I won't stand for any silliness today. I'm your maid of honor, and I take my duties very seriously. So, young lady, you will get up and prepare yourself to marry that big hunk snoring away in the next room," Marti said through bursts of laughter, tears rolling down her cheeks. "No more tantrums."

"Arrrg!" Darcey exclaimed as she rolled over, laughing, and threw the pillow at Marti. When nothing else could, Marti was always there to pull her out of a funk and make her laugh.

∽∾∽

Luis was up early to meet Aicha. She had asked to meet with him this morning while everything was still calm.

Jose showed Aicha to Luis's office where he waited.

"*Buenas días*, Aicha." Luis greeted her with a warm smile. "Tea?"

"Yes, *por favor*," she replied, seating herself in one of

the chairs in front of Luis's desk. "I want to get right to the point. I am ill. The doctors have diagnosed me with leukemia. They say I have maybe six months to a year left."

"Aicha, I am so sorry. What can I do for you?" Luis asked, stunned, as he slowly sank into the chair next to her. Never in a million years would he ever have imagined something like this happening to Aicha. She had always been in good health and active. She had to be to keep the family business running. Luis had lost all respect for Ahmed when he walked out after his father's death, leaving Aicha to struggle with keeping the company running. It had not been easy in a male-dominated world to conduct business, but she had preserved.

"What I need from you, Luis," she said, pointedly, "is for you to contact your attorney. I wish to change my will, and I do not trust the company's attorney. He is still in touch with Ahmed, and I do not want him to know about this. I am afraid, if he learns of my situation, he will try to take the business from me. I have found out he has bribed someone on my board, so I must be careful how this is handled. No one knows about my illness, except for my doctors and now, you.

"Even though I have gained some standing in the business community, I am still a woman in a man's world. I fear, with the right support behind Ahmed, it would be easy for him to persuade the rest of the board that it is not a woman's place to be the head of the company. Especially one who is terminally ill. I have no doubt he would be ruthless in his attempt to take the business from me. Plus, I have a strong suspicion that Ahmed was behind ORCA's trouble on the Bio Dome Project."

Luis immediately leaned forward. Had he heard correctly? *Has that little bastard been the cause of all the trouble? If it is so, I will slit his throat,* he swore to himself. Luis placed his hand on Aicha's. "What are you saying? Are you saying Ahmed was involved with Javier?"

"Not just involved, I believe he was behind the whole

thing from the start. I have a friend on the Eastern Alliance board that has been keeping me apprised of Ahmed's movements at considerable risk to his own life. They have told me that Ahmed is now big into the heroin trade and has been funneling millions of dollars to the EA to fund that sabotage attempt on the dome. His goal was to run his heroin business out of the dome where he could not be touched by the authorities." Aicha paused, taking a drink of her tea before she continued. "His plans included taking over OR-CA and using it to front his operation. Fortunately, the entire operation was bungled from the start."

"I will do my best to protect you," Luis said. "I will call my attorney immediately and have him meet with you in my office right after the ceremony."

"Thank you, Luis," she said. "I was confident I could count on your discretion."

Aicha sank back against the chair's back. A feeling of relief washed over her. Once she had her will changed, the biggest worry would be over. She would have secured Darcey's inheritance and blocked Ahmed from contesting it.

Watching Aicha out of the corner of his eye, Luis could see just how tired she looked now. Something he had not noticed before as she had kept up a strong façade for the public, hiding her illness.

೮ುಲ

Brad hurried down to breakfast, hoping for a quick glimpse of Darcey before Marti sequestered her until the ceremony. Surveying the dining room, he did not see her but noticed Marti filling two cups with coffee.

"Where's Darcey," he asked, sidling up to Marti.

"She's in her room, and you can't see her." Marti poked him in the chest with her finger, accentuating her point.

"Ouch! I just wanna say 'Hi,'" he said, looking all hurt and dejected as he rubbed his chest.

"Well, you can say your 'Hi' through the door." Marti giggled. "You'll not be seein' Darcey 'til she walks down the aisle, mister," she said, over her shoulder as she walked out the door. She carried the two cups of coffee up to Darcey's room and placed them on the table outside on the balcony. "Brad says 'Hi,' 'n I'm tellin' you, right now, you're not to see him—no matter how much he begs," she said in her I'll-stand-for-no-nonsense' manner, her hands on her hips.

"Okay, not to worry." Darcey giggled. "I promise." Solemnly she crossed her heart as she stepped out on the balcony. She looked at the clock on the bedside table as she passed by. It was a little before ten. *Four more hours.* Sipping her coffee and looking out over the grounds, she was lost in thought. *It still doesn't seem real. Has it only been four years since I graduated? I had had my life all planned out—graduate college, get a good job, save for five years, start my own business. Yes, that had been the plan, and then Brad happened, and my world hasn't been the same since.* She smiled. *I wouldn't change a thing.*

Marti stuck her head around the door. "What time do you want Marla to come? I've told Ashley and the girls to be ready no later than one. The ceremony starts sharply at two according to Luis," she finished.

"I guess around twelve-thirty would be soon enough. I plan to spend the next hour or so pampering myself with a long hot soak in the tub." Darcey said, stretching her arms up over her head. "Really, I don't need you girls. Madam Chelsea and Catherine will be here to help me dress." She frowned a little at that. She really didn't want them here, but since Madam Chelsea had decided she was featuring Darcey's gown in her show catalogue, she wanted the full effect—from design to down the aisle. "I'm not telling you not to be here. It's just that there will be nothing for you to do once Madam Chelsea 'takes over.'" She did finger quotes for "takes over."

Marti started laughing. "Yeah, well, I'm gonna be here

anyway," she said. "'N Marla 'n the girls will probably feel the same way."

"Okay, that's fine by me."

❧

In a flurry, at twelve-thirty sharp, Madam Chelsea burst into Darcey's room, followed by Catherine carrying *the* gown. Madam Chelsea had insisted that the gown could not be out of her sight until Darcey walked down the aisle.

"Come, come, Catherine, hang the dress up before it wrinkles," Madam Chelsea twittered. "Marshall!" she shouted. A frown creased her forehead as she turned around, looking behind her. "Where is that boy? Marshall!" She stuck her head out the door and hollered again, pushing a wayward strand of hair, that had escaped the alligator clip that held her hair on top of her head, behind her ear.

Darcey shook her head and slipped into the bathroom to wait until the chaos subsided. A gentle tap on the door told her it had to be Catherine. "Yes?"

"We are ready for you, senorita," Catherine said. "Madam has the dress unwrapped, and she's ready for you to put it on. Please hurry," she whispered.

"I'll be right out," Darcey said, grabbing the makeup tray, just in case something might be needed at the last minute.

Just as Darcey opened the bathroom door, there was a loud knock on the bedroom door. Marti rushed over and opened it just a crack.

"Yes?"

Darcey heard her Uncle Jack's voice asking to speak with her. "Let him in."

"I need to speak with you," Uncle Jack said walking over to Darcey. He looked around the room, "In private."

"Okay, let's go out on the balcony," she said, motioning toward the balcony doors. "Now, what's so important you have to talk to me in private?" she asked, pulling the doors closed.

"Please sit down." He indicated the chair across from him. "Luis wants me to ask you if you would consider letting him walk you down the aisle, instead of me," he spit out in disgust.

Darcey stopped in mid air, then, fell the rest of the way to the chair. "He what?" she asked in disbelief.

"You heard me," Uncle Jack returned none too quietly. "He wants to walk you down the aisle."

Oh, shit! Damn! WHY? Darcey looked across the table at Uncle Jack. "What did you say to him?"

"Didn't say a damn thing. Just said I'd have to ask you."

"Did he give a reason why?"

"Said somethin' about he thought of you as a daughter and knew your dad was gone, and he didn't want you to walk down the aisle by yourself," he fumed.

"Well, didn't you tell him you were walking me down the aisle?"

"Yeah, but I don't think he heard me."

"More likely he just ignored it. Luis is good at that," Darcey said, rubbing her forehead. *This is a dilemma, one I had not even considered. I had always planned for Uncle Jack to give me away. Just where does Luis come off asking this?* "What're your thoughts on this?" Darcey already knew the answer before she asked the question, but she still wanted to hear it.

"I'm mad—damn mad. But, ultimately, it's all up to you. It's your wedding. You need to do what you think is best. Whatever your decision, it will be okay with me."

Uncle Jack stared at the tabletop as he spoke. Even though he said he would be okay with her decision, Darcey could tell he would have trouble abiding by it, but he would do it without complaint.

"Well, this is certainly unexpected, yes indeed. Give me a half hour, and I'll give you my decision." Darcey stood and opened the balcony doors and escorted Uncle Jack out.

"Madam Chelsea, Marti, Catherine, I need you all to leave. I have something I have to consider, and I need to do it alone, in peace and quiet." Darcey smiled sweetly at them as she stood holding the bedroom door open.

"Humpf," Madam Chelsea snorted. "Come, Catherine, Marshall. Don't dawdle."

Marti gave Darcey that "what-the—" look and pulled the door shut.

Darcey dug her cell out of her purse and punched in Brad's number. She needed his advice. He knew Luis.

"Hey, beautiful!" Brad answered. "Having wedding jitters?"

"*No!*" she shouted, letting her frustration show.

"Whoa! What brought all that on?"

"*Luis!*"

He chuckled. "What's he done now?"

"He wants to walk me down the aisle. That's what he's done," Darcey fumed, pacing the floor.

Brad let out a low whistle.

"I need your thoughts on this. How upset will he be if I say no?"

"I don't know, but I think he would understand if you said no. He's a reasonable man. You know how he views you. You're Saleem's daughter, and to him, you would have been his daughter."

"Yeah, I know, and that's what makes this so hard. But I promised Uncle Jack he could do it."

Brad laughed. "You know, you could have both of them walk you down the aisle. That would solve the whole problem."

Darcey rolled that around in her mind for a few moments.

"Hey! You still there?" Brad wanted to know

"Yes, I've been considering what you just said."

"That was a joke, silly."

"No, I think it could work," she said, suddenly feeling like a weight had been lifted. "Later." She hung up and dashed for the bedroom door. She found Uncle Jack leaning against the wall a short distance from her room, and she asked him to come back in.

"I think I have the solution if you will agree," she said, searching his face.

"Well, let's hear it." He looked none too happy, anticipating her decision.

"I want you both to walk me down the aisle." She waited for his reaction.

The frown didn't go away, but he answered. "I suppose that would solve the problem. Not sayin' I'm happy about it, but I'll do it, as long as I'm the one who gives you away."

"Oh, Uncle Jack! Thank you!" Darcey threw her arms around him and hugged him as hard as she could. "You're the best!"

He laughed and kissed her on the forehead. "Yeah, I know. That's what you always say when you get your way."

"Will you ask Luis to come to my room? I want to tell him myself."

"Yes."

"Will you also tell Madam Chelsea that I will be ready for her as soon as I speak with Luis?" Darcey laughed. "She wasn't too happy about having her plans interrupted."

After Uncle Jack had left, she flopped down on the bed and stared at the ceiling, immediately dismissing the now-solved dilemma, and wondered how she would feel when she woke up tomorrow as Mrs. Brad Daniels. *Will it just be like any other day or will it be the first day of a glorious, fantastic adventure? Marti has said this was my fairytale coming true. I've always leaned toward practical and believed fairytales only happened in books, not real life. But now, I'm not so sure. What could be more of a fairytale than what has happened to me these last two years? I met Brad, my knight in shining armor, was rescued from the clutches of evil, not once but twice, found a new family, and now a fairytale wedding.*

A knock on the door brought her back to earth. She opened the door and asked Luis to come in. "I have come to a decision," she said, as she walked over and stood looking out the balcony doors. "I cannot hurt Uncle Jack or you, so I have decided that you both will walk me down the aisle. But," she said, turning to face Luis, "Uncle Jack will be the one to answer the question 'Who gives this woman to this man.'"

"Yes, yes, wonderful!" Luis exclaimed in delight as he rushed forward, stopping just short of embracing her. Slightly embarrassed, he slipped his hands into his jacket pockets. "Yes, Jack may have that privilege."

"Yes, he has earned it," she said flatly. "Now that that is settled, please inform Madam Chelsea that I am ready for her now."

CHAPTER 11

And Then They Were One

Reverend Callaway stood in the middle of the room, reading over his notes before the ceremony. He and Mrs. Callaway hadn't been able to come over with the rest of the guests from Dallas because of a prior commitment, so they had arrived just three days ago. He was still feeling slightly jetlagged, even though he had slept most of the day after they had landed. Reverend Callaway hoped that he didn't fall asleep in the middle of the ceremony, like he almost did at the rehearsal dinner last evening. If it hadn't been for his wife, he would have fallen face first into the second-course plate. Thankfully, everyone at the table had been engrossed in lively conversation, and no one noticed his almost-disastrous faux paw.

A rap on the door jolted him back. "Oh, yes, do come in," he said, adjusting his collar. There was a big smile spreading across his face as Brad entered followed by Ty carrying a steaming cup of coffee, with Scott, Matt, and Hot Dog trailing behind.

"Glad to see you, boys. You can help me stay awake." Reverend Callaway laughed, yawning. "I haven't been able to keep my eyes open."

"Not to worry, Rev.," Ty drawled out. "We'll make sure you keep them peepers open." He gave Reverend Callaway a hearty slap on the back as he handed him the cup.

"Yes." Reverend Callaway laughed, holding up the cup. "A couple more of these might do the trick."

Brad barely heard the conversation as he looked out the window, watching the guests as they made their way to the chairs that the gardeners had arranged in the garden for the wedding. His mind raced as he thought about the call he had made to Asad telling him he was onboard with the project and all that it entailed. Asad had been elated, although he had had no doubt that Brad would accept the position. That taken care of, all Brad had to worry about now was the wedding.

He hadn't thought he would be nervous, but his stomach was churning, and his heart raced every time he thought of Darcey. He missed her. He hadn't been able to see her since the rehearsal dinner when Marti had swept her away as soon as the dessert course was over, leaving him with only the guys to keep him company. They had adjourned to Luis's library where they had helped themselves liberally to Luis's hospitality. Stepping away from the window, Brad walked over to Ty. "Got it?" he asked.

"Got what?" Ty asked, winking at Matt.

Brad stepped closer to Ty. "The ring, you idiot."

"Oh, that." Ty laughed. "Yeah, man, I got it. You ain't nervous or nothin', are ya?" he asked, grinning, patting his pocket as he walked away.

"No, I'm not nervous, I'm terrified. Can't you tell?" Brad joked. "Seriously, I didn't think I was going to be nervous, but, man, this is a huge step."

"Yeah, man. One I'm contemplating jumping into my-self. Remember?" Ty said.

"Yeah, you're getting a great gal there," Brad said. He laughed, shoving Ty on the shoulder. "Don't screw it up."

Ty grinned. "Not to worry."

"Gentlemen," Reverend Callaway said. "I believe the time has arrived."

Brad swallowed, inhaled, and walked out the door, fol-lowed by Reverend Callaway and the guys.

∽∾∽

Madam Chelsea directed Catherine in making the final adjustments to the veil before stepping back, her hands clasped together as she admired the beautiful bride before her. "Oh, I have done it again," she gushed, clapping her hands. "Your beauty is the perfect complement to my creation."

Darcey was still dazed from all the chaos that had surrounded her as she dressed, but as she looked in the mirror at the woman standing there, she still couldn't believe it was her. She had been transformed into an enchanted princess enveloped in a shimmering gown of silk adorned with jewels.

The woman in the mirror took her breath away. Butterflies erupted in her stomach, and her palms were wet as she thought about what was about to happen.

Darcey heard movement behind her. She turned to see Marti rush to the door. Someone must have knocked, but she hadn't heard it.

"¡*Dios mio*!" Luis exclaimed, clasping his hands together. "How beautiful. Your mother would be so proud." Luis walked over to Darcey. He did not hesitate as before, but reached for her hands and held them in his.

Darcey did not jerk away as Luis took her hands. Somehow, it felt right as he held them. She couldn't think of a reason why it should, but at that moment, it did. She glanced over Luis's shoulder and saw Uncle Jack standing there, staring at her as if he was seeing her, for the first time.

She smiled at Luis, removed her hands from his, and stepped around him to Uncle Jack, who let out a long, low whistle. She wrapped her arms around him and hugged him tightly. "I love you," she said. "Thank you for being there for me. For keeping me on the right path."

"I love you, too," Uncle Jack said, holding her away and

placing a kiss on her forehead. "You know I'll always be here whenever you need me."

"Yes, I know—"

"Yes, well enough of this," Madam Chelsea interrupted. "If you don't get a move on, the wedding will start without you."

"I hardly think so." Darcey smiled sweetly at her. "Can't have a wedding without a bride, you know," she quipped. The butterflies in her stomach increased, and her mouth went dry. "I need a drink," she said, heading for the water carafe on the bedside table.

"Take it easy," Marti cautioned as Darcey gulped a couple of mouthfuls.

Darcey swallowed the last bit of water in the glass. "Okay. I'm ready."

‮e/ɔe/ɔ‬

The last of the guests had been seated, and a hush fell over the crowd. A slight lull in the music indicated the ceremony was about to begin, as Brad stepped to the altar where Reverend Callaway stood.

Brad's hands were wet and his mouth dry as he waited for Darcey. He couldn't stop thinking about how much he loved her. He didn't know if he could hold himself back until the ceremony was over before he grabbed her up right here in front of everyone and planted the biggest kiss ever on her delicious lips. His arms longed to hold her. It had been over twenty-fours since he had been able to hold her— an unbearable twenty-four hours.

The orchestra started up again, and the procession began. Ty escorted Marti down the aisle followed by Ashley and Scott, Melanie and Matt, Wendy and Hot Dog, and last Marla and Nicho. Darcey was surprised as she saw him standing beside Marla, looking a little guilty. Luis said he would have someone to walk with Marla. He just neglected to tell Darcey it would be Nicho. She had seen him off and on with Jenny since she had arrived but had never attempted to talk to him. She felt a slight twinge of guilt as she remembered she still hadn't told Brad about meeting him in Lima. *Too late to worry about that now* she reasoned.

Everyone stood and turned toward Darcey as Marla and Nicho reached the altar. Darcey's body went ice cold and then super hot as she saw Brad standing at the end of the aisle. The most gorgeous hunk of maleness she had ever seen, grinning that heart-stopping grin, and he was hers—all hers. She could feel their connection pulsating, stronger than ever.

Darcey took a deep breath, looked at Luis on her left and the Uncle Jack on her right. "Okay, boys, let's do this."

Brad stood in complete awe as he saw Darcey, her body hugged by the gown, revealing all of her womanly curves. She took his breath away. The heat began to rise, as he caressed her with his eyes and the connection between them pulsated.

ℛℛ

Luis had opened the ballroom on the third floor for the reception. Darcey didn't even know there was another ballroom. She had just assumed that the reception would be held in the Bel Ami Gala ballroom but was pleasantly surprised when he announced he was opening the Grand Ballroom for the reception. *I am glad. The other holds too many ghosts.*

As she and Brad stepped onto the dance floor, the orchestra began to play "This Guy's In Love With You," that Brad had asked them to play for their first dance. Moving into each other's arms, she and Brad felt the world melt away as they floated around the floor. Brad pulled her closer, and Darcey could feel his desire as she melted into his body.

A gentle tap on Brad's shoulder told him Uncle Jack wanted a dance. *Damn!* he thought, but relinquished Darcey into Jack's arms.

"You're all grown up," Uncle Jack said, searching her face. "No more little brat breaking into my liquor cabinet." He laughed and gave her a squeeze. "You know your folks would be so very proud of you and all you've accomplished, and I think they would have approved of Brad, too."

"Aren't you ever going to let me forget about the liquor cabinet?" she asked, blushing. "I was sixteen and headstrong and knew everything. Besides, I have never been so sick in all my life as I was then." She giggled as Uncle Jack twirled her around. "I'm glad you like Brad. I would have married him anyway, even if you hadn't, you know."

"Yes, I know."

Darcey saw Luis coming across the floor. "Looks like someone else wants to dance with the bride," she said.

Uncle Jack bowed graciously as Luis took her in his arms. It was a feeling she wasn't quite ready to deal with, but she contained herself, hoping Brad would come to the rescue shortly.

"My lovely Darcey, I am so proud of you," Luis said admiringly. "Your mother would have been so proud to see what a beautiful young woman you have become."

"Thank you," she said quietly.

"You know your grandmother is also proud of you," he said, as he turned her around so that she was looking at Aicha over his shoulder.

Darcey saw her sitting at the table next to the Bride's Table where the immediate family members were seated. She noticed a gentleman speaking with her, then Aicha rose and left with him. Darcey looked back at Luis with a raised eyebrow.

"She is going to speak with my attorney. She will be okay. It is nothing for you to concern yourself with tonight. Tomorrow will be soon enough."

ℰↈℰↈ

The music played, wine flowed, and the food was never ending as the night wore on. Darcey's feet hurt unbearably, and, finally, she took her shoes off and finished the rest of the evening barefoot. Marti and Ty were lost in each other in their own little world, and it looked like the others had paired off as well. Darcey smiled at the thought of all of them finding their prince charmings five miles down on the ocean floor. Of course, hers had been topside when they first met.

Darcey noticed that Marla did not lack for a dance partner, either. Luis had been making himself available at every opportunity to keep her company. Darcey looked around for Nicho and found him at a table at the far end of the room sitting with Jenny. They seem quite absorbed in each other. She hoped that Nicho had found his girl.

Darcey leaned over and put her head on Brad's shoulder. "I'm ready to leave anytime you are,"

"Thought you'd never ask." He laughed, giving her a kiss. "Let's go."

She giggled. "We can leave out the back, and they'll never know."

They headed for the dance floor and did one circle, keeping to the outside. When they were in front of the door, they backed off the dance floor and hightailed it down to Darcey's room. They were laughing so hard, it was a wonder they didn't fall down the stairs.

Brad opened the door and pulled Darcey inside, quickly shutting and locking it. Leaning against the door, still holding her hand, he pulled her into his arms. She melted against him as he slowly trailed kisses down her neck, across and up the other side. Suddenly there was no air to breathe as her arms found their way around his neck and her fingers wound themselves in his hair, pulling him closer.

"I didn't carry you over the threshold, Mrs. Daniels, so

this will have to do." He grinned as he picked her up and carried her over to the bed. He was aiming to toss her on it, but she held on tight, and they both fell onto the bed, laughing. He pushed himself up and looked deep into her eyes, now dark with passion. "I love you, Mrs. Daniels," he breathed, his tongue circling the outer rim of her ear, his passion pressing hard against her.

Slowly he rolled over, taking Darcey with him, settling her on top of him. He ran his hand up her back, feeling the tiny buttons that held the silken gown on her lovely body.

Darcey felt his hands checking the buttons at the small of her back and decided she had better take it off before something happened to it, causing Madam Chelsea to go ballistic.

"Here, let me get up, and you can unbutton the back while I unbutton the neck," she breathed. "We can't have anything happen to this dress. Madam Chelsea would have my head." She giggled as she turned her back to Brad and felt him began to fumble with the tiny buttons. "Take your time, so you don't tear anything," she cautioned as she undid the buttons at her neck.

Thankfully, she had talked Madam Chelsea into fastening the neckline with only three tiny buttons at the back of her neck. The back was left open to a few inches below her waist, using ten, tiny buttons to close it.

"I don't know if I can," Brad said, exasperated at the slow progress he was making with the buttons, wanting to rip it off her body. Then he smiled wickedly as he watched the top of the dress fall in a silken cloud around her waist. He leaned forward and kissed her skin, loving the feel of it under his lips. He felt her gasp as his lips touched her. His hands found the round mounds of her breasts. He could feel her heart rate increase as he caressed her creamy skin, feeling the nipples harden under his touch.

Darcey closed her eyes and inhaled sharply as she felt his lips on her back and then his hands slid gently around and caressed her breasts again. There was no air to breathe; her heart beat wildly as she placed her hands on his. "Hurry up with those damn buttons," she said breathlessly, pushing his hands behind her. *Just a few more buttons and my body will be free.*

She felt the last of the buttons give way, and the gown puddled on the floor around her feet. She turned and faced Brad, his eyes dark with a passion that equaled her own. Her arms wound around his neck, and her lips parted in anticipation of his kiss. His lips claimed her, and the world spun out of control, time stood still as they became one.

CHAPTER 12

Moving Forward

The chaotic clamor of well wishes and goodbyes faded away. Darcey snuggled up to Brad in the backseat of the limo as they headed for the airport.

"Well, how does it feel to be Mrs. Brad Daniels?" Brad asked, holding her hand, his thumb gently moving the simple band that complimented the engagement ring on her finger.

"Feels pretty much the same as yesterday," she said casually, sneaking a look at him from under her eyelashes. "Sure haven't noticed any earth shattering events happening, yet." Darcey let a little snicker escape as Brad pulled away, feigning a hurt expression.

"What about last night?" he exclaimed. "Personally, I thought that was pretty earth shattering. Well, at least from my perspective and, quite frankly, I didn't notice any complaints coming from you, unless that was what all the groaning and gasping was about." He laughed and dodged her hand as she attempted a half-hearted swipe at him.

"That was a silly question anyway," Darcey told him. "I'll have to have at least fifty years before I can truly say how it feels to be Mrs. Brad Daniels, and maybe not even then. I have a suspicion that our life is going to be one big adventure after another." She turned and snuggled into Brad's side.

His arm draped around her shoulders pulled her closer.

Yes, and tomorrow I'll find out just what our first one will be, she contemplated.

Darcey still wasn't completely onboard with this Moon/Mars thing. Although she had no idea what space travel entailed, she did know that if something went wrong up there, there wouldn't be any nine-one-one to call. Brad would be on his own, and she didn't like that one little bit.

Brad noticed Darcey had slipped into a serious mood as she looked out the window. He knew she was worrying about the new project and, in spite of all of his assurances that it was perfectly safe, he knew he had not convinced her one iota. Maybe after seeing and hearing everything about the project, she would be less worried. He hoped so, anyway.

The limo stopped in front of the ORCA hangar. Brad helped Darcey out while the driver unloaded the luggage, placing it on a cart for the attendant to load on the plane. Brad thanked the driver and asked him to tell Luis he would call when they were settled at the hotel.

Darcey slept most of the nine-hour flight, exhausted from the stress of the last two days. She woke three or four times to eat or chat with Brad as he took a break from studying the materials Asad had given him about the project when he had left Dubai.

Sometime later Brad put the binder he had been reading down and gazed at Darcey sleeping. His heart filled to overflowing with love as he gazed at the gentle rise and fall of her breasts.

He marveled at her flawless complexion, the soft curve of her cheek as it rested on the pillow. The small smile that would appear on her soft lips as her eyes danced under her creamy eyelids in REM sleep. He had no doubt that *he* was the reason for the smile.

Brad turned back to the materials that Asad had wanted him to read about all phases of the new project in the hopes that it would further tweak his engineering curiosity and persuade him to accept the position, which it most definitely had.

Reading through the technical information, Brad accessed the logistics of building the Moon and Mars habitat modules in his mind. He could see it would be simple once he knew what they would be dealing with. Presumably, the major concern would be the atmospheric conditions on both the Moon and Mars, which he guessed, would not be hospitable without substantial cover. For that, he trusted the ORCA scientists who had been researching the conditions both places and compiling the data. As he read through the materials, he began to visual how the modules would come together and realized he would need a crew that was familiar with the Bio Dome Project—he would need Ty, Matt, Scott, and Hot Dog for the technical end, plus his handpicked crew for the construction. Their expertise in underwater construction would be invaluable in the weightlessness of space on this project.

"Ummmm," Darcey mumbled, rubbing the back of her neck. "What time is it?"

"It's about five, I think. We should be landing around five-thirty or six." Brad said, not raising his head from the book he was reading.

Darcey stood and stretched, to straighten out her back. "I'm going for something to drink," she said, walking toward the galley. "Want something?"

"Naw, I'm fine. I'll finish this," he said, holding up a glass almost empty of an amber liquid.

Darcey reached the galley door just as it opened and almost collided with the flight attendant.

"Oh, my, gosh!" the attendant exclaimed. "I didn't get any of the hot coffee on you, did I?"

"No," Darcey said. "I'm fine. You didn't get any on you, did you? I'm so sorry."

"That's quite all right," the attendant said, overdoing her smile. "You just go back and sit down, and I'll bring you a hot cup of coffee, unless you'd like something stronger," she added as an afterthought, glancing back over Darcey's shoulder at Brad.

"No, coffee will be just fine." Darcey watched as she turned and walked back into the galley.

Darcey hadn't remembered seeing her when they boarded and certainly not any time when she had been awake. She wondered what had happened to Thomas. *Hmmmm?* "What happened to Thomas," Darcey asked casually, sitting down in the seat next to Brad.

"Ummm, yes, Thomas," Brad said, adjusting from reading to answering her question. "Well, it seems Thomas decided to take a few days off, just like that, out of the blue." Brad snapped his fingers.

Immediately the attendant poked her head out of the galley door. "Did you want something, Mr. Daniels?" she purred.

Darcey eyed her suspiciously.

"No," he said flatly.

"So who's that?" Darcey asked, raising an eyebrow and indicating the galley with her thumb.

"I think someone said her name is Monica. Didn't catch the last name," Brad said absently, turning back to his reading.

"Hadn't you better start packing that stuff up before we land?" Darcey asked, poking the stack of manuals on the table. "Didn't Asad say that stuff was highly confidential?"

"Yeah, you're right. Hand me the briefcase."

Darcey watched as Brad carefully packed the manuals and pamphlets away in the briefcase and locked it. She half expected him to whip out a pair of handcuffs and handcuff himself to it. She giggled at the thought.

"What's tickled your funny bone?" Brad wanted to know, grinning.

"Oh, I just had a vision of you handcuffing yourself to your briefcase James Bond style."

⁂

Darcey lay back in the wicker chez lounge on the balcony off their room, watching the lights of Dubai twinkle in the fading evening light, thinking how they looked like fairy lights and reminded her of the crystals on the hem of her wedding gown. She wondered how Madam Chelsea was coming along with her new catalogue. Marshall had almost driven her crazy with the incessant clicking of his camera. The only privacy she had had was in the bathroom, and she smiled at that. It seemed like the bathrooms at Luis's had been her own personal sanctuaries ever since she first arrived there. And that brought her back to the fact that she still hadn't told Brad about meeting Nicho in Lima or any of the other things that had happened to her. She turned toward the balcony door just as Brad stepped out and walked over to her.

Well, this is as good a time as any. I can't put it off forever. I don't want any secrets between us—not ever. She patted the empty space next to her on the lounge.

"Why so serious?" Brad asked, sitting down next to her.

She hadn't realized that her expression had changed. She attempted a small smile. "Well, I want to tell you some things about my time before I remembered who I was," Darcey said, swallowing and looking into his eyes. "I think I can do it now."

"It's okay if you don't really want to tell me. If you do or don't, it will never change how I feel about you," Brad said, taking her hand and kissing the palm. "You are my life, my reason for existing."

The sensation of the kiss jolted through her body and was almost her undoing. If she hadn't already had her mind made up, she knew she would have let the moment slip away, never to mention it again. But, once again, she had made her decision, so it was, *Damn the torpedoes. Full speed ahead.*

Gently, Darcey pulled her hand back, rested it with the other one on her lap, and proceeded to relate everything that she could remember from the time she woke up in that dirty little room until the Gala. She quickly glossed over the boat trip leaving out the encounter with Quin, deciding it would serve no purpose now since Quin was long gone and only a faded memory.

She paused and inhaled before telling Brad about meeting Nicho in Lima. He didn't seem surprised when she had finished. He just smiled and pulled her into his arms.

"I know you said it didn't make any difference whether you knew what had happened to me, but I don't want any secrets between us," Darcey said, searching his face.

He grinned that heart-stopping grin. "Well, if that's the case, I have something to tell you, too."

"Okay, what is it?" *I can't imagine any secret he would have kept from me. He has already told me about his girl-friends, his college days. What else could there be?* She gazed expectantly into his eyes and then turned away. *Maybe this is something I don't really want to hear.*

"Well, I already knew most of everything you just told me. Luis had filled me in on some things and Nicho some, too. Especially the bathroom incident." Brad stopped, placed his finger under her chin, and turned her head toward him.

She could see the laughter in his eyes. "Humpf!" she snorted and jerked her head away.

"And, I also knew about you meeting Nicho in Lima."

Her eyes flew open, and she looked back at Brad. He just grinned and nodded his head. He reached out to pull her into his arms.

"Why didn't you tell me?" She pushed him away and glared at him. "Here I've been stressing over not telling you and feeling guilty because of it, and you already knew *everything!*" Her voice raised and grew louder. "How could you not let me know you already knew all of it?" She was feeling hurt and betrayed. *Now I wished I had told him about Quin,* she thought, wanting to hurt him back.

Brad flinched under her cold, steady glare. *I should have kept my mouth shut* he realized and sighed. He hadn't meant to hurt her. He hadn't pushed her to talk to him. He knew she would talk about it in her own time, and if she never did, well, that would be all right with him, too. He only wanted to assure her that what had gone before in no way would change his love for her. He reached for her hand and held it firmly as she tried to pull it back. "I'm sorry," he said, pulling her hand to his lips. "I didn't mean to hurt you. Nicho told me the last time I was at Luis's. He had no idea that you had not told me about your time here when we spoke."

He gently reached for her and pulled her into the circle of his arms. He felt her stiffen, but she did not pull away. "I didn't say anything about any of this because you didn't seem ready to talk about it, so I let you take your time and decide when or if you wanted me to know. It makes no difference to me one way or the other," he breathed in her ear. "You are mine. Now and always."

In spite of the anger she was feeling, Darcey's body ran hot and cold at the same time, and there was no air to breathe as he pulled her up and lifted her into his arms. How could she stay mad at him? In light of everything that had happened to her, he had backed off giving her time to heal, letting her set her own timetable when to talk about it. He had only been thinking of her wellbeing.

The love she felt for him burned strong. She buried her face in his neck and inhaled his scent, and her heart went soring. She was his totally and completely his, now and forever.

CHAPTER 13

Old Friends and New Mysteries

The phone rang. Fumbling around to find it, Brad knocked it on the floor.

"Damn!" he mumbled. "Yeah!" he said, finally finding the receiver.

"*Buenas días*." Luis chuckled. "Sleeping in, are we?"

"Yeah, something like that," Brad said, yawing.

He glanced over at Darcey, who had just rolled over and was looking at him through bleary eyes.

"What time is it?" she mouthed.

Brad shrugged his shoulders, pointed to the phone, and mouthed, "Luis."

"What time is your meeting with Asad?" Luis wanted to know.

"Four this afternoon," Brad yawned.

"Well, you had better get a move on as it is now coming up on noon. I am in the lobby. I have just checked in and will call you when I reach my room. I wish to treat you and your beautiful bride to lunch."

Brad could hear Luis laughing as the line went dead. He rolled over and caressed Darcey's cheek. "Time to get up, beautiful," he said, leaning in to place a kiss on her still-swollen lips.

"Ummmm," she said, returning the kiss and pouted when he pulled away.

"We've got to get ready. Luis is here. He wants to take us to lunch," he said, running his hand through his tousled hair. "I didn't know he was coming, not that it makes any difference, but it would have been nice to know he was planning on being here."

As Brad headed for the bathroom, Darcey got up, walked over to the balcony, and opened the doors. A blast of hot air slammed her in the face, and she quickly closed the doors. She had hoped to have coffee on the balcony this morning, but they had slept in until almost noon, and the heat of the day was well on the way to topping the hundred-degree mark or more. Maybe it had already, it felt like it. She made a mental note to get up earlier tomorrow before the temperature became too unbearable to sit on the balcony.

Darcey heard the water in the shower stop as the phone rang. "Hello," she answered.

"*Buenas días*, Señora Daniels," Luis said, all dignified and proper.

"*Buenas días*, to you, too, Señor Vargas." Darcey tried to sound equally as dignified, but it came out in a giggle.

"Are you ready for the day?" Luis wanted to know.

"No, not quite yet. We sorta slept in." She giggled, feeling giddy like a schoolgirl as she glanced toward the bathroom door where Brad lounged against the doorframe—completely naked.

"Well, do not take too much longer. I am taking you to lunch. I will meet you in the lobby in an hour."

"Umm…ah…yeah, in an hour."

☙❧

The heat of the afternoon was left behind as Brad and Luis entered the refreshing cool of the lobby in the building where ORCA's headquarters resided. Several other ORCA board members and a few men Brad didn't know waited for the elevator. Luis greeted them, and Brad presumed he was familiar with everyone, as they all seemed to know him. Brad wondered if any of them had been at one of Luis's galas. Shaking his head, Brad let that thought go as the elevator doors opened.

Asad's reception area was full of ORCA board members and members of the other corporations joining in on the project. Brad hadn't expected to see so many. Not counting the ORCA board members, he guessed there were at least twenty, maybe twenty-five men who represented the other corporations. He had assumed there would only be the primaries involved with the project at the contract signing. Of course, he had never been privy to this level of confidentiality either, so he didn't have a clue how things were handled before he had gotten the go ahead to start a project. This was a learning experience, and he wondered just why Asad had involved him from the beginning on this one.

"Gentlemen, *por favor*. It is time," Asad said, indicating the conference room's doors. "Leave your cell phones in the basket. You may pick them up after the meeting."

Adara, Asad's receptionist, stood smiling holding a basket at the conference room door carefully watching and making sure everyone placed their cell phone in the basket. As the last man entered, she quietly shut the door.

❦❦❦

Left to her own devices after Brad and Luis left for the meeting with Asad, Darcey decided to explore the area surrounding the hotel. She didn't want to be gone too long since Brad had said they would be back, he thought, somewhere around seven, just in time to make the reception Asad had arranged at eight. She figured she could spend a couple of hours exploring before she dashed back to get ready.

Darcey stopped at the concierge's desk and asked what points of interest there might be within walking distance. The gentleman behind the desk smiled broadly as he told her about the small open-air market he thought she might be interested in. It boasted a wonderful selection of jewelry, rugs, tapestries, and other fabrics as well as fresh produce. It was a local market and mostly visited by neighbors in the area so he was sure she should be able to find many bargains.

He wrote down the directions, and Darcey thanked him, draped the hijab that Aicha had given her over her head, put on her sunglasses, and started out. She had gone maybe a half a block and decided this wasn't the smartest idea she had ever had—starting out in this late afternoon heat that felt like one-hundred-twenty. The concierge had said it was only a few blocks to the street where the market was located, so she walked on. Checking the directions again, she saw it was just a little ways up ahead.

Turning the corner onto the market street, Darcey took in the little open-air market filling the street with booths of colorful clothing, rugs, fabrics, jewelry, produce items, and that was just what she could see from where she stood.

૯౧౬౭

Darcey had taken no notice of the tall, dark man sitting at a table in the hotel's alfresco café as she started down the street. He waited until she was far enough ahead before he rose and followed her. In spite of hijab and sunglasses, he knew it was her. Her perfume had floated on the hot afternoon breeze as she passed by, and he had inhaled the scent that was uniquely her. In spite of the many months that had passed, he would know her scent anywhere. He had stored it in his memory, and his heart remembered.

Quin followed a short distance behind the woman, watching and remembering her body, as he had held her in his arms, and her complete surrender to him. He had held that memory all these months while he searched for her. Now, she was within his reach, but she was now married, and he still did not know if it had been an arranged marriage. He would deal with that after he had—he stopped the thought. *After I what? Kidnap her again? That would be barbaric*, he thought, *I do not want her to be afraid of me. I want her to love me as she most certainly did while we were at sea.* He paused, waiting while she turned the corner into an open-air market. *But if she has no love for this man, what difference would it make if I just take her? She would be forgiving and overlook that small detail. She would remember us, and that is all that is necessary* he rationalized.

Quin adjusted his sunglasses and closed the distance between himself and the woman. He stopped within a few feet of her as she bartered with a shop owner for a coral necklace. Her scent filled him with a desire to touch, to hold, to taste her again.

Slowly closing the few feet that separated them, Quin observed two unsavory-looking men intently making their way toward the woman. He could see one of the men had a gun tucked into his trousers and figured the other one would have one, too. Without a second thought, Quin moved swiftly to the other side of the woman and placed himself between her and the two men. He picked up a pair of earrings that matched the necklace.

"These would look lovely on you," he said a bit too loudly, holding the earrings up to her ear.

Darcey had felt someone move and stand beside her as she bartered for the coral necklace. It would match the new silk blouse she had purchased before they left Agadir.

"Excuse me?" Darcey said, turning to glare at the man standing next to her holding up the pair of earrings. She fully intended to tell him to buzz off. "Quin!" she gasped as she recognized him. "Quin, what are you doing here? Where did you come from?" she asked in rapid succession, resisting the immediate impulse to throw her arms around his neck.

What-are-you-thinking? she scolded herself, immediately tamping down the urge.

"I have been looking for you for months," Quin said, placing his hand on her arm. "Let us go somewhere and talk. You can tell me all about what has happened to you since we last met." He gently maneuvered her away from the booth, sensing the two men quickly closing the distance between them. "Come, we have much to catch up on."

Darcey was too overwhelmed at seeing Quin, and also trying to understand the feelings that he had aroused in her just now, that she took no notice that he had taken the necklace from her hand, or that he had dropped it back on the table. He was now gently but firmly, moving her away from the booth and back toward the main street. When they turned the corner and headed back in the direction of the hotel, she finally realized what was happening.

She stopped and pulled her arm away. "What do you think you're doing?"

"I am taking you somewhere where we can talk," Quin said innocently, glancing over his shoulder to see if the two men were following. "I did not mean to scare you. Forgive me, *por favor*."

Quin looked so hurt that Darcey had to smile. "No harm done," she replied, placing her hand on his arm. "Of course, we can talk. My hotel is just there," she said, pointing in that direction. "They have a lovely little café where we can talk."

Quin's heart was doing double time as he walked beside her, her scent rising sensually to his nose. *I will have to keep control of myself,* he cautioned himself as he seated her at the table and signaled the waiter. "First, you must tell me your name, *por favor*," he said, removing his sunglasses and taking the chair that faced the sidewalk entrance to the café. "I was not allowed to know your name. Carlos knew it, but he would never tell it to me. So, you must tell me now, *por favor*?" He reached across the table and gathered her hand in his, glancing over her shoulder as he did, watching the café's entrance.

The warmth of his hand triggered the memory of that

night those many months ago. The night she had surrendered herself to him. The night before Carlos had handed her off to Nicho. The night her life became insignificant. His touch brought back everything—everything she wanted to forget.

Darcey pulled her hand back, inhaled, and cleared her throat. "My name is Darcey Marie Callahan Daniels," she said, liking how it rolled so easily off her tongue.

"Darcey," Quin repeated, a slow smile spreading across his face. "I like it," he said as the waiter placed two coffees on the table. "So, tell me what has happened since we were last together?" He sat back in his chair, covertly watching the people as they passed the café entrance.

"Well, let's see," Darcey said hesitantly, fidgeting with her hands, wondering if she wanted to tell him everything or just give him the highlights. "Of course, you know I lost my memory. I believe you and your friends were actually the cause of it." She looked pointedly at Quin, who lowered his eyes. "After I went to Vargas's, I was sold to Brad Daniels, who was actually my boyfriend and had come to rescue me, although I didn't know it at the time. He took me to Lima and to the Bio Dome, which is an underwater habitat, where he helped me regain my memory." She paused, gathering her breath as she gazed lovingly at her wedding ring. "He is now my husband. We were married on the twenty-sixth and are on our honeymoon here in Dubai. There you have it in a nutshell." She glanced up at Quin, who, at that moment, seemed to be somewhere else. "Hey!" She gave the table a small shove, the coffee cups rattling in their saucers. "Sorry to bore you, but you asked," she quipped, her eyes narrowing as she looked at him.

"Sorry. I just thought I saw someone I knew pass by on the sidewalk," Quin said, smiling warmly at Darcey. He had observed one of the two men who had been in the market walk slowly by, surveying the café patrons. By design, Quin had seated Darcey with her back to the entrance so he could keep an eye out for the men. He placed his hand on hers again and gave it a small squeeze. "You could never bore me, *mi querido.*"

"Thank you," she said softly as the corners of her mouth lifted slightly. The feelings she'd had for Quin stole back in, and she didn't like it. Darcey immediately pulled her hand back and glanced at her watch. "Oh dear!" she exclaimed, pushing her chair back. "I'm late. We have a reception to attend tonight, and I'm not near ready. Please excuse me. Perhaps we can meet again before Brad and I leave," she said over her shoulder as she made her way to the lobby entrance.

Quin stood half way out of his chair, staring after her. The sinking feeling he had been carrying around since the stranger had told him about her impending marriage turned into to a knife twisting in his heart. It had not been an arranged marriage as he had hoped. That would complicate things, but he could tell she still had feelings for him. He could see it in her expressive hazel eyes, even though she tried to hide it. He could see the desire that they had had for each other still shone there in their depths. He would turn it to his advantage once he had her all to himself. He would make her forget the other man.

His feelings for Darcey still very much on his mind, Quin sat back down, continuing to watch the passersby, and then he saw them, the two men from the market talking just outside the café entrance. He had no way of knowing if they had seen his face in the market, so he bent down pretending to pick something up off of the ground. With his head down and looking under the table, he could watch the men from between the table legs unobserved.

As they talked, the shorter of the two continued to watch the café patrons. The one with the gun visible in his waistband kept pointing to the hotel, as if trying to make a point. Just then, a black sedan pulled up alongside of them, and the window in the rear door opened slightly. The two men looked at each other, turned, and walked over to the car. Quin could not see their faces, but their body language spoke volumes. Whoever was in the sedan, the men were afraid of them. Possibly their boss, he guessed. After a few minutes, the widow went up, and the sedan drove off. The two men looked like they were arguing over something, but Quin was too far away to hear.

"Excuse me, señor," the waiter said, bending down and looking under the table at Quin. "Is there something I can help you with? Have you lost something?"

Quin jumped, and his head hit the edge of the table. "*¡Ay! ¡Maldito!*" he exclaimed. "No, I just thought I dropped a coin, but I guess I was wrong. *Gracias.*" He smiled sheepishly at having been caught spying. The waiter walked away, and Quin glanced toward the entrance again. The two men had disappeared. Tossing some coins on the table, he quickly made his way out to the sidewalk. Quin looked in both directions for the men then saw them heading back toward the street with the open-air market.

Quin slipped his sunglasses in place and followed. The men turned down the street and headed into the market area. Afraid he might lose them in the crowds of the busy market, Quin shortened the distance between him and the two men. Thankfully, they seemed unaware of him as he followed them deeper into the market.

Quin watched as the men left the market behind and continued down the street for several more blocks and let the distance between them lengthen so they would not suspect he was tailing them. The men slowed and turned down a dark, narrow alley. Arriving at the alley, Quin cautiously peered around the corner and observed the men as they entered a doorway at the other end of the alley. He waited a few minutes before stepping into the shadows and following.

Carefully, Quin pulled his Glock from his waistband as he made his way down the narrow alley to where the two men had entered through a solid wooden courtyard gate. Slowly he pushed it open. The hinges groaned. He stopped and waited, but heard nothing, then continued to push the gate open. It opened onto a small, over-grown, courtyard that had been neglected for years. Quin looked around. No one was in sight as he stepped through the opening. What once must have been a beautiful home now stood in disrepair, its windows and doors boarded up. Tiles that had slipped from the roof lay broken on the ground. Quin wondered why the men had entered here as he stealthily approached the only door not boarded up.

Quin turned the door handle and pushed on the door. It swung quietly open. Obviously, it was being used quite frequently. Quin silently slipped inside and flattened himself against the wall, letting his eyes adjust to the low light of the interior. His finger was on the trigger of the Glock, as he listened for any sounds coming from elsewhere in the house. All was silent. No footsteps, no talking—nothing, except his breathing and the pounding of his heart.

There was only one other door in the room, and Quin silently made his way across the floor toward it, the Glock in his hand. He turned the knob. The latch clicked, and the door opened into a dimly lit room stacked floor to the ceiling with wooden crates. As he slipped farther into the room, he could see a couple of the crates had been opened and inside were burlap bags. One of the bags had been cut open, and several small reddish brown blocks of some substance had spilled out into the box. Quin picked up one of the blocks and smelled it—morphine. He had stumbled on someone's stash of morphine, and morphine meant heroin, and heroin meant trouble. Quin wanted nothing to do with heroin trafficking. Granted, there were more bucks to be made there, but it was a cutthroat business, and the risks were higher. With heroin, once you were in, there was no way out but feet first. Human trafficking was not much better, but he had been lucky, and Carlos had let him walk. Of course, Carlos was too much of a coward to play like the big boys. He only catered to private and select cliental like Vargas, who only wanted one or two at a time.

Quin dropped the block back into the box and started to

move forward when a door opened on the other side of the stack of crates he was behind. Crouching down, he slipped farther back into the shadows of the crates, his heart pounding as he listened to footsteps coming closer. His gun was ready.

"Hurry up, he's waiting," someone shouted from the outer room. "Just grab a damn bag. He wants one right now. There's a buyer, and he wants to sample the product. Get it out of that open crate, there, at the end." The voice sounded angry and impatient.

Quin heard the sound of the bag as it scraped across the edge of the crate, then the footsteps retreated, and the door slammed. He waited a few moments before moving forward and quietly slipping around the stack of crates until he saw the door that the man must have used. His ear to the door, Quin heard nothing coming from the other side.

Do I dare open the door, he wondered. *Maybe wait a few more minutes* he debated. He did not like where this was heading. *Morphine bricks meant heroin, and heroin meant drug dealers. The question is—why would drug dealers be interested in Darcey?*

He needed to find out more information. Something was not right about this. Cautiously, he turned the handle and pushed open the door. The room on the other side was not much to look at. A wooden desk that had seen better days, a couple of filing cabinets with padlocked drawers, a few chairs, and an old leather sofa. The light that filtered through the boarded up windows gave the room a sinister feeling. Quin shivered as he stepped in and closed the door behind him.

There were several papers scattered on the desk. He quickly rifled through them but found nothing that would indicate their interest in Darcey. He opened and looked through the desk drawers. Nothing there either. He walked over to the filing cabinets and tugged on one of the locks.

"*¡Mierda!*" he said out loud.

There has to be something here, he thought. *Otherwise,*

they would not have been tailing Darcey. Quin was sure, as he thought back that they were not just tailing her, they had fully intended to take her. But why?

He peered through the nailed up boards across the window. He saw another neglected yard area surrounded by a high, deteriorating brick wall that had been at one time covered in red stucco. Now, only parts of the faded stucco remained. The wall separated the yard area from the street. He could see at the far end of the wall a large solid wood gate with an odd-shaped opening cut into the center of the gate. The gate itself was big enough for a car to drive through. A small walk-in gate identical to the large one was in the wall at the end of the stone walkway that ran from the covered porch area to the wall. In spite of being in the house, he could hear the muffled sounds of traffic on the street beyond the wall. No one was in sight, but he decided to leave the same way he came in.

CHAPTER 14

The Break In

Darcey rushed through the lobby, still excited about seeing Quin, and headed for the bank of elevators. She glanced again at her watch and saw she had maybe an hour before Brad would be back and they left for the reception. Her head down, thinking how she was going to explain meeting Quin to Brad, she started to enter the elevator and slammed into a man as he was exiting.

"Oh!" Darcey exclaimed. "I am so sorry. Are you all right? I should have been watching where I was going," she babbled, blushing as the man ignored her.

He stepped around her and moved quickly away.

Really? What's his problem? Darcey thought, watching the man as he disappeared quickly through the lobby doors. *He could have at least asked if I was all right. Oh, well.* She shrugged. *I don't have time to worry about that now.*

Doing an "eeny, meeny, miney, moe" in her head between the two dresses she had picked out to wear to the reception, she slipped the key card in the slot and pushed the door open. Her eyes and her mouth flew open, and she stood rooted to that spot just inside the door, staring in horror at the ruins of their room.

Darcey couldn't believe her eyes.

Oh-my-God! What the hell happened in here?

Everything had been tossed. The clothes in the dresser

had been ripped from the drawers and were now scattered all over the floor, even the clothes in the closet had been yanked from the hangers and trampled on, and then, she noticed that the linings and pockets of Brad's sports jackets had been slashed.

Darcey stepped back, pulled the door shut, and ran to the elevator, panicked. Frantically, she kept pushing the down button, watching as the numbers indicating the floors crept their way up to hers.

"I should have taken the stairs. I'd already be there," she muttered to herself, as she pushed past the woman getting off.

The woman glared at Darcey and started to say something, but the doors closed and her words were lost. Darcey pushed the lobby button and prayed that no one called for the elevator before it reached there.

She burst through the elevator's door before they had completely opened, scaring a group of Chinese tourists waiting to take the elevator.

Slow down. You'll have everybody staring at you. The damage is done and whoever did it is long gone. You just need to report it to the hotel and call Brad.

Pacing the floor in the manager's office, Darcey called Brad. It went to voicemail. She left a message and hoped she had made sense and didn't sound too hysterical.

"Mrs. Daniels, please, have a seat," the hotel manager said as he walked in. Taking his seat behind the desk, he calmly straightened a pile of papers before looking up at her. "Now, tell me what has you so upset," he said, clasping his thin, spidery hands together as he tried to sound sympathetic, but it came out condescending.

Darcey glared at the hotel manager, whose name badge read Nigel Radcliff. He was small in stature with a receding hairline and spoke with a faint English accent. His thin lips were drawn up in what Darcey supposed was meant to be a smile.

"Someone broke into our room and ransacked it. That's

what has me 'so upset,'" She did finger quotes, thinking she probably shouldn't have done that, but at that moment she was so angry, she really didn't care what he thought.

Astonished, the hotel manager sat back in his seat and placed his hands flat on the desk in front of him. "Are you sure?" he asked, in utter disbelief. "This is a five-star hotel, and we do not have this sort of thing happen here—ever." He looked so indignant, waving his hand in the air as he peered at Darcey over his rimless glasses. If the situation hadn't been so serious, she would have laughed.

"Am I sure?" Darcey's voice rose. "Yes! I'm sure!" she hissed through clenched teeth. "Here is the key to our room. Go see for yourself!" She tossed the key card on the desk, taking deep breaths, trying to hold it together. Between being infuriated and scared to death, it wasn't easy.

"Please, calm yourself. I did not mean to upset you further. It is just that this sort of thing is unheard of at this establishment," he said, still unconvinced but trying to defuse Darcey's tantrum. "I have been manager here for fifteen years and not one—let me repeat—not one of our guests has ever been robbed," he stressed, leaning forward. "I pride myself on running a crime-free establishment, so I am sure you will understand why I find your claim a little hard to believe." He leaned back in his chair, a smug expression on his face that only added fuel to Darcey's now volatile state.

"No, quite frankly, I don't understand how you can dismiss this out-of-hand without even seeing for yourself." Darcey glared at him, throwing her hands in the air and walking toward his desk. "Unless you are afraid that it just might be true," she challenged, placing her hands on his desk, leaning forward, and looking him in the eye.

The manager glowered and then shoved his chair back, stood up, and snatched up Darcey's key card. "I am sure there is an entirely logical explanation for what you thought you saw." His thin lips clamped together in a patronizing smile.

Darcey bristled, "Yes! The logical explanation is that

someone broke into our room and ransacked it!" She stormed out of his office, heading for the elevator, not waiting to see if he followed.

Nigel followed Darcey to the elevator, his lips forming a thin straight line, his jaw muscles hard as he fumed inwardly about this American woman who dared to suggest that her room had been broken into. That just did not, could not, happen under his watch.

Darcey stood back, letting Nigel open the door, and waited for his reaction.

He stood dead still. Darcy even thought he might have stopped breathing at one point. He turned to look at Darcey. All the blood had drained from his gaunt face, making his pointy cheekbones even more prominent. "I...I...I do not know what to say." He turned and looked at the room again. "I will call the authorities and have this cleaned up immediately." Nigel backed out, never diverting his eyes from the shambles that the intruders had left the room in.

Darcey stepped aside, letting him pass, catching the door before it closed. She went inside. Carefully stepping over clothes and other items strewn on the floor so as not to disturb anything until the authorities had had a chance to check it all out, she made her way to the balcony. That seemed to be the only place spared from the upheaval. The balcony was now in shadow since the sun had dropped behind the hotel, and it was considerably cooler than this morning. She sat down on the chez lounge, to wait.

❧❧❧

The gavel hit the mahogany block with a resounding whack as Asad gaveled the meeting adjourned. The meeting lasted a little longer than Brad had anticipated. As soon as he had retrieved his cell phone, he saw there was a voicemail message from Darcey. Playing it back, he signaled Luis from across the room.

"We gotta go," Brad said quickly to Luis. "Someone broke into our room at the hotel. Darcey found it when she came back from her walk. I'll tell Asad while you call for the car."

Brad walked away, leaving Luis staring after him.

Broke in? Luis thought. *Why would anyone want to break into Brad and Darcey's room?* he wondered. *It makes no sense—unless something about the new project has been leaked.* Luis buzzed for the car and waited for Brad at the elevator.

Asad looked worried as Brad told him about the break in. "Is anything missing," Asad wanted to know.

"I don't know. Darcey only said the room had been ransacked. I can't imagine what they would have wanted. We have nothing of great value with us. I will let you know as soon as I find out," Brad said. "We may be a little late to the festivities this evening."

"Never mind about that," Asad said, placing his hand on Brad's shoulder as they walked to the elevator where Luis stood waiting. "Do not worry about the reception. You take care of what needs to be done."

Asad watched as the elevator doors closed. A sense of foreboding swept over him—a feeling that someone had leaked information about the Lunar-Mars Project. But why would they have thought that Brad would have had anything of importance in his possession? Asad had been careful to make sure no one knew he had given Brad the details of the project to study while he was back in Morocco or that Brad had given them back this afternoon. Asad turned and walked into his office, closing the door. A quick call to the ORCA hangar confirmed everything pertaining to the project that was stored there was locked in the safe, and there had been no break ins, or attempted break ins—everything was secure.

If someone had leaked information about the project, it would have had to have been someone who was at the very first meeting. But none of the Lunar/Mars Project materials had been allowed to leave the conference room, and Asad was finding it hard to believe that he had been betrayed by one of them since everyone in that room he had personally handpicked for their position on the board and trusted completely. However, this development seemed to indicate that he had been betrayed, and whoever it was, was a traitor.

I will have their head, Asad thought, slamming his fist down on his desk.

A gentle tap on Asad's office door, then Adara appeared carrying a cup of tea. "I thought you might like a cup of tea," she said, sitting the cup on the desk. "Will you be needing me anymore this evening?"

"*Gracias,* Adara. Yes, the tea is most welcome." Asad smiled, reaching for the cup. "No, I do not believe I will need your assistance any more this evening. You may go and get ready for the reception. I presume you will be there."

Adara blushed and smiled sweetly. "Yes, I am being escorted by my brother."

"Very well. Enjoy your evening."

Softly closing the door, Adara hurried and collected her handbag and hijab. Draping the hijab over her head, she moved swiftly, avoiding the men from the meeting who still lingered in Asad's outer office, and stepped into the elevator. The last glow of twilight greeted her as she walked out of the building, only stopping briefly to locate the black sedan. In three graceful steps, Adara reached it as the back door swung open. Quin stood in the shadows across the street watching as the sedan drove off, making a note of the license number.

ळळळ

Brad could see Darcey through the balcony doors as he entered their room. He sensed her mood the minute he opened the door. Darcey looked up and, instantly, and he knew she felt it, too. Brad knew their connection ran deep, but it had always been the passion they felt for each other, this was a whole other level they'd never experienced. This was not a connection of passion, he felt now. It was anxiety, fear, and something else that he couldn't put his finger on.

Darcey didn't see Brad enter their room, she felt him. She sensed his fear and worry for her. She sensed his anger about being violated, and she sensed an inner strength so intense that she immediately felt safe. Meeting him halfway across the room, she threw her arms around his neck and held him tightly.

"Hey, I need a little breathing room," Brad said, a little short of breath.

She loosened the grip on his neck and relaxed slightly. "Sorry," she breathed into his shirt. "I'm just so upset about the whole stupid thing, 'n then the damn hotel manager didn't believe me, 'n I couldn't reach you…" Her voice trailed off as she raised her head and saw Luis standing across the room, studying Brad's briefcase.

"Luis," she said, "I didn't know you were here."

"Yes, I came with Brad," he said, walking across the room, bringing the briefcase with him. He looked Brad in the eye. "It appears that someone's been trying to break this open, and I can guess what they were after."

"Wouldn't have done them any good if they'd gotten it open, there's nothing in there now," Brad said, taking the case from Luis and sitting it on the sofa. "I took all the project stuff with me to the meeting and handed it back to Asad. I just felt it would be safer if he had it all back." He turned and surveyed the tumbled mess of the room. "Looks like I was right."

"Look around and see if there's anything missing," Luis said, picking up a lamp that had been knocked to the floor and setting it back on the end table.

A sharp knock on the door caused Darcey to jump, and she turned to see Brad moving across the floor to open the door. The man standing there introduced himself as the Paul

Moore the hotel's security inspector. He was rather rotund with a ruddy complexion and slightly balding. He reminded Darcey of a detective in a B-grade movie. The only thing missing was the wrinkled tan suit and the stub of a cigar sticking out of the side of his mouth.

Totally not interested in anything the hotel's inspector might have to say, especially after the run in with the manager, Darcey busied herself checking through the closet and her jewelry case to see if anything was missing. The contents of the jewelry case had been dumped onto the bathroom floor, and the case itself had somehow wound up in the bathtub. Nothing appeared to be missing. She had brought only a few of the jewels that Luis had given her, and those were only worth a few thousand dollars. All appeared to be accounted for as she placed them back into the case. The links on one of the gold chains had been damaged and squashed together as if someone had stepped on it in their haste to leave. And, then, it hit her.

That man that had rushed off the elevator as I was getting on, the rude one, who didn't even acknowledge my apology or presence. Could he have been the person who did this? He certainly was in a big hurry to get out of the hotel.

"Brad," Darcey shouted as she hurried from the closet, the gold chain still in her hand. "I think I ran into the guy who did this. As I was getting on the elevator coming back from my walk, this man rushed out of the elevator and almost ran me down in his hurry to leave. I didn't think anything about it then, except that he was rude for not apologizing. He just rushed right on out the front door."

"Do you think you could recognize him if you saw him again?" the inspector asked, moving over to stand by Darcey.

"I don't know, maybe," she said, eyeing him suspiciously. "Do you have mug shots for me to look at?"

"No, not here," the inspector sneered, "but I can get some from the police station for you to look at if you wish.

However—" He surveyed the room again. "—I doubt that it will be necessary because, as you have said, nothing appears to be missing. Therefore, I see no need to file charges unless, of course, the hotel wants to do it. All of the damages appear to have been done to the hotel's property." He dismissed Darcey with that you're-just-an-insignificant-woman look, and it was all she could do to keep her cool.

There it was again. That condescending attitude. First the hotel manager and now this oversized asshole.

Darcey was fuming inside. She looked across at Brad, and he was grinning. If she didn't know better, she could swear he was reading her mind.

CHAPTER 15

The Reception

While Darcey was in the shower, the hotel manager had sent up two housemaids to help with the cleanup, and they had just left as she stepped out. The shower had done wonders for her attitude, to say nothing of how wonderful it had felt letting the hot water wash over her body, releasing the tension in her muscles.

I almost feel like a new woman, she thought, letting the cool silk of her baby blue robe caress her body.

"Look what we have here," Brad said, as he closed the door to their room. "The manager just sent this up. Looks like it's a check to cover the repair of your gold necklace and the loss of my four jackets. There's also a note," he said, handing it to Darcey.

She pulled the note out of the envelope and began reading. The manager had written an apology for the *unfortunate* incident and saying there would be no charge for their stay at the hotel. *After all*, he wrote, *it is the least that the hotel could do under the circumstances.*

"Really?" she exclaimed, handing the note back to Brad. "The cheap little jerk didn't even have the balls to say it to us in person."

Brad just smiled and stuffed the note in his pocket. "We still have time to make it to the reception," he said, giving Darcey a shove toward the bathroom. "Go slip into one of those gowns you brought, and we can still make the ball, m'lady."

He gave a mock bow, grinning that lopsided grin, and her heart started doing crazy things as she looked into his emerald green eyes, now dark with passion.

"Don't look at me that way or we won't make it past the bedroom," Darcey teased, breaking free of the trance, he had her in. "Give me a couple of minutes, and I'll be ready. You men have it easy," she said, as the bathroom door closed. "Pull on a pair of pants, a shirt, jacket, and tie, and you're ready in ten minutes."

She laughed as she hurriedly stepped into her favorite Dior gown, knowing full well he knew she could be ready in half the time if she put her mind to it, in spite of what Marti thought. She giggled as she heard a "Humpf" from the other side of the door.

⌘⌘

It was late when they arrived, but by the sound of the laughter and music, the guests of honor had not been terribly missed.

Asad spotted them and made his way across the crowded room. "*Bienvenido!*" he said, shaking hands with Brad and giving a slight bow in greeting to Darcey. "I presume all has been taken care of?" He looked from Brad to Darcey then indicated that they should follow him.

Brad smiled, as he took Darcey's elbow and maneuvered them across the room. "Yes, I believe it has."

"I knew this was going to happen," Darcey leaned into Brad, her eyes darting around the room. "I don't know any of these people," she whispered.

"Not to worry." He squeezed her hand. "Just relax and enjoy yourself. There, see, here comes someone you know."

Darcey looked in the direction Brad had indicated and saw Luis making his way toward them.

"I am so happy you made it," Luis said, his eyes never leaving Darcey as a wide smile spread across his face. "You will come and sit with me. Dinner is about to be served." He extended his arm to Darcey. She looked at Brad, who nodded approval, and reluctantly she placed her hand on Luis's arm. In spite of everything, she still couldn't feel at ease with Luis. Maybe it would come later. She hoped.

As they neared the table Luis had indicated, Darcey noticed a beautiful, blushing Marla occupying one of the chairs at the table. She smiled sweetly as they approached. Darcey quickly looked at Luis, who had transferred his gaze from her to Marla, his face softening and his eyes speaking love.

"What's this?" Darcey asked, smiling, giving Luis's arm a gentle push. She stopped a short distance from the table and turned to look at Luis with raised eyebrows.

"That is my most precious jewel, next to you, of course," Luis said, dragging his eyes back to Darcey. "Of all of the women who have come and gone through my home, Marla is the only one who, whenever I made a conscious decision that it was time for her to go, I would always find some excuse for her to stay. I did not realize I was even doing it until you arrived, and I found out that you were Saleem's daughter." While Luis was talking, he had guided them out into the courtyard. "It was then when I realized that all hope of finding Saleem had vanished, that I saw Marla for the first time as a woman, not property. I supposed subconsciously I had seen her that way all along, and that was the reason for all of the excuses I had made for her to stay."

"Oh, Luis," Darcey said, placing her hand on his arm. "That is wonderful news. Marla is such a fine person."

"Yes, I know." Luis looked at Darcey, his eyes twinkling with mischief. "I have asked for her hand in marriage, and she has accepted."

"Luis, how wonderful" Darcey exclaimed, resisting the sudden urge to hug him. "Another wedding. When?"

"I do not know. That will be up to Marla, but until then

we are happy with this arrangement." Luis turned, taking Darcey with him. "Come, I am sure they are wondering what happened to us."

೮ఎ೮ఎ

The final course of the delicious dinner had been served and dishes cleared by Asad's efficient house staff. Asad captured everyone's attention, and, after a small speech, he introduced Brad and Darcey. Immediately they became the center of attention, with everyone gathering around them to wish them much happiness. It was during one of the lulls between greeting people that they managed to squeeze in a couple of dances. As Brad twirled Darcey around the floor, she noticed a tall, dark man at the edge of the dance floor who seemed extremely interested in them. She covertly watched him for several minutes as he circled the room, following them with his eyes.

Almost to the exact moment that Darcey started feeling apprehensive about the man, Brad also looked in the man's direction and pulled Darcey closer. They both looked at each other in amazement.

"What was that?" Darcey asked. "Did you feel it too?"

"I don't know, but whatever it is, it looks as though we are both on the same wave length. Just like when we know each other is in the room and sparks begin to fly, we feel this, too, when danger is around." They both turned and looked for the man, but he had already vanished.

"Who do you suppose that was?" Darcey asked, not really expecting an answer.

೮ఎ೮ఎ

Making his way across the room with Marla on his arm, Luis went in search of Asad to introduce Marla to him. That was when he spotted an unpleasantly familiar face. Luis was not sure as he only managed a brief glimpse of the man before several dancers twirled across the floor, blocking his view, but he thought it was Ahmed Kaddur.

Why would he be here? he wondered.

Luis was positive that Asad would not have invited Ahmed, under any circumstances. Asad had, on many occasions, forcefully expressed his displeasure with Ahmed for abandoning Aicha. Aicha's late husband, Hakim, and Asad had been long time friends. After Hakim's death, and Ahmed had deserted her, Asad had taken Aicha under his wing.

He had advised her, assisted in opening doors that would have otherwise been closed to her, and, in general, kept the wolves at bay, as she fought against discrimination of a woman in a man's world. She owed much to Asad for his assistance and compassion.

Asad had also spotted Ahmed and was heading in his direction when Luis found him.

"Asad—" Luis began but was cut off as Asad stepped quickly past him. *What the—* Luis thought then understood as he looked in the direction Asad was heading.

Asad, followed by two burly bodyguards, was quickly closing the distance between himself and Ahmed. Ahmed had not noticed them yet as he was intently watching a couple on the dance floor. Luis glanced in the direction of the couple, saw that it was Darcey and Brad, and wondered why Ahmed would find them so interesting.

Out of the corner of his eye, a flurry of activity drew Luis's attention back to Asad. The two bodyguards, one on either side, had seized Ahmed's arms and were forcefully dragging him out the double doors into the courtyard. Luis quickly excused himself and rushed over to offer assistance. Stepping out into the courtyard, he caught the tail end of an argument between Asad and Ahmed.

Ahmed turned and glared at Asad. "You will get what is due you, this I promise." He shook his fist at Asad. "You are not so big that you cannot be taken down, and I have the power to do it. I am not someone you want to cross swords with."

"I do not turn and run at idle threats," Asad sneered.

"I do not make idle threats," Ahmed bristled. "I will have your head. No man stands in my way and gets away with it!"

Ahmed jerked his arms free of the bodyguards, straightened his Armani suit coat, and glared back at Asad. Turning sharply on his heel, he stormed, stiff backed, head held high, out the courtyard gate into the street.

"What was that all about?" Luis asked, walking up to Asad.

"It was an uninvited guest, that I asked to leave," Asad said, still glaring at the courtyard gate that Ahmed had gone through.

"Was that Ahmed?" Luis inquired.

"Yes."

"Yes, I thought so," Luis agreed. "It has been many years since I last saw him, but I thought it was him. He was watching Darcey and Brad, you know?"

"No," Asad said, turning to Luis, a look of worry on his face. "Are you sure?"

"Yes."

"Then we must take precautions. I believe this might be connected to the break in at their hotel room and the project," Asad said, as he signaled the two bodyguards. "I am reassigning you to keep a close watch on Mr. and Mrs. Daniels for the rest of their stay in Dubai. If you need more men, get them. I want a daily report on anything that might be suspicious, regardless of how small you deem it to be."

The two bodyguards nodded in understanding.

"We must talk," Luis said. "I have important information that I believe might be connected to all of this."

"Very well." Asad inclined his head. "Let us go into my office. This way, *por favor*."

Luis followed Asad a little ways down the courtyard to another set of doors that opened into an office. Both men settled themselves in two of the over-stuffed leather chairs, and Luis proceeded to tell Asad all that Aicha had relayed to him regarding her son, Ahmed.

"This all makes sense now," Asad said thoughtfully. "He seems to be the missing piece in this puzzle. I wonder if the entire Eastern Alliance Board knows about this."

"I do not know," Luis said. "I do know that my friend on the EA Board did not know about Ahmed, or he would have told me. He only knew about Javier so there must be someone else on the board that Ahmed has been dealing with. He had to have had an inside connection with power."

"Yes, I agree, but who?" Asad asked, and not waiting for an answer, continued. "That person, most likely, also has an inside connection on the ORCA board. I am betting that it is the same person who stole the information about the Lunar/Mars Project." He stood up. "Come, let us get back to the celebration of the happy couple. We will take this up tomorrow. Come to my office around ten."

Luis nodded as they stepped out into the hallway.

Luis and Asad walked side by side down the wide hallway that led to the festivities. Luis spied Marla, excused himself, and walked off in her direction.

Asad stood a moment, viewing the guests in the room. Mentally, he made note of those who were there, comparing them the guest list.

A sudden splash of bright color caught his eye. He turned and saw Adara preparing to leave with a gentleman, who he assumed to be her brother, although he had never formally met him. He had seen him several times from a distance when he had picked Adara up at the office. "Adara, so good of you to come," he said, walking up to them. "Please introduce me to your friend."

"This is my brother, Jamal," Adara said, casting her eyes down and blushing.

"How very nice to meet you," Asad said, extending his hand.

"Ah—yes," Jamal stammered, as he hesitantly shook

hands with Asad, looking very uncomfortable and glancing covertly at Adara.

The awkward moment was not lost on Asad. "I believe I saw you arrive with a tall gentleman as well. Is he a friend of your brother?" Asad asked Adara.

"Yes, but he had to leave early. He will be sorry he missed meeting you," Adara said quietly, still keeping her eyes down.

"Ah," Asad sighed. "And what is your friend's name?" He turned his attention to Jamal but did not miss Adara quickly looking up at her brother, a look of pleading and fear in her eyes.

"Ahem…well…ah, he is not exactly a friend. More of an acquaintance, I would say," Jamal cleared his throat. "We only just met him a couple of days ago. Ah…he is acquiring some property from our family and…ah…is staying with us until the transaction goes through." Droplets of perspiration began to form along the side of Jamal's face as he lied.

"I see," Asad said suspiciously. He had not missed the moisture forming on Jamal's face. "So does this *acquaintance* have a name?" he prodded again. He could see that both Adara and Jamal were becoming uncomfortable, and he it piqued his curiosity as to why.

"We were asked not to mention his name." Adara blurted out, her eyes wide as she nervously looked around.

"Why not?" Asad asked, his left eyebrow raised in speculation, looking from one to the other. "Is he of such disreputable character that he fears the authorities or is it, per chance, that he is not an invited guest?

"I do not know. I only know we were instructed not to tell anyone he was here or his name if we were asked," Adara sobbed, the questioning wearing on her. "After I had told him of our invitation to the reception tonight, he insisted on coming with us. He said he had to see someone who would be here but would be here only long enough to meet with this person and leave, promising to come back to pick us up later. Only he has not come back for us," she finished, wiping away the tears that had made glistening silver streaks down her cheeks.

Asad watched as the brother and sister became increasingly nervous under his scrutiny. Adara jumped as a soft buzzing sound came from her purse.

"You'd better answer that," Asad instructed softly.

Her hands shaking, Adara fumbled through her purse and found the phone. "Yes," she said, barely audible. "Yes, we will leave right away." The blood drained from her face as she put the phone back in her purse. "That was him," she whispered. "We are to meet him outside, now."

Adara grabbed Jamal's hand and rushed for the door before Asad had a chance to ask more questions.

An idea began to form in Asad's mind that greatly disturbed him, as he watched the brother and sister disappear through the door. Although they had not said the name, Asad felt sure that the mysterious friend was Ahmed Kaddur, as he was the only person to leave early. Asad knew of Ahmed's violent and vicious reputation, and it worried him that Adara and her brother might be mixed up with him. However, the most troubling question that remained was why he would be interested in Brad and Darcey?

CHAPTER 16

Quin had been unable to find out anything on his own about the house where he had followed the two men. He had then decided it was time to call the number scrawled on the scrap of paper the stranger in Agadir had given him. As it turned out, the number belonged to the stranger's cousin, Omar, who had quickly informed Quin he was the only one who knew everything about everything that concerned the comings and goings in the underbelly of Dubai, and he was more than willing to help Quin—for a price—of course.

Omar told Quin the license number of the black sedan that Quin had given him belonged to Ahmed Kaddur, a local drug lord with ties to the human trafficking underworld.

"It is an extremely good idea to steer clear of him," Omar had whispered. "He has a reputation for violence and is considered mad by some." He shuddered as he proceeded to tell Quin about Ahmed.

From the seat of his newly acquired mode of transportation, a beat up old Nissan that his new friend Omar had procured for him, Quin had followed the black sedan around Dubai most of the day. The tall, dark man, presumably Ahmed Kaddur, had made several stops. At each stop, he entered empty handed but returned carrying a briefcase. The last stop had been early evening at a business office downtown, where a man and a young woman got into the sedan. Quin followed the sedan as it stopped at a swank restaurant downtown.

He found a place to park and waited. Around eight, the three emerged from the restaurant and drove off in the sedan. Quin followed as it wove its way around the streets to a residential area on the other side of town.

Parking a short distance away but with a good view of the residence where the sedan stopped, Quin watched the three people get out and go inside. The sedan moved on down the street and parked. From his vantage point, he saw several more people enter the residence. Later, a woman who looked a lot like Darcey and a man entered, but he could not be sure if it was her. Her head was covered with a hijab.

Time passed slowly, and Quin found it hard to stay awake the later it became. After dozing off several times and jerking himself awake, he got out of the car and walked around in the shadows. It felt good to move about and stretch.

Sometime after that, a disturbance at the residence caught Quin's attention. The tall, dark man he believed to be Ahmed Kaddur stormed out of the courtyard door. Quin slouched farther down in the seat, but he was still able to see out the window and watched as the man stomped out onto the street, his hands curling and uncurling into fists, and motioned vehemently to the black sedan parked a little ways down the street. The sedan backed up to where the man was standing and sped away quickly after he had entered.

Quin slowly pulled away from the curb and followed the sedan. For half an hour, he followed it as it went through the residential area, circling back to the residence. It stopped, and the back door opened. A man and young woman, who he remembered had arrived with Kaddur, rushed out of the gate and hurriedly entered the sedan. Quin waited then followed the sedan.

Forty-five minutes later, the sedan pulled up to a residence, stopped, and the man and young woman got out. The sedan sped off, barely waiting until the door had closed. The couple stood staring after the sedan.

Quin drove the Nissan slowly past where they were standing, deep in a conversation that, on the surface, appeared to be an argument. Neither noticed as the Nissan passed by, but Quin observed that both looked more frightened than angry.

After dropping the couple off, the black sedan made a right-hand turn at the end of the block. Quin slowed and waited a few seconds before also making the turn. He slowed the Nissan, keeping a good distance between him and the sedan, but still keeping it in sight as he followed it back across town to the downtown area where Darcey's hotel was located. Before the sedan reached the actual area with the hotel, it turned down a street and traveled several blocks before slowing as it approached a residence.

Quin immediately recognized the wall, and the odd shape cut into the gate. *This has to be the front of the drug house,* he thought, swallowing hard.

The sedan slowed and waited for the gate in the courtyard wall to open. The sedan's taillights disappeared through the gate as Quin drove by.

Figuring it would not be a wise idea to just walk right up and knock on the front door, Quin drove the Nissan around the next corner and continued until he found the street he was looking for. Parking at the curb of the street where the open-air market was located, he got out and walked the short distance to the narrow alley that led to the back of the house, and the back courtyard entrance.

Glock in hand, Quin cautiously pushed open the gate, cringing as its rusty hinges groaned at being disturbed in the middle of the night. He waited, listening, before he stepped into the back courtyard. It was dark. No lights from the neighboring houses shone over the high walls into the courtyard, and there were no streetlights.

In the time it had taken him to sneak down the narrow alley, his eyes had adjusted somewhat to the dark, but still, he moved stealthily across the courtyard, trying to remember just where most of the broken roof tiles were located so he would not trip over them.

Reaching the door, Quin tried the door latch. It was unlocked. It still baffled him about what kind of drug operation would leave its back door unlocked. It reeked of arrogance and the knowledge that whoever was in charge had nothing to fear from anyone, not even the authorities.

Taking a deep breath, he pushed the door silently open, remembering from his earlier visit that its hinges had been well oiled. Cautiously, he proceeded across the room to the other door and listened, his heart pounding in his ears. He could hear muffled sounds coming from the other side. He waited. After several minutes of hearing nothing, he turned the knob and pushed the door open.

Quin could see a low light shining from somewhere behind the stack of crates putting them in silhouette. Holding his breath and hearing nothing, he crept forward and knelt down behind the crates, listening for any sounds coming from the room on the other side of the stack of crates. From the glow of a dim light bulb in an old lamp sitting on the floor, he saw the crate that had been open there earlier was gone. In fact, he could see several crates were missing.

Quin crept around the stack of crates to the door leading to the outer room and listened. He could hear loud voices on the other side of the door, but could not make out everything they were saying, but what he could hear told him the two men disagreed violently about something. What that something might be, he could not discern.

A loud crash on the other side of the door shook the whole wall and caused Quin to jump. Then right on the other side of the door, he heard, "You sonofabitch! You will do as you are told. I do not care what you think. You are not paid to think. You will dispose of that woman, and I do not care how you do it. Just get it done, or else!" the voice growled. "She will not stand in the way of what is rightfully mine. That old woman will not defeat me nor will that bastard who runs ORCA."

There was a shuffling sound, and then a door somewhere slammed. All was quiet.

Slowly Quin relaxed. He had not realized just how much he had tensed up. Carefully, he placed his hand back on the knob when he heard a chair scrape across the floor. Jerking his hand back, he stepped quickly away from the door, knelt down behind the crates, and waited. A phone rang. Quin crept back to the door, but could only hear one part of the conversation.

"Very well. Wait until tomorrow," a disgruntled voice said. "Keep an eye on her. Do not let her out of your sight. When the opportunity comes—take it! Do not wait!" A slight pause, and then, "I do not care if people get in your way! I want this taken care of! Have I made myself clear?" the voice thundered.

Quin heard the phone receiver slam down.

The sound of pacing on the other side of the door increased and then something heavy hit the wall.

"Damn her!" the voice yelled.

Quin moved closer to the door.

"I got rid of the bitch. Got her out of my life and out of my way, and for what? She goes and has a damn kid!" the voice stormed.

A loud thunk and then the sound of something sliding violently across the floor.

The voice continued muttering, "I should have killed her then. It was just that the thought of seeing her suffer at the hands of those men was too much to resist. Her high and mighty ways had to be brought down. I so enjoyed watching as they stripped her down to nothing and left her bleeding on the floor—" The voice paused as if in reflection.

Quin thought he could almost see him smiling.

"If I would have known she was such a survivor, I would have asked twice the price." The voice chuckled and paused again.

Quin could smell the cigarette smoke as it drifted under the door.

The pacing stopped then the creak of a chair as if someone had sat down on it, a drawer opening and shutting, the tapping of something hard against wood, and after a few seconds, the voice continued amidst the frantic shuffling of papers.

"The old lady is going to croak. It is just a matter of time, according to her doctor, but I plan to hurry that along as soon as I dispose of the spawn..." The voice trailed off, and the shuffling of papers stopped.

"No—not kill. I sold her *puta* of a mother; I will sell her, also. She will fetch a much higher price than her mother." The voice paused again for several seconds. "Marco! Listen, there has been a change of plans." A pause. "Yes, I know what I said, and now I am telling you something else," the voice snapped. "I want you to grab her and bring her to me. I will take care of the rest."

Quin heard the phone slam down, followed by a chair scraping on the floor and a bang as it hit the wall, and then a door slammed shut with force. All was quiet.

Cautiously, Quin turned the doorknob and pushed the door open. It was dark inside the room, but from the dim glow of the lamp by the crate, he could make out the desk, an overturned chair, several papers and file folders scattered on the floor, and a photo of Darcey with a big black X scrawled across her face laying on top of the heap.

Quin's hand trembled as he slowly picked up the photo, and the cold finger of fear touched his heart as he stared at it. *What is she to them?* he wondered. Omar might know about this, he thought as he stuffed the photo in his pocket. Slipping the Glock back into his waistband, he left the house by the back way.

CHAPTER 17

The Project Begins

It was well onto one in the morning before Darcey finally convinced Brad it was time to go. She was dead on her feet, and her eyelids were lead weights. Around eleven, Brad, Luis, and Asad and gone to Asad's office to discuss the project, while Marla and Darcey had spent time catching up on each other's lives. Darcey had congratulated Marla on her upcoming wedding. Marla blushed as she talked about Luis. Darcey could see she was deeply in love with him, and it warmed Darcey's heart that Marla had at last found love and a home but wished it were with anyone else besides Luis.

Deep in her heart, Darcey felt Marla was too good for Luis, but she would never speak it aloud. Marla glowed with love, and Darcey would do nothing to diminish that glow, no matter how she felt about Luis.

Darcey cautiously asked about Nicho and Jenny. Were they an item? she wanted to know. Marla was a little hesitant to answer, and Darcey wondered why, so she pushed her to give her an answer.

"I do not know," Marla said reluctantly. "I know Jenny is head over heels in love with him. You can see it all over her face when she looks at him. But I am not so sure about Nicho. You see, he was devastated after the auction where you left with Brad." She looked at Darcey with sad eyes.

"All of us were concerned about him. He has never been the same because I think he is still in love with you."

"Yes, I know." Darcey sighed. "We met in Lima when I visited ORCA's offices, and he told me of his feelings, but I thought he would have moved on by now, knowing I didn't return them. Are you sure he hasn't fallen under Jenny's spell?"

"That is just it," Marla sighed. "With Nicho, you cannot always tell. He is attentive to Jenny and spends a lot of time with her, but he has never looked at her the way he looked at you."

My heart hurts for Nicho. I so want him to be happy. He deserves it, but what can I do? Darcey thought, pulling her lower lip between her teeth.

Whether by design or maybe it was just the way things played out, Nicho and Darcey saw very little of each other in the days leading up to the wedding. Then only briefly as he had escorted Marla down the aisle. During the reception, Darcey had seen him from afar several times with Jenny and thought they made a great couple, and she had been happy for him.

Maybe I need to have a talk with him when we get back, she decided.

Now, don't go meddling in where you haven't been asked. Things will work out as they should be without your help.

Darcey's inner voice was back. It had been absent these past days, so Darcey guessed she hadn't done anything too impulsive that warranted her inner voice's attention to keep her on the straight and narrow. She smiled inwardly as she started to get up to go find Brad.

"I am so happy for you, and I will see you back at the ranch in a couple of weeks," Darcey said, as she gave Marla a big hug. "Let me know how things progress with Jenny and Nicho. I think they make a lovely couple."

"Yes, I will," Marla agreed, returning her hug. "Maybe all Nicho needs is a little more time."

"Yes, I'm sure that's it."

ↁↁↁ

Darcey snuggled up to Brad in the backseat of the limo on the way back to the hotel, thinking about Nicho and Jenny. She had noticed that Nicho and Brad had become quite friendly, so she decided to see if Brad could shed some light on Nicho and Jenny's relationship.

"It's good to see that you and Nicho are on friendly terms now," Darcey said. "I'm glad."

"Yes," Brad said. "He's a good guy."

"Has he said anything to you about Jenny," she asked absently.

"No, should he have?"

"No, I guess not. I just noticed they have been spending a lot of time together, that's all."

"Yeah, now that you mention it, they have," Brad mused. "You don't suppose there's something there, do you?"

"That's what I was wondering. Marla thinks Jenny is in love with him, but she's not sure he's in love with her," she said.

"Well, don't worry your pretty little head about it. It will all work out," Brad said, patting her hand, indicating that that was all he was going to say on the subject.

Ummm—that's what Marla said.

Deciding Brad wasn't going to offer any more words of wisdom on the subject, Darcey snuggled closer, and Brad wrapped his arm around her as her eyelids slowly slipped down. She thought, although she wasn't sure, she heard him say something about a meeting in the morning through the fog in her brain as she drifted off to sleep.

ↁↁↁ

Brad slipped out of bed, punched the alarm off before it

could ring and wake Darcey, dressed, and wrote her a short note.

Babe, I will be at Asad's today. The timeline for the project has been moved up. Don't know why right now. I will call and let you know what's going on. See you tonight. Sorry, babe, I'll make it up to you. Promise. All my love, Brad.

Softly closing the door, Brad pulled out his cell and called Luis.

"I'm on my way down. Meet you in the lobby." Brad slipped the phone back in his pocket and stepped into the elevator.

He watched as the floor numbers descended, thinking about what Asad had said last night about this Ahmed character. Even though Asad hadn't said he was the reason the timetable had been moved up, Brad was sure he had something to do with it.

The elevator doors opened, and Luis met Brad with two large to-go-cups in his hands. One, with steaming rich, black coffee, and the other, Luis's favorite, sweet green tea. Hasan had the limo waiting as they came out of the hotel.

"What's up with this Ahmed guy?" Brad asked, sipping his coffee.

Luis preceded to tell him about Ahmed and how he was related to Darcey. A feeling of uneasiness swept over Brad as he listened to Luis.

"If he's such a threat, why don't you just take him out?" Brad wanted to know. "You have the resources."

"Ah, therein lies the rub," Luis replied, staring into his cup of tea. "He is Aicha's son, and even though he is the scum of the earth, I could not hurt her like that. She has disowned him, but that does not stop her from loving him. He is her flesh and blood, and she has already lost one child," Luis said sadly. "I would rather settle this without that happening if it is possible."

"What has he to do with the Lunar/Mars Habitat Project? I thought he was the one suspected of masterminding the sabotage of the Bio Dome Project."

"Yes, he is, but there's no proof he was ever involved with that. All I have is second-hand information from my friend on the EA board and, unfortunately, there is no way to prove he had a connection to Javier, or Lilly, either. He is a ghost," Luis said. "My gut is telling me that this is not so much about this project, as it is about him seeking revenge against you and Asad for spoiling his plans for the Bio Dome. My big worry is that he may try to harm Darcey, in order to get back at you. Asad has assigned some of his bodyguards to shadow Darcey, and I have called in some men from my Elite Force as well. We will see that Darcey is kept safe."

"Will Nicho be coming?" Brad inquired. "I would feel more comfortable knowing he was the one watching over Darcey."

"Yes, he will be in charge of the Elite Force. I called him last night. He will be here this morning, and his main priority will be protecting Darcey. That way you can concentrate on getting the Lunar/Mars Habitat Project underway without trying to protect Darcey yourself," Luis said as Hasan stopped the limo in front of the ORCA office building.

Brad followed Luis into the building, his stomach churning with anxiety over the Ahmed situation. He tried to wipe away all of the possible scenarios that could happen to Darcey his mind had suddenly conjured up.

Thank goodness Nicho is coming, he thought. *It will give me some peace of mind knowing he is watching over her.* The elevator doors slid open, and Brad's cell buzzed. It was Darcey.

"Hey, babe," Darcey heard Brad answer, noticing that his voice lacked the usual cheerful tone. "What's up?"

"I was going to ask you the same thing," Darcey said. "I've had this weird feeling come over me, and I don't like it. It's the same feeling I had when I saw our room ransacked and the other night at the reception. I want to know what's going on," she demanded.

"I know. I got it, too," Brad said quietly into the phone.

"I don't know what's going on, but don't worry about it right now. Can't talk now. We're here at Asad's. Call you as soon as I can."

"Okay, I'll try not to worry if you say so, but I don't like this. Something's not right. I can feel it." Darcey paused, rubbing her forehead.

"Yeah, I know. Grab a book and read. Stay in. We'll talk this evening."

"Love you."

"Love you, too, babe."

She heard voices in the background as Brad ended the call.

Read a book? Stay in? Why on earth would he suggest that, let alone think I would do it?

Regardless of the feeling of dread that nagged at the back of her mind, Darcey had no intention of sitting in the room all day reading a book. She wanted to go back to the market and get that necklace that she had been bargaining for when Quin showed up. *Now that I think about it, it was strange how he rushed me out of the market that day. As if he was getting me out of the way of something. Strange.*

A cold chill ran up her spine. She shook her head and shrugged, trying to shake off the feeling of impending doom, but that nagging little tickle in the back of her mind refused to go away.

∽∾∽∾

Luis gave Brad a questioning look, as they stepped off the elevator, "Darcey?"

"Yeah. She's worried that's something wrong," Brad said, as worry lines creased his forehead. "I can feel it, too. This thing with Ahmed has me worried. What if he tries to hurt her, and I'm not there? I couldn't live with myself if that happened."

"Yes, I understand. Nicho will not let anything happen to

Darcey. He will take care of it, if it comes to that," Luis said, walking on. "I just hope it does not," he said under his breath.

"Gentlemen." Asad greeted them warmly. "This way, *por favor.*" He turned and started down the hallway that led to the conference room, but walked on past it. He paused at the door at the end of the hallway and unlocked it, revealing a large room full of drafting worktables and several computers stations.

"Brad, this is where you and your crew will be developing the plans for the first set of the lunar modules," Asad said, surveying the room. "I presume you have your people already picked and notified."

"Well…no, actually, I don't." Brad hesitated. "Stepping up the timetable caught me off guard. I was only informed about it yesterday." He talked as he walked around the room looking at the equipment. "I have decided on my men but have not had time to notify them. My technical team is still in Morocco, I believe, so getting them here on short notice is possible. The construction crew will take a little longer." Brad stopped and looked at Luis. "Have Ty and Marti left on that cruise yet?"

"They are scheduled to leave tomorrow," Luis said. "I think the others are taking a few days exploring Morocco, but they should be easy to contact. I will have Nicho do that before he leaves." Luis turned and pulled his cell from his pocket as he walked out into the hall, the door closing behind him.

Brad opened the door and leaned out. "Tell Ty to bring Marti, and I'll make this up to them later."

Luis smiled and nodded in agreement.

Letting the door close, Brad mentally congratulated himself on that last minute piece of brilliance—having Marti here would keep Darcey company while he got the project underway. He wouldn't have to worry about her being alone or getting into trouble.

Asad opened the safe and pulled out a flash drive and

hardcopy files containing the Lunar/Mars Project. He carefully placed the hardcopies on one of the worktables and plugged the flash drive into the nearest computer, looking up as Brad stopped beside him.

"Here is the project in detail," Asad said. "I know you have been studying the logistics, but here are the final ones," he said, placing his hand on the stack of binders, then he reached over and turned on the computer. With a couple of keystrokes, a holo-image formed over the worktable behind the computer.

"Although these will not be your main concern, you will need to familiarize yourself with the ILC, FTLHE, IDE, and the EGLS," Asad said as he turned off the computer and removed the flash drive. He handed it to Brad. "This is never to be out of your possession when you are working and in the safe when you are not or leave the building. I have assured Granston and Aries that their prototype schematics are safe here."

He paused and sorted through the binders. "All of the pertinent information concerning surface temperature, atmospheric pressure, and any stress factors you might need to know are all in these files. Our scientists have compiled all the information necessary for you to build the Moon and Mars' modules." He watched Brad thumb through a binder as he continued. "All of this information is being transferred to your tablet, and these files will be locked in the safe. Even though your tablet is password protected, you must keep it with you twenty-four-seven from now on. There is a self-destruct built in that will be initiated if someone tries to access it without the proper password."

Asad paused before continuing. "All of the materials have been ordered according to the specifications provided in these binders and await your inspection. Look these over and inspect what has been ordered to see if there is anything else you will need."

"Ummm, yes," Brad mumbled absently. He had already slipped into the "zone" where everything else simply faded to whispers, in the background.

Asad turned to Luis as he walked back into the room and smiled. He had seen Brad drop into this state as he had started the Bio Dome Project. *This is a good sign*, he thought. *I have chosen wisely for him to head this project also.* As Asad watched Brad, he was glad he had brought him into the inner circle, although some had opposed it at the time. Asad had been sworn to secrecy, as had everyone else involved in the Environmental Research Consortium—ERC—as to the real reason behind these projects, and why they could not fail...

It had all started ten years ago when a group of scientists at the International Conference on Environmental Issues had been reviewing ozone data from the 1970s and comparing it to the current data. That was when they discovered that the ozone layer was depleting at a rate far more rapid than earlier scientists had calculated. According to the new calculations, it was estimated, that at the present accelerated rate of depletion, and the increased solar activity, dangerous levels of UVB wavelengths from the sun would begin to pass through the earth's atmosphere. They calculated that it would happen sometime in the next fifty to sixty years. The resulting exposure to these UVB wavelengths would cause a variety of biological outcomes, making life on the earth's surface extremely hazardous for its inhabitants.

The scientists took their findings to the small, but powerful ERC. Shocked at the data, the ERC called a secret summit meeting to discuss the new data and to formulate a solution to the situation. After weeks of discussions, a solution was finally reached. The representatives from the nations joining in the summit signed a pact to keep everything that transpired at the summit secret until such time there was no other option than to go public.

It had been touch and go, the first few months as the project got underway when the news media tried to make headlines by saying ORCA was working on a top secret project. To quell such rumors and to keep the United Federation of

Nations—UFN—Earth's central government from snooping into the project, Asad called a press conference. He announced that, due to the recent severe droughts throughout the globe, ORCA would be working on an experimental habitat for their new Oceanic Research Division. The exploration would consist of cultivating the oceans' floors as a new food source.

The media soon lost interest in the project, as no earth-shattering developments, accidents, or scandals surfaced from the project. Plus, the UFN in all of its governmental wisdom, had labeled ORCA's project as a foolish venture that would be a waste of time and money. Citing that years ago, when the ocean temperatures began to rise, and marine life began to vanish from the oceans, the UFN had done an extensive study on the possibility of farming the ocean floors. It had been abandoned shortly after it began with the UFN acknowledging it was too expensive and dangerous. Further exploration there would not be practical, and instead, they looked to the stars when NASA scientists proclaimed they had discovered several new planets they deemed capable of sustaining human life. Trillions of dollars had then been funneled into the UFN's new space program, much to the detriment and well-being of Earth's citizens.

During that same time, ocean temperatures were still rising, marine life continued to disappear, and several countries around the globe experienced severe droughts. Global food supplies were dwindling, and, still, the UFN refused to acknowledge that these events were anything but cyclical. It had now been ten years ago that the first UFN exploration mission had been launched and still nothing of any value had been realized in the search for a habitable planet.

The ERC began working quickly under the guise of the ORCA research project to come up with a workable design. During the months that followed the ERC had gone through several failed designs before they stumbled on Brad Daniels. His groundbreaking design for the Bio Dome with its Biosphere Ecosystem had proved to be both practical and workable.

The Bio Dome Project had taken five years to complete, but it was now ready for habitation by the first five hundred, preselected families. Asad had not told Brad that there were fifty more Bio Domes under construction around the world, each capable of housing and sustaining five-hundred families underwater for years to come.

Recent calculations by the ERC scientists had revealed that there were probably now less than thirty years before the UVB wavelengths would begin penetrating the Earth's atmosphere. And, considering the newest report on the rapid rate of deterioration, if it increased over the next five years as it had been over the past five years, there might not be enough time left. Time was of the essence as the estimated completion time for each the Moon and Mars habitats was five to ten years and a possible five years more to transport people to the sites.

After receiving the last report just six months ago, the ERC had stepped up its own timetable for the next phase of the plan—the off-world plan—the Lunar/Mars Habitat Project. An exploratory mission into space had been made just after the Bio Dome had been started. It was determined that Earth's Moon and Mars would be the closest and most suitable for the next habitats to be constructed within the time constraints. The habitats would be constructed simultaneously on the Moon and Mars. Then with the additional ILCs and the new FTL hyperdrive engines now under construction, it was estimated that several million people could be transported in just little over a month after the completion of the domes.

Decades earlier the UFN had sent a manned exploration to Mars, but it had proved unsuccessful, as it had been determined that the Mars atmosphere was too harsh to sustain life, even with shelter. After that, the government dropped the colonization of Mars, and the story disappeared from the headlines when the UFN turned to exploring the outer limits of the galaxy where planets capable of sustaining life had been discovered. Then, when ORCA sent up an exploration party to the moon and then on to Mars, it caused barely a ripple in the headlines, and again, the UFN belittled ORCA for such foolishness—

Asad's cell phone buzzed, bringing him back to the present. As he answered the phone, he noticed that Brad had his head buried in a stack of reports, writing notes and calculations, and Luis had left.

"Yes," Asad answered. "I will see where he is. Have him come on up, *por favor.*"

Asad touched Brad on the shoulder causing him to jump. "Sorry, but I have to find Luis. Did you see him leave?"

Brad looked up and chuckled. "No. I've been so wrapped up in this, a bomb coulda gone off, and I wouldn't a heard it."

"I will see if I can find him. His man from Morocco is here."

"Nicho?"

"I presume so. I was not told his name, only that he had arrived."

"I need a break. Let me go find Luis. He has sent for Nicho to help protect Darcey." Brad rolled his chair back, stood up, and stretched. "The exercise will do me good."

"Very well. I will be in my office if I am needed," Asad said as they walked out of the room.

Brad turned off the lights, slipped the flash drive into his jeans pocket, and locked the door.

CHAPTER 18

Omar's Warning

Quin had tossed and turned as he tried to sleep on the narrow excuse for a bed. But the things he had overheard and the photo of Darcey with that black X scrawled across her face, kept running through his head. He was sure that Darcey was "the woman" the voice had been ranting about. There had been no doubt in his mind after he had found her photo in the pile of papers scattered on the floor.

Grabbing a to-go cup of Turkish coffee at the small café down the street from his cheap hotel, Quin started up the old Nissan and drove to Omar's apartment building. Omar had just stepped out onto the sidewalk when Quin pulled up outside. He showed the photo to Omar, who looked at it apprehensively and declined to even touch it before answering.

"Yes. This looks like something Kaddur would do," Omar said, hesitantly pointing a shaky finger at the photo. "I have seen several photos like that and then—" Omar drew his forefinger across his throat for effect, "—the person shows up dead." He shuddered. "I would stay away from this."

"I cannot," Quin said, placing the photo in his jacket pocket. "I have to find this woman and protect her."

"You are a crazy fool then," Omar chided. "You will get

yourself killed. No woman is worth a man's life." He shook his finger at Quin. "Mark my words—you will die, and for what—a woman? You are a stupid fool."

"Not if I am careful, and I am always careful. And, yes, she *is* most definitely worth it," Quin confirmed, over his shoulder as he walked away, leaving Omar standing on the sidewalk frowning and shaking his head.

Slipping in behind the steering wheel of the old Nissan, Quin adjusted the rearview mirror and noticed a black sedan pulling up to the curb in front of Omar's apartment house.

Interesting, he thought as he watched two men climb out and walk up to the entrance.

Quin saw Omar slide back into the interior shadows of the entrance. The men walked right by him. Quin shrugged and started the Nissan. He had to go find Darcey, but before he could pull away, Omar was pounding on the door, motioning to Quin to unlock it.

"Go!" Omar shouted as he clamored in. "Go! Go! Go!" he yelled, frantically pounding on the dashboard, craning his neck, and looking out the rear window.

Quin hit the accelerator, and the old Nissan chugged away from the curb. "What is going on?" he asked, looking at Omar and then in the rearview mirror.

"Those were Kaddur's thugs. I do not know who they are looking for, but I am not going to hang around to find out," Omar said, out of breath.

He stretched his neck to watch out the rear window, his eyes big and round with fear, his breathing coming in short gasps. Little beads of sweat had formed on his forehead and were trickling down the side of his face. From Omar's reaction, Quin suspected that he knew Kaddur's thugs were looking for him or soon would be.

The old Nissan coughed and sputtered, as Quin shifted into first gear, hoping the men did not come after them because there was no possible way he could outrun the sedan in this old rust bucket. He remembered another time in Lima when he and Ricardo had been chased by that black

SUV. They had barely escaped then with the Jaguar, he had hotwired. Quin knew they were doomed now if that black sedan came after them. This old girl could barely hit fifty when pushed, but at the time it was all he could afford.

Quin kept watching in the rearview mirror for any sign that the black sedan was following. Just in case, he decided to take a short detour down a small side street. Halfway to the next street and still no sedan on his tail, Quin let himself relax. Maybe luck was on his side—he hoped.

He dropped Omar off at what he had called his "safe house" before heading back downtown to stake out Darcey's hotel. If the chance presented itself, he would snatch Darcey and take her away. She might be upset for a while, but all would be forgiven when she realized how much he cared for her and that he had saved her from a horrible fate.

જ્ઞજ્ઞ

Darcey stepped out of the shower and grabbed one of the big fluffy towels from the towel rack as the phone rang. Quickly she wrapped the towel around her damp body and went to get the phone. "Yes?" she answered, sitting down on the side of the bed.

"Hey, girl!" Marti gushed, "Guess what? We're coming to Dubai!" she said enthusiastically. "Brad has called in the guys to start on the project now instead of December, and I'm coming with Ty. Just think of all the shopping we can do while the guys are working."

"Wow!" Darcey exclaimed. "This is great." She tried to sound excited but was slightly pissed off that Brad hadn't told her about it, but she couldn't let Marti know she was upset. Marti was so excited. "When do you get here?"

"We leave this afternoon, I think," Marti said. "We're waiting for Ashley and Scott to get back from Casablanca. If they get back this morning, we leave shortly after one. If not, it will be first thing in the morning. I'm so excited, I can hardly wait."

Darcey could almost see Marti twirling around in excitement, and she laughed. "Yes, I can hardly wait, either."

They hung up, and Darcey went to the closet to find something to wear. She flipped through the hangers, still miffed that Brad had neglected to tell her about Marti.

Calm yourself. He probably wanted to surprise you, her inner voice chided her.

Yeah, well, he could have called, she snapped back.

Shaking her head and dismissing her sensible inner voice, Darcey found a dress that color coordinated with the hijab that Aicha had given her and slipped it on. Making sure she had the room key and money, Darcey left the room.

Stepping into the hallway, she saw two burly men, who apparently had been lounging in the chairs in the common area of her floor, coming toward her. A cold sinking feeling came over her, and she hoped she didn't look scared out of her wits, which was exactly how she was feeling at that moment. Covertly, Darcey looked for an escape route. There wasn't any—they were between her, and the door that led to the stairs. She knew she'd never make it past both of them.

In the amount of time it took them to reach Darcey, she thought about screaming, wished she'd listened to Brad and read a book, and tried to remember some of the moves from the self-defense class she had taken several years ago, none of which she had time to do.

"Señora Daniels?" the first man inquired hesitantly.

Looking from one to the other, Darcey swallowed and said with force, "Yes."

Don't show them you're scared.

Both men looked relieved, smiled, and the first man extended his hand, saying, "I am Alex Westphal, and this is David Cross. We are from ORCA. Señor Damji requested that we escort you wherever you would like to go today. We will be discreet and not interfere with whatever you will be doing today."

Darcey shook both their hands, wondering as she did if this had something to do with the incident last night at the reception.

"Nice to meet you," she said, "but there is no need for you to accompany me. I'm quite sure I will be fine." She wasn't about to let these two bozos follow her around all day, and she pushed past them on her way to the elevator.

"I'm sorry," Alex said, matching her steps. "We have our orders, so you're stuck with us." He smiled as he pushed the Down button.

"Humpf!" She snorted, as she stomped into the elevator.

Alex's smirk, as he winked at David, didn't go unnoticed by her.

Oh, calm down, girl, her inner voice admonished. *Just think, you have two big hunks to escort you around, and you know they are only doing this to protect you. Brad wouldn't let anything happen to you, and he can't be here, so he had Asad send the next best thing.*

Yeah, you're probably right, but that doesn't mean I have to like it.

The elevator doors slid open, and Darcey stepped out, never giving any indication that she knew who the men were, and walked quickly out the front door of the hotel. She could sense them behind her, but she was bound and determined to totally ignore them and, if she could figure a way to give them the slip, she was going to.

You'd better be careful. You don't know this city. Anything could happen, her inner voice poked again.

Realizing that good judgment should trump her usual, *Damn the torpedoes. Full speed ahead!* attitude, Darcey sighed and resigned herself to her two unwanted escorts. She made sure she walked well ahead of them. They followed her the few blocks to the open-air market where she went directly to the booth with the coral necklace that she was bargaining for when Quin interrupted her. Out of the corner of her eye, she could see her escorts standing a short distance away, but keeping watch.

"So sorry, señora." The shop's owner grinned and shrugged. "It is gone. Perhaps one of these?" He directed Darcey's attention to a tray where fifteen or twenty coral necklaces lay.

Frowning, she picked out another necklace, not quite like the one she had wanted but thought the color would work just as well. "How much?"

"One hundred American," he said, grinning.

"I will give you twenty American," Darcey countered.

"No, no, no." He shook his head and waggled his hands, palms toward her. "Sixty American," he countered.

"No, still too much. When I was here the other day, we settled on thirty," she said, hoping he didn't remember that they were still haggling when Quin pulled her away. "I will pay thirty and not a penny more." She gave him her take-it-or-leave-it look and waited.

"It is much too pretty for so little money," he said, holding the necklace up. "I cannot let it go for so little."

"Well, then I guess I will have to go to another booth. I will pay thirty American, and that's all," she said bluntly and turned as if to leave.

"Wait!"

She stopped and turned back to him.

"I will do thirty American—cash," he said. "No, credit card." He waggled his finger at her.

"Yes, cash," she said, smiling.

Darcey leaned forward and selected another one as a surprise for Marti.

"I will take this one as well, *por favor*," she said as she handed him the money.

He carefully counted the money before stuffing it in his tunic, then, dropped both necklaces in a small bag. "May Allah be with you." He gave a slight nod as he handed Darcey the bag.

Darcey wandered on farther into the market, enjoying the

beautiful array of colors and the many items for sale, stopping at various booths to sift through their wares before moving on.

She stopped at one booth that had, what she thought must be, antique jewelry, it was so beautiful. Admiring the many beautiful pieces, a necklace caught her eye and drew her to it. It had a faceted emerald stone dangling from a slender gold chain that had been threaded through emerald cabochons and pearls separated by tiny gold balls. It was breathtaking, and she knew she had to purchase it, which was strange because it was not at all anything she would normally wear or even consider buying, for that matter.

Darcey paid the merchant, dropped the necklace into the bag with the other two, and moved on, still wondering what possessed her to buy it. Twice she considered turning around and returning it, but each time she drew it out of the bag, she immediately changed her mind.

Strange.

Covertly, Darcey glanced back to see where her babysitters were. She giggled as she watched them trying to navigate through the crowded booths and shoppers and still keep an eye on her. *Now would be a perfect time to slip away. I could be clear on the other side of the market and out of sight before they realized I was gone.* She giggled to herself again, at the thought of them rushing after her.

Dismissing the thought, Darcey turned and walked back toward them. It was close to lunchtime, and she was famished since she hadn't taken the time to eat breakfast. "Gentlemen," she said, walking up to them. "I believe it is time for lunch. I'm going back to the hotel. You may go with me or get something on your own, but you are welcome to dine with me if you wish," she finished, not stopping to wait for an answer. She glanced back over her shoulder and saw they had been temporarily held up by a group of women haggling at a produce stand. Darcey smiled and walked on.

By the time Darcey had reached the hotel restaurant, the

men had caught up with her, and the maitre d' showed them to a table that overlooked the fountain with the Koi pool. Darcey loved the splashing water from the fountain—it was soothing. It smoothed out some of the annoyance she was still feeling over her two babysitters.

The dining room started filling up, and Darcey watched as the people entered, hoping she would see Luis, but he never came in. Finally, she decided he must have gone in with Brad, leaving her feeling a little lonely, even though Alex and David were dining with her for lunch. She sighed.

CHAPTER 19

A Spy Among Us

Brad found Nicho in the reception area talking with Adara. She was pouring Nicho a cup of tea as Brad entered and walked over to Nicho. Brad gave him a hearty slap on the back, and Nicho extended his hand in greeting.

"Good to see you," Brad said. "How was your trip?"

"Good," Nicho said, returning Brad's handshake. "We had a tail wind. We landed twenty minutes ahead of schedule."

"Did you get in touch with the guys?"

"Yes. Ty will be arriving this evening with Marti as you requested," Nicho answered. "The others will be here tomorrow."

"Great! Have you checked in at the hotel?"

"No, I came here first to find out exactly what I need to do," Nicho said, setting his cup down.

"Well, let me find Luis, and we will go get you checked in and discuss what needs to be done," Brad said as he started across the room toward Asad's office. "Come on. I'll introduce you to Asad," he offered over his shoulder.

Nicho took a final swallow from his cup before following Brad. He was feeling anxious about the whole business of protecting Darcey. It would be hard because of the little piece of his heart that still harbored feelings for her. Ever since that unexpected meeting in Lima, Nicho knew he should push it out, but his heart refused to let it go. Jenny had made the piece shrink, and he had let her push it into a corner of his heart, but it was still there, waiting. He cared deeply for Jenny, but nothing like he had cared for Darcey—no, still cared. He knew it wasn't fair to Brad or Jenny for him to have these feelings for Darcey. They both deserved better from him. Now, he would have to keep a close watch on that piece and make sure it stayed hidden.

Brad poked his head in Asad's office. "Asad, I'd like you to meet Nicho," he said.

Asad came around his desk and shook hands with Nicho. "It is good to meet you. I have heard wonderful things about you from Luis."

Nicho shook Asad's hand. "Good to meet you also, and likewise, I have heard many good things about you, also."

"I am going to search for Luis. You wouldn't by chance have happened to know where he's gotten to, would you?" Brad asked, his Texas drawl coming to the surface.

"I believe I last saw him on the phone in the conference room," Asad replied.

"Great! I'll go round him up and meet you all out front," Brad said to Nicho as he walked out of Asad's office and headed for the conference room.

Brad found Luis on the phone and noticed he had quickly hung up as he walked in.

Strange, Brad thought, *I must've interrupted something.* He knew Luis was secretive about his business affairs and shrugged it off as that. "Nicho is here," he said, standing just inside the door. "He hasn't checked in at the hotel yet, so I thought we'd take him over and get that done 'n then set down 'n work out a plan for protecting Darcey."

"Yes, that seems like a good idea," Luis said, somewhat distracted as he slipped his phone back into his pocket, then he paused for a couple more seconds before continuing. "Yes, I will have Adara tell Hasan to bring the car around." He smiled as he stood up.

"Okay, I have some things to put away in the work lab. I won't be but a couple of minutes," Brad said, leaving Luis at the door. "See you out front."

Brad thought that Luis looked distracted for a moment but seemed his old self now. *Still,* he thought, *Luis has a lot on his mind.*

He remembered Luis had been notified last night after they got back to the hotel from the reception that Aicha had had a spell and had been rushed to the hospital. Luis had asked Brad not to say anything to Darcey just yet. He did not want to alarm her since the doctors had assured him that it was nothing serious, and she would be going home this morning. Maybe that was who he was on the phone to, Brad speculated as he unlocked the door to the work lab.

Gathering up the file folders and his notes from the worktable, preparing to put them back in the safe, Brad noticed that a few of the folders were not where he had left them, and some he had not gotten to yet were laying open. *What the—* he thought, flipping open one of the folders; it was the guidance and landing system, EGLS folder. It was easy to see that the file had been gone through—pages had been shuffled out of sequence as if someone had been in a big hurry looking for something.

"Who could've done this, but the better question is— who would've had a key to this room besides me and Asad," he wondered aloud, as he checked the other folders. It was most likely that whoever had done this had made copies of some of the pages, as none were missing—but which pages? It didn't appear that all of the folders had been disturbed; only the folders with the Granston engines and the EGLS seemed to have been targeted.

I haven't been gone that long, he thought. *This must have just happened.*

Brad gathered the folders, tucked them under his arm, and went directly to Asad's office, forgetting he was to meet Luis and Nicho.

"Who else has a key to the work lab?" Brad demanded,

startling Asad as he burst through the rear door to Asad's office.

"What do you mean by that?" Asad demanded.

"I mean I wanna know who else has a key to the work lab," Brad exclaimed, as he laid the stack of folders on Asad's desk. "Someone got in 'n rummaged through the files. I believe that they might've made copies of some of the pages in these folders." He poked the stack of folders for effect.

"No one else has a key but you and myself," Asad said, reaching for the folders. He was astonished when he saw which folders they were. "Do you know what they copied?" he asked as he looked through the folders on the engines and the EGLS.

"Not sure, but only the pages on top seem to be outta order, so, I'm gonna guess those were the ones copied or at least looked through." Brad sat down and ran his hand through his hair. "Can you tell by looking at those pages just what they might've been after?"

Asad was deep in thought, as he shuffled through the folders in question. It was clear that whoever had done this, did not know exactly what they were looking for, or maybe this was just a trial run. They had looked at, or worse, copied, only the parts that explained the FTLHE, IDE, and EGLS. It also included the overview with the purported function of the domes and a brief explanation of where and how the modules would be transported and assembled. Nothing in those pages would cause alarm.

The real reason for the project was not in any of those reports. Neither were any of the diagrams of the landing craft, engine or guidance system. However, it was the fact that someone had obtained the key to the work lab that bothered Asad the most. It meant that there was a spy his midst.

Asad's brow furrowed as he reached for the phone and placed calls directly to each of the other partners, explaining the situation and cautioning them to double security. Brad noticed he had not requested Adara to make the calls as usual and wondered why.

Leaning back in his chair, Asad looked Brad in the eye. "I think I have a spy. The only way anyone else could have gotten a key is if they handled the keys before I received them. And, I have an idea that that is exactly what happened because until I gave you your key, no one but the locksmith, Adara, and myself had access to them," he told Brad.

Asad paused, looking down at the file folders on his desk. He did not want to believe that Adara could have done this, but there was no other answer. She was the only one the locksmith had handed the keys to when he left. Asad had had no reason to distrust her. She had been a loyal employee, one, he could always count on. Now, he was afraid she might have been the one to leak information about the Bio Dome Project also.

He had trusted Adara to prepare all of the materials for those meetings. It would have been a simple matter for her to make an extra set and hand it off to whomever she was working for. Asad still did not want to believe that it was Adara. However, with her connection, or rather her brother's connection to Ahmed Kaddur, and what Luis had told him at the reception, it seemed extremely likely she was responsible. Whether willing or unwilling, the finger of guilt pointed directly at her.

"I am afraid that Adara may be behind this." Asad sighed and raked his fingers through his hair. "I do not want to believe it, but there does not seem any other explanation. All of the evidence points to her."

A knock on the door caused both Asad and Brad to look up as Luis opened it.

"Are you coming?" Luis inquired of Brad.

"Yeah. Come in for a moment," Brad said. "We've gotta problem."

Luis looked questioningly from Brad to Asad and back. "Problem?"

"Yes," Asad said. "Someone has gotten into the work lab

and apparently made copies of some of the files relating to the project." He picked up the stack of file folders and held them out to Luis.

Luis took the folders and sank down into the chair next to Brad. "What does this mean?" he inquired. "Does this mean we have to put the project on hold?"

"No, we will continue as if nothing has happened while a quiet investigation is held. However, I am sure it will not take long as I have a good idea who has done this. The matter will be taken care of discreetly. We do not want any adverse publicity at this point. The media has treated our press release on this project as nothing of major importance and have not given it much coverage. I want it kept that way. All they need to know is that we are constructing more domes as base camps for ORCA's newly developed space exploration program."

"Yes, well, if this person has already passed on the information, it might be hard to keep it under wraps if they think it is to their advantage to publicize it. Then along with the speculations about the ozone layer that has surfaced lately, it could cause the UFN to become suspicious. We have worked too long and too hard on this project to let it be derailed now," Luis said, laying the file folders back on the desk.

"But remember, we purposely did not put anything in the reports that went to the public about the ozone, and there is nothing in these files about it either. So, I do not see anything coming of this," Asad said. "Only a select few on the board actually know the real reason for the domes. What concerns me now is the rumors that have recently been surfacing about the ozone. I do not know where they are coming from. Certainly not from the ERC or us."

"We cannot afford any unfavorable publicity about this. If the UFN gets wind of what we are doing, they will take it over, and that will be the end of it. ERC is trying to keep this all quiet until it is absolutely necessary to go public," Asad told Brad. "So for now, all anyone needs to know is that we are constructing habitats for ocean research and base camps for the new ORCA space program."

"There are fifty more Bio Domes being constructed quietly on the oceans' floors around the world, but at this point, those will not be enough to support the world's population," Luis said, frowning. "Many more are needed."

"That is why it is imperative that the Lunar/Mars Project stay on schedule and with no adverse publicity. The more domes we complete before the ozone layer reaches the critical point somewhere in the next fifty years when we do have to go public, the more people we can save," Asad said.

"But what would having these copies gain them?" Brad wanted to know. "There's nothing in what was copied that says anything about the ozone layer depleting or for that matter anything about what the domes will be used for, except research. How can their releasing that information benefit them?"

"It could be spun to raise suspicions and cause the UFN to look more closely at ORCA and bring into question the ERC's roll. There have always been hard feelings between them since the ERC split away from the central government, and that may be exactly what whoever is doing this wants. The UFN is being advised by a group of scientists who do not believe that the rising temperatures of the oceans or the droughts have anything to do with the ozone layer depletion, and it may not. I am no scientist. However, if the UFN does wake up and realize just how critical things really are with the ozone layer, it will demand to take over the project for the 'greater good.' If that happens, there will not be any more domes built for the masses. The UFN will use the existing domes and any future ones constructed for the elite of the world, selling them to the highest bidder with no thought to the rest of the populace. Our projects are privately funded through the ERC, ORCA, and the other corporations involved in the project. At present, we have control over the domes, but if the UFN gets involved, all of that goes away." Luis said, sadly.

Nicho had slipped in and had been sitting quietly, listening to the conversation. He did not like the sound of any of it and was not particularly happy knowing that life on Earth was about to change shortly. *Maybe it will not happen in my lifetime,* he thought, *fifty years is still quite a ways off, and a lot can happen in that time.*

"Well, let's hope it doesn't come to that," Brad said, as he looked over and saw Nicho. "Nicho, sorry to keep you waiting."

"No problem," he said. "I have found this all very interesting, and not to worry, I will not divulge anything I have heard here today."

"Thank you," Asad said. "I am glad you understand the urgency of this situation."

Nicho inclined his head and smiled. "Most assuredly."

CHAPTER 20

It was early afternoon as Hasan patiently waited, reading the morning papers as Brad, Nicho, and Luis emerged from the building. He folded it neatly and placed it on the seat beside him before he got out to open the door for them.

"Sorry about the delay, Hasan," Luis said, sliding into the back seat beside Brad.

"No problem, señor," Hasan said, waiting for Nicho to get in. "The hotel?" he inquired of Luis.

"Yes, *por favor.*"

Brad left Luis and Nicho at the registration desk and went to his room. Slipping the key card into the slot, he pushed the door open.

"I'm home," he called out.

No answer.

"Darcey?"

No answer.

He checked the bedroom, the balcony, and the bathroom. No Darcey. He looked for a note.

On the desk, a neatly penned note saying, *Didn't feel like reading a book. Went shopping instead. See you this afternoon. All my love, Darcey.*

Brad smiled as he read it. He should have known she wouldn't stay in.

He heard voices in the hall outside the door and went to see what was going on. Brad opened the door and was greeted by Darcey and two burly men loaded down with packages.

"We've been shopping," Darcey said as she breezily brushed past Brad. The two men followed her in. She giggled as they struggled past Brad, packages bumping against him. "Just put the packages on the bed, please," she said, smiling sweetly at them. "Darling," she said, putting her arm around Brad's waist, "this is Alex Westphal and David Cross. Asad sent them to escort me around today, so we went shopping."

"Glad to meet you." Brad shook hands with them. "Thanks for looking after my wife."

"No problem, sir. It was our pleasure," Alex said, with a sideways grin to Brad as his hand reached for the doorknob. "I presume we will see you tomorrow?" he questioned, looking at Darcey.

"Most certainly. I will have company tomorrow. My friend Marti will be here, and we're going shopping again. I can hardly wait." Darcey giggled, watching a slight frown on David's face, but Alex took it in stride. She cast a sideways glance at Brad in time to see him give her an eye roll.

"In the morning, then. Good evening, Mrs. Daniels, Mr. Daniels," Alex said, closing the door.

Brad walked up behind Darcey as she was slipping off her shoes and put his arms around her.

"Hmmm, I've missed you." He sighed, hugging her closer to his body inhaling the soft fragrance of her hair.

Immediately Darcey was all goose bumps and butterflies, and no air to breathe as she turned in his arms and planted a kiss on his parted lips. She felt the zipper of her dress slowly open then felt it slip to the floor. Time stood still, and the world stopped spinning as they drowned in each other's passion, surfacing only when there was a loud banging on their door.

Damn! That's probably Luis and Nicho, Brad thought.

He had completely forgotten all about them the moment he saw Darcey.

Darcey rolled over and looked at Brad, his green eyes still dark with passion as he pulled on his jeans and went to answer the door. She sighed, her desire totally not satisfied.

Bummer, she grumbled to herself.

She heard male voices coming from the outer room. She recognized Luis's then Nicho's. *Crap!*

Darcey jumped up quickly, found a pair of jeans and a tee, and slipped them on, not bothering to put on shoes. She ran the brush through her hair, spritzed some Joy on, a dab of blush and a swipe of gloss. She opened the bedroom door.

"Evenin' all!" She gave a big Texas greeting, putting on the biggest smile she could muster to cover the annoyance she was feeling at their untimely interruption. She closed the bedroom door a little harder than intended. "Luis. Nicho, I didn't know you were coming. So good to see you."

From across the room, Brad looked at Darcey with a raised eyebrow and that lopsided grin. The air in the room instantly evaporated as it always did when he grinned at her. She dragged her eyes away from him to look at Nicho.

A brief smile crossed Nicho's face as he inclined his head. He could not trust his voice not to waver if he spoke.

"Darcey, my dear." Luis rushed forward giving her a big hug. He felt her stiffen but gave her an additional squeeze anyway before letting her go. Turning to Brad, "We will order room service this evening. We have much to discuss, and it will be better if we do it in private."

"Yes, I think you are right," Brad said, walking over to Darcey, placing his arm around her waist as he spoke.

Darcey looked from Brad to Luis to Nicho and back. "What's going on here?" She pulled away from Brad and put her curled fists on my hips. "What are you all cooking up?"

"We are not cooking anything," Luis said with a raised

eyebrow. "We are putting plans together to keep you safe. We have reason to believe that your room being broken into and the incident at the reception are connected and most likely to the new project, also." Luis looked Darcey in the eye as he spoke.

"How is it related to the new project?" Darcey wanted to know, worrying that Brad might also be in danger.

"We don't know for sure, babe," Brad said, placing his arm around her waist sensing her anxiety. "But there was an incident at Asad's office this morning that could be related, so we're not taking any changes."

"What kind of incident?" she demanded, her voice rising as she pulled away from Brad.

"Nothing for you to worry about, someone got in the work lab and copied some of the project's files. Asad is conducting an investigation as we speak. He is sure he knows who did it, but not why," Brad told her.

"What has *that* to do with protecting me? You should be more worried about whoever this is doing something to *you*," she exclaimed, pointing her finger at Brad.

"No," Luis chimed in, "we do not believe that they will try to harm Brad directly, but they will try to get at him through you. What we do not know yet is why. Personally, I think it is something that goes back to the attempted sabotage on the Bio Dome." Luis paced as he spoke. "Aicha's son Ahmed is believed to be the mastermind behind all of that, and I believe he is seeking revenge for Brad's and Asad's role in putting a stop to it." He turned a looked at Darcey. "And, that is why we must protect you. You will have Nicho and Asad's men as bodyguards until this is all sorted out."

Darcey slowly sank down on the sofa as she listened to Luis. *This can't be happening. This. Cannot. Be. Happening*, she repeated to herself.

Brad sat down beside her, put his arm around her shoulders, and drew her close. He placed a soft kiss on her hair, and she scooted closer.

"It will all be fine," Brad whispered.

Yeah, all fine, with me or you hurt, or worse—dead, she fretted.

Oh, come on. Now is no time for a pity party, girl. Where's Uncle Jack's girl? her inner voice asked.

Yeah, you're right. Enough of this. This is not all just about me.

Atta girl. I knew you had it in you. Just remember Uncle Jack.

The little argument with herself over, she was ready to tackle "protect Darcey" head on. She straightened up and looked at Brad. "Okay, how's this thing gonna work?"

CHAPTER 21

A Threat Revealed

Quin stopped and picked up a case of water before heading downtown to Darcey's hotel. He found a spot on the street across from the hotel and parked, giving him a good view of the hotel's front doors. He had looked for a shady place, but, short of parking in the hotel's parking garage, there was none that would give him a view of the hotel's front doors.

It was too hot to keep the car running with the air conditioner on. It would soon overheat. So, he sat, with all the windows down and a goodly supply of water on the seat beside him.

An hour into watching, he saw Darcey, followed by two burly men, head in the direction of the street with the open-air market. Quin slipped down into the seat as he watched them stroll by, then he turned his rearview mirror so he could watch them as they turned the corner. He waited until they were out of sight and then he slipped out of the car to follow them. He watched from a distance as Darcey shopped and the men waited. He found a shady spot alongside one building, squatted down, and waited. With those two guys watching her, he figured there would not be any trouble.

Around noon, Darcey approached the bodyguards, had a short conversation with them, and walked away. They followed shortly after. After seeing they were going back to the hotel, Quin had made his way back to his car.

The early afternoon faded into late afternoon when the need to find a bathroom and something to eat both struck at the same time. Quin decided to take the chance and walked across the street to the hotel. It was risky, but in spite of it, he went anyway. The only one who would recognize him would be Darcey.

Entering the hotel, he went straight to the men's room, off the main lobby. As he reached for the flush handle on the toilet, he heard the outer door open, and a familiar voice sent chills up his spine. It was the voice from the drug house.

"I do not want any more excuses," the voice said sternly. "You will get this done tonight."

"Look," a second voice said. "It ain't that easy. Alex sticks like glue to her, and he won't leave me alone with her. Besides, we've been dismissed for the night. We will pick her up again in the morning. It will have to be tomorrow."

"Well then, tomorrow. It looks like you will have to take Alex out first and then grab her," the voice said snidely. "Really, it is not that hard. A knife in the right place will quietly take care of Alex, and then you grab the Daniels woman. How hard can it be?" The man chuckled. "Just do it! Is that understood?"

"Yes."

"Well, then we have nothing more to discuss."

Quin heard the outer door open and close, followed by a loud crash as something hit the wall, and then the door opened and closed again. He waited several more minutes listening, before leaving the stall.

His hunger pangs forgotten, Quin made his way back across the street to his car.

Tomorrow, he thought. *Okay, I need a plan. What time? The damn guy didn't say what time.*

He knew he could not park on the street overnight. It

would look suspicious. Plus, he would run the risk of being towed. The hotel's park parking garage would be perfect. From there, he could go into the lobby and watch.

Quin pulled up to the parking attendant's booth and was stopped by a mechanical gate.

"Your parking voucher, sir." The attendant inquired.

"Parking voucher?" Quin questioned.

"Yes, sir. I will need your parking voucher from the hotel before you may enter."

"Oh, yes," Quin cleared his throat. "I have not checked in yet."

"Well, I am sorry sir, but I must have your parking voucher before I can let you in." The parking attendant shook his head. "You must register first. They will give you the parking voucher there."

¡Maldito! Quin thought. "Very well," he said as he put the car in reverse and backed away from the gate. *¡Maldito!* he thought again as he stopped the old Nissan under the hotel's portico and entered.

⌒⌒

Nicho and Luis left Brad and Darcey's room, heading to theirs. Brad closed the bedroom door and stood leaning against it, watching Darcey. Her jeans, tee, and undies had been carelessly tossed on the floor. She stood naked, arms raised above her head letting her baby blue silk nightgown float down over her seductive body. His heart was doing double time as he watched.

"Well, Mrs. Daniels." He pushed away from the door as she turned and smiled at him. "Looks like I finally have you all to myself."

She giggled slyly, looking at him from under her eyelashes. "So it would seem," she responded. "Just what do you intend to do about it?"

"Ummm, I can think of a few things," Brad said as he

walked up to her and gently pulled up the gown that accentuated her curves so perfectly. He slid it up over her head and let it slip to the floor. His lopsided grin highlighted the mix of passion and mischief in his emerald green eyes.

Brad reached for Darcey and drew her into his arms, and suddenly there was no air for her to breathe. Her body ran hot and cold all at the same time as his hands caressed her body. Butterflies of passion erupted in her stomach and fire raced through her veins as his lips claimed hers and his tongue invaded the sweetness of her mouth, and she tasted him. A small groan escaped as Darcey melted against his desire. Streaming hot kisses up her neck and murmuring unintelligible nothings Brad nibbled then circled her ear with his tongue. She gasped, pulling her arms from around his neck, and sexily let her hands slid down his muscular chest, down to the belt buckle that held his growing desire prisoner. Deftly, Darcey unbuckled his belt and pulled the zipper on his jeans down. Slowly her hands slid under the waistband, and she relished in the feel of his warm, firm flesh beneath her hands. Darcey felt the jeans slip off his hips and fall to the floor freeing him. Her hands caressed his firm bottom, and she pulled him closer. His maleness warm and hard with desire pressed into her body. She could feel him throbbing, and she pushed closer as her passion rose, matching his. Brad stepped out of his jeans and sent them flying with a swift kick before he scooped Darcey up in his arms and together they tumbled onto the bed, lost in their own world of love and passion.

⁊⊃⁊⊃

Some time later, after the heat of passion, had dimmed to a warm glow, Darcey began to worry if this job that Asad wanted Brad to head up was worth it.

It was bad enough that someone had tried to sabotage the Bio Dome and put my life in jeopardy, but now, both of us, and this project as well is in danger. What I don't understand is why anyone would want to sabotage this project. I could understand, maybe, about the Bio Dome. It was first of its kind, but this? Space exploration was old hat. Everybody and their brothers are into space exploration now. There have to be at least a half dozen other corporations doing it, to say nothing of the UFN's own projects. So, what makes this one so different? Brad owes me some answers.

Sleep crept up on Darcey. She moved over and snuggled up to Brad. A soft rumble came from his chest as he rolled over, draping his arm across her, subconsciously pulling her closer. His soft, rhythmic breathing made her feel safe as she drifted off.

♥♥♥

Bam! Bam! Bam!

Darcey bolted upright in bed. *What the hell?*

The room was still dark, but soft defused light filtered in around the edges of the drapes. She checked the clock. It was five-thirty in the morning.

UGH!

She looked over at Brad, and he was still in dreamland, so she gave him a none-too-gentle shove.

"Huh?" he muttered, rubbing his eyes and slowly turning over.

Darcey's heart did a flip as she looked at that handsome face with scruffy beard and tousled hair falling softly across his forehead. He was perfect, and he was all hers.

Another Bam! Bam! Bam! interrupted her dreaming.

"I think someone's at the door," she whispered.

"Ummm. Okay, I'll go see who it is." Brad rose up on one elbow and caressed the side of Darcey's face, sending sparks coursing through her veins.

She sat in bed pulling her knees up to her chest and wrapped her arms around them watching Brad as he pulled on his jeans thinking how sexy he looked at that moment. Suddenly, an explosion of butterflies erupted in her stomach.

Damn, he's sexy, she thought. *My sexy man.*

Darcey could hear voices coming from the other room, and then the door to the bedroom flew open, and Marti came rushing in. She jumped on the bed and gave Darcey a big hug.

"I couldn't wait," Marti gushed, sitting back on her haunches, a big grin spreading across her face. "We just got in, and I had to see you!" she exclaimed. "Ty said we should wait at least until seven, but that was way too long, so I didn't give him much choice in the matter 'cause I just dragged him along with me."

Marti stopped to catch her breath, giving Darcey time to say something.

"Great to see you, too," Darcey said, swinging her legs over the side of the bed and grabbing her robe. "What time did y'all get in?"

"The plane landed about an hour ago, and we came straight here to the hotel," Marti explained. "Checked in and then up here." She giggled.

"Well, let me get dressed, and we'll order up some breakfast," Darcey said over her shoulder as she closed the bathroom door.

"Great. I'm starved!"

It took Darcey only a few moments to pull on a pair of jeans and throw on a tee.

Thank goodness for short hair, she thought, as she ran the brush through it. "Come on, let's see what the guys are up to." She grabbed Marti by the hand, and they went into the living room where she saw Brad and Ty deep in conversation out on the balcony.

Darcey slid open the balcony door and stepped out.

"What are you two up to?" she asked with a raised eyebrow, speculating it had something to do with the project.

"Just filling Ty in on the job," Brad said, as he walked

over and put his arm around Darcey's shoulders giving her a squeeze.

"Okay, but that's enough business for right now. How about ordering up some room service for breakfast for these starving folks?" Darcey directed her question at Brad as she turned and looked at him.

"Sounds like a plan, babe," Brad said, planting a kiss on her forehead. "I'll order up some extra coffee, too. Ty and I have a lot to discuss this morning before going to the office."

"I figured as much. That's why Marti and I are going shopping as soon as the 'babysitters' get here." Darcey turned and giggled when she saw Marti's expression.

"Babysitters?" Marti mouthed, her eyes wide.

"Yep. Asad thinks I—we—need babysitters. I don't see the need, but if it makes him happy, well, what can I say? They're okay. They don't get in the way, and they're excellent at carrying packages."

The girls laughed.

After breakfast, Darcey dressed for the day and then walked Marti down to her and Ty's room.

"Well?" Darcey asked.

"Well, what?" Marti countered.

"You know. Did he?"

"Oh, that," Marti giggled as she held out her left hand with a huge diamond on it.

"OMG!" Darcey exclaimed, taking a closer look at the ring. "It's fabulous!"

"Yes, isn't it," Marti smiled smugly, wiggling her fingers, admiring the ring as it sparkled in the light.

"Well, when's the date?"

"Not sure yet," Marti paused. "Ty wants to wait and see what this job's all about first."

"Well whenever you decide, I'm ready to help." Darcey gave her a hug.

CHAPTER 22

Lawsuits, Shopping & Other Sundry Things

Quin barely slept, tossing and turning all night, worrying about Darcey and the man who wanted to harm her. Finally, when he could not stand another minute in the tangled mess he had made of the sheets, he got up, showered, shaved, and went down to the lobby. He paced, waiting for the hotel's coffee shop to open. The sign said *Open at 6 A.M.*

As he was the first one in line at the coffee shop's door, it was only a matter of minutes before he sat sipping a cup of dark, rich Turkish coffee. Shortly after sitting down, he observed a man and woman checking in. Quin did not pay much attention to them until he heard the woman telling the man she was going to Darcey's room. The man tried to talk the woman out of it, but in the end, the man lost.

Quin smiled. He wondered who those people were and how they were connected to Darcey as he made note that the elevators stopped on the twelfth floor. His stomach rumbled as he headed across the lobby to the restaurant. Tapping his fingers on the side of the to-go-cup, Quin fidgeted, shifting his weight first on one leg and then the other as he waited to be seated.

An elderly woman walked up behind Quin and said, "Patience, young man. Nothing good ever comes from letting your frustrations get the better of you. Patience always wins." She smiled sweetly at Quin, who had turned to stare at her.

"Yeah, I guess," he said sourly.

"You will see. Patience is what is needed."

Quin was about to answer her when the maitre d' tapped him on the shoulder.

"Right this way, señor."

Crazy old woman, Quin thought as he followed the maitre d' to the table. *My patience is worn thin, very thin.* He glowered at the maitre d' as he placed the menu on his table.

Quin reached for the menu and noticed that he had a clear view of the bank of elevators from where he sat. Trying to read the menu and keep an eye on the elevators at the same time proved frustrating. So, he finally decided it would just be easier to order the breakfast special. That way he could keep his eyes on the elevators. His stomach rumbled again. At this point, Quin did not care what the special was as long as it was edible.

A short time later, the waiter placed the breakfast special on the table. It consisted of a small omelet with cheese sauce drizzled over it, an assortment of sweet breads, fresh butter, and fruit. His stomach rumbled again. He stuffed a forkful of omelet in his mouth as he noticed two men walk up to the elevators. Quin recognized them from yesterday—black suit, clean-shaven, close-cropped hair, and sunglasses. He watched as they got in and waited to see on which floor it stopped. It stopped on the twelfth.

Quin quickly wolfed down the rest of the omelet, paid his over-priced bill for the meager breakfast special, and headed for the parking garage. He needed to be in his vehicle, so he could watch in case they left by car.

ↂↂↂ

Marti and Ty's room was two floors below Darcey and Brad's. It was not a suite, but still large and comfy with a king sized bed and seating area complete with sofa and two matching chairs.

"This is great!" Darcey exclaimed, looking around the room. "You'll love this king sized bed," She giggled and winked at Marti, who blushed.

"Yeah, I know," Marti said, still blushing as she opened her suitcase. "Ty's already mentioned that on our way up in the elevator." She grinned. "Give me a couple of minutes to change, and I'm ready to go *shopping*," she shouted through the bathroom door.

Darcey laughed and sat down on the sofa and turned on the TV, thinking maybe she needed to catch up on the news. It had been days since she had watched a TV or read a newspaper for that matter. Most of the newspapers that Luis had at the ranch were either in Spanish or Arabic so she couldn't have read them anyway. Besides, everything was in such chaos getting ready for the wedding, and she was so worn out at the end of the day that world news was the last thing on her mind. However, with everything that had been happening with the project, she decided it would be prudent, on her part, to know what was going on.

Darcey surfed around the dial until she found an English speaking station. The morning news report was just starting, and she moved to the edge of her seat as she heard the news anchor reporting.

"…this just in. Mustafa Hassan head of the Asteron Corporation has filed a lawsuit with the Dubai Courts against the ORCA Corporation for breach of contract. The lawsuit alleges that ORCA signed a contract with Asteron to develop an engine system to power the new Aries Global spacecraft to be used in ORCA's new space exploration project. It further alleges that Asteron had the engine already in production when ORCA terminated the contract without notice or explanation. Asteron Corporation is seeking to stop all progress on ORCA's new space project, as well as two-hundred million dollars in production costs, and another two-hundred million in punitive damages. So far, there has been no comment from ORCA's CEO Asad Damji. More on this later when information becomes available."

Darcey fell back against the sofa. "Wow! Did you hear that?" she hollered at Marti. "ORCA's being sued!" Quickly she pulled out her cell and called Brad. "Are you watching the news?" she asked excitedly.

"Yes."

"Well?"

"I don't know. I've called Luis, but he's not in his room, and his cell is turned off." Brad sounded frustrated. "I've also just tried to call Asad, but I can't get through. You and Marti stay close to the hotel until I can find out what's going on. Ty and I are going to the office."

"We'll be fine. Remember we will have the 'babysitters' watching out for us," Darcey reminded Brad. "Besides, Marti has her heart set on shopping, and I can't disappoint her," she said in a pouty voice.

"Well, all right, but I don't like it," Brad said, hesitantly. "I want you to call me every hour, on the hour while you're out. Am I clear on that?" he demanded.

"Yes, sir!" she snapped back, coming to attention, and then she giggled. "We'll call you every hour, on the hour, sir."

"Hold on, there's someone at the door." She heard Brad open the door. "It's Alex," he said to her. "Alex, come on in. The girls are getting ready. Make yourselves at home. There should be coffee in the carafe, help yourself. Alex and David are here to collect you. How much longer will you be? Ty and I want to get going."

"Marti's ready, and we're heading out the door. Be there in a few."

"What's goin' on?" Marti wanted to know.

"ORCA's bein' sued," Darcey told her again.

"Oh," she said, "Oooooh!" Marti's mouth formed a big O as what Darcey said just hit her. "Like with lawyers 'n stuff? Like *that* sued? Over what?" she asked in rapid succession.

"Yeah, seems like they signed a contract with the Asteron Corporation to build an engine, and then canceled it and didn't tell them why," Darcey explained. "Now Asteron wants to shut down the project 'n two-hundred million for costs 'n another two-hundred million in punitive damages."

"What does that mean for Brad's project? Are they going to shut it down? This is terrible!" Marti threw up her hands.

"I don't know. Brad and Ty are going to the office to find out what's going on," Darcey said, opening the door. "Come on, we gotta get goin'. The 'babysitters' are here."

Two minutes later, the girls walked into Darcey's and Brad's room where Brad was pacing the floor, Ty was leaning against the bedroom doorframe, and Alex and David were lounging on the sofa.

"Good. You're here now," Brad said, walking up to Darcey. "We've gotta get going. Finally got ahold of Asad 'n he's waiting on us. Oh, and Nicho won't be going with you today as you have Alex and David. He will be going with us. You take good care of our girls," Brad said, turning to look at Alex and David, who were now standing. "I'll call and let you know what's going on," Brad said, turning back to Darcey, then planted a big kiss on her lips.

She immediately felt the electricity through their connection, but this time there was also the underlying feeling that something bad was going to happen.

Darcey could tell Brad felt it too as he backed up and searched her face with questioning eyes. "You be careful," he whispered in her ear as he pulled her into his arms. "I don't like leaving you. You call me if something doesn't feel right."

"Yes, I will," she said softly and kissed him back.

"Come on Ty, let's go," Brad said, opening the door.

"Right behind ya, Boss," Ty said, planting a kiss on Marti's upturned face.

"You be careful, too," Marti told Ty.

"Always," Ty said, shutting the door.

Darcey turned to see Alex and David looking uncomfortable with the situation and grinned at them. "Okay, boys," she said, "I think we're ready for a day of shopping. Right, Marti?"

"Oh, most definitely!" Marti exclaimed. "It's a 'shop 'til you drop' day."

Turning to pick up her bag, Darcey heard a low groan from David and smiled quietly to herself.

"Alex, get the door," Darcey instructed as she gave the room one last look to see if she forgot anything. She checked her bag for the room key, money, credit card, and makeup. All were in their proper places.

David didn't wait for Alex to open the door. He was out it before Darcey had finished telling Alex to open it. They found him waiting, holding the elevator door open, a pinched expression on his face. Darcey thought he looked a little frazzled but dismissed it as having to follow two women around on a shopping spree. She supposed he would rather be out doing "man things" instead. *Well, you'll just have to deal with it, buddy*, she thought as she stepped into the elevator.

The ride down to the lobby seemed to take forever. It made two stops, one a mother with two unruly children got on. She had them both by the hand and asked David who was standing closest to the button panel to push the button for floor three. He jabbed at the button and glared at the mother who was trying to keep the little girl from kicking her brother. The little girl missed and hit David in the shin. Darcey was sure all hell was going to break out, but David knelt down, looked the little girl in the eye, then grinned a big ugly toothy grin.

"That's once," he said and stood up, looking down his nose at her.

The little girl scrunched back against her mother's side and stared wide-eyed at him. The brother, undeterred, leaned around his mother and stuck his tongue out at his sister just at the doors opened on the third floor. A sigh of relief could be heard from everyone as the doors closed.

The elevator stopped again at the second floor. An elderly gentleman got on and rode down with them to the lobby.

Grabbing Marti by the hand, Darcey dragged her along to the concierge's desk. She wanted to find out where the best place for shopping could be found. Much to Darcey's delight, this morning the usual gentleman behind the desk had been replaced by a very fashion-conscious looking woman.

"How may I be of assistance?" she inquired.

"We are looking for the best place to go shopping," Marti jumped in. "A mall or something like that."

"Yes, we have several beautiful malls." She smiled as she reached over to pull out several brochures, each one featuring a different mall. She handed them to Marti.

"Gee, thanks! This is great," Marti said, turning to Darcey and handing her two of the brochures.

"Yes, thank you," Darcey said. "Do you have any suggestions about which ones are the best?" she inquired.

The woman smiled sweetly and pointed to the brochure that Marti was holding. "I would suggest Mall of the Emirates. It is my favorite."

"Well, thanks again," Darcey said, turning toward the front doors, and looking around for Alex and David. She spied them standing just a short distance away. Alex seemed keenly aware of what they were doing, but David appeared to be preoccupied with something else.

Darcey touched Marti on the arm getting her attention. "I think David would rather be anywhere else but here," she whispered to her. "He really looks like he hates being here."

Marti looked a David over the top of the brochure she'd been reading. "Yes, I suppose you're right," she surmised. "He does look a little out of sorts."

"Well, he'll just have to put his big-boy pants on and deal with it." Darcey giggled. "We're going shopping."

Darcey grabbed Marti by the arm and rushed out the hotel doors with Alex right behind them. David reluctantly followed. Alex quickly stepped to the curb and signaled for the black limo parked a short distance away in the hotel driveway.

Darcey was surprised to see Hasan jump out and open the door for them.

"*Buena días*, Hasan," Darcey said smiling. "I didn't know you were going to be driving us around."

"*Si*, señora. It is my pleasure," he said with a slight bow.

"Marti, this is Hasan," Darcey introduced Marti. "Hasan, this is Marti Campbell, my very best friend."

"Nice to meet you," Marti said, then climbed into the back seat.

Alex and David waited until Darcey had gotten in and settled before they also climbed in. Alex told Hasan where they wanted to go and settled back in the seat while David sat glumly staring out the window.

Darcey sat watching David. There was definitely something bothering him. *I have the feeling I should say something to him, like telling him I'm sorry he has to follow us around today, and that it really wasn't my fault. My husband and Asad have given me no choice in the matter. Or maybe inquire about his health. Maybe he isn't feeling well, and that is the reason for his mood,* Darcey worried. *Oh, silly, it could be any number of things bothering him. Your best bet would be to just thank him for escorting you today,* she finally decided.

While she'd been debating on saying something to David, they had arrived at the mall. Hasan pulled up in front and helped them out.

"Thanks, Hasan. We'll probably be here a while. I'll have Alex call you when we are ready to leave," Darcey told him. "Please give Alex your cell number."

Alex and Hasan exchanged cell numbers, and Darcey and Marti headed inside the mall. They were browsing in the first shop by the time Alex caught up with them. Surprisingly, David had stayed right with them, although he remained outside the store.

CHAPTER 23

Another Clue

Quin turned into the mall parking lot shortly after the limo carrying Darcey pulled up to the curb. He drove past and watched out his rearview mirror as two burly looking men climbed out of the limo. The last one helped Darcey and another woman out. After a few words directed at the driver, Darcey grabbed the other woman's hand and quickly headed into the mall. Quin pulled into the parking space just vacated by a fire-engine red Mercedes convertible. The driver, a bleached blonde with overly large hoop earrings, looked with disdain at the beat up old Nissan as it pulled to a stop in the parking space she had just left. Quin smiled broadly and winked at the woman driving the Mercedes. She flipped her head around sending her blonde hair flying out, stuck her nose in the air, and accelerated away. Quin shook his head and laughed.

He approached the entrance and was pushed aside as a group of noisy teenage girls shot out of the door. He let them pass before entering. Quin's eyes quickly adjusted from the bright glare of the sun outside to the lower light of the interior. Quickly his eyes scanned around, searching for Darcey or the men. Seeing neither, he walked on into the pulsing throng of shoppers, keeping an eye out for Darcey as he moved forward. A large, angry woman clutching the hand of a small boy, who was frantically trying to pull his hand out of hers, bumped into Quin. The boy screamed at the top of his lungs as the woman tried to get him under control, never acknowledging that she had bumped into Quin. He stopped and blocked her way as several other shoppers began to gather around watching the woman and the boy. Sensing that people had actually stopped and were watching her, the woman immediately started to cajole the boy. She smiled as best she could as she realized she was the center of attention. Her eyes frantically scanned the crowd, and her face turned a flaming red. The boy finally succeeded in freeing his hand and darted into the crowd that had gathered.

"Just wait 'til I catch you, you little bastard!" the woman screamed violently as she fought her way through the crowd, pushing and shoving the gawkers out of her way.

Quin had gradually inched his way to the back of the crowd, sensing there was nothing more to see, and he needed to find Darcey. A few shops farther down from where the crowd had gathered, he spied Darcey and the other woman. The two bodyguards were following a little distance behind them. Quin heaved a sigh of relief.

Staying a safe distance away but still keeping Darcey in sight, Quin followed the group through the mall, noticing that on more than one occasion, the men did not follow the women as they entered a store. Quin watched as the men stood outside a lingerie shop while the women turned to go inside. Darcey stopped and said something the taller of the two. He shook his head and motioned to the seating area that surrounded a fountain in the middle of the mall's walkway. She grinned and shrugged then followed the other woman inside.

Quin sauntered over to the seating area that consisted of two circular rows of wooden benches set back to back. The inner circle of benches faced the fountain, and the outer row the mall shops. Quin stepped through the opening to the inner circle of benches. He positioned himself on the bench diagonally from the men, just off to the side where he could hear their conversation, but not be in their direct line of sight. The tall one deposited the bags and packages he had been carrying on the bench beside him, then he reached in his jacket pocket and took out a pack of cigarettes. He lit the cigarette and blew a perfect smoke ring as he offered one to his partner who declined. Quin heard him say he had to go take a leak and watched him walk on down toward an overhead sign that had *Restrooms* painted on it in several different languages.

Quin settled himself on the bench and picked up a discarded newspaper that had fallen to the floor. He opened it and pretended to be engrossed in an article about a Formula One racing event. His ears picked up as he heard the other man's phone ring.

"David here," the man answered, and Quin immediately recognized his voice as the other man he had heard in the hotel restroom the previous evening. "No. I have not had a chance. I told you Alex sticks like glue to her." He paused, his brows furrowing as he listened to the person on the other end. "No, he's taking a leak," he answered. "They are in the store." He paused again, his lips forming a straight line. "*No*! I can't just run in and haul her out. We're in the goddamn freaking mall!"

The man held the phone away from his ear, squeezing his eyes tightly shut. Quin could hear the man on the other end yelling, but could not understand what he was saying.

"Listen," David said through clenched teeth, "if you want her so damn bad, you come and get her! I am done!"

With that, he shoved the phone into his pocket and started pacing, running his hand through his hair. Quin covertly watched him out of the corner of his eye, noticing his hands had balled into tight fists at his side.

The other man who David had called Alex strolled back up to where David stood fuming. "What's up?" Alex asked, noticing David's agitated state.

"I gotta go, man," David said. "Something's come up, and I gotta take care of it. If Asad doesn't want to pay me for today, that's fine." He turned on his heel and quickly walked away, leaving Alex staring after him.

What the hell? Alex thought as he watched David disappear into the crowd of shoppers. Alex had never seen David walk out on a job in the two years he had known him. *Something's not right here,* his gut told him. *Time to collect the ladies and head for the hills.*

Alex pulled his phone out. First, he called Asad, telling him what had happened with David, and he called then Hasan. He picked up the packages and braced himself as he prepared to step into the lingerie shop to collect the women.

Quin continued to sit, pretending to peruse the newspaper as Alex entered the shop, then, moved to where he could watch the store over the top of the paper without turning his head. Quin watched as Alex escorted two very displeased women out of the shop. He could see Darcey arguing with Alex, but to no avail. Alex simply shook his head as he placed his free hand under Darcey's elbow and moved her toward the exit.

"We gotta go," Quin heard Alex say as they passed by the bench where he sat, his face buried in the newspaper.

CHAPTER 24

Plans? What Plans?

Brad, Ty, and Nicho exited their taxi in front of the ORCA building, amazed at the throng of reporters and television camera crews already lining the sidewalk. Brad motioned to Ty and Nicho to stay on his tail as he quickly wormed his way through the crowd to the lobby doors. Several of Asad's security force stood, feet apart, arms behind their backs in parade rest, behind the closed and locked tempered glass doors. Upon seeing Brad approach, the guard nearest the doors quickly opened them, letting Brad and the guys escape the sea of microphones being shoved in their faces. They could still hear the shouts from reporters clamoring for a quote and the paparazzi hoping for the money shot.

"Whew! Thanks," Brad shouted to the guards who were now pushing the hoards back and securing the doors again. The three of them headed for the bank of elevators.

"Just like a bunch of vultures," Ty said, stepping into the elevator.

"Yeah," Brad said shaking his head. Nicho stood quietly.

The elevator doors hissed open on Asad's office floor, and they stepped out into the reception area. Brad noticed that someone new was behind Adara's desk. She looked up. Her clear blue eyes sparkled as she smiled.

"How may I help you," she inquired sweetly.

"We're here to see Asad. Just tell him Brad is here." Brad smiled back at the woman who blushed as she realized who he was.

"Oh, Mr. Daniels, I am so sorry I did not recognize you. Please forgive me. You may go right in. He is waiting for you." The woman continued to blush as Brad, Ty, and Nicho walked toward Asad's office.

Brad tapped lightly on the door before opening it. Asad was on the phone and motioned for them to come in and sit down.

"*Si*, I will take care of it," Asad said running his hand through his hair. "No, there is nothing to worry about. That has already been handled." He paused listening to the voice on the other end. "The lawyers have already done that." He listened again. "*Si*, I will call if anything else happens. You need not worry." A pause. "*Si*, goodbye."

Asad replaced the receiver in its cradle and stared across the room, seeing nothing. He had been on the phone all morning, trying to calm the fears of the board members, who had awoken this morning to the breaking news that Asteron was suing ORCA. Asad had immediately called the lawyers and found they were already on top of the situation.

The whole staff of Harkmann, Hatteruss, and Johnson had been up all night working on the case and informed him they could find no legal grounds for the lawsuit. The one thing opposing council had overlooked in their eagerness to file the suit was that the date of ORCA's cancellation on the contract came well before the listed date of Asteron beginning work on their engine. In fact, the date on the cancellation papers was a full two months prior to the start date that Asteron had listed in the suit. Asad assumed heads would roll at Asteron's law firm over that mistake. Then, this morning the lawyers received word from a confidential informant that Asteron had actually had their engine in production months before ORCA even approached them about negotiating a contract.

Apparently, the reason Asteron did not mention their engine already being in production had to do with the hyper-drive propulsion system failing to perform at faster-than-light speed. Asteron had hoped that the influx of money from the contract with ORCA would allow them to correct it, and ORCA would be none the wiser.

Asad had been surprised at hearing that, as that particular bit of information had never been disclosed in any of the negotiations. ORCA had only considered canceling with Asteron after Granston International had approached them with a hyper-drive engine of their own, already in full production and fully tested. Test results on Granston's FTL engine showed that it would outperform everything that Asteron had proposed their engine would do.

That had been one of the bright spots of Asad's morning. The other came when the realization that the break-in in the work lab had been to get information on the company that ORCA had hired to build the engine—not about the ozone. That knowledge more than made up for any frustration the Asteron suit would cause.

Asad shook himself out of the stupor he had let himself slip into and turned to greet the men. He stood and walked over to them. "Gentlemen, welcome."

"Asad, this is Ty Horton, my main man," Brad said, placing his hand on Ty's shoulder. "And, of course, you have already met Nicho."

Nicho inclined his head in greeting.

"Mighty glad to meet you, sir," Ty said, extending his hand to Asad, who took it in his firm grip. "I've heard good things about you from Brad."

"As I have about you," Asad said, giving a slight nod of his head. "Come, be seated. I will have Cala prepare some coffee and tea." He stepped over to his desk, pushed a button on the intercom, and asked her to prepare beverages for his guests. "I think we are in the clear on the ozone question," he said as he walked over and sat down across from Brad. "I think the break-in had to do with getting what information they could on the company we contracted with to build the FTL engine. That is the only explanation that seems plausible in light of the speed with which Asteron filed their lawsuit. They must have had it in the works and only needed information on Granston before filing."

"Yes, that makes sense now," Brad said. He looked over at Ty, who had a concerned expression on his face. "I'll explain all of that later. No worries. We're all good."

Asad checked his Rolex then stood, and walked to the door just as Cala entered with the coffee and tea. "Carry that on down to the work lab, *por favor*," he instructed Cala.

"Gentlemen, sorry to cut this short, but I have another matter to take care of this morning," Asad said, looking at Brad, who gave a slight nod indicating he understood. "So, if you will follow me, I will show you where you will be working for the next few months." He directed his comment at Ty. "Nicho, if you would, *por favor*, wait here. I will be back shortly."

Nicho inclined his head. Brad gave Asad a questioning look as he followed him out the door.

Asad paused at the door, placing his thumb on the screen of the biometric identity scanner. A light flashed under his thumb as the computer scanned his thumbprint. A message then appeared on the monitor above the scanner to *Please lean forward for retinal scan*. Asad leaned forward. The message on the monitor changed to *Welcome, Asad Damji*.

The tiny red light beside the door turned green, and the lock on the door clicked. Asad opened it and waited for Cala to proceed him into the room. Cala placed the tray on one of the workstation tables and walked casually to the door. It closed softly behind her.

"I have had all of the locks changed and biometric identity scanners installed at all of the highly sensitive areas," he told Brad. "You are to have all of your workers scanned. Their information will be programed into the areas they are to access."

"Understood," Brad said, nodding his head in agreement.

"Well, I will leave you to show Ty around and get him

acquainted with the project," Asad said. "I am taking Nicho with me. We will be gone the rest of the morning, figuring out how to handle the situation with Adara. Sad business that," he said, shaking his head as he left.

Watching the door close behind Asad, Brad shook his head, wondering too what would happen to Adara and why Asad had wanted Nicho to go with him. Brad had brought Nicho along with them this morning because Alex and David had shown up to guard the girls, and Brad had thought it would be a perfect opportunity to acquaint Nicho with the project. However, he had not expected Asad to step in and command Nicho's time. Brad paused then turned to Ty. "Are you ready for this?" he asked Ty, who still had a concerned expression on his face.

"Yeah, I think so, boss," Ty said, but it lacked conviction. "Just what's goin' on around here?"

"Well, I really don't have permission to tell you this, but I'm gonna anyway," Brad said as he motioned Ty to pull out one of the drafting table chairs. "I feel since you are my friend, and we are in this together. I owe you an explanation so you know exactly what you're getting yourself into."

"I appreciate that," Ty said as he pulled out a chair and sat down. He poked the underside of his hat's front brim with two fingers shoving it back on his head.

Brad filled two cups with coffee, handed one to Ty, pulled out a chair for himself, and sat down. He then proceeded to bring Ty up on all that had happened since the wedding, and then the reason behind building the domes.

Ty exhaled, his eyes wide. "Whew! That's pretty impressive shit and damn scary at the same time."

"Yeah, I know. Now that you know, you can make the decision whether to tell the guys or not," Brad suggested. "If you do, they must be sworn to secrecy just like on the Bio Dome Project. It is imperative that none of this is made public until the time is right."

ာင်္

Ty looked at Brad and wondered if he had the right to keep this information from the guys. The shit Brad just laid on him was heavy stuff and a lot more than he really wanted to know. Yet, he didn't like the idea that sometime in the near future everything on Earth was going to sizzle like steaks on a grill.

His mind was having a terrible time wrapping itself around that vision. He wondered if he had known all of this stuff at the time he signed on to the Bio Dome Project, would he have signed on anyway. He didn't know for sure but figured he probably would have if nothing else, just for the excitement.

He wasn't one of those do-gooders who jumped on their soapboxes for every little cause that came down the pike, but he was willing to help the legit ones where he could really do some good, and this was definitely one of those.

He rested his ankle on the knee of the other leg and leaned forward with his forearms resting on the crossed leg staring at the floor. He had been working shoulder to shoulder with Brad for the past year going on two and the other three guys five years before that. They were his family, and he had to be upfront with them. *No beatin' 'round the bush with this one,* he decided.

Ty straightened up, picked up his cup, saw it was empty, and scooted it across the table for a refill. He waited until Brad had added the coffee to his cup before speaking. "I think I don't have a choice on this one." Ty cocked his head slightly to one side and looked at Brad. "I brought the guys in on this, and they need to know, before we go any further, what's ahead of them." He paused, looking Brad square in the eye. "But let's get this straight—regardless of what they decide, I'm in all the way." His face broke into a big grin. He took off his hat and slapped it across his leg. "Hell, I'll never get another chance like this to go to Mars. Hell, yes, I'm in!" he exclaimed, grinning as he stood and reached to shake Brad's hand.

A big Texas grin spread across Brad's face as he shook

Ty's hand. "You. Have. Made. My. Day!" Brad exclaimed, jumping up out of his chair and giving Ty a big thump on the back. "Man, that's a load off my mind. I don't know what I would've done if you'd said no."

"Hey, ain't no big deal," Ty drawled out. "Ya always help out family."

What was left of the morning was spent going over the preliminary plans for the project.

Since Brad and Ty had not emerged from the work lab by twelve thirty, Asad sent Cala to escort them to the dining hall. She knocked lightly on the door and waited for it to open.

Brad barely heard the tap. He swung his chair around and stared at the door. He had been so in the zone that he had lost all track of time. He had even tuned Ty out after he had handed all of the technical stuff over to him to study.

Brad shook his head as he stood, resetting his mind to the here and now. He opened the door to see Cala standing there, her blue eyes wide in expectation.

"Mr. Damji asked me to escort you to the dining hall for lunch," she said sweetly as she tried to see around Brad to peer into the work lab.

Brad moved, blocking her view and pulled the door closer to him so that it was only open wide enough for him to stand between it and the doorjamb.

"Why, that's mighty nice of him," Brad drawled out. "Give us a few, and we'll be right out." He stepped back and shut the door. He glanced around at Ty who still had his nose in one of the schematics printouts for the communications systems. "You ready for a break?" he asked, jolting Ty back to reality.

"Yeah, I could do with some chow," he said, grinning as he grabbed his hat off the table and slapped it on his head.

Brad opened the door allowing Ty to go first. He followed, closing the door behind him. He slipped the flash drive into his jeans pocket.

"This way, gentlemen," Cala smiled and, started down

the hallway, her hips swaying sexily. Brad and Ty looked at each other, shrugged, and followed.

Asad and Nicho were waiting as Brad and Ty entered the dining hall. Asad motioned to them to follow him to a table that had already been prepared for them.

"Gentlemen, *por favor*," Asad said, signaling the waiter, and their meal was brought and placed on the table before them.

They ate in silence for a few minutes before Asad laid his fork down, cleared his throat, and said, "Brad, I know you are expecting Nicho to take over watching Darcey. But I have asked Nicho to shadow Adara and her brother Jamal for a few days. With your permission, of course." He paused and looked at Brad. He did not want Brad to think that he took their relationship of employer/employee for granted or presumed too much on their friendship. "I have a suspicion that one or both will lead us to Ahmed, and I am positive that he is involved in this somehow."

Brad narrowed his eyes, sat back in his chair, and looked at Asad closely. He was not completely sure he could approve of this plan. Nicho had come at Luis's request to protect Darcey.

"And what do you say to this?" Brad directed the question at Nicho, wanting to hear his thoughts on Asad's request.

"I will do whatever you decide. I have already told Asad that my first priority is protecting Darcey," Nicho said, glancing at Asad then back at Brad. "However he assures me that his two men are more than capable of protecting her. I have seen their files, and I have to agree I believe they can handle the job. That does not mean that I am completely happy with relinquishing my responsibility to you or Luis in this matter."

"What type of surveillance did you have in mind for this?" Brad asked Asad.

"My thoughts were to have Nicho tail Jamal for a couple of days, in the hopes that he would be in touch with Ahmed.

Neither, Jamal or Ahmed would recognize Nicho. However, I am sure that Jamal would most assuredly remember my men from the many times he has picked up Adara at the office." He shrugged. "If that does not pan out, then Nicho can take over for Alex and David, and I will find another way."

Brad turned again to look at Nicho, who was sitting quietly, but his jaw muscle flexing belied his calm exterior. "I will give you two days. If nothing has happened by then, Nicho will resume his job protecting Darcey," Brad said slowly, still not feeling good about it but realizing that to refuse Asad would put their relationship on a shaky footing.

At this point, he did not feel that their relationship could stand an outright refusal from him on this, even though his gut told him it would be the right thing to do.

That foreboding feeling of impending disaster gnawed at his stomach.

ↄↄↄ

Nicho stared at his plate. He was feeling like a pawn in a chess match as he listened to Brad and Asad. He knew he did not have the authority to refuse Asad, but he had at least hoped that Brad would have stepped in and said no. He did not know the reason for Brad's decision, but he assumed it must have something to do with the project. He did know that Asad was Brad's boss and as such would have the final say in most matters.

But protecting Darcey was personal and had nothing to do with the project as far as he could see. But then again, he did not know the history behind this project or all of the ins and outs of the office politics that might be related to it.

He much preferred his arrangement with Luis. It was straightforward—no bullshit, no song, and dance. With Luis, you always knew where you stood on any job.

"Well, it is settled, then," Asad said, grinning. "Come let

us finish our meal." He turned to Nicho. "If we only have two days, you and I have much to do this afternoon."

CHAPTER 25

David Takes A Hike

Quin watched as Darcey and her friend disappeared into the crowd of shoppers followed by the lone remaining bodyguard, then he worked his way quickly through the crowd to the front doors of the mall. He had just fastened his seatbelt as Darcey's limo pulled up to the curb. He waited until they had pulled away before following them. As he turned out of the mall and onto the street, he thought he caught a glimpse of the other bodyguard walking, hunched over, his hands in his pockets.

Quin shadowed the limo carrying Darcey as it drove directly back to the hotel. He slowed his speed to match the limo as it slowed to turn into the hotel's portico driveway. He drove on slowly past, watching as they emerged from the limo. Dropping his speed to a crawl, Quin turned into the hotel's driveway that led around to the parking garage. Last night's parking voucher lay on the dashboard; he reached up and grabbed it. Covering the time stamp with his thumb, Quin held it up for the attendant to look at it. The attendant glanced up from the newspaper he had been reading, clearly agitated at being disturbed, pressed the button to raise the security arm, and grunted something unintelligible at Quin.

The spot Quin had parked in last night was still vacant, so he pulled the old Nissan in and shut the engine off. It sputtered twice and died. Quin shook his head, slid out from behind the steering wheel, and locked up the old thing out of habit. There was not anything worth stealing in there. Everything Quin owned of any value, he had on his person or tucked under the floorboard he had jimmied loose in his room's tiny closet.

Quin hustled on into the lobby and entered just in time to see Darcey, her friend, and the bodyguard step into the elevator. He stood for a moment debating whether to register for another night or just sit in the lobby and wait on the off chance that she might go out for the evening.

He sighed and shook his head as he walked over to one of the many sofas that made up several cozy conversation areas populating the enormous lobby. He plopped down on the closest one.

It had been a long day, and doubts began to creep in Quin's tired mind. What was he really doing here anyway? What did he expect to gain by following her around? What did he really expect the outcome to be?

Where are you going with this? he asked himself, running his hand through his hair? *Do you expect her to come running and throw herself into your arms? Stupid fool,* he chided himself with a frown. *She is married to a man of her own choosing. How are you going to compete with that?*

Unconsciously, his hand slipped into his pocket and pulled out the photograph of Darcey with the black X scrawled across her face. He stared at it for several minutes before folding it in half and stuffing it back in his pocket.

Like it or not, he knew he could not let anything happen to her. He closed his eyes and let his head fall back and rest on the back of the sofa. It was his fault what had happened to her.

When he had started his search for her, it was with the hope of finding her and, in some way, making up for all the hurt he had caused her. He wanted to tell her how sorry he was and beg for her forgiveness. In the end, if he was truthful with himself, what he really wanted was to pick up their relationship right where it had ended on the boat. *What rela-tionship?* he asked himself, opening his eyes and staring at the elegant mosaic scene on the ceiling? *One night does not make a relationship. How can I even think that she would feel the same for me? She did not know who she was then, and now she does. Face it, fool, if you do this, you are the villain here. No amount of begging for forgiveness is going to change that.*

The feelings he still harbored tugged at his heart, but he began to realize that too much time had passed for her, maybe even him, if he was truthful with himself. What he had fantasized faded in the cold light of reality. He could see she had pulled her life back together and put the past behind her. But, still, he could not just give up and leave her. He had learned too much about what Ahmed Kaddur had planned for her. Her life was in danger. He supposed he could go to the authorities and inform them of the situation. Or, he could try to get a message to Darcey to meet him so he could tell her, or as he originally planned, he could handle it all on his own. He figured he owed her that much for being such a selfish-assed coward for not freeing her when he could have. His decision made, Quin walked over to the gift shop, picked up a newspaper, then settled himself back on one of the sofas to wait.

℘℘℘

It was a little after two when Darcey and Marti flopped down on the sofa in Darcey's room. Alex had put all the packages on the floor as Darcey requested.

"If that's it for the day, we'll see you tomorrow," Alex said, standing by the door waiting for Darcey to answer.

"I guess so," she finally said.

She was still miffed at having to cut their shopping spree short, and Alex had not given her a good enough answer as to why he thought they should leave. His only reason was that Asad had said it was a two-man job, and with David leaving, he did not feel comfortable carrying on by himself.

I guess I can't really blame him. He has to answer to Asad, she thought, watching him standing there.

"What time do you want us back tomorrow?" Alex asked.

He really hoped the women would decide to do something that would not require a security detail. He needed to find out what was up with David. David had been his partner for two years now, but he didn't know him all that well and didn't have a clue what could be wrong. He just felt it in his gut that he had to do something.

"I'm not sure right now. I'll let you know," Darcey answered. "And, Alex, thank you."

CHAPTER 26

Ahmed Kaddur

The heavy wooden door to Ahmed Kaddur's downtown office slowly opened, the visitor, obviously hesitant to enter.

"Where have you been?" Ahmed yelled, the veins on his temples visibly pulsing. "Is it done!?"

"No," Jacques said calmly as he pushed the door fully open and stepped in then stopped just inside the door. He had been a bystander to this scene too many times, just never on the receiving end of one of Ahmed's tirades. When he was in this mood, it was best to remain alert, just in case a quick exit was called for.

"What happened? *Why not*?" Ahmed's face turned a deeper shade of red.

Jacques braced himself for the onslaught he knew was coming when he told Ahmed what he would not want to hear. "I do not know. I could not find David. One of our men at the hotel reported that they came back to the hotel around two, without David." He flinched slightly as a knife whizzed by, barely missing his ear, and buried itself in the thick wooden door behind him. "Hey! Don't kill the messenger," he growled at Ahmed, who stalked past him to retrieve the knife from the door.

"If I wanted you dead, you would be dead," Ahmed ground out through clenched teeth. He gave one strong yank on the knife, and it came loose. "I will kill *him*!" he yelled, holding the knife in his hand so tight his knuckles turned white. He spun around and pointed the knife at Jacques. "*You*! Bring him here! *Now*!" Ahmed stormed across the room and flung himself down in the leather executive chair behind his huge mahogany desk, his hand closing and un-closing rapidly on the knife's handle. "Well? What are you waiting for?" He glared at the man still standing calmly by the door. It irked him that he had never been able to crack the calm exterior of Jacques Rousseau. The man had nerves of steel.

"I looked for David before coming here. He is nowhere to be found," Jacques replied calmly.

"Unacceptable! Find him!" Ahmed waved his hand in dismissal. "And do not come back without him! Is that un-derstood?"

Jacques inclined his head and backed out the door, knowing it would be highly unlikely David would be found right away, at least not until he was sure Ahmed had cooled off. From what little he had observed of David, it was obvi-ous to everyone, except Ahmed, that he was a flake and to-tally incompetent of doing any job that required any type of physical injury to another person. David had been a child-hood friend of Ahmed's. He had followed Ahmed around like a faithful puppy back then, and not much seemed to have changed with the passage of time. Jacques could not imagine why Ahmed put up with it, but when it came to David, Ahmed had a blind spot. *However, that may not save him this time*, he speculated.

Jacques had never seen Ahmed quite so obsessed as he was this time. He was blinded by hate and revenge after he had been thwarted in the attempt to take over the Bio Dome. There had been many who found out the hard way that you did not stand in the way of Ahmed Kaddur getting what he wanted.

Ahmed sat and stared at the closed door. *Is everyone working for me incompetent idiotas? Is there not one of them I can trust to carry out my orders? Just a bunch of spineless* pendejos, *his mind seethed! I'll get rid of the lot of them!*

He wanted to hit something, destroy something. He wanted to wring David's neck, and he wanted Asad Damji and Brad Daniels to pay, and pay dearly. He picked up the paperweight sitting on the front of his desk and flung it violently at the door. It hit with a resounding thwack, leaving an indentation on the wooden surface, and then fell with a soft thud onto the carpeted floor, its energy spent.

Minutes passed while the raging storm in Ahmed's mind slowly calmed, and he slouched back in his chair. Reaching inside of his suit jacket, and into the pocket that held his favorite gold cigarette case, he pulled it out and selected a cigarette. Snapping the case closed, he thoughtfully ran his thumb across the etched monogram. It was not his initial ornately etched in the gold case. It had been one of the many spoils from another brief, but deadly encounter. Just another stupid *pendejo* in a long line of *pendejos* who had tried to take what was his. Smiling, he laid it on the desk beside the jewel-encrusted lighter, a gift from one of his South American cartel clients. He lit the cigarette, inhaling deeply, before he let the smoke escape slowly. He drew his mouth into an O, breathed out a perfect smoke ring, and idly watched it drift up toward the ceiling.

The red haze finally lifted, and he began to think clearly. He recognized his mistake in not sending Jacques to handle the pick up of the woman. But when that *culo* Asad had assigned David as one of the bodyguards for the woman, it had been too good of an opportunity to pass up. After all, he should reap some reward from the money he had spent getting David on Asad's payroll. It had been easy after he had "gently persuaded" one of Aicha's lawyers to vouch for David. Of course, he should have remembered that David was not emotionally equipped to handle this type of job. Ahmed shook his head and pulled another long drag on his cigarette.

Was he becoming too complacent? Too arrogant? Too over-confident that everything would go his way just because he demanded it to? He supposed that could be true but seriously doubted it. For the last decade, he had had total control of the heroin trade in the Middle East, North Africa, and South America. Every interloper who had stepped forward to challenge him had been squashed like a bug. No one questioned Ahmed's power or authority. Until now.

Now, the sister he thought he had rid his life of long ago had come back to haunt him. The bitch, claiming to be his sister's daughter was upsetting everything, and he could not—would not let that happen. He stabbed the cigarette out in the crystal ashtray and reached for the bottle of Jack Daniels. He poured a healthy glass full.

I should have killed that puta, *Saleem, when I had the chance,* he reflected angrily, taking a swallow of the amber liquid. *Then there would be no spawn of hers to challenge me now. On the other hand, if I had,* he smirked, remembering, *I would not have had the pleasure of hearing her pleading, screaming in pain, and watching her humiliation as they stripped her down and forcibly took her like a piece of whore trash.* Yes, he had watched it all and felt nothing but satisfaction.

The money he had received for selling his sister he'd used to buy into the local heroin operation. The operation had been small back then, and Ahmed had made himself invaluable to Fadi Kamir, the head of the organization. Fadi was a small man with a small vision. He listened politely as Ahmed had excitedly explained his ideas of expansion. But Fadi had simply shaken his head as he had patted Ahmed on the shoulder, saying it was too risky, besides he was happy with the way things were. He enjoyed a good living with no interference from the local cartel since he had worked out an equitable arrangement with them to pay a small monthly amount for protection. In return, they had agreed to leave his operation alone. Everyone was happy he had told Ahmed—no need to upset the apple cart.

That did not deter Ahmed. He had a vision with bigger plans and set about accomplishing them by any means necessary. He had been ruthless in his pursuit of power. He could not remember how many lives he had disposed of to reach where was his today, not that it mattered to him—the ends always justified the means.

There had been no love lost between him and his mother, Aicha. When his father had passed, Ahmed had been glad. Now he could claim his rightful place as the head of the house and owner of the family business. However, that was not to be. His father had left everything in the hands of his mother. Ahmed had raged at his mother, saying she had no right to assume his father's position in the family. In a fit of rage, he had left his father's house, declaring he no longer looked upon her as his mother. He could no longer live under a roof where he was refused the honor as head of the house. She did not know her place, he had screamed as he had stalked out the door. He would have killed her, too if Asad Damji, who considered himself her protector, had not been there. It was just another reason that fueled his hate for Damji.

After that, Aicha had publicly disowned him, but privately she still held out hope that one day he would come to his senses. She had not cut him entirely out of her will.

Over the intervening years, Ahmed had kept tabs on his mother through a paid informant within her company. Then several months ago the revelation about her illness had reached him. He had paid the informant an additional fee to obtain a copy of the doctor's report. The report indicated that she had possibly six months, a year tops left. He decided to wait, knowing the business would revert to him on her death. It was only after this spawn of his sister's had shown up that things changed drastically.

Days before the wedding word had reached his ears that Aicha was having a new will drawn up. Infuriated at that news, Ahmed immediately sought an audience with his mother in the hope of convincing her he had turned his life around and changed. He was ready to cry, plead even, that he desperately wanted them to be a family again—even willing to accept her as head of the household.

Ahmed had his speech all rehearsed and ready to go. He could even bring tears to his eyes on demand. He knew her soft heart would forgive him, but to his utter disbelief—she had flatly refused to see him. That had further fueled his rage. In a fit of anger, he had ordered Jacques to kill her, but Jacques had persuaded him to let nature take its course. There was no need to hasten the inevitable by calling attention to himself needlessly. Then at the wedding, Aicha had outplayed him when she had had Vargas's lawyer draw up the new will. Frustrated, Ahmed had to assume the new will would cut him out entirely and make that *puta* sole heir.

At the time, he had thrown one of his temper tantrums. But he decided it would be just a matter of time before he found someone who would be willing to get him a copy of the new will, just as he had done with her doctor's report. That had cost him a pretty penny, but it had been worth it to find out just how sick the old hag was. There was still time to correct the situation once he had the Daniels bitch out of the way. Once she was gone, and the old lady was dead, he could contest the will as sole surviving heir.

The piercing ring of the phone sliced through Ahmed's thoughts. He turned and glared at the phone.

"*What*?" he shouted, pissed off at being interrupted.

"I have him."

"Well, why are you not here?"

"He is at the house. I thought it would make less of a scene if you handled it here," Jacques replied.

Sometimes Jacques could not understand what made Ahmed tick. He had no rhyme or reason to some of the things he did. He was volatile and vicious and lately unpredictable. Like the other evening when he showed up at Asad's house uninvited during the reception so he could get a look at Daniels and his wife. Jacques would not have known about it, except Asad's receptionist Adara had mentioned it to her brother who in turn told Ahmed. Jacques could see the kid was getting in too deep. He worshiped the ground Ahmed walked on, just like David. But, unlike David, he was willing to do anything Ahmed asked him to do—no matter what.

Jacques worried for Adara, too. He had seen the way Ahmed looked at her and knew what happened to the women he had favored with that look. He feared that once her usefulness in obtaining information about the ORCA projects was through, Ahmed would make her disappear like all the rest.

For months, Jacques had sat and listened to Ahmed as he laid out all of his plans for the Bio Dome, making it his own underwater country. It had everything he needed. The hydroponic gardens to grow the poppies, the hospital with its state-of-the-art labs for producing the heroin, the fleet of subs to deliver it undetected around the world, and the best part—it was located in international waters, untouchable by any authority. Yes, he had told Jacques, it was perfect. Then all of his well-thought-out plans had been derailed by one stupid person failing to complete a simple task. Ahmed had quickly ordered him eliminated.

Jacques then had to listen while he ranted about Daniels and Damji and how they had ruined all of his plans for the Bio Dome and how he was going to make them pay. Ahmed had been obsessed with making Daniels pay by doing away with his wife, but that was before he found out she was his sister's daughter. That news had only made it sweeter in Ahmed's eyes. He could hit Daniels where it hurt and destroy his mother at the same time. He had yet to improvise a plan to take down Damji, but that somehow took a backseat to the woman. He would worry about that tomorrow.

"*Si*, well, I suppose you are right," Ahmed reluctantly agreed. "I will be there shortly."

CHAPTER 27

Timetable Moved Up

Well, now what?" Darcey questioned no one in particular still miffed that their shopping spree had to be cut short.

Marti jumped up off the sofa and grabbed her bags of goodies. "I for one—" She grinned at Darcey. "—am going to put away my purchases and change into my swimsuit," she finished as she glanced over her shoulder on her way out the door. "Meet you at the pool."

"Yeah, okay." Darcey smiled back at her. She sat a few more minutes before picking up her parcels and carrying them into the bedroom thinking a nice cooling swim sounded excellent and probably was just the stress reliever she needed. It sure would help her get out of the funk she was in now.

She sat on the edge of the bed, peeled off her shoes, and wiggled her toes, wondering if she should have taken the time to talk with David. It worried her that she hadn't. Maybe she could have done something to help. If nothing else, she was a good listener and sometimes that's all a person needed. Tomorrow, she would make it a point to talk to him.

Darcey sorted through her purchases and organized them, putting each away in their proper place before sitting back on the bed. She picked up the peach and white striped dress box from the Galleria Boutique and carefully lifted the lid. Under the layers of peach-colored tissue, lay the beautiful ivory-colored Carolina Herrera dress. She had fallen in love with it immediately.

Even though she thought it was a little pricey, it had just been just too juicy to pass up. The flirty hem of the sleeveless silk faille dress ended just above her knee. The scoop neckline flattered her bust line, and the asymmetric pleating at the bodice accentuated her tiny waist perfectly. It had fit her as though it had been personally designed for her. Lifting the dress out of the layers of tissue the sales lady had gently wrapped it in, Darcey held it up to herself and stood in front of the full-length mirror. She knew Brad was going to love it on her.

Turning around, she laid it out on the bed and stood back admiring it. Suddenly she knew exactly what piece of jewelry to wear with it—the antique necklace that she had bought at the open-air market. It would be absolutely stunning with it. Lifting the necklace out of the jewelry case, she gently laid it on the bed in the open area above the neckline. The emerald pendant glowed. It mesmerized her. The beauty of it was unbelievable. She was so glad she had not returned it that day at the market.

The phone's loud thring, thring startled Darcey. She hadn't realized she had been so wrapped up in studying the necklace until the phone's shrill ringing broke in.

"Hello," she said, shaking her head to clear it.

"Hey, babe." Brad's velvet voice washed over her. "How was shopping?"

"Humph!" She snorted. "Some shopping spree! We had to cut it short because David just up and left," she grumbled, plopping down on the bed. "Alex refused to let us keep shopping after that. Said he wasn't comfortable with him being the only one."

"What'd ya mean 'David just up and left'?" Brad asked as a stab of anxiety hit his chest.

"I mean he gave Alex some flimsy excuse about having

to take care of something and just left," she said as a wave of anxiety hit her too. She sat up. "Is there something going on?"

"No, I don't think so, but it's strange that he would just leave. Asad said both Alex and David were some of his best bodyguards. I will check with Asad and call you back," he said. "Don't go anywhere until you hear from me."

"I wasn't planning on it, except I'm going to meet Marti at the pool in a little while," she replied. The feeling in her chest sank like a stone to her stomach. "You think there's something wrong, don't you?"

"No. It's just strange that David would leave in the middle of a job, that's all." He didn't want to alarm Darcey any more than she already was. He knew she would be feeling the same wave of apprehension through their connection and tried to hold his unease in check until he had spoken with Asad.

"Okay, but you will let me know as soon as you find out anything, right?" she said, the knot in her stomach easing.

"Yes. Gotta run, babe," he said, feeling her anxiety ebbing. "Enjoy your swim with Marti. Love you," he breathed into the phone.

"Love ya back," Darcey said quietly, and she sent a silent kiss as she hung up the phone.

Brad slipped his phone back into his pocket as the image of Darcey in her tiny coral bikini floated through his mind. A sharp barb of jealousy hit him when he thought about the men at the pool who would be ogling her perfect figure. He was seriously considering calling her back and asking her to cancel her swim with Marti when Asad walked into the work lab with Nicho.

"Say, you're just the person I want to see," Brad said, sliding off the drafting stool. "I just got off the phone with Darcey, and she said David walked off the job—"

Before Brad could continue, Asad held up his hand and interrupted. "Yes, I know. Alex has just informed me about David. That is what I have come to tell you," he said somberly. "I will not need Nicho. I have asked Alex to investigate what is going on with David. And the issue of Jamal will have to wait, for now." Asad headed for the door, pausing as his hand gripped the door handle. "One more thing," he said, turning around. "The timetable has been moved up. Have your construction crew here by the first of next week. We go into production immediately." He did not wait for a response.

Brad watched the door close and turned to Ty. "Well, let's get the ball rolling," he said, giving Ty a sideways grin. He slid one of the personnel folders across the table to him. "That has the names and numbers of the construction crew from the Bio Dome. Start calling them. Be sure they all know that all travel expenses are paid, they will receive a twenty percent increase in salary, and they will have a five-thousand-dollar-bonus waiting for them when they arrive. Tell them all questions will be answered when they get here. And don't take no for an answer."

"Yes sir, boss man." Ty saluted with an oversized grin and grabbed the folder from the table. "Am I at liberty to negotiate someone away from their present job?"

"Yeah, but let me know who it is first," Brad said, pausing. "I may be able to offer a better deal, depending on their expertise. There are a few I definitely want on this job." He picked up the other folder and settled himself behind one of the workstation desks.

"Have you heard anything from the rest of the guys?" Ty asked Brad.

"Yeah, they should be here sometime today," Brad said. "I guess they waited until the girls took off for Dallas. Otherwise, they would have been here yesterday."

☙❧

Nicho paced, waiting for Asad to return from seeing Brad. A small niggle in the back of his mind made him anxious to leave and get to the hotel and Darcey. The need to protect her had not faded in the passing months. It was still as strong as ever, and he would keep her safe at all costs. She was and would always be a very special friend, just never the love his heart desired. He let out a long slow breath and tried to clear his mind of her.

Unbidden, the image of Jenny drifted into his mind, and a pang of guilt wormed its way to the pit of his stomach. He had feelings for Jenny. He could not deny that. Although, it was not the burning, unrequited passion that he hid in a small corner of his heart for Darcey. But something else that was strong and steady. It warmed his heart, and it felt like home. A place he had not felt in his heart for a long time. He smiled as he envisioned Jenny with her softly curling, honey-brown hair that smelled of spring. The soft curves of her body as she fit perfectly in his arms and her whiskey-gold eyes that reflected the love she felt for him in their depths. At that moment, the secret corner of his heart shrank a little more.

He stood, staring out Asad's office window watching the ships in the Dubai Harbor when Asad walked in.

"Nicho, I am sure you heard part of my conversation on the phone concerning the bodyguard detail assigned to Darcey," he said as he strode over to his desk.

"Yes," Nicho responded. "I gathered that there was some sort of problem."

"*Si*," Asad said. "Suffice it to say that you will be protecting Darcey from now on," he said, turning to face Nicho. "The thing with Jamal will have to wait." He stepped around and sat down at his desk. He looked up at Nicho. "You must go. Check in on her and apprise her of the situation if you feel it is necessary," he said somberly. "But there is no need to say anything other than that you are taking over the responsibility of protecting her." He smiled briefly. "I believe you already had a plan in place before I asked you to help me?"

"Yes. I will inform Luis that your plans have changed

and that we will proceed with our plan as scheduled" Nicho reached his hand out to Asad. "I wish you well in the Jamal situation. Until later, then."

Nicho made his way down to the main lobby and out the front doors. The gaggle of news media had dissipated considerably since the morning. A few looked in his direction, but they either did not recognize him, or he did not look important enough to bother running after—they left him alone. He smiled as he walked away, pulling his phone out to call Luis, then Darcey.

CHAPTER 28

The Wheels Are Set In Motion

The black sedan pulled out of the parking garage and turned onto the street. Ahmed was alone in the car. He did not trust the new driver enough to let him drive to *the house* just yet.

The drive across town was a blur as Ahmed thought about how he wanted to handle David. The rage he felt against David for disobeying his orders still colored his thinking. He wanted to beat David to a pulp. He wanted to make him pay.

He wanted to blame David for his own error in judgment for not sending Jacques. But he could never admit he was wrong. To admit that was a sign of weakness, and he could not have that. There were too many just waiting for a chink in his armor to show. No, he would never admit he was wrong about anything.

The house came into view, and Ahmed pushed the button on the steering wheel that controlled the gate—it swung open. He pulled up beside Jacques's car that sat at the end of the driveway and shut off the engine. He sat a while, waiting for his mood to level out before he entered the house. He couldn't afford to do anything he would regret later.

❧❦❧

Jacques had been watching the past half hour through the boards that covered the window. He could hear David sniveling somewhere in the room but paid him little mind. He was more worried about Ahmed's temper and what he might do to David if he had not cooled off sufficiently by the time he arrived. He knew that Ahmed cared for David. Hell, Ahmed had been picking up after David and getting him out of scrapes since they were kids, but this time…well, Jacques just did not know.

He knew David could sense it too. He had been cowering ever since Jacques had shoved him through the door. Jacques cared what happened to David, he really did, but his hands were tied. He had told David that when he had pleaded to let him go.

"Just tell him you could not find me." David had begged Jacques. "I promise I will leave Dubai and never return." Tears had streamed down his face as he pleaded.

Jacques could not be swayed. He knew that would be a dangerous game to play with Ahmed. Yes, he could let David go and say he could not find him, and David could leave Dubai. But, sooner or later, and David being David, he would screw things up, and Ahmed would find out Jacques had lied. Then, all hell would rain down on him. No, Jacques had decided, it was not worth it. *It is too late now anyway* Jacques thought as he watched the black sedan drive through the gate.

Ahmed opened the door with purpose and strode in, looking around for David. He knew this was not going to be pleasant for David, but right now he really did not give a shit. Upon not seeing David immediately, he spun around and glared at Jacques. "Why are you still here?" he demanded. "Go get the damn *puta* and bring her here. I do not care how you do it—just do it!" he screamed. "*Now!*"

Jacques raised his eyebrow at Ahmed and then shrugged and turned toward the door.

Ahmed was right, he realized. *Why* was *he still here? After all, David's fate was now in Ahmed's hands.*

Jacques pulled the door closed behind him and walked slowly to his car. He knew it was not going to be easy to find the woman in a place where he could just scoop her up and stuff her in his car. No, he would have to think about it for a while—make a plan.

๛

"David!" Ahmed shouted as he did a three-sixty turn around viewing the room. "Where the hell are you? I can smell the fear on you, you sniveling little coward. Show yourself!"

In a huff, Ahmed stomped across the room to the time-worn, scarred wooden desk. He slammed his body down on the ancient wooden, swivel office chair behind it. As his eyes roved the room, his fingers drummed a tattoo on the desktop.

"Daaaviiid," Ahmed said in a singsong voice. "Don't make me wait."

A shuffling noise came from behind a stack of wooden crates in one dim corner of the room. A scared and shaking David inched his way out from behind them and approached the old wooden, straight-back chair that sat like an executioner's chair in front of the desk. Slowly his body sank down on it. Closing his eyes, he rested his chin on his chest, his hands resting on his thighs, and waited for whatever punishment Ahmed had planned for him. He drew a ragged breath and opened his eyes but was unable to look up at Ahmed. Instead, he stared at an abandoned cobweb. The empty shell of a dead fly hung limply in the web that stretched between the scared leg of the desk and the dirty wooden floor.

That is me, he thought. *I am that fly caught in Ahmed's web that I have let him spin around me.* He sighed. Nothing would stop the inevitable that was going to happen.

It had become all too clear to him that afternoon at the

mall that he did not have the intestinal fortitude to do what Ahmed wanted. His stomach had recoiled at the thought of killing Alex—he knew he could not do it. In spite of his life-long friendship with Ahmed, he knew that would not protect him now. Ahmed was only loyal to those who were loyal to him and refusing to do what Ahmed had demanded of him was an act of disloyalty.

"David, David, David," Ahmed said, shaking his head as he surveyed what he saw as a cowering excuse of a man in front of him. "I cannot have this. You understand you deliberately disobeyed me, and I cannot let that stand. I can forgive you of many things, but *this* I cannot." He shrugged. "If I do, I will be considered 'soft.' You know I cannot allow that." He leaned across the desk waiting for David to look up. When he did not, Ahmed slammed his open hand violently on the desktop.

The loud, jarring *smack* reverberated off of the desktop caused David to jump. His eyes flew up. Ahmed's bored into him. Cold chills ran up David's spine as he looked at the evil glinting in Ahmed's eyes. The inevitable was here. A lone drop of sweat slid down David's temple.

☙☙☙

Jacques pulled out onto the main thoroughfare, heading for downtown. He did not have any idea how he was going to accomplish what Ahmed wanted. Hell, he did not even know what the woman looked like for sure. Ahmed had had a photo of her, and he had gotten a brief glance at it once. But it had somehow disappeared from *the house*. The best he could do at this late in the game was to check with his sister. She worked as one of the concierges at the hotel where the woman was staying. The situation between them was tenuous at best since he had been working for Ahmed. He could never tell her why he felt he owed Ahmed. She would not understand. But he hoped she would reconsider and give him the information he needed or at the very least point him in the right direction.

The sun was just dipping behind the hotel when Jacques walked through the hotel's front doors. Stopping to orient himself, he glanced over at the concierge's desk and seeing it was empty, turned, and headed toward the door marked *Hotel Personnel Only*.

The door swung shut behind him with a slight swooshing sound. It had been a while since he had been down this hall, but he supposed things were still located in the same place. He found the door he wanted. It was closed. He tapped lightly on it before pushing it open. The cramped room, which was hardly more than an oversized walk-in closet, was devoid of any person. The room was lit by the harsh glare emanating from the row of bare bulbs ringing the mirror of the dressing table. On the dressing table, an open pack of cigarettes, and a half-smoked one lay smoldering in the ashtray among the numerous dead butts. On the floor, beside the dressing table, a scattering of objects spilled out in front of an upturned purse as if someone had knocked it off but had not taken the time to pick things up.

Jacques paused, eyeing the room with unease, but decided to wait anyway. If he knew Angeline, she would be back shortly. She never went anywhere without her purse, and definitely not without her cigarettes. Jacques stubbed out the smoldering butt before he squatted down, shoveled the spilled items into the purse, then he set it back on the dressing table. Eyeing the large, over-stuffed chair in the corner, he squeezed past the bench in front of the dressing table over to it. He plopped down, his knees coming up almost level with his eyes as the springs in the old chair offered no resistance to his weight.

"¡*Merde*!" he said out loud as he squirmed his way out of the chair. *Sonofabitch!* He fumed inwardly checking his trousers for any damage. Hiking his leg, he perched himself carefully on the arm of the chair, balancing his weight so the chair would not tip.

Jacques had just gotten himself situated when Angeline burst through the door. "What the hell are you doing here?" she started when she saw Jacques. "I told you, *you* are not welcome here anymore." She glared at him, her hands on her hips. "As long as you persist in being a flunky for that asshole Kaddur, you are no longer a brother of mine. When are you going to get it through that thick skull of yours that he is evil? *Evil!*" she screamed, pointing an accusing finger at him.

Jacques stared at the petite bundle of fury that was his sister. Not that he could ever make her understand his situation or that he would never leave Ahmed, but he knew she was right. In spite of everything, he loved his sister and contacting her had been a difficult decision and a long shot at best. But right now she was the quickest way to get the information he needed.

"Hi to you, too," Jacques said, standing up. "I will not be long. I need some information about a guest staying here—"

"*No!*" she shouted, interrupting him. "I will *not* tell you anything about our guests." Her eyes were shooting daggers at Jacques. "*Get out!*" She whirled around, pulled the door open, and pointed out into the hall. "Don't ever come back!"

"I am sorry, *mon cher*," he said sadly as he reached out. One hand pushed the door closed, the other he laid on her shoulder. "But I cannot do that. I need this information. It is a matter of life and death." But neglected to say whose life or death. "I will have this information, and you will give it to me." His fingers tightened on her thin shoulder, and his tone left no doubt that he meant business.

She stared wide-eyed as Jacques. Her petite body began to shake. "How can you demand this of me? I owe you nothing. *Nothing!*" Tears pricked at the corner of her eyes. She winced as she jerked back out from under his hand, totally unprepared for the broad-handed slap across her face that followed.

"Angeline, I am truly sorry," he said, his voice soft, his

eyes sad as he grabbed her shoulders, "but you leave me no choice. I have to have this information."

Her hand flew to her cheek and tears welled up in her blue eyes. "You bastard!" She flew into him, pounding his chest with her small fists. Startled, Jacques pulled her to him and cradled her in his arms for one brief moment. Looking up, the image in the mirror stared back at him. Illuminated by the harsh glare of the lights, he looked like the monster she thought he was. The man holding his sister was a stranger. He sighed then shoved her down on the bench, his fingers biting into her shoulders. A sadness filled his heart with what he had to do.

"Now," he said, squatting down in front of her. "I need to know what you can tell me about Darcey Daniels."

CHAPTER 29

Darcey in Danger

The last four hours had dragged by while Quin kept an eye out for Darcey. Growing bored, he checked his watch for what seemed like the hundredth time when a girlish laugh reached Quin's ear. He would know that laugh anywhere. Turning his head in the direction of the elevators, he saw Darcey and her friend emerge wearing swimming attire. His heart skipped a beat as her gauzy cover up flowed around her body as she walked. It did little to hide the curves he remembered so well. Quin followed shortly afterward, stopping in the shadows of the hallway to watch.

Darcey sat down on the edge of one of the chaise lounges, turned, and stretched out, her graceful body kissed by the sun. A small smile played around Quin's mouth as he remembered every detail of her perfect body, the feel of her flesh under his, the smell, and taste of her as they had made love. Taken aback by his reaction to the memories, he shoved his hands into his pockets and entered the men's room. It had been too long since he had had a woman.

After his quick jaunt to the restroom and things were back to normal, Quin stepped out and briefly watched the women before returning to the lobby area. He noticed that there was only one-way in or out of the pool and that was through the hallway where he stood.

Quin surveyed the lobby from his vantage point in the hallway, studying the people who came and went through the front doors. A tall man caught Quin's eye as he stepped through the doors and paused. He reminded him of someone, but he could not place him. The man looked toward the concierge's desk then turned and walked directly to and through the door marked *Hotel Personnel Only*.

Odd, Quin thought. *I am sure I know that man from somewhere. But where?* He stood several minutes pondering it then turned back for one more look at Darcey.

Quin shook his head, made his way out of the hallway, and into the lobby area. He was still puzzled about the man and why he so looked familiar. Nothing came to him as he strolled toward the seating area off to the side of the front doors. It offered the best view of the elevators and the hallway to the pool.

Before sitting down, Quin glanced briefly over the sofas, chairs, and low tables that made up the area he was about to occupy and noticed it was devoid of any reading material, quite unlike the other areas he had occupied during his vigil. In those areas, there had been plenty of discarded magazines, books, and newspapers. However, he had looked through or read everything that interested him in those. Now, he needed something new. Gazing around, he saw the hotel's gift shop. Mentally shrugging, he walked over, spent several minutes browsing through the shop, and several more minutes before deciding on which magazines he wanted. He paid for his magazines and picked up a local newspaper on his way out the door.

With his cache of magazines on the seat beside him, Quin unfolded the newspaper. He glanced through several pages, reading the headlines before a small article caught his attention. It was about a supposed drug deal that had gone bad, leaving several people dead or injured. But what had caught Quin's eye was a picture of Omar. According to the report, Omar was listed as among the dead. The article stated that Omar and three other men were believed to have been innocent bystanders who had been in the wrong place at the wrong time. Along with the pictures of the men, someone had captured a picture on their cell phone of the alleged perpetrator's fleeing vehicle. It was a black sedan. The car looked identical to the one that Omar had said belonged to Ahmed Kaddur. A cold chill ran down Quin's spine as he looked at the picture of the car and then back at Omar's picture. Then, it all fell into place—the tall, dark man was one of Kaddur's men that Quin had seen that day outside of Omar's apartment building. He quickly raised his eyes and scoured the lobby for the man.

This could only mean one thing, he thought, alarm bells sounding madly in his mind. *They have come for Darcey!*

Quin folded the newspaper, laid it on top of the magazines, and directed his eyes to the *Hotel Personnel Only* door. He had not noticed the man leaving, so he assumed he must still be somewhere behind it. Cautiously, Quin walked toward the door, casually turning his head from side to side to make sure no one was watching him. Then he quickly slipped through the door. It swooshed shut behind him.

A long hallway loomed in front of Quin. He was thankful there were no hotel employees in sight. All was quiet. No outside noises filtered in. Only the muffled hum of the florescent overhead lights broke the silence. An odd thought passed through his mind that maybe this part of the hotel was sound proof. Taking a deep breath, he started walking, noticing there were doors on either side of the hall. Most doors were closed, but two were open giving all indication they were a break room and some type of exercise room, but both were unoccupied now.

Quin proceeded on farther down the hall, pausing when he heard loud voices coming from somewhere just ahead. He could not hear what was being said, but a door suddenly swung open, and he heard a woman shout something like "Get out and don't ever come back," but he could not be sure. He tried the door beside him, found it unlocked, and quickly ducked inside. Waiting several minutes before peeking out, he saw and heard no one. Stepping out into the hall, he moved forward toward the door where he thought he had heard the voices.

Just as he reached the door, it swung violently open, and a man barreled out the door, slamming into Quin. The force of their collision moved Quin back a step. He immediately recognized the man and swung at him. The punch that should have connected to the man's jaw glanced off, throwing Quin off balance. However, it was just enough for the man to rebound and hit Quin squarely in the face. The hit propelled Quin back into the wall, knocking the wind out of his lungs. He saw stars as he slid to the floor and blackness threatened to envelope him. He fought it, trying to regain his footing, but the man was on him in a flash, grabbing him by the front of his shirt and pulling him up to deliver another blow to Quin's face. This time there were no stars, only blackness.

"Who the hell is that?" Jacques bellowed at Angeline, his face distorted with anger as he gave the man a hard kick for good measure. "Is this some boyfriend of yours?" he asked, glaring at her. Hell, what did he care if she had a boyfriend? She was twenty-six years old. She could have a dozen of them if she wanted. He was just pissed and needed someone to direct his anger at that wasn't unconscious.

Jacques looked again at the mangled mess he had made of the man on the floor. He did not have any idea who the man was or why he would have attacked him. He did not have time to find out now. He had finally gotten the information he wanted from Angeline and could waste no more time. Ahmed was waiting, and Jacques knew he would not wait long.

"I don't know," Angeline said, peering around the door-frame at the man on the floor. "I have seen him in the lobby off and on for a couple of days," she said, recognizing the scar down the side of his face. She knelt down and gently moved a lock of dark hair that had stuck to his battered face. "You know," she said looking a Jacques, "like he's waiting for someone. I think he even checked in for a night," she said softly, her eyes returning to the man's battered face.

She had noticed him the first day he started hanging around, thinking he was kind of cute in a dangerous sort of way, with his dark good looks, sculpted body, and the scar. She tingled at the bad boy vibe he projected. One she had fully intended to explore further, but the hotel guests had been particularly demanding of her time over the last couple of days so she'd had no opportunity to do so.

"Well, whoever he is, get rid of him. I do not want him following me," Jacques glared at Angeline. "I do not care what you do with him, just make sure he does not follow me."

Turning down the hall, Jacques left, leaving a bewildered Angeline with the man to take care of. Jacques's focus was now solely on getting the woman. Angeline had given him her room number and what she knew about her routine, which mostly consisted of shopping. She had said the husband was usually gone until early evening.

Jacques left the employee area through the door at the other end of the hallway that opened into the hotel's laundry facility intending on taking the service elevator from there to the twelfth floor. According to the floor plan that Angeline had shown him, the service elevator opened on the twelfth floor around a corner and just a few yards from the Daniels woman's door. It was perfect. He could get in and get out with her quickly. He pushed the up button on the elevator.

ℜℛℜℛ

Angeline sank down on the floor beside the man and stared into his handsome face. She reached out and touched the place where Jacques had hit him. It was already turning bluish purple. She ran her finger down the scar on the side of his face and wondered how he got it.

"Well, I can't have you lying about in the hall," she said to the man, who was beyond hearing her. "What will people think?"

She giggled as she reached under his arms to drag him into her small room. Struggling, she finally got him into her room then maneuvered his feet out of the way so she could shut the door. Exhausted she plopped down on the bench, rested her elbows on her knees, and watched the even rise and fall of his hard chest. She let her eyes wander over his body, taking in his sculpted frame wondering what it would feel like to be held in those arms and kissed by those lips.

"*Bonté divine*," she said aloud. Placing her hands on either side of her face her eyes wide in astonishment. "What am I thinking?"

She shook her head. She did not know who this man was or why he would have attacked Jacques, which had been a big mistake in her estimation. Regardless, she had to get him out of her room. Tentatively placing her foot on his leg, she prodded him. He groaned but did not come around. Finally, after several more attempts at prodding, he still gave no sign of regaining consciousness. Angeline reached around behind her, picked up the full bottle of water sitting on the dressing table, and poured it on his face.

The cold water hitting Quin's face startled him awake. "What th—" He bolted upright, almost ramming his nose into a very shapely knee. Looking up and to his left, he saw a cloud of chestnut waves encircling a flawless porcelain complexion out of which two of the bluest eyes he had ever seen stared back at him. "Whoa! Who are you?" he asked, mesmerized by her eyes then, slowly the surroundings came into view, and the urgency of the situation kicked in. "Where am I? That man. Where did he go?" Quin asked in rapid succession as he struggled to get upright in the cramped quarters between her legs and the closed door.

"Well, to begin with." She smiled at him. "My name is Angeline Rousseau. You are in my dressing room and that man—" She shrugged her shoulders. "—*mon ami*, he has left." She saw no reason to mention he was her brother. She would no longer claim him as a brother anyway if he kept working for Kaddur. As she studied his face, she felt no reason to afraid of him. "Now, tell me who you are."

"Quin. Quin Alvarez, and I do not have time for this." He growled at her. "Tell me where that man has gone!" he demanded, working his feet back under him. "There is a woman who is in danger if he finds her. She will be killed! *Now*, where did he go?" He finally had his feet back under him and stood up glaring down at her.

Angeline tried to stand up, but there was not enough room. Quin was taking up too much space as he loomed over her. He reached out, grabbed her shoulders, and shook her. Her chestnut hair floated around her face.

"Where did he go?" he demanded again squeezing harder on her shoulders.

"What do you mean she is going to be killed?" Angeline demanded now, her anger rising to the surface. "That man would not hurt a fly," she insisted, defending Jacques, as she twisted out of the man's grip. *What's with grabbing my shoulders?* she thought angrily. *First Jacques, and now this guy. My shoulders are going to be black and blue.*

"I mean if that man gets his hands on her, she will be killed," Quin said through clenched teeth. "I have heard them talking, and they are going to kill the woman. Do you understand, *kill*?" he yelled, exasperated at the woman's inability to comprehend the seriousness of the situation.

"Yes, I know what kill means, and I'm telling you that man would not do that!" she screamed back at him, her face turning red in anger. If she could have stood up, she would have stomped her foot.

"I do not know how you are so sure about that, but let me tell you if he does not kill her, the man he works for most certainly will. I heard them planning it." He stared into her eyes for a few seconds. "If anything happens to her because you have not told be where that man has gone, I will come back here and kill you myself," he said with deadly calm in his voice. He watched as the color drained from her face and her eyes turned into blue saucers.

Angeline blinked and swallowed. A stab of fear struck as his words sank in. She knew Jacques would not harm that woman, but she was not so sure that Kaddur wouldn't. If what this man was telling her was true, she could be a party to murder, and so could Jacques.

"He—the man left and has gone up to her room by the service elevator, but I am telling you he would not harm her."

"What is her room number?"

"Twelve-forty-five. He won't hurt her!" she shouted at Quin's back as he raced down the hall.

જ⁄ઝજ⁄ઝ

The service elevator doors hissed open, and Jacques pushed the laundry cart he had snagged from the laundry room out into the hall. The hall was empty. He pushed the cart around the corner and down the hall checking the room numbers until he found hers. He gently tapped on the door and waited. No response. He maneuvered the cart against the wall then, pulled the master key card that he had forced Angeline to give him out of his pocket. He was sorry that he had to use force to get it, but he would make it up to her— someday.

The lock light turned green. He opened the door and stepped in. All was quite. He checked the bedroom and then the bath. No one was home. He would wait. It was just a little after four as he made himself comfortable on the sofa.

Checking his watch again, he saw it was now just a little before five. He began to worry. Angeline had said the husband usually arrived back at the hotel in the early evening. That could mean anywhere from now until eight. He was beginning to feel uneasy, and his usual calm exterior began to slip.

Several minutes had ticked by since the last time he looked at his watch. He started to check it again when he heard the female laughter out in the hall getting louder as it approached the door. Quickly he stepped into the cloak closet by the door. It had been empty when he had checked earlier and appeared that they were not using it.

Quietly he shut the door as he heard the key card slide in the slot. Seconds later the outer door opened and banged into the cloak closet door. He jerked as the door rattled. Through the door louvers, he watched the woman as she tossed her towel and beach tote on the sofa and walked out onto the balcony. She had her back to him. It would be easy now.

With one swift and silent movement, Jacques was across the floor and through the balcony doors. He grabbed her from behind, placing his hand over her mouth stifling any screams. He spun her around and slammed his fist into her jaw. She went limp. Jacques caught her up before she hit the floor and hoisted her up over his shoulder. Quickly he made his way across the room to the door. Cautiously, he opened the door and looked out. Surveying the hall, he saw no one. The woman's unconscious body began to slip, so he jostled her back upon his shoulder. He was unaware that the movement had caused one of her sandals to slip off and fall to the floor. Grunting, he dumped her unconscious body into the cart and pulled the dirty linens from beneath her to hide her body. Casually, he pushed the cart back to the service elevator. Now, it was just a matter of transferring her to the trunk of his car. He wondered exactly what Ahmed had in mind for the woman as he waited for the elevator to arrive. It could not be good.

℘℘℘

Quin scrambled out of Angeline's room and sped down the hall in the direction of the service elevator. He thought he heard her shout something, but it did not matter what she had said, he had to hurry. Sliding to a stop in front of the doors, he pushed the up arrow. He reached back and pulled the Glock out of his waistband. He took it off safety. Shifting his weight from one foot to the other, he anxiously waited for the elevator to arrive. He pushed the button several more times before the doors finally opened and Quin rushed in.

Frantically, he jabbed at the twelve button, hitting it several times in succession before the door closed, the motor engaged, and the elevator rose. The floor numbers seemed to be moving in slow motion as he stared at the digital display above the doors.

The doors opened in slow motion. The two men stared at each other. Jacques was first to move, and he rammed the laundry cart into Quin, pinning him against the back wall of the elevator car flushing all the air out of his lungs. The gun flew out of Quin's hand and skittered across the elevator floor. Before Quin could regain his breath, Jacques had shoved the cart out of the way and had Quin by the front of his shirt pounding away on his face.

Quin slumped to the floor his head throbbing as Jacques gave him a hard kick to the side. A stabbing pain shot through his body. He was sure he had some broken ribs or at least some cracked ones. Struggling to raise himself up off the floor, he was rewarded with another kick. This one, coming up under and catching his stomach. It sent him slamming into the elevator wall. Stars exploded behind his eyelids and darkness threatened to engulf him. He struggled once more to get up, but the toe of Jacques boot came at him again and caught him under the chin—the lights went out.

The whole altercation had taken just a little over a minute. Jacques looked around, thankful they had not drawn any attention. He pushed the cart on into the elevator so the doors could close before the alarm sounded. Reaching down, he grabbed the gun and then Quin by the waistband of his jeans. Jacques hefted Quin up into the laundry cart and tossed the gun in on top of him. He turned and pushed the express button to the basement.

CHAPTER 30

Where is Darcey?

Settling himself in the back of the limo, Nicho waited for Luis to answer. He did not. Nicho left a message. Leaning forward, he told Hasan to take him to the ORCA hangar at the airport. Then, he called Darcey. She picked up after three rings.

"Hello," she said out of breath.

"Nicho here," he answered concerned at her breathless state. "Are you all right?"

"Yes, I was just on my way out to meet Marti at the pool when I heard the phone," she said as a little twinge of alarm percolated in the back of her mind. "Is everything all right?"

"Yes. I just wanted to inform you that I would be taking over for Alex and David. They have been reassigned to another detail," he told her. "I will be there shortly. I am in route there now."

"That is good news," she said smiling into the phone. A warm, safe feeling engulfed her at the thought of Nicho being her protector. "Marti and I will be at the pool. See you there," she said light hearted.

"Yes, I will look for you there," Nicho said and hung up. He had to make a stop at the ORCA hangar to retrieve his Sig nine millimeter from his locker and pick up a rental car. He did not like being without his own transportation.

Slamming home the clip in the Sig, Nicho slipped it into

its holster. He dropped two more clips into his jacket pocket before closing and locking his locker. Outside he commandeered an ORCA golf cart shuttle and headed for the rental car place in the terminal.

The perky little brunet behind the Hertz kiosk greedily eyed Nicho as he stepped up to the counter. Her overly cheery greeting did nothing to enhance his attitude. He was in a hurry and in no mood for come-on banter. The one-syllable answers and grunts he offered to her sometimes too personal questions did not deter her from asking more. Finally, seeing that she was not going to get him to warm up to her, she finished processing his rental agreement with a scowl on her face. That suited Nicho just fine. He was in no mood to make new friends. It had already taken longer than he anticipated and he was anxious to get to the hotel to check on Darcey.

❧❧❧

Walking down the hallway, Nicho stepped out into the bright sunlight of the pool area. The sunlight reflecting off the azure-blue water in the pool made it difficult for Nicho to see across to the other side in spite of his Ray-Bans. He looked for Darcey as he circled the pool. Darcey was nowhere to be seen.

Damn, he thought as he headed for the elevator. *Calm down*, he told himself. *She probably got tired of waiting and has gone back to her room.*

The elevator stopped on the twelfth floor. The doors hissed open. Nicho stepped out and held the door for a flustered-looking woman who had been waiting for the elevator. He turned and walked the few feet to Darcey's door. Even before he reached it, he knew something was wrong. The door was open a few inches. There appeared to be something blocking the door. His heart dropped, and his anxiety level rose as he realized it was one of Darcey's sandals. Nicho cautiously pushed the door open. He scoured the suite. No Darcey. No sign of a struggle. Just the sandal, in the doorway.

Nicho whipped out his phone and called Brad, then Luis. Both men were alarmed at the news. Brad said they were on their way and asked Nicho to check on Marti. Brad gave him the room number.

Nicho rushed out the door and up one floor to Marti's room. He pounded on the door repeatedly until an angry Marti yanked the door open.

"What the hell do you want?" she blurted out angrily before she recognized Nicho. "Oh! It's you."

"Is Darcey here?" he asked quickly, pushing past Marti into the room.

"No. She went to her room," Marti answered him frowning. "Why?" she snapped at Nicho.

"She is missing," he said through clenched teeth.

"*What*?" Marti exclaimed, her eyes wide. "What do you mean missing? I just left her not twenty minutes ago."

"I went to check on her just now and found her sandal wedged in the door," he said, running his hand through his hair, "and no Darcey." He pulled out his phone and called Brad.

"*Si*, Marti is okay. The last time she saw Darcey was about twenty minutes ago," he told Brad as he stood staring out the balcony door. "*Si*, I will meet you there." Nicho put his phone back in his pocket and turned to face Marti.

"I am going back to Darcey's room to wait for Brad," he informed Marti, "and you are to come with me. Ty is coming with Brad. He said you are to stick with me."

"Oh, dear! Oh, my!" she muttered to herself as she headed for the door, and she then turned and snapped at Nicho. "Well, come on. What are you waiting for?" She was halfway to the elevator by the time Nicho caught up with her.

☙❧

Jacques popped the trunk on his Mercedes as he tried to decide what to do about the creep that had attacked him. As far as he could determine, there had been no reason for him to do that. He did not recognize the guy, so why? Maybe he'd gotten him confused with someone else. Regardless of the reason, he had to do something about him. As he saw it, there were two options open to him. One, he could tie the guy up and leave him somewhere, or two, he could pop him right now and dump the body. Number two seemed the best option. Neat and tidy.

In the meantime, Quin had come around. He could feel Darcey's body underneath him. Cautiously he felt around until he could feel her breathing. He knew he did not have much time before the man would be dragging him out of the cart. It had to be now or never. So, when the man reached in to grab him, Quin grabbed the man's arm and pulled him, head first, into the laundry cart. A sharp pain shot through Quin's side, but he ignored it as he swung his other arm around the man's head and tugged hard bringing his feet into the air. Off balance, the man fell forward, his legs over to the other side. The cart lurched and then tipped over onto its side spilling Quin, the man, and Darcey out onto the concrete floor.

Quin scrambled to his feet before the man could recover and landed a well-placed kick in his groin. The man rolled up into a tight ball groaning in pain. Quin gave him another kick in the kidney area for good measure. Delivering that last kick had caused an intensely sharp pain in his side. It now hurt to breathe.

Standing up, as straight as his side would allow him, Quin paused and looked at the man, who was still writhing in pain on the floor. Out of the corner of his eye, he saw Darcey. She lay tangled in the sheets from the laundry cart. They were wrapped around her like a toga. Quin stepped quickly over to her and checked her pulse. Her breathing was shallow. Gently he untangled the sheets from around her feet. As he did, he noticed his Glock on the floor next to

Darcey's feet. As he reached for it, he heard a shuffling noise behind him. He turned just in time to see the man bearing down on him. Quin rolled to his side, grabbed the gun, and fired three quick shots, hitting the man in the chest.

The man stopped and looked bewildered. "*Pourquoi?*" he asked as he crumpled to the floor.

"Why? You ask me why, you sonofabitch," Quin screamed. "Because you were going to kill her, that is why." He was on his feet, staring down at the man, but the guy was already beyond hearing or feeling Quin's wrath.

Quin turned back to Darcey, who was just beginning to come around. She was sitting up looking dazed at her surroundings. The filmy swim wrap she had been wearing was doing little to cover her body. It had ripped and was hanging off of one shoulder. Her bikini top was now all askew. She was seemingly unaware of it. Quin took it all in as he walked up to her, his heart beating wildly.

"Where am I?" she asked rubbing her jaw where Jacques had hit her. "What happened?" She looked around and saw Quin. "Quin, what are you doing here? Where did you come from? Where's Brad?" she asked question after question, fear and frustration building in the pit of her stomach.

"It is okay. You are safe now," Quin knelt at her side, pulled one of the sheets up, and placed it around her shoulders. "That man over there was trying to kill you," he said, pointing at Jacques body lying in a growing crimson pool of his own blood.

"But why? Who is he?" she asked, unable to make any sense out of it. Why would a man she didn't know want to kill her? What had she done that was so terrible that he felt he had to kill her? She dragged her eyes away from the dead man on the floor and looked questioningly up at Quin.

"It is a long story," he said softly. "But first I need to get you back to your room," he said as he helped her up.

Quin had her on her feet and an arm around her waist helping her to the elevator when the doors hissed opened. Brad, Nicho, Ty, and Luis came storming out. He did a double take as he saw Nicho step out of the elevator.

Maybe he won't remember, Quin thought as he tried to quell the lump forming in the pit of his stomach.

"Oh, my God! Darcey!" Brad yelled. Rushing to her side, he pushed Quin out of the way and gathered her in his arms. "Are you all right?"

His heart pounded madly as he hugged her tightly then ran his hands up and down her body, making sure everything was okay. Cupping her chin and turning her face up, he kissed her gently as if she were a piece of fine porcelain.

She opened her eyes and saw relief and love flowing from Brad's eyes, covering her with a blanket of love, and she knew she was safe. She placed her forehead on his. "Yes, I think so," she winced as she gently placed her palm on her bruised jaw.

Brad pulled back and turned her head to the side, examining the swelling and bruise. His eyes immediately turned hard as he looked over Darcey's shoulder at Quin.

"Did you do this?" Brad demanded as he gently handed Darcey off to Luis and stalked up to Quin.

"No!" Quin shouted his hands out in front of his body in a defensive position, palms toward Brad. "I would never hurt Darcey. It was him. He was going to kill her," he said emphatically as he spun around and pointed at the dead body that Nicho and Ty were examining.

"Who is he?" Brad demanded.

"I do not know. I just know he was going to take her and kill her!" Quin exclaimed in frustration.

Brad ran his hand through his hair as he looked at the body. He knew they should call the authorities to handle this. He turned to Luis, "Have you called Asad?" he asked.

"Yes, he should be here shortly," Luis answered, adjusting the sheet around Darcey's shoulders as she leaned against his body.

"Right. Well, we can't just leave the body like this," Brad said, looking around at the overturned laundry cart. "Ty set that cart upright and put him in there," he said, surveying the basement area. He noticed a door across from where they stood and walked up to it. Testing the knob, he found the door unlocked and looked inside. It was maintenance closet full of buckets, mops, brooms, and shelves full of cleaning supplies. Stacking a few of the buckets and adjusting them, made room enough for the cart. "Put him in here," he said, turning around to face Ty.

"Brad!" Luis hollered as Darcey collapsed in his arms.

"What happened?" Brad asked, panicked as he lifted Darcey in his arms.

"I do not know," Luis replied. "She began to shake. Then she looked at me, and her eyes closed, and she passed out."

Brad was beside himself as he rushed to the elevator cradling Darcey in his arms. "It's going to be okay, babe," he murmured frantically, his heart pounding wildly. "You're safe. I'm here." Fear ripped a hole in his heart as he held her limp body to his chest. Nothing could happen to her—he wouldn't let it. She was his life, his reason for living. "I love you. I will not let anything happen to you."

Worry lines creased Luis's brow as he watched the pain on Brad's face, a pain he also felt in his heart. The pain fueled his anger that was building, and he needed someone to direct it at. He would talk to Asad and offer him the use of his Elite Force. Together they would find out who was behind this and take care of them. This time he would let Brad have the pleasure of eliminating whoever was behind this.

തെയ

Ty finished loading the body into the cart, pushed it inside the closet, and was just shutting the door when he heard a cell phone buzzing. He stopped, backtracked to the body, and lifted the sheet. Digging in the pockets, he found the phone and pulled it out.

It was a text. *Where the hell are you?* was all it read.

There was no name identifying who the text was from—just a bunch of numbers. Knowing he probably shouldn't take the phone because the authorities would consider it evidence, he thought about it for half a second, then slipped it into the pocket of his jeans and shut the door. Smiling as he headed for the elevator.

∽∾∽

The seriousness of the whole situation finally hit Darcey as she stood by Luis. Traumatized at the realization of how close she had come to death, her body began to shake, and she felt lightheaded. She had looked at Luis, intending to tell him she needed to lie down and then everything went dark.

Some time later she had been vaguely aware of gentle hands washing her body, and then she felt her silk nightgown being slipped over her head. She drifted in and out of consciousness. At one point, she felt herself being carried. She inhaled his scent and knew it was Brad. A warm blanket of love and protection flowed over her. All anxiety slipped away, and she relaxed.

"Darcey," Brad said softly. "I'm going to call the doctor. You need to have that bruise looked at."

Darcey's eyes were still shut, but she was shaking her head from side to side. "No doctor," she mumbled. "No doctor. I don't need a doctor." She briefly opened her eyes and smiled up at him as he had tucked the sheet up under her chin. But as quickly as her eyes had opened, they closed again. "No doctor."

Brad barely heard her as he felt her relax and her anxiety fade away.

Brad lay down beside her his thumb lightly rubbing the back of her hand. He stayed until he was sure she was fast asleep before he reluctantly stood. Placing her hand under the covers, he kissed her forehead, and left, softly closing the bedroom door behind him. Turning, he was met with five pairs of worried eyes.

"She's asleep," Brad finally said. "She won't let me call a doctor."

"Well, you should anyway," Marti said sharply. "I don't like the looks of that bruise on her jaw."

"I called room service for an ice pack," Brad said, walking over and sitting down at the dining table. "It should take the swelling down."

Ty stood and walked over to Brad, tossing him the cell phone he had taken from the dead man. "Here, I took this off the body," he said with a sideways grin. "Probably shouldn't have, but I thought it might be important." Brad caught the phone as Ty continued, "I think we can find out who that text was from. It might give us a clue to what is going on."

Brad read the text. "Yeah, see what you can find out. I'm damn tired of all this cloak-and-dagger shit! I want to know what's going on and why!" Brad cast his eyes toward the closed bedroom door. Had he known accepting Asad's job would be putting Darcey's life in danger, he would never have accepted it. They would have gone back to Dallas and done the house-in-the-burbs-white-picket-fence thing and lived happily ever after. His face turned hard as he looked back at Ty and flung the phone back to him. "Find the son-ofabitch!"

"You got it, boss."

An urgent tap, tap on the door jerked everyone's attention to it, indicating just how on edge everyone was. Nicho being the closest to the door opened it. Asad, along with four of his men, entered the already crowded suite.

"How is Darcey?" Asad asked, concern in his voice as he walked up to Brad.

"She's resting," Brad said, standing and shaking Asad's outstretched hand.

"Have you called the authorities?" Asad questioned. He hoped they had not. It would be difficult for his people to investigate if the authorities became involved. The authorities were notorious for taking bribes and overlooking or destroying critical evidence.

"No, we were waiting for you," Luis said, standing. "We left the body in the basement, but we will have to do something quickly, or it will be discovered, and then it will be too late." He motioned to Ty. "Ty can show you where it is."

Ty nodded, stood, and walked toward the door. Asad signaled one of his men to go with him.

Asad placed his hand on Brad's shoulder. "We have to get you out of here. I will have my men arrange to bring you to my home. There is more than enough room for you and Darcey as well as Ty and Marti. You will be safe there. I have twenty-four-seven security."

"Thanks," Brad said. "I appreciate that. I've got to keep Darcey safe." He rubbed his hand across his forehead, closing his eyes. Yes, he had to keep Darcey safe at all costs. Opening his eyes, he glanced around the room. His eyes narrowed as they fell on the man who had been holding Darcey when they entered the basement. "Who the hell are you?" Brad's eyes bored into the man, who had taken a chair in the farthest corner of the room.

Quin swallowed nervously. "Ah...I am Quin Alveraze," he said, his eyes darting around the room at the men who were now scrutinizing him. No need to tell them everything just yet, in case Nicho did not remember him. So, he simply lied. "I was a deck hand on Carlos Santiago's boat. That is how I know your wife. Then, the other day I ran into her here by accident," he explained but noticed a flicker of recognition in Nicho's eyes.

Brad was taken aback by Quin's words. "What the hell were you doing with my wife here in the basement?" he growled.

"I was trying to save her life," Quin answered defensively. "It is a long story, but I will tell you what I know," he volunteered. Clearing his throat, he began to recount what he had found out about the man who wanted to kill Darcey. He filled them in on his suspicions about who the man might be, and how he wound up in the basement with her in his arms.

"I knew it!" Luis stormed, his face livid at the mention of Ahmed's name. "That no good sonofabitch! I should have killed him when I had the chance. We must never let Aicha know this," he said, looking from Brad to Asad.

Asad gave his men a silent signal, and they quietly left the room just as Ty came in.

"Your man," Ty said to Asad, "has loaded up the body and is on the way to dispose of it."

"Good," Asad said, nodding his head.

CHAPTER 31

Negotiations

Ahmed fumed after Jacques's phone went to voicemail for the fortieth time. Since arriving back at his downtown office, he had been calling and texting for the past two hours.

"I will kill that son of a pig when I find him," he swore out loud. His fist was clenched tightly around his phone as he paced on the expensive Persian carpet in front of his desk.

Rounding his desk, he forcefully tossed his cell on the desk. An angry frown played across his face as he slouched down in his desk chair and drummed his fingers on the desktop.

Where the hell is he? Ahmed fumed. It had been over four hours since he had sent Jacques out to get that woman. *How hard can it be to snatch one woman?* he groused silently.

Steepling his fingers, he tapped his chin, mentally listing all of the delightful things he would do to the *puta* once he had her in hand. He even thought of ways of getting Aicha there to watch.

Oh, how he would enjoy watching her face as he made her watch the delicious revenge he had planned for her granddaughter. He grinned wickedly, thinking that just might be the thing that pushed the old bat over the edge—

sort of like killing two birds with one stone. He chuckled.

The b-bloop of the inter-office communication system sounded, and the image of his receptionist appeared on the monitor.

"*What*?" he shouted at her.

"A—Ammon Bustani is here to see you," she answered, flustered.

Bustani? What the does he want now? he pondered. *Do I not have enough to worry about without the Eastern Alliance plaguing me?* "What does he want?" he growled.

"He—he says it is urgent and he must speak with you immediately," she stammered.

"Humph!" he snorted. "Send the *pendejo* in!"

He could not imagine what could be so urgent that the EA would come crawling back to him. Especially after his vicious tirade over the botched job on the Bio Dome. He had reminded them all that what had had happened to Javier could also happen to any one of them—at any time.

The door opened slowly, and Ammon Bustani cautiously stepped into Ahmed's office. A small bead of sweat popped out on his forehead, and he swallowed the huge lump that suddenly appeared in his throat.

Why do I always have to be the one to meet with Kaddur? he wondered rhetorically. He knew exactly why he was always the one. He occupied the last seat on the board, and the other members were too afraid of Kaddur to confront him. So the shitty stuff, like delivering bad news, was palmed off on him. But today he had good news, so why was he still scared shitless?

"Well do not just stand there like a *culo*," Ahmed growled at him. "Sit down!"

Ammon moved quickly, almost tripping over the corner of the Persian rug, to the chair that Ahmed indicated he should sit on. The bead of sweat, followed by two more, trickled down and slipped in the corner of his eye causing him to blink repeatedly to clear it out. Nervously, he perched straight-backed on the edge of the chair his hands flat against his thighs to keep them from shaking.

Ahmed studied the stupid little man in front of him. *Why am I plagued with incompetent* pendejos*? Just once can they not send me someone with* cojones*?* He sat for several minutes, staring at Bustani just watching him squirm before he finally spoke. "What is so damn important that the EA had to send a little *el gusano* like you to me?" Ahmed asked rudely.

"Ah…em …" Bustani cleared his throat and straightened up. "Well, our informant within the UFN has brought us news that the UFN is going to force the ERC to turn over all of their research files on the ozone." He paused, waiting for a response from Ahmed.

Ahmed raised an eyebrow. "And this concerns me how?"

"Well…ah…the chairman thought you might be interested as it is connected to ORCA and their new space project," he explained, running his finger around the inside of his collar that suddenly seemed to be choking him. "He knows how important the Bio Dome was to you and hoped that the offering of this information might in some way make up for the unfortunate Bio Dome situation."

"Go on," Ahmed said, waving his hand at Bustani, indicating he should continue. The audacity of the board mentioning the Bio Dome intrigued him.

If possible, Bustani stiffened his back more and sat up straighter. His tongue snaked out to wet his lips before continuing. "Well, you see—" He swallowed. "—the chairman has discovered, through his informant at ORCA, that the ERC is partially funding this ORCA project." He paused, wetting his lips again. "However, the UFN is unaware of that connection at this time." He paused again, pulling a handkerchief from his pocket, and blotted his brow then continued. "However, if the UFN does succeed in forcing the ERC to turn over the files, the connection with ORCA and the project will be discovered. It will not take long for the UFN to force ORCA to turn the project over to them," he finished, wishing he could get up and move about the room. He hated being shackled to the chair by Kaddur's eyes. His stomach churned, sending bile up into his throat as he watched Kaddur digest what he had just told him.

"Hmmmm—interesting," Ahmed said, looking at Bustani but not really seeing him. *Interesting indeed*, he thought but to Bustani he said, "And what does the chairman want me to do about it?" He already had in mind what *he* would like to do, but it would not hurt to see what the chairman thought.

"*Si*, well, the chairman would like you to exert your…ah…influence in certain quarters to take over the project for the EA," Bustani said, feeling a tiny bit more comfortable now that Ahmed's eyes had lost some of their menacing glare.

Ahmed leaned back in his chair a wicked grin tickling the corners of his mouth. "And what is he offering in return for my…ah…influence?"

"Ah…*si*…well…" He fidgeted with the handkerchief in his hands. "I was not informed of any…ah…offering to bring to you. Only to inform you of the situation and…ask for your assistance," Bustani said hesitantly. His mouth went dry, and his comfort zone sank to zero as Ahmed's eyes narrowed.

"You can go back and tell your *pendejo* of a chairman that I am not interested." Ahmed leaned forward and half stood then braced his body with his arms on the desk and scowled at Bustani. "I am not a charity. I do not work for free!" he said through clenched teeth. "It is an insult to me that he did not think enough of my influence to send an offer. However, if he wants to make an offer for my influence, then I might be interested in listening. Now. Get. Out." Ahmed fully stood, using both hands in a shooing motion toward Bustani.

"*Si, si,* I will tell him," said Bustani hurriedly, his eyes wide. He all but leaped from the chair and began backing toward the door, bowing slightly and wiping his brow as he went. "*Si*, I will tell him." He was thankful he was leaving with his body still intact.

Ahmed turned around to the credenza behind his desk and picked up a crystal glass and the matching crystal decanter of whiskey off the silver tray setting there. Filling the glass half full of the amber liquid, he swirled it around before downing it in one gulp. He enjoyed the burn as it flowed down his throat. The heat felt good.

After refilling his glass, he sat down and contemplated what Bustani had told him. He wondered why the UFN would be interested in the ERC's files on the ozone. Some time ago there had been rumors that some scientists thought that the ozone was in trouble and had issued a report to the UFN. But that had been shot down by the central government's own scientists who had refuted every point in the argument. So why were they so interested now? Could it be that there really was something happening to the ozone? But what would that have to do with ORCA's space project? True they were building habitats similar to the Bio Dome, but those, according to everything he had heard, were to be staging areas from which deep space exploration crafts would be launched.

He was not interested in space exploration. If it could not further expand his heroin empire, he was not interested. However, the possibility of destroying ORCA greatly appealed to him, but not nearly as much as seeing that *culo* Daniels's wife dishonored. Which reminded him he had still not heard from Jacques.

He tried again calling Jacques's cell phone. It went to voicemail. It was now going on six hours since he last saw Jacques. Jacques never failed to return his calls or to let him know when he would be late. Ahmed began to worry that maybe something had happened to him. He scrolled through his contact list and punched Marco's number.

"Marco!" he shouted. "Where the hell is Jacques?" He waited, listening to Marco's response, the scowl on his face deepening.

"That's not acceptable!" he stormed. "Find. Him!" He flung the phone on the desktop. It slid across the smooth surface, slowed, teetered on the front edge of the desk, and slipped over. It landed with a soft thump on the Persian rug. "¡*Maldito*! Where is that *culo*?" he stormed out loud, running his fingers through his hair.

He needed Jacques. Jacques was the only one he really trusted to have his back. The only one he trusted to handle everything, and it gave him a sinking feeling in the pit of his stomach that something bad was on the horizon.

However, business must go on. Money and time waited for no man, and neither did opportunities like the one EA just dropped in his lap. The EA chairman was a greedy little *mierda* who wanted everything handed to him on a silver platter. Ahmed knew the EA had billions, if not trillions of dollars, in reserve stashed in banks all over the world, so for the chairman not to have sent an offer for his services was an affront to him. Of course, he did not intend to help them take over ORCA or their space project. He intended to destroy it!

I will make a nice bonfire of their warehouses. There will be nothing left but ashes, he thought gleefully. *And, what I cannot burn, I will blow up.*

Draining the last of the whiskey in his glass, he got up and retrieved his phone from the floor. He scrolled through his list of contacts looking for the man he knew would find this venture right up his alley—Julio Lopez.

"*Hola*, Julio!" Ahmed said.

"*Hola*, Ahmed," Julio replied half-heartedly. "It has been a long time, *mi amigo*."

"*Si*. Too long," Ahmed replied, taking in Julio's tepid greeting. Nevertheless, he knew once Julio knew about the project, he would be all for it. "I have a proposition for you."

"What is it you have in mind?" Julio queried.

"I am in need of some intense pyrotechnics. The kind you like to play with," Ahmed said.

There was a moment of silence before Julio replied. "Exactly what do you have in mind?"

"Something big. But we cannot talk about it on the phone," Ahmed replied. "Meet me in two hours at the house, and I will explain." He gave Julio the address and then rang off.

CHAPTER 32

Safety in Moving Forward

Making his way as quickly as possible and keeping his head down, Quin slipped out the hotel's side door and headed for the parking garage. Thankfully no one took notice of him, and the parking attendant barely acknowledged his presence when he entered the garage. He had not taken the time to clean the dried blood from the cuts where the man had used his face as a punching bag. Unlocking his car, he eased into the seat. His ribs hurt and he knew he probably should get them wrapped, but he was not going to a hospital. There would be too many questions that he did not want to answer.

Maybe I can find someone at my dump of a hotel to help me out, he thought. He had purposely picked a hotel where everyone minded their own business. He needed to stop by a pharmacy to pick up some Ace Bandages to wrap his ribs with. His gut told him not to trust the day clerk, but maybe the night clerk would help, if he could hold out until the clerk came on duty at ten. A sharp pain shot through his side as he turned the key in the ignition and drove his car out of the parking garage.

The pain was worsening as he made his way to his room. He barely made it to the bed before he passed out.

☙☙☙

Brad sat through dinner with Luis and Asad. He tried to relax, but there was no way in hell he could do that, still knowing that Darcey was in danger, even though he knew Nicho would protect her. It was Brad's responsibility to protect her, not Nicho's. But he couldn't be in two places at once. And, it really pissed him off that this Ahmed guy was screwing things up.

As soon as it was feasibly possible, Brad excused himself and headed for the elevators. He rode up to the twelfth floor to give the illusion that he was going to his room then, took the service elevator down to the basement where Hasan waited. He gave Hasan instructions to head for the airport and the ORCA hangar to pick up his guys—Matt, Scott, and Hot Dog. He called Darcey's cell phone. It went to voicemail. He tried Asad's home number and the butler answered.

"Hello, Darcey please," Brad said.

"One moment, sir. I will see if she is available."

Brad listened to several seconds of silence before Darcey picked up. He heard a stifled yawn.

"Mmmmm—hey, babe," she said, her voice husky from sleep. "I've missed you."

"Missed you too. How are you feeling?" Relief filled his body and it responded of its own accord to her voice.

"Better now that you've called," she purred into the phone, butterflies exploding in her stomach as the velvet tones of his voice flowed over her.

"I'm on my way to pick up the guys. They just got in," he told her, feeling their connection beginning to pulsate through his body. He ran his fingers through his hair, aggravated that he could not be with her right now, holding her in his arms, feeling her body pressed against his. He sighed before continuing. "We will be going right to the office after I pick them up. Asad wants everything underway tonight. Apparently, there are some rumblings in the UFN about ORCA's project." He paused.

"What kind of rumblings," she asked, beginning to feel a twinge of foreboding.

"Don't know. Asad didn't go into detail. But he has it all under control. So don't worry your pretty little head about it," he assured her. "By the way, your cell needs charging," he said as an afterthought.

"Yeah, I forgot to put it on the charger. Sorry."

"Did Marti get there okay?"

"Yes. She is beside herself with worry. I gave her a couple of Tylenol and sent her to bed. It wasn't easy, but she went," Darcey giggled, remembering how Marti had sputtered and fussed, telling her she was supposed to be taking care of her not the other way around. She had hugged Darcey and then burst into tears. Darcey had finally settled Marti down and she was sleeping.

"Where's Nicho?"

"He's right here," she said, looking across the room and smiling at Nicho. "Would you like to speak to him?"

"Yeah, actually I would."

Darcey smiled and held the phone out to Nicho, who was already on his way across the room.

"Nicho here," he said, taking the phone from Darcey and returning her smile.

"What's it look like there?" Brad wanted to know. "All's been quiet around the hotel as far as we could discern. Asad assigned a couple of men to keep it under surveillance."

"Same here," Nicho replied. "No one followed us from the hotel, and Asad has his men stationed around the compound. Everything is secure."

"Okay. I am going to the office as soon as I pick up the guys. It will be sometime tomorrow before I can get away. Asad wants the first loads ready for liftoff day after tomorrow, so we are pushing everything hard," Brad said. "I'm counting on you to protect our girl, and I want you to call me if anything comes up."

"I understand," Nicho said, as a feeling of family hit him when Brad said "our girl," and he discovered that the love he carried for Darcey in his heart was no longer that for a lost love, but the warm love of a sister.

☙❧

At that time of night, the halls of the ORCA Corporation were silent with the exception of the echoing footsteps of the patrolling night guards.

Brad paused at the front door, sliding his ID card for access to the building. He pushed the door open and entered, followed by Matt, Scott, and Hot Dog.

"Wow!" Hot Dog exclaimed. "Will ya get a load of this place?"

"Yeah, not too shabby, eh," Matt said, eyeing the giant waterfall and mini oasis that surrounded it at one end of the lobby area.

Just then the elevator doors opened, and Ty sauntered out to meet the guys with a wide Texas grin on his face. "Well ain't you guys a sight for sore eyes," he guffawed sarcastically, reaching his hand out.

"Hey, man. Long time no see," Matt said, returning the sarcasm and shaking Ty's hand.

Brad grinned as he watched the guys shake hands and backslap as if they hadn't seen each other for over a year instead of just last week. He stepped into the elevator and let out an ear-splitting whistle, causing the guys to jump and stare.

"You wantin' somthin' boss man," Ty asked, grinning slyly.

"Yeah. Time to get things underway."

☙❧

Brad gave the guys a tour of the facility then handed out the information packets he had prepared that contained a complete overview of the project and the critical information each would need to carry out their individual part of the project. Brad walked with them back to the work lab where they spent the next few hours absorbing the information. By the time the sun was peeking over the horizon, each man had his responsibilities down pat and was, to quote Ty, "rarin' to go."

Waiting for the guys to finish breakfast, Brad made a call to Darcey's cell. This time it went through. It was early, he knew, but she wouldn't mind.

"Hey! Morning," she said, pouring herself a cup of coffee from the carafe that one of the housemaids had placed on the table.

"Hey to you, too!" he said. "Sleep well?"

"Yes, actually I did." She smiled, reaching for her cup of coffee. "Marti's still in bed though. She had a tough time getting to sleep."

"Yeah, I think Ty was worried about her. He seemed a little distracted, so I told him to take a break and give her a call," he told her. "After that, he was back to normal. Well…as normal as Ty can be." He chuckled.

"Well, good. I'm glad," she said. "This whole thing has her tied in knots." She paused. "Say, when are you coming back?"

"Probably won't be until sometime tomorrow before I can getaway. We should have the first modules ready to load by the end of the day tomorrow," he said, finishing the last of his coffee. "The ILCs are already in the launch area." He could feel her tensing, and he sensed her wanting to ask *the* question, all the while knowing the answer would not be what she wanted to hear. The question he didn't have the answer for her either.

He missed Darcey in the worst way. He missed the smell of her skin still damp from her shower, the feel of her body that fit perfectly with his, the taste of her as they made love. These next few nights would be the first they had not spent wrapped up in each other's arms as they fell asleep for some time.

A pang of longing struck a chord deep in his soul, and he knew she was feeling it, too.

Darcey frowned as a sudden feeling of loneliness struck her. She could sense it in Brad, too. And she had to decide whether to ask if he would be on that first flight. In her heart, she knew he had to be. He was the project manager, and Asad would expect him to be there to make sure there were no glitches. He had already been through the crash course from Aries Global on the ILC and passed with flying colors, and it wouldn't be like he was really flying the ship himself. The guidance system would take care of that. It was just…well, it was *outer space* for crying out loud—millions of miles of black nothingness. That was what scared her the most. Hell, she had even considered asking Asad if she could go with him, but she figured he would laugh her out of his office and call her a silly woman. But—on the other hand—what would it hurt to ask? Nothing ventured, nothing gained, her old art professor had always said when he introduced a new concept to the class.

"Ah…how many ships will there be leaving?" she asked, avoiding asking if Brad would be onboard one of them leaving him the opportunity to tell her himself.

"There will be two heading to the Moon and two to Mars," he said. "One will carry the modules components and the other the workers. There will be enough components to build one unit on the Moon and one on Mars. They will be the living quarters for the men while they construct the actual domes." He paused, noticing the guys were finishing up breakfast. "Gotta go for now babe. I'll call you as often as I can so you won't worry. I love you," he said softly.

"I love you, too," she said. "Be safe. I'll be waiting for your call."

"Always," he said and rang off.

Brad sat a few minutes, collecting his thoughts. She hadn't asked *the* question, but he knew she would sooner or later. What was he going to tell her? He was torn between telling her he was going or letting her find out after they had lifted off. But that would be a real chicken shit thing to do, and he could not, would not, do that to her. He didn't know why he even considered it as an option in the first place.

What's the matter with you, Daniels? he chided himself. *You're thinkin' like a real prick now. Get your head out of your ass and tell the woman you love the truth—You. Want. To. Go. She already knows you've had the training, so it should be obvious to her that you're going. Besides, Asad had already told me I had to be on the first flight to the Moon to get that part underway. Then I will take one of the ships to Mars to get that one underway also. I've gotta tell her. I don't have a choice.*

Brad heaved a sigh and stood, motioning for the guys to follow him. He'd have to deal with his dilemma later. Right now, he had to get his head in the project.

He hustled them down to security where each one had their thumbprints and retinas scanned and received their ID badges. From there, Matt, Scott, and Hot Dog headed back to the tech lab to upload the software into the ILCs system that would be needed for the project.

Brad walked with Ty to the launch area. He introduced him to the technicians in the master control room who were monitoring the progress of the uploads. A wave of excitement swept through Brad as he looked out the control room window at the four silver-skinned ships on their launch pads. If all went well, the day after tomorrow, he and Ty would be rocketing through space on their way to the Moon.

CHAPTER 33

The Plan

The wooden gate slowly opened as a black sedan approached the driveway. The movement caught Julio's attention. He had purposely arrived early. He wanted to get a feel of the place—to see what vibes it gave off—checking for anything out of the ordinary. Once, he had made the mistake of walking in cold to a meet. He barely made it out alive. A mistake he had never repeated.

It was not that he did not trust Ahmed, but rumors had been circulating that certain people felt Ahmed might be letting his ego get in the way of seeing things clearly. Like the scene, he made at Damji's home the other night. No one threatened a powerful man like Damji and then expect it to go unnoticed by your business associates. Especially, if those associates happened to engage in questionable business practices that could wind up in the spotlight. He loved his craft too much to let some egomaniac ruin his reputation just for revenge.

Finding both the front courtyard gates locked, Julio sought out the back entrance. Much to his surprise, he found both the courtyard gate and the back door to the house unlocked. Cautiously, Julio stepped in and took a quick tour through the house. The house was void of any living person. However, he did discover a corpse on the floor by the back door. It had been covered over with a blue plastic tarp. Satisfied there were no surprises waiting for him, Julio went back to his car to wait.

The taillights of the black sedan disappeared behind the wall. Julio could not tell how many were in the car. If there were anyone with Ahmed, it would be Jacques. He did not go anywhere without Jacques. Jacques seemed to be the only one who could keep Ahmed in line these days.

Time to go, Julio thought as he turned the key in the ignition and pulled away from the curb.

ഊഊ

Ahmed bounced out of the car, excited to tell his plan to Julio. He opened the door and stepped across the floor to turn on the small lamp on the desk. It was not very bright, but it was bright enough to conduct business by. It still worried him that his men had not been able to find Jacques. It was as though he had dropped off the face of the earth.

He placed his hand on the back of the wooden chair that David had sat in and frowned at the dried bloodstains on the floor around the chair.

Business is business, he thought, shaking his head. *David should have understood that. Yes, David should have understood that,* he repeated to himself, his mouth drawn into a straight line.

Reaching down, he tugged the old Persian carpet from in front of the leather couch to cover the stains. Then removed the wooden chair and replaced it with a more-comfortable-looking leather armchair.

"There. That should do it," he mumbled, straightening the chair just as he heard a knock on the door. "Julio, *mi amigo!*" Ahmed held the door open. Smiling broadly, he extended his arm into the room. "Come, come. We have much to discuss."

"*Si,*" was all Julio said as he walked into the dimly lit room. He noticed the newly repositioned carpet and the new chair in front of the desk. He wondered if the corpse at the back door had also been repositioned.

All smiles, Ahmed quickly sat out two glasses on the desktop and filled then half full from the crystal decanter of whiskey. He passed one to Julio. *"Salud!"* Ahmed said, holding his glass out.

"Salud," Julio returned as he touched his glass to Ahmed's.

Both men took a healthy drink from their glasses.

"Now, down to business," Ahmed said, grinning. "We have much to discuss."

The next few hours Ahmed laid out his plan. His spies had informed him of the pending launch in the next day or two. To say he wanted the launch stopped was putting it mildly—he wanted it blown to smithereens. In fact, he wanted the whole damn compound blown up and burned. The launch area, the warehouses, and anything else that Julio would like to blow up, he was free to do so. Ahmed did not care as long as there was nothing left of ORCA. He gave Julio complete control of the job.

"What about backup?" Julio wanted to know. "There are bound to be armed guards in those areas."

"Not to worry," Ahmed said, leaning back in his chair, grinning as he steepled his fingers. "I have more than enough men to take care of any guards they might have. Not to worry." He leaned forward and refilled their glasses. "I have a special favor to ask. It is small but very important to me." He grinned, looking at Julio over the rim of his glass as he took a sip.

"What is this 'special favor' you require of me?" Julio looked suspicious. Favors after a job had been settled spelled nothing but bad news.

"Nothing really." Ahmed smiled charmingly. "I have been working with a young man, Jamal, my new protégé. I am grooming him so to speak to take over for Jacques, which, may be sooner than expected." He paused but did elaborate on why he might need to replace Jacques. "Nevertheless, I want you to take him with you on this job. He needs to learn and what better way to learn than from the master." Ahmed was all smiles again, stroking Julio's ego.

Julio was not impressed with Ahmed's attempt at flattery. "I do not take beginners on a job. They are a liability, and the chances of something going wrong increases substantially," he said, shaking his head. "No, I cannot take him. You want this done right. If I take him, it only increases the probability of something going wrong. I cannot be responsible for some idiot blowing himself up."

"Tsk, tsk," Ahmed said, still grinning widely. "You worry too much. Jamal will do as I say, and I will simply tell him he must do exactly as you say," he said, brushing Julio's concerns away.

"I am very uncomfortable with taking this young man," Julio started again, but Ahmed raised his hand interrupting him.

"Nonsense!" he exclaimed. "I will hear no more of this. You will take Jamal, and that is the end of it." In a flash, Ahmed's face turned red and the blood vessels in his temples pulsed visibly. "*Understood?*" he shouted, his eyes narrowing in anger. He half stood and braced himself with his arms as leaned over the desk, staring at Julio.

Julio's face remained deadpan as he stared into the raging fury shooting from Ahmed's eyes. He had no doubt that Ahmed intended to do bodily harm if his demands were not met. He had heard rumors about Ahmed's tirades but had never seen one in person. A cold chill swept over him. There was no doubt that if he did not agree to the terms, he would be on the receiving end of one now.

Julio forced himself to relax. He picked up his glass, leaned back in his chair, and crossed his legs, as if seeing Ahmed raging at him was an everyday occurrence. He drained the remaining whiskey in the glass and set it back on the desk before speaking.

"As long as you guarantee he will follow my orders, I will consider taking him along," Julio said calmly. He did not intend to let Ahmed see just how rattled he was. You did not let a man like Ahmed see he could intimidate you. If you did, he would own you forever, and Julio would be owned by no one.

"See, that was not so hard to agree to," Ahmed said, sitting back down, his face all smiles again. "I knew you would see it my way." He chuckled as he sipped the whiskey in his glass.

"I have only agreed to take him if you guarantee he will listen to my direction," Julio said, leaning forward in his chair. "The first time he does not listen to me, I am sending him packing." Julio narrowed his eyes. "Is *that* understood?" *I may be playing with fire, but I cannot let him know he can get to me.*

Ahmed eyed Julio over the edge of his glass as he finished the last of the amber liquid. He admired the man's courage for standing up to him. He reminded him of Jacques. His thoughts quickly turned to Jacques. He was beginning to worry that something had happened to him. It was not like him to not answer his phone regardless of where he might be. And it was curious that none of his men could locate him. As a last resort, he would contact Jacques's *puta* of a sister, but it would be doubtful that she would have any information.

Julio watched Ahmed's attention drift as if his thoughts were miles away. *Now is a good time to take my leave*, he thought. "Send him to me tonight. I will start making him familiar with what I am going to do," he said, standing. "Make it clear to him he is to do everything I tell him, exactly as I tell him without question." He turned and headed for the door then paused and looked back, "Have your men ready tomorrow night. I will call you with the time." Not waiting for a response, Julio pulled the door open and walked out.

Julio's comments jerked Ahmed back to the present. "Ah…*si*." He cleared his throat. "I will send him to you tonight," he said as the door closed.

CHAPTER 34

Foolish Boy

Adara came to a halt just outside the door to Jamal's bedroom, intending to tell him that the evening meal was ready. The door was slightly ajar, and she could hear Jamal talking on the phone. She froze as she heard him mention "ORCA," followed by "It will be as you wish, Ahmed."

What has he gotten himself into? she asked herself. *He promised me that he would have nothing more to do with that awful man Kaddur. How could he break his word to me?*

She waited until he had ended the call before bursting into his room. "How could you?" she admonished her brother. "You promised."

"I only told you what you wanted to hear," he said curtly. "I promised you nothing, sister."

"Are you crazy? You know what kind of a man he is."

"Yes, he is the kind of man I want to be," Jamal said, turning to his sister. "He has money and power, and I will have it, too. He has promised to show me everything he knows. I will be a rich and powerful man."

"You will dishonor our family if you do this," Adara said with tears in her eyes.

"No, I will not. You are thinking about the old ways," he said, shaking his head. "I am progressive. I will not be bound by the old ways. Ahmed will show me the way," he said, walking around the room. "Why, he has already given me a job to do for him." He stopped and grinned at Adara. "It will be only a matter of time until I will be standing by his side, advising him." His chest puffed out as he strutted over and stood in front of Adara. "You will see."

"What I see," Adara said, "is a foolish boy who thinks he is a man. That is what I see," she sniffed. "What is this job he has trusted you with?"

His eyes sparkled with excitement as he told her about what he was going to do. He told her all about Julio and how he would be helping him to blow up ORCA—the space ships, the buildings—what a wonderful sight it would be, and Ahmed had entrusted him to help carry it out. Of course, as this would be his first job, he would be following Julio's lead, but after Ahmed saw how wonderful he had done the job, he would be giving him many more jobs to do.

Adara's heart beat rapidly as she listened to Jamal's blathering about how wonderful Ahmed and Julio were and how fantastic it was going to be blowing up ORCA.

No! No! No! Adara's mind screamed. *I cannot let this happen. It is all my fault that any of this has happened. I should have listened to my conscience and never did what that awful man asked of me. I am so ashamed. I was weak, so weak that I could be bribed by the glitter of a few baubles. How could I have been so blind?* "Jamal, you cannot do this," she said, placing her hand on his arm. "Señor Damji has been good to us."

"He fired you," he yelled.

"Yes, with reason," she said, lowering her eyes. "I cannot fault him for that. I did a very bad thing." She raised her eyes and looked into Jamal's. "I smuggled out information that that awful man used to try to destroy Señor Damji. He lied to me, to us. How can you defend him?"

"You worry too much, sister." Jamal waved his hand, dismissing her concerns. "That is all in the past." He turned around to admire himself in the full-length dressing mirror.

"However, Ahmed regrets very much that you lost your job on his account and has promised that our family will be well taken care of. As for Señor Damji," he said, turning to look at Adara, "he does not warrant your concern. He is but a piece of dung that *I* will be helping Ahmed sweep out of the way," he declared, puffing his chest out farther as he walked out of the room.

Adara stood for a moment, giving Jamal time to reach the dining room before she scurried to her room. She quietly closed the door, moved into the bathroom, and closed that door, too. Phone in hand she sat on the edge of the marble tub and placed a call to Asad Damji.

"*Hola*," Asad answered, curious why Adara would risk calling.

"Señor Damji, please do not hang up," she pleaded. "I know I am violating my agreement with ORCA by calling." she rushed on, "But I have terrible news, and it is urgent that I tell it to you."

"You are correct, it is," Asad said curtly. "But since you have, what is this terrible news that is so urgent?" he asked, his curiosity tweaked. It must be extremely important for her to risk violating her agreement with the ORCA Corporation and risk prison.

She took a deep breath and proceeded to tell him everything that Jamal had bragged to her about. Asad's hand clenched into a fist as he listened to what Ahmed had planned.

"When is this going to happen?" Asad asked.

"I do not know," Adara replied. "Jamal only said he was meeting with Julio tonight to learn what he would be doing." Her heart jumped into her throat as she heard her bedroom door open. "I have to go," she whispered. "I cannot talk anymore." She ended the call and slipped her phone into her pocket. Jumping up, she pushed the handle on the toilet and turned on the tap to wash her hands.

⌘⌘

Asad hung up and immediately called Brad on the com-link. "We have a problem. Bring all your men and meet me in the conference room." He opened a comlink to his security office and directed all off duty men to meet him in the conference room, also. Lastly, he placed a call to Luis at the hotel, instructing him to get all available men in his Elite Force on a plane to Dubai. He did not know how much time they had, but he had a feeling it was not much.

Asad knew of Julio Lopez's reputation—a very dangerous man with explosives and an expert arsonist. The authorities knew him well, too, but they had never been able to make a case against him. He was careful to never leave any incriminating evidence behind. *It is well known that Lopez works alone, so why has he all of a sudden taken on Jamal,* Asad wondered as he walked toward the conference room. *It does not make sense unless—he has been forced to by Ahmed.*

Brad, Ty, Matt, Scott, and Hot Dog along with and Brad's project crew of forty men and women were already crowded into the conference room when Asad arrived.

"Gentlemen, ladies," Asad said. "As soon as my security people arrive, I will tell you what this is all about." He turned and with a few keystrokes, a 3-D holo-image of the ORCA compound appeared to hover over the center of the conference table.

The last of the security force arrived. Asad took note of the men and women seated and standing around the conference table before he began relaying to them what Adara had told him. It weighed heavy on him that if it came down to a firefight, some of these people's lives would be lost. His security force of ex-military men knew the consequences. It was what they trained for, but Brad's people had not been prepared for this. However, from the determined looks on their faces as he told them what to expect, he had no doubt that they were committed to the fight.

"We will have the element of surprise on our side," Asad assured them. "They will not be expecting any resistance, but we cannot expect this to be easy. I am sure Kaddur will have his men accompany Lopez as a precaution." He paused before continuing. "This must be handled quickly and as quietly as possible. We do not want the authorities showing up and spoiling our party. Are there any questions?"

"Yes," Justin Miles, the head of Asad's security force, stepped forward. "We have several here—" He turned to indicated Brad's team members. "—who are not combat ready—"

Asad raised his hand interrupting him. "*Si*, I know. We have little time, but I expect you to acquaint these men and women with our weapons. They do not need to be crack shots, but they do need to know how to protect themselves. I expect you and your men to coordinate the training and develop a strategy for protecting our facility." He paused as Luis entered the room. "Luis, *bienvenido!*"

All eyes turned in Luis' direction as he stepped forward to shake Asad's hand.

"Let me introduce *mi amigo*, Luis Vargas. His men will be arriving shortly to help us out. With Luis's men, we will have a formidable force to handle anything Kaddur might have planned." Asad turned and faced his security chief, "Justin, you will be in charge of coordinating yours and Luis' men. I will expect your plan on my desk within the hour. Training is to begin immediately."

"Yes, sir!" Justin turned to Brad, "Have your people follow Mick," He pointed to the man standing at the door. "He will take them down to the firing range and start their training." Without hesitation, Brad's people followed Mick out of the room. "Sir, I will have our plan ready within the hour," Justin said as he turned and signaled to his men to leave.

Asad nodded. He then turned to Luis. "How soon will your men arrive?"

"They will all be here by tomorrow morning. There are fifty of my finest coming, coupled with your force of one-hundred-fifty we should be in good shape," Luis said.

"Yes, that is my feeling also," Asad replied. "Kaddur does not have a large force, and he will not be expecting us to be ready for him. We should easily overpower him. However, my concern is Lopez. He is excellent at what he does. We will have to double security around the perimeter, and we still may not stop him from gaining access to the compound. He has been known to avoid detection and gain entry to highly secured areas."

"In that case," Luis said, "would it not be more prudent to double the security around the launch area?"

"Yes, you are right."

ↄ৵ↄ৵

All through the meeting with Asad, Brad's phone had continually buzzed. He knew it was Darcey, so as soon as he left the conference room, he called her.

"Where have you been?" Darcey all but screamed into the phone as she stopped her pacing. "What's going on? And don't tell me it's nothing." She had been trying to reach him for over an hour after the tingling sensation in the pit of her stomach from her connection to Brad had started doing double time. She knew there was something wrong, and it was big.

"Whoa, slow down," Brad said calmly, although he was not feeling calm. He had tried to keep his anxiety level down during the meeting, but it had been next to impossible with what Asad was telling them. "We have had a situation come up at the compound. It's being handled," he said, not really wanting to go into detail and get her more upset than she already was.

"What situation?" she asked curtly, her stomach churning. "Brad Daniels, you had better tell me what is going on this instant!"

Brad heaved a sigh and ran his fingers through his hair as he walked back to the work lab where he sat down at his desk and proceeded to explain to her what had been happening.

"Oh. My. Gosh!" she said, finally collapsing on the sofa and staring across the room at Nicho, who was on his cell. She bombarded Brad with questions. "What are you going to do? What can I do? Is Ty okay? Has he called Marti?"

"First off, you and Marti are going to stay right where you are with Nicho. We don't believe there will be an attempt to take you, but for my piece of mind—stay put with Nicho!" he said a little more forcefully than he had intended. "Second, everything is under control here. Asad's and Luis's men are here, so we have plenty of protection, and third, I'm sure Ty is calling Marti right now."

None of Brad's assurances stopped Darcey's mind from forming all sorts of "what if?" scenarios, and none of them were good. She wanted to be with him, she wanted to feel his arms around her. If something bad was going to happen, she wanted to be with him. Whatever it might be, they could face it together. She did not want to go on without Brad. She closed her eyes and rubbed her forehead, where a headache was beginning to form. Yet, she knew being with Brad at the compound was not going to be possible. To Brad, her safety came first, and she knew, no matter how much she pleaded, he would not give in on this.

"Okay," she sighed. "I love you. Don't you go and get yourself killed. You hear me?" she told him. The anxiety level of their connection was still high, but she could also feel the love, passion, and desire begin to push it out.

"That's my girl," Brad said, love flowing from his heart. "I love you, too. And, I promise, I won't let anything happen to me. I'll be okay as long as I know you are safe." He could feel her now. The passion of their connection was flowing stronger.

CHAPTER 35

The Job

Snap! Snap! Julio worked his slim fingers into the latex gloves—a precaution against leaving any identifiable fingerprints. He counted the bricks of C-4 before he placed them in his "boom-bag," as he liked to call it. Snagging up the detonators, he placed them on top of the C-4 then checked the box of PIDs before carefully slipping them into the side pocket of the boom-bag. He stuffed an extra box of latex gloves in the other pocket. Finished, he ripped off the gloves and tossed them into the glass jar on the kitchen counter. A few drops of nitric acid took care of the gloves.

As Julio watched the gloves dissolve, he thought about Jamal. Earlier he had sent Jamal home, telling him to be back the next day at five for further instructions. He did not intend on taking the kid with him. Jamal was too full of himself to listen to what Julio had been trying to show him about handling the C-4. After several attempts to show him how to place the C-4 and attach the detonator correctly, Jamal had finally gotten it correct. After that, Julio did not dare try to show him how to operate a PID. Unfortunately, he did not have the luxury of time waiting for Jamal to learn how to do things correctly. Ahmed wanted the job done tomorrow night. Julio would get it done, but he would not take the kid.

❦❦❦

The sound of gunfire greeted Brad as he stepped through the door into the indoor firing range. After finding out that Ty and the boys were expert marksmen, Mick enlisted their help with the training. Ty looked up and saw Brad enter. He waved him over to his position.

"Hey there, boss man," Ty said. "Grab one of those AKs and see how ya do."

Brad selected an AK-47 from the rack, shoved a banana clip into place, and stepped to the line. He fired off ten rounds and then brought the target forward. There was a neat grouping directly in the heart area of the target.

"Not bad, boss man," Ty said, grinning. "Where'd you learn to shoot like that?"

"My dad was an ex-marine and an avid hunter. I've been shooting since I could walk," Brad said, pulling the target down. "How's the training going?"

"Not too bad," Ty said, looking around. "Luckily, several members of the crew already knew how to shoot, and those who didn't are really learning fast. Not sure how'd they do on the front line, but should be okay as back up for Asad's and Luis's men."

"Okay, as soon as you feel everyone knows what they are doing, send them back to work," Brad instructed Ty. "We've got to get those ships loaded and ready for liftoff. Where are you on uploading the software?"

"Almost finished," Ty said. "All that is left to do is to run the diagnostics to make sure there are no glitches," he said, taking his rifle apart to clean it. "It's getting late, and some of the guys need to get some rest. I'm going to send half for a few hours' sleep while the rest carry on, and then switch them out."

"Sounds good. Let me know as soon as you're finished with the diagnostics. I want to take one of the ships for a short spin before all hell breaks loose. I want to see what the real thing feels like. The Sim was great, but the real thing has to be a hundred percent better." Brad turned and waved to his crew as he headed for the door. He needed to call and talk to Nicho and let him know what was going on. He was sure Luis had already informed him, but Brad needed to make sure he had.

Rounding the corner in the hallway that led back to the elevators, Brad collided with Luis.

"Ooof!" Luis expelled the air from his lungs as Brad's body hit him in the stomach.

"Luis, are you okay?" Brad asked, taking him by the shoulders. "I wasn't paying attention to where I was going. So sorry."

Luis smiled and straightened his suit jacket. "Not to worry. I am tougher than I look." He laughed. "I was just coming to find you. I have called Aicha and informed her of what is going on. I did not want her to hear about it from someone else or from the news if we cannot keep this under wraps."

"Yes, I think that is a wise idea," Brad agreed. "How did she take it?"

"I do not know," Luis said his eyes sad. "I sometimes do not know how to read her. She sounded okay, but it was as if she had been expecting my call. Regardless, she wants to be kept informed."

"Walk with me," Brad said. "I am on my way to the work lab. I have a few things to wrap up, and I want to call Darcey."

"Yes, I have been on the phone with Nicho," Luis said, falling into step with Brad. "He is aware of the seriousness of this and has taken extra precautions at the compound. The security at the compound is state-of-the-art, but Nicho is old school. He likes hands on and being in control of a situation."

"Yes," Brad agreed. "We are lucky to have him."

⌘⌘⌘

"Why can't we have dinner on the patio?" Darcey glared at Nicho, her hands fisted on her hips. "It's a beautiful night, and the weather is perfect. I don't see why we can't eat on the patio."

"It is too dangerous," Nicho said, exasperated at her stubbornness.

"I know you said it was dangerous, but the compound is surrounded, and that wall has to be at least fifteen feet high," she argued.

"That is not what I am concerned about," he said, running his fingers through his hair and walking over to the patio doors. He carefully pulled the draperies that covered the doors open a small crack and pointed to the full moon that was just beginning on its nightly journey through the heavens. "That is what concerns me," he said as he stepped aside so she could peek through the crack. "You and Marti would be setting ducks for any would-be sniper."

"But there are no buildings around the compound that are high enough for a sniper to use," she argued back.

"A sniper does not have to be within close proximity to kill you. A good sniper can take you out at a mile distance," Nicho explained.

"Oh," she breathed. "I didn't know that. Until a year ago, I didn't know any of this existed. An X-Acto Knife was the closest thing to a weapon I owned." She threw her arms wide, making her point. "You—you deal with this all the time. How can I be expected to think of everything?" She flopped down on one of Asad's comfy upholstered sofas in a huff, her arms folded tightly across her chest.

"What's up with you two?" Marti asked, coming in and sitting down beside Darcey. She looked questioningly form Darcey to Nicho.

"Well, for one thing, we won't be eating on the patio tonight or any other time soon," Darcey said, glaring at Nicho who gave a half grin and sat down on the arm of the upholstered chair across from Darcey.

"Explain, please," Marti said, drawing her legs up under her getting comfy on the sofa.

"It seems like we *might* have a sniper problem," Darcey said, playfully kicking her foot out in the direction of Nicho. "He thinks we would be 'prime targets' for a sniper if we dined on the patio." She did finger quotes for prime targets, looking steadily at Nicho.

"Huh?" Marti said. "With that big wall out there? No way." She shook her head at Nicho.

"Humph! That's what you think. Go ahead, Nicho. Tell her what you told me."

"A sniper can hit his target even if he is a mile away. So you see that wall isn't going to protect you."

"Oh! Wow!" Marti said with a little shiver, her eyes big and round. "I should've known that. At the store, we sell rifles with scopes that can do that. One of our customers is a championship marksman. He competes all around the globe. Just last year his winning shot was one-point-five miles." She looked over at Darcey, who was fidgeting with the arm of the sofa. "Look, all is not lost," she said, putting on her best Texas grin. "We can just have Nicho bring in the table and chairs from the patio, turn out all of the lights, light some candles and volia! It will almost be like dining on the patio."

Darcey turned, looked at Marti, and grinned. Leave it to Marti to come up with the solution. Although it wasn't what she wanted, it was a solution nonetheless. She had to agree that it even sounded like fun. It brought back warm memories of her mom when she would make quilt tents and pretend bonfires so the girls could pretend they were camping out.

"Okay, let's get this done," she said, grabbing Marti by the hand and pulling her off the sofa then giving Nicho's foot a whack as she passed by him.

Nicho's phone buzzed. "*Hola*!" he answered.

"Hey! How's it goin'?" Brad wanted to know.

"Fine. We are just getting ready for *al fresco* dining inside." Nicho laughed and explained the situation to Brad.

"Hummm, if you say so." Brad laughed. "I mean about the dining part. Wise move, though, considering you could be right about a sniper." He paused, explained the situation at the ORCA compound, and asked that he say nothing to either Darcey or Marti. The women were already stressed enough. He didn't want to add more.

"Is that Brad?" he heard Darcey asking in the background. He frowned. His indecision, whether to tell her about going on the flight, tugged at him. Right now, it looked like he didn't have a choice. He would be lifting off for his preflight test in just a few hours.

Maybe I should wait until after the test flight. Things could go wrong, and I might not be able to make the flight he reasoned. But he knew, regardless of what happened on the test flight, he was going. "Hey, would you mind handing your phone to Darcey?" he asked Nicho.

"Sure."

"Hey, babe," Darcey breathed. "I've missed you. When are you coming home?"

"It won't be until this situation is taken care of," he told her. "I—I have something I need to tell you," he stammered. "You'd better sit down."

"*What*?" she exclaimed as her heart began to pound madly. "I'm not going to like this, am I?"

"No, probably not," he said, leaning forward resting his elbow on the desktop and placing his head in his hand. "Just remember that I love you more than life itself."

"I know," she whispered and listened to him as he told her about the test flight and that he would be going with the ships when they lifted off.

CHAPTER 36

Boom Bag

A black sedan pulled up to the curb and stopped, long enough for the young man who had been standing there to enter, then drove away. Adara watched from her darkened room as her brother got into the sedan. Even though she could not see who was driving, she knew in her heart that it was Ahmed Kaddur. Wiping a tear that had slid down her cheek, she picked up her phone and called Señor Damji.

"*Hola,*" Asad answered.

"Señor Damji, this is Adara," she said meekly. "I have more news."

"*Si,* what is it?"

"I think they are going to do it tonight," she whispered. "Jamal was bragging about Ahmed going with him to see the bomb guy. He said he was sure Ahmed was going to let him lead the attack." She paused, swallowing before continuing. "Oh, Señor Damji, Jamal is in so much trouble. I am afraid for his life."

"Did Jamal happen to mention the time of the attack," he queried, ignoring her plea.

"No, only that it would be sometime tonight. I am so very sorry. Very sorry."

Sniffling, she wiped the tear from her cheek and pushed the button ending the call. She was not going to plead for

Jamal to be spared. He needed to be taught humility and pay the price for his misdeeds. She was glad her mother and father were not alive to see the dishonor Jamal would bring to the family.

Asad quickly opened a comlink to Brad. "It will be tonight. We do not have much time. Where are things?"

"We are as ready as we can be. Justin has his and Luis's men ready. My crew is armed and ready, also. All personnel will be linked to the comm, so everyone will know what is going on," Brad told him. "I've called Darcey and Nicho, and everything is under control there."

"Good. I will be down there shortly," Asad said and tapped the button, turning off his comm. He had one more stop before heading down to the control room—the science lab. ORCA's scientists had been working on a new weapon—a pulse rifle. It had been scheduled to be tested later in the year, but he figured this was as good a time as any to test it. The ORCA pulse-action assault rifle was designed to use an electronic pulse action to fire titanium pellet projectiles at 1000 miles per second. It had been very effective in the indoor firing range but had not been tested under simulated battle conditions. However, this test would not be a simulation.

⌁∽⌁∽

Julio looked at the clock. It was five on the dot when he heard a knock on his front door. He slammed the clip to his Sig p226 home and holstered it before opening the door.

"Well, do not just stand there," Ahmed said curtly. "Invite me in."

Without waiting for Julio to step aside and invite him and Jamal in, Ahmed brushed past Julio, shoving him to the side. "Where is all of this wonderful boom-boom stuff?" Ahmed asked, rubbing his hands together as his eyes scanned the room in search of it.

"It is all packed and ready to go," Julio said flatly. "What are you doing here anyway?"

"I came to see the big bonfire," Ahmed said, spinning around pinning Julio with his eyes. "You did not think I would miss this, did you?"

"I had no idea what you intended to do," Julio responded with a shrug. "I presumed you would watch from afar. I know how you don't like to get your hands dirty," he said snidely as he walked into the kitchen and stowed the glass jar that he had dissolved the latex gloves in under the sink.

Ahmed followed him into the kitchen. "Come, come. No need for unpleasantries. I just want to see the stuff I am paying for," he insisted.

Julio sighed and walked back into the living room with Ahmed on his heels. He gave a glance in Jamal's direction and noticed that the young man was noticeably quieter this evening. He chuckled to himself. Not quite the big man when the boss was around. He grinned at Jamal, who frowned and turned away.

"All right, enough of this *mierda*," Ahmed slammed his fist down on the top of the bookcase that sat next to the kitchen door. The force of the hit jarred everything on the shelves. The picture frame with Julio's daughter's picture toppled over and fell to the floor. "Now see what you made me go and do," he said as he reached down to pick up the bent frame. "Your daughter has grown. Does she still live with your wife?" he inquired casually. "Hmmm. Let me see, where was that? Oh, now I remember. It was the Arabian Ranches," he said, forgetting for the moment that he wanted to see the explosives. He grinned maliciously at Julio.

Julio felt a cold chill run up his spine as he looked into Ahmed's eyes. *Keep your cool. Do not let him see you are afraid,* he cautioned himself silently. "Yes, she still lives with her mother," he replied with false bravado as he reached for his boom-bag setting by the door. "Here, you wanted to see what I will be using," he said, hoping to redirect Ahmed's attention away from his daughter's picture.

He pulled two latex gloves from the box in the side pocket and pulled them on. He did not offer any to Ahmed. Julio carefully laid out the detonators, the bricks of C-4, and the box of PIDs.

The first thing Ahmed reached for was the box of PIDs and tipped the box side to side as he tried to open it. Julio gasped along with Jamal, who was halfway across the room ready to grab the box if Ahmed fumbled it to the floor.

Before either Julio or Jamal could say anything, Ahmed opened the lid and peered inside the box. He started to reach for one of the PIDs.

"Stop!" Julio shouted. "You want to burn us all up?"

"Ahmed! Stop!" Jamal shouted at the same time as Julio.

Julio reached for the box of PIDs in Ahmed's hands that began to tremble slightly.

"Why did you not caution me before I picked it up?" he shouted, red-faced at Julio. His heart pounded wildly at the thought of going up in flames.

"I did not know you were going to pick the damn thing up," Julio replied curtly as he carefully replaced the box in the side pocket. "I thought you just wanted to look at the stuff. You did not say anything about wanting to handle it."

Ahmed was truly shaken, but he was not going to let Julio know that. It would be a sign of weakness on his part, and he did not display weakness in front of subordinates. He would think of something to repay Julio for letting him almost burn himself up. Perhaps a visit to his daughter was in order. Or maybe, an unfortunate accident during the demolition of ORCA. Both thoughts cheered him. "We are wasting time here," he said sharply. "What time are you planning on starting our little party? He glanced at his watch. It was early yet, but the adrenaline was pumping through his body. The excitement was seductive. He felt himself growing hard as he visualized what he was going to do. No woman had ever affected him like this. He adjusted himself before walking over and looking through Julio's entertainment center.

"Where is your booze?" he asked, flinging doors open and poking through the contents.

"It is in the kitchen. I will get it for you," Julio said, glancing over at Jamal, who was still standing nervously by the front door. "Find yourself a seat," he told Jamal as he headed for the kitchen.

Jamal quickly sat down on the end of the sofa.

Julio grabbed two glasses and the bottle of Jim Beam he kept for special occasions. He guessed this was about as special as it was likely to get tonight. If both Ahmed and Jamal tagged along it would be a miracle if they made it out alive.

CHAPTER 37

The Lights Go Out

The hour hand on the clock crept by agonizingly slow. The waiting was wearing on everyone. Brad had been around three times, checking on everyone. Asad seemed to be the only one calm through the whole thing, besides the ex-military men in his and Luis's security forces. They were used to "hurry up and wait."

Brad and Asad both were pleased with Justin's strategy. He had said that if he were planning the attack, he would take out the ships first and then blow the buildings. Basing his plan on that, he had put Luis's men stationed around the launch area while his men would patrol the perimeter. Should Lopez by some chance gain access to the compound, Luis's men would take care of him. Justin had left Brad's crew and the other ORCA personnel to guard the buildings. There was just one minor glitch in his plan. One that he had no control over but he would rectify immediately after this was over. The power station that powered the electric fence around the compound was off site. It was three-quarters of a mile away from the compound and owned by a private company who had assured ORCA that their facility was secure. But on the outside chance that Lopez did manage to take out the power grid, everyone had been issued night vision goggles.

Brad needed something to eat. He hadn't eaten in over

twelve hours, and his stomach was beginning to protest. On his way back from checking on the warehouse, he stuck his head in the control room to see if anyone there wanted anything from the vending machines down the hall. Asad had unlocked them earlier for anyone who wanted something to eat or drink. Brad had gotten halfway to the vending machines when the lights went out.

"Shit!" he said out loud. "Damn it to hell!" He turned and ran back to the control room.

Lopez or Ahmed's men had taken out the power grid. The whole compound was now dark. Perimeter guards reported no activity yet, but it would be just a matter of minutes before Lopez would be at the compound. It was just a matter of keeping a sharp eye out to see where he would try to enter.

Tat! Tat! Tat! Tat! Tat! Tat!

A burst of gunfire exploded on the south end of the compound.

Tat! Tat! Tat! Tat! Tat! Tat!

An all-out gun battle erupted. Brad grabbed his AK and goggles and rushed to the door leading to the compound. Slowly he pushed the door open.

Zing! Ping!

A stray bullet ricocheted off the concrete parking stop in front of him, sending fragments of concrete his direction. He searched the area and saw nothing. Keeping close to the ground, he crept out the door and made his way toward the battle raging fifty yards away. He could see the flashes from the guns as they fired into the compound and the return fire from Asad's men.

Asad picked up his pulse rifle and his goggles and followed Brad out into the compound. Asad was about ten feet behind Brad when a movement along the fence line caught his eye, but by the time he had trained his goggles on the spot where he thought the movement was, he could see nothing.

Tapping his comlink for Brad, he said, "I saw something

off to the left over by the fence line. I am going to check it out."

"Okay. I'm going to check on Justin."

"Right." Asad tapped his comlink off.

Brad turned to his right. He located Justin and his men who were taking cover behind several large concrete pylons. The compound was in total darkness except for the orange muzzle flashes and the red flashes from the tracer bullets that made an abstract display of red lines in the darkness. It would not be long before the full moon would light up the compound. That might work to their advantage, but it would also make it easier for Ahmed's men to see them.

Brad tapped his comlink for Justin. "I'm on my way," he said, keeping low and running in the direction of the pylons.

Tat! Tat! Tat! Tat! Tat! Tat!

Bullets whizzed past him as he zigged and zagged his way toward Justin's position.

"We got 'em pinned down for the moment," Justin said, squeezing off a quick dozen rounds.

Tat! Tat! Tat! Tat! Tat! Tat!

Brad could see the red of the tracers as Justin returned fire with his OM-12. He saw two of Ahmed's men crumple to the ground and a third scream as a bullet ripped through his arm. Another two of Ahmed's men made a run for the pylons to the right of Justin's position and were quickly cut down by some of Asad's men hunkered down behind a loading skiff.

Tat! Tat! Tat! Tat! Tat! Tat!

"But I think they just got some reinforcements," Justin said, rising again and firing. "I saw movement in behind them." Catching his breath, he turned and rested his back against the pylon. Bullets hit the pylon sending chunks of concrete flying. He picked up a spent casing and sent it spinning across the concrete pad in frustration. "We lost two good men and have four wounded. I don't know what their count is, but I feel that we have hurt them bad." He flipped around and let rip with another burst of bullets from his OM-12 as more bullets pounded his position. His frustration obvious, he emptied the clip in the direction of Ahmed's men.

"What about the grenade launcher?" Brad asked as he slid in beside Justin and began firing.

Tat! Tat! Tat! Tat! Tat! Tat!

"Didn't want to pull it out unless necessary," Justin said, slamming a new clip home. "I want to contain the noise as much as possible." He squeezed off another burst of bullets and taking out two more men. "We gotta shut 'em down without using it. I'm gonna have to move some of Luis's men to our flanks."

He quickly gave instructions to Jason, who was in charge of Luis's men over the comm to send up twenty men to flank their position on the right and left. Ahmed's men were on the move, and he didn't want them getting past their position in the dark, so he ordered Jason to send up some low-level flares to light up the compound. The new low-level flares hovered just a little over nine meters in the air over Ahmed's men's position, sending them scrambling back toward the fence.

Tat! Tat! Tat! Tat! Tat! Tat!

"Where's Asad?" Justin wanted to know. He hadn't seen him since the fighting started.

"He thought he saw something over by the fence. He's on his way there now." Brad fired and took out one of the four men making a dash for another set of pylons.

Tat! Tat! Tat! Tat! Tat! Tat!

"I'd better check on Ty." Brad opened a comlink to Ty, ducking down as a barrage of bullets hit the pylon. "Hey! How's it goin' over there?" He flipped over on his belly and fired at the three men behind the pylon.

"All's quiet at the moment," Ty said. "Had a couple try to get in, but took 'em out with no trouble. Sounds like your keepin' busy, though."

Tat! Tat! Tat! Tat! Tat! Tat!

"Yeah, ya could say that." Brad squeezed off another burst, hitting a man as he stood to return fire. "Well, keep a sharp eye out. I think Lopez is in the compound. He needs to be taken out before he has a chance to do any damage," he said, squeezing off another round, taking out another of Ahmed's men.

CHAPTER 38

The Battle Begins

Julio had climbed into the back seat of the black sedan, allowing Jamal to sit in the front seat. He liked it better this way. No one was behind him. He sat with the boom-bag on his lap, cradling it in his arms. He did not know how he was going to ditch Jamal and Ahmed so he could work his magic. He could not do it with them under foot. Ahmed had already contaminated the PID box with his fingerprints, which Julio conveniently had not wiped down. If everything went as he hoped, he would leave the PID box behind. He smiled, thinking how extremely carless of him that would be.

Ahmed pulled the sedan up into the shadows, behind the power station and turned the engine off. "We will wait," he said. "My men will be here shortly, and they will take care of the power station."

They waited fifteen minutes before an SUV parked beside the sedan. Two men got out and walked around to the driver's side of the sedan.

Ahmed powered the window down. "Well, it is about damn time you got here," he said through clenched teeth. "Where are the rest of the men?"

"They are already stationed at the compound and in place, ready to begin as soon as the power is shut down," the man said, placing his hand on the door. He glanced in the back at Julio. "That your guy?" he asked, nodding his head toward the back seat.

"Yes. Now get on with your job." Ahmed powered up the window, almost catching the man's hand. He watched as the two men entered the power station before starting the engine and heading for the compound.

All was quiet, except for the nocturnal sounds of early morning as Julio stood beside the sedan down the hill below the compound fence. He watched Ahmed continually adjusting himself and wondered if something was wrong with him. The compound lights blinked and then went dark. Julio waited a couple of minutes before approaching the fence. He picked up a discarded soda can and tossed it at the fence. It bounced and fell to the ground. The power to the fence was off.

He picked up his boom-bag and pulled his wire cutters from his pocket. The cutters easily sliced through the chain link fence. He cut through just enough of the fence links to pull it back and slip through. Bending the fence back, he pushed his boom-bag through before he scooted through himself. He had hoped that Ahmed and Jamal would stay with the car, but that did not look like it was going to happen. Ahmed was already breathing down his neck and had not given Julio enough time to clear the fence before he started through. In his haste, he fell across Julio's foot twisting it as he wiggled his way through the opening in the fence.

"Move it along!" Ahmed growled in a whisper.

Julio stopped, still in a squatting position he swung around to face Ahmed. "Get off my ass and I will," he hissed at Ahmed, noticing that Jamal was still outside the fence. He hoped he would stay there. The mission had not even started, and it already had the makings of a full-fledged FUBAR.

Julio turned, rose up into a bent over stance, and started cautiously toward the first launch pad, his boom bag strapped securely across his back. The closest one was some twenty yards away, and there was no cover between the fence line and the ship. The moon had not yet risen, so he figured he had about forty minutes to place the explosives and get out. How he was going to do that with Ahmed right on his ass, he did not know.

The sound of gunfire cut through the night air and acrid smell of sulfur from the gun powder assaulted Julio's nostrils as he crept his way to the first ship, thankful for the diversion that Ahmed's men had created at the other end of the compound leaving this end unprotected. He realized that Jamal was not with them when he stopped to pull his boombag around in front of him, and Ahmed slammed into his back.

"Back off!" Julio hissed at Ahmed, who took a step back as Julio thumped him in the chest.

Ahmed gritted his teeth but said nothing as he watched Julio pull out the first of the C-4 and mold it to fit into the heat sink ejection port. Julio pushed it into place and attached the detonator setting the timer for thirty minutes. It would be cutting it close, but if Ahmed stayed out of his way, it would be enough time.

Julio started for the next ship when he noticed a dark figure silhouetted by the gunfire and some flares floating in the air at the other end of the compound. The figure appeared to be making its way across the launch area, heading toward the fence line where they had opened it up. He worried that Jamal would be found. If the kid had any smarts, he would be long gone by now, but the kid had never struck him as being overly smart.

Julio tapped Ahmed on the shoulder and pointed toward the dark figure. Ahmed seemed unconcerned. He forcefully grabbed Julio by the arm and shoved him in the direction of the next ship, causing him to stumbled and lose his balance.

Pffft! Pffft!

A bullet zipped past Julio's arm, riffling the sleeve of his hoodie.

Mierda! his mind screamed as he ducked back behind

the ship. *Suppressors! Where the hell are they?* He had not noticed any muzzle flash.

Pffft! Pffft! Pffft! Pffft!

Drawing his Sig, he returned fire in the direction he thought the shots had come from. Ahmed worked his way around to the other side of the ship and shot recklessly at anything he thought moved. Julio could hear the bullets from Ahmed's MHS ricocheting off solid objects in the launch area.

Ping! Blang! Blang! Blang! Ping!

"Ahmed!" Julio said in a loud whisper. "Save your damn ammo until you see something."

Blang! Blang! Blang!

Pffft! Pffft! Pffft! Pffft!

Julio quickly moved around behind Ahmed. "Hold your fire!" He grabbed his arm. "We have to move! I am going to make a run for the next ship. I want you to laydown cover as soon as I start out. Keep them pinned down until I can get there."

Ahmed was still taking pot shots as Julio was talking to him. "You got that?" Julio asked.

"Yeah, I know what you want." He turned viscously on Julio. "You want to leave me here to get shot." Ahmed grabbed Julio by the shirt. "You listen to me, *culo*. We will go together. Got that?" He shoved his gun up under Julio's chin.

"Sure. Whatever you say," Julio agreed. With a gun at his head, he would have agreed to anything the mad man wanted.

There was no way in hell I am going to get out of this alive now, he thought as he backed away from Ahmed and returned fire. *We have already wasted ten minutes since I set the timer. Twenty minutes left.* He reached around the side of the ship and fired again. More bullets whizzed by and ricocheted off the ship's hull.

Pffft! Pffft! Ping!

No, I can see no way this is going to work in my favor,

he reasoned, ducking as a bullet struck the ship just above his head. *Best to cut my losses and scram. Leave Ahmed to clean up his own damn mess.* He paused. *No sense in letting a good chunk of C-Four go to waste either,* he decided as he reached into the heat sink ejection port and pulled it out. He had no desire to blow these people up now, and he was positive he would not see even one fils from Ahmed in payment for the job. Pulling out the detonator and stuffing the C-4 in the boom-bag, he crouched down and began retreating back the way they had come. Ahmed was too busy shooting his gun to notice Julio's retreat.

CHAPTER 39

The Coward

Asad reached the spot where he thought he had seen movement. He quickly searched the area and discovered the opening in the fence and the sedan parked a short distance away down the hill.

He crawled through the opening heading for the sedan to check it out. Bent over, he cautiously approached his rifle ready. He waited several seconds, crouched beside the driver's side door to see if he heard the noise again. Yes, there it was again, a small whimper. He hadn't imagined it. Slowly, he crept to the back door and opened it. The dim dome light inside the sedan came on exposing Jamal, who had wedged himself on the floorboard between the back of the front seat and the bench of the back seat. His eyes round saucers and his face white as a sheet.

Asad hit the comlink for Justin. "I got us a prisoner. What do you want me to do with him?"

"I'm a bit busy right now," Justin said. "Tie him up and leave him. We'll pick him up later."

Tat! Tat! Tat! Tat! Tat! Tat!

Asad could hear the gunfire in the background and Justin barking orders to his men. "I'll see what I can find." He tapped the comlink off.

He looked at Jamal before shoving the barrel of the rifle under Jamal's nose. "Get out."

Jamal sat there petrified. His muscles refused to move. The cold of the gun barrel shoved up his nose triggered a rush of warmth that flowed between his legs.

"Last time, kid. Get out!" Asad growled.

Jamal flailed his arms, trying to get leverage to push himself up. It was useless. The connection between his mind and his muscles was frozen with fear and embarrassment. He closed his eyes and prayed to Allah to deliver him from his misery as Asad's big fist reached in and dragged him out. The smell of fresh urine permeated the night air.

Jamal fell to the ground and buried his face in his hands. How could he ever raise his head again? The only good part of this was that Ahmed was not there to witness his disgrace. As ashamed as he was, he would never admit to Adara she was right.

"Lopez is on the grounds," Asad whispered into the comlink as he stuffed Jamal into the trunk of the sedan. "Everybody be ready. Shoot on sight."

With his night goggles, Asad had noticed the dirt had been disturbed, and the scuffed up ground led away from the fence. The marks soon disappeared as the dirt turned into concrete. He paused, keeping an ear on the gunfight at the south end of the compound. The gunfire seemed to be getting closer to the launch area. He tapped his comlink for Justin. "What's happening?" he asked. "It sounds like you're moving this way."

"Yeah, they keep moving. They were trying to work their way around behind us. I've sent up flares, and we've dropped their numbers by half. Unfortunately, we've lost two men and have four wounded in the process. The wounded I've sent back to the control room. The dead will have to wait." The sound of Justin's rifle firing rang in Asad's ear. "I have moved some of Luis's men to the perimeter to cover our flank," he said, popping off single shots as a dark figure moved out from behind their cover. He dropped him with the second shot. "The rest are still by the ships."

"I think Lopez is somewhere in front of me," Asad said. "I can hear gunfire close." He opened a second comlink to Jason. "Jason, what does it look like from your position?"

"We have two pinned down by ship four. I think it may be the ones you are looking for," he said. Asad heard gunfire come over the comm. "I am just coming up on the concrete pad for ship three. I am about twenty yards from there. Keep them occupied while I get closer. If you get a shot, take it," he instructed Jason.

"Roger that."

Asad could just make out ship four from his position as erratic muzzle flashes popped from beside the ship. He could not imagine why someone of Lopez's training would be firing like a wild man. It had to be the second person Jason had seen. Jason and his men were doing a good job of keeping the two men distracted as Asad crept ever closer to ship four. He made his way to a forklift still loaded with pallets of modules. He paused to get a read on the men behind the ship through the scope on his rifle.

Through the scope, Asad could see the men but could not make out their faces. He was sure one was Lopez, but not sure about the other. The man farthest away appeared to be moving back in the direction of the fence line. The man closest to Asad had not noticed the other man and was still firing wildly. Asad took aim and fired his pulse rifle at the man. Just as he fired, the man bent down out of sight. The projectile missed. The man flattened himself out on the concrete and once again began to fire erratically, several of the bullets hitting the forklift. Asad again took aim this time scoping out the retreating man who was now almost to the fence line. He squeezed the trigger. The projectile sliced through the air and struck the man in the back. There was an immediate explosion as the projectile struck the PID box in Julio's boom-bag.

CHAPTER 40

The Great Escape

A re you ready to go?" Ahmed growled, still firing. He could not see what he was firing at. He did not care. He loved the control that surged through his body as the gun vibrated in his hand when he pulled the trigger. He loved the white-hot flash as the bullet exploded from the barrel sending an extension of his power out to annihilate everything that it touched. His body tingled with the seductive stimulation of it. He loved it. He could feel himself getting hard as pleasure coursed through his body but quickly softened as the "dead click" of the trigger signaled the clip was empty. Angry that his pleasure had been interrupted, he ejected the empty clip and bent down to grab a full one. As he did, a bullet went whizzing over him.

"What the—" he exclaimed as he flattened himself out on the concrete. He slammed the clip into place and started shooting again. "Julio!" he shouted. "Julio!" Hearing nothing, he flipped over onto his back just in time to see Julio running toward the fence line, and then he exploded.

Ahmed lay there a few seconds, stunned at what he'd just witnessed. *Puta madre! Tengo que largarme de aquí!* he told himself as he scrambled to his knees.

He was hearing gunfire coming from all directions. He could not make out if any of it was being directed at him, but he stayed crouched down just the same. The explosion—that had once been Julio—fully lit up that end of the compound and the heat radiating from it was unbearable from where he stood. All he could think about was running as fast as he could. And that was exactly what he did. He ran as though the hounds of hell were nipping at his heels. He skirted the human torch and made a beeline for the opening in the fence and the sedan.

He could hear shouts coming from behind him as he wiggled himself through the opening, catching his jacket on the sharp links that had been cut. He ripped himself loose and stumbled his way down the hill to the sedan. His breath came in short gasps as he fumbled through his pocket for the keys. Finally, he had them, but his hand was shaking so much it took him several tries to get them in the ignition. The engine roared to life, and he slammed the sedan in reverse barely missing a utility pole as he floored it leaving gravel flying in his wake. The glow from the fire dimmed in the rearview mirror as he sped away. No one followed.

EPILOGUE

That's the last of it," Ty said as he closed the door to the cargo bay. "We're ready for lift off anytime you are." He slapped Brad on the back as they walked toward the cockpit.

It had been a tense two days after Julio went up in flames. The authorities had swarmed over the ORCA compound, investigating the explosion even though Asad has assured them that it had been an accident.

The wounded of Ahmed's men along with ORCA's wounded had been flown to ORCA's infirmary in London for treatment. Ahmed's men were later conscripted aboard one of ORCA's tanker ships headed for Cape Horn on their way to Peru. Ahmed's dead had been incinerated in ORCA's waste disposal unit. And what was left of Julio had been covered with a highly corrosive chemical compound so now the area looked like a chemical explosion had happened. After two days of intensive questioning and probing, the authorities finally left, seemingly satisfied with their results.

Ahmed was nowhere to be found. His downtown office was closed and locked. His receptionist had arrived for work that next morning to find a handwritten note taped to the locked door. *You are fired.*

Jamal had been found two days later, delirious and wandering around half-naked, several miles out in the desert. He had been rushed to the hospital where he was recuperating.

He still could not remember who he was or what had happened to him.

The crisis over, Nicho had returned to Luis's ranch to resume his duties there and to see Jenny. He had missed her but had not known just how much until he had observed Brad and Darcey, and the love they had for each other. He finally realized that was how he felt about Jenny but had been afraid to admit it to himself. He had called her several times during the last few days and each time saying goodbye became harder. Darcey would always be his very special friend, but Jenny had completely captured his heart.

Ty had taken Marti to the airport along with Brad and Darcey to say goodbye. There had been many tears shed and long hugs before Marti boarded the ORCA jet for Dallas. She had wanted to stay, but Ty wanted her home and safe. He promised to call her daily on the Interstellar Video Link—IVL—and Asad had a special computer prepared for her so she could send and receive over the IVL in Dallas. She hugged Darcey and Brad then turned to Ty. He folded her in his arms as he kissed her passionately. Her arms snaked around his neck as she returned his kiss. The sun reflected off the huge diamond on her hand as her fingers played with Ty's hair.

As a last ditch effort, Darcey had finally worked up the courage to approach Asad to ask, no, plead to go on the ship with Brad. In her heart, she knew it was probably hopeless, but she had to try. This was not going to be like Brad leaving for Peru, which was only on the other side of this world. No, he was going to leave this planet and head into space to the Moon or Mars where only God would know what might happen, and the thought of him going without her was unbearable. On the other hand, she didn't have a clue about what might be required of her for space travel. The only things she knew about space travel was what she had gleaned watching old reruns of Star Trek, but that was just a TV show with actors pretending to be in outer space. If she did this, she would not be pretending.

Her appointment time set, she arrived at the ORCA building fifteen minutes early. Excitement and dread both building in her stomach at the same time.

Am I doing the right thing? she kept asking herself repeatedly as the elevator rushed up to Asad's office floor. The doors hissed open. She swallowed the lump in her throat and stepped out of the elevator.

"Good morning, Señora Daniels," Cala said, smiling brightly. "Señor Damji is ready for you. Go right in, *por favor.*"

"Hmmm…yes, thank you," she swallowed. The tension twisted in her stomach as she placed her hand on the doorknob. *This is it,* she thought, straightening her back and inhaling as she pushed the heavy teakwood door open.

"Ah, Darcey," Asad said, smiling as he came around his desk to greet her. "Your appointment could not have been more fortuitous. You are just the person I wanted to see." Holding her hand, he escorted her to the seating area in his office. "Make yourself comfortable, *por favor.* I will have Cala bring in some refreshments." He stepped away to instruct Cala about the refreshments.

Darcey fidgeted, smoothing the hem of her dress over her knees, as she waited for Asad to sit back down. Her mouth had gone dry, and she had to run her tongue over her teeth several times to make enough saliva to swallow.

This is silly, she told herself. *I have nothing to be afraid of. Asad is my friend. He will understand.* She smiled apprehensively as he approached.

"Now then," he said, sitting down across from her. "I have a most exciting proposition for you." He smiled as he spoke the words, and then his face turned serious. "Unfortunately, during the attack the other night, one of our data technicians was seriously wounded, and we do not have a replacement for him." He paused while Cala placed the refreshments on the table beside him. "*Gracias,* Cala," he said, smiling. "Coffee?" he asked Darcey.

"Y—yes, please," she stammered and quickly regained

her composure from the shock at what Asad had just said. Was she reading him right? *Is he hinting that he is going to offer me the job?*

He poured coffee into both cups and handed one to Darcey. "I have discussed this with Brad," he continued, "and he thinks it is an excellent idea, but he wanted me to present it to you. I know this is short notice and that you are not familiar with any of our systems, nor have you had the flight orientation, but Brad believes, and so do I, that you are more than capable of stepping into this position." He paused taking a drink from his cup.

Darcey was afraid she had that deer-in-the-headlights expression on her face, but she couldn't help it. This was so unexpected. She had been prepared to plead even beg, for the chance to go with Brad, and here Asad was offering her a job to go.

How ironic, she thought and grinned.

Asad sat, waiting for Darcey to give some sign that she had heard what he had proposed. Instead, she was sitting there with a sweet, girlish grin on her face.

Darcey blinked her eyes and focused on Asad. "You mean you want me to take over for the other technician. You really want me?" she said, placing her hand over her heart. "Really?"

Oh, please, her inner voice admonished her. *You sound like a gushing schoolgirl instead of a grown woman. Get your act together.*

Asad chuckled at her disbelief. "Yes, I really do want you to take the position. Brad tells me you minored in Computer Science, and I feel that more than qualifies you for the position which will consist mostly of entering, sending, and receiving data from ORCA and the job sites on the Moon and Mars."

What are you waiting for? Her little inner voice poked her. *Say YES for crying out loud!*

"Ah…em…yes, yes, I will do it!" She clasped her hands to keep from throwing her arms wide in jubilation. "Yes," she said again. "Oh, thank you so very much!" She closed her eyes for just a second and prayed silently. *Oh, thank you, God.*

Asad grinned as he held out his hand for her to shake, sealing her acceptance of the job. He did not know quite how to read her reaction but believed her to be completely overwhelmed.

"Now, that that is settled," he said, reclining back in the chair. "What did you want to see me about?"

"Oh, that. Well…ah…nothing really." She smiled sheepishly and blushed. "I just wanted to ask you if you would consider letting me go on the flight with Brad."

"Well then, it seems that the fates have truly smiled on you today." He grinned. "Welcome to the ORCA family." He stood, offering her his hand in assistance. "If you will come with me, we will get you ready for your space journey."

☙❧

Asad called all of the ships' crews together in the center of the launch area for a send-off. "Ladies, gentlemen," he said, addressing the crowd. "You are about to embark on a momentous journey for mankind. The building and completion of these domes will mean that the human race can continue into the future. We do not know how long we have to complete our mission, but we will do it with all due haste." He turned and motioned to the several wait staff in white coats to bring out the trays loaded with glasses of champagne. "Everyone take a glass, *por favor.* We will toast to our new venture and the naming of our new ships. Although not very creative, but in the short time allotted us, these will have to do. Ladies and gentlemen, I give you *Luna One* and *Luna Two* and *Mars One* and *Mars Two. Saluda!*"

Loud cheers rose from the crewmembers, and they downed their glasses of champagne.

Although the ships were equipped with the EGLS and pilots were not necessary, the ships still needed captains. The captains could also pilot the ships should the EGLS fail for any reason. Each ship carried four crewmembers to man the ship. The *Luna One* and the *Mars One* were each carrying twenty construction workers and six months of supplies. The *Luna Two* and the *Mars Two* each carried four crewmembers and the modules for the temporary Bio Domes.

Brad gathered his crew. He would be taking the *Luna One*. He had selected Tony Lupo from Asad's technicians for the co-pilot and navigator. Tony had experience as a marine pilot and navigator. Matt, Scott, and Hot Dog drew straws to see which one would go with Brad. Matt drew the long straw and would be systems technician on the *Luna One*.

Darcey would handle the data and communications. Ty would be taking the *Mars One*. Hot Dog would be his co-pilot and navigator, Scott the systems tech, and Lana Wyatt would handle the data and communications.

Troy Nash, an ex-navy pilot, would captain the *Luna Two* and the *Mars Two* would be piloted by Lucas Diaz, also an ex-navy pilot. Brad did not know much about the other members of their crews. He had only had brief introductions but figured he would have plenty of time to get to know them better.

The pre-flight checklist completed, Brad powered up the impulse engine, switched to the EGLS, and the *Luna One* lifted off heading for space. Reaching the exosphere, Matt laid in the coordinates for the Moon. Brad opened the new holo-comm, and a holo-display of him appeared on all the ships.

"I want to congratulate each and every one of you for your hard work in getting everything ready in record time," he said, feeling a little awkward using the holo-comm for the first time. It was a little unsettling seeing the crews of each ship as if he were actually on board their vessels while knowing he was already thousands of miles from each ship and getting farther with each second. He supposed he would get used to it in time.

"Hey, no problem." Ty laughed. "You ask, and we do."

"Here! Here!" came from Nash's ship followed by cheers from all vessels.

"Thanks!" Brad grinned. "Now, I would suggest that everyone take the time to look out the Sky Port Deck windows. It will be six months before we get back there."

He closed the holo-comm and took his own advice. He grabbed Darcey by the hand and together they made their way to the Sky Port Deck. Brad raised the shield, and the blue orb of earth came into view. He placed his arm around Darcey's shoulders as her arm wrapped around his waist. She laid her head on his shoulder and watched the Earth become suspended in a sea of black surrounded by thousands of twinkling lights of stars thousands of light years away. A cold chill rippled through her body. She wasn't sure if it was excitement or dread.

Brad felt her shiver. "Are you okay?" he asked, kissing her hair. He too felt something, but he knew his worry was about the responsibility Asad had placed on him for this project.

"Yes, I'm fine. It's just the excitement of it all," she said and snuggled closer to Brad.

"Yes, it is exciting in an inexplicably dangerous way," he replied. "Who would have ever thought we would be doing something like this together?" he said, turning her around and pressing her body into his.

"Yes," she breathed. Butterflies exploded in her stomach as his lips claimed hers. It was their first kiss in outer space, and it was erotically breathtaking.

☙❧☙

The image of Brad and Darcey's passionate kiss flashed on his QuantiumX microcomputer screen. The Sky Port

Deck camera was just one of many microcams he had hidden throughout the ship. He smiled, running his arm behind his head, propping it up as he reclined on his gravmatt in his sleep cubby. He traced Darcey's image on the screen with his finger. *It is going to be a very interesting journey. Yes, very interesting.*

About the Author

Madge Gressley lives in Missouri with her granddaughter and three dogs (Pixie, Lily, and Milo). An award-winning visual artist for over thirty years, she decided to trade her paintbrush and canvas for paper and pen but, in this case—computer and keyboard—and started her writing career in 2013. She works from home where she squeezes her writing in between jobs for her graphic design business and letting the dogs in and out—a full-time job in itself. Gressley self-published her first book in the *Inescapable* series The Beginning in May of 2014, and the second book *Remembering* in June of 2014. Book three *Tomorrow*, made its debut July 2015. There is a possible book four simmering on the back burner.

She is currently working on the second book in the Sophie Collins Mystery series, her version of a modern-day Nancy Drew. Book one in the series, *The Red Coat* is out and book two, "The Secret of Trail House Lodge," came out in 2016.

Gressley is an accomplished, award-winning visual artist. She is a Signature Member of the Missouri Watercolor Society and Best of Missouri Hands Juried Artist. The scope of her artistic talent covers a wide range of media, including acrylic, oil, watercolor, clay, and graphic design. Her work is proudly displayed in the collections of numerous corporate and private collections throughout the United States, Great Britain, and China.

She is also co-owner and graphic designer for Art & Graphic Innovations, LLC, a Missouri based graphic design firm, and owner of MEG Originals Fine Art.

Follow Madge on Twitter: https://twitter.com/mgressley1
Face-
book:https://www.facebook.com/groups/1460702867501390/
https://www.facebook.com/MadgeHGressleyArtistAuthor/
Blog: http://mhgressley.com/
Website: http://www.meg-originals.com

www.ingramcontent.com/pod-product-compliance
Lightning Source LLC
Chambersburg PA
CBHW060939120726
47910CB00002B/401